Pete's Crossroad

J.P. Osterman

Pete's Crossroad

CreateSpace, Charleston SC

Published by JPOsterman.com

ISBN-10: 061598276X
ISBN-13: 978-0-615-98276-2
Date of Publication: June 2014
Printed in the United States of America

Cover Photo: Bowie15| Dreamstime.com

Pete's Crossroad

DEDICATION

To my Grandpa Pink

ACKNOWLEDGMENTS

I thank Drew and Liz C. for helping me edit the book, along with artist Bowie15 for my cover art.

Pete's Crossroad

Part I

George Gibson

Pete's Crossroad

Chapter 1 – Borrowed Time

George opened his eyes to sunlight streaming through the blinds. He heard his 1957 Woolworth alarm clock's *tick tick*, smelled coffee wafting in from the motel breakfast area, and popped wide awake when he heard the pitter-patter of children's feet as their parents rolled luggage through the hall. Yawning and sitting on the edge of his bed, he said his morning prayer: "God, I hope I make it through another day. I just haveta! I got too much to do, and I can't die just yet! Please help me, God. Thank ya."

Donning his glasses, he read the time: "9:17 a.m.! I gotta get movin'!" Jiggling a cord out of a socket, he stuffed his clock into his carry-on next to his giant suitcase containing everything he owned in the world. "Darn clock keeps breakin' on me. The alarm was supposed to go off at 7:30!"

He sat up and stretched. "Another day! Another day o' life!" He yawned and smacked his lips—the taste of morning-breath bitter. He inhaled and exhaled, imbibing the Santa Monica ocean air as he made his way step-by-step to the bathroom.

Feeling worn out like an old turtle, he grabbing the edge of the sink. "Thank God!" He lathered up to shave, leaning into the mirror. "One more day…just one more day and I'll be in Albuquerque," he said to his reflection as he flicked a line of gritty cream into the sink. "Boy, won't Donny and the kids be surprised to see me. I'll sure be happy to see them!" He felt suddenly downhearted. "If I can find 'em all."

Standing half out of breath, he tried to remember the last time he had seen his son Donny. He squinted hard into the mirror, straining to recall his face. "Lemme think…" He tapped the tip of his razor on the porcelain. "Donny moved away from the farm in Indiana to Chicago in nineteen-ninety seven…or nineteen-ninety six?" He nicked himself on a tough curve of his chin. "*Ahhh*!" He swiped off a piece of tissue, licked it, and pressed it on the cut. Then, he saw his shaking hands, the swollen joints reminding him again of the little time he had left.

Suddenly, he heard *tick tick*…the sound now coming from his pocket watch inside his suit coat. "The time! I'm wastin' it!" Lumbering over to the jacket draped over a chair, he steadied himself, grabbed his watch, and opened up the glass face. "9:43 a.m." He rushed to see the notice posted on the back of the door. "When's check-out time?"

He remembered the bus was leaving at 2:45 p.m. "The Greyhound station's a half-an-hour's drive away! Gotta go!"

He saw his keys in one spot, his wallet across the room on a small table, and his clothes still hanging in the closet. "I gotta get outta here." He stumbled around, grabbing them all, clutching them to his chest, until he spotted his reflection in the mirror above the desk.

He stopped dead in his tracks. "Oh my! I'm still half naked, my face splattered with shavin' cream, and my false teeth missin'!" He raced to the bathroom, dabbed lather off his chin, spread Polygrip on his dentures, thrust his teeth into his mouth, and bit down to secure the fit. "Great!" He smiled at his reflection. "If I were thirty years younger, I'd look like the Skipper on *Gilligan's Island*!"

Huffing, he began dressing: each action—from sliding on

Pete's Crossroad

his socks to tying his shoe laces—felt as if it took minutes.

"I don't have much time!" he gasped as he packed his clothes into his giant suitcase and arranged some gifts among his folded shirts and socks. He had four wrapped gifts, three not big and one not too heavy, but all just the right size to fit among his clothes and all his possessions. He had another small carry-on and a cooler he had yet to pack. "I haveta make sure that if the baggage handler tosses this big trunk into the baggage compartment, all these things won't break." He treated each wrapped gift like china, packing them among his shirts and socks to form a perfect line. Then he fluffed their little shiny Christmas bows. "But these little things are gonna get crushed! I don't want that!" Seeing paper cups on the sink, he covered the bows with them, arranging some clothes in between them to make sure the cups would remain upright and straight. "They gotta be perfect, so when I give these gifts to Donny and my grandchildren, they'll look fresh wrapped!"

After packing his carry-on and filling his little cooler, he stood up and took a deep breath. "There…done." He glanced out the blotchy motel window that gave him a crack-of-a-view of the Pacific Ocean in the distance. The waves were rising like chop sticks. Behind the motel noises, he could hear their steady pulses on a shoreline he couldn't see. They made him panic. "Holy moly…my life is swooshing away in waves! I gotta get movin'!" He took out his pocket watch, clicked open the glass face, and stretching it out in front of him to see the time: 10:31. "I gotta get outta here!" Now, he felt as if he were at a starting line. He called the front desk to help him with his luggage.

Ambling out of his motel room, he rolled his large suitcase and carry-on into the hallway and called, "Can someone help me, please?" His back hit the wall and he closed his eyes. "Please! Can someone help me?" The dizzy spinning of the ceiling made him think he was falling, until he steadied himself against the wall.

A maid quickly dashed out of the room next to him. "Are you all right, Mister—Mister—"

J.P. Osterman

"Gibson!" he gasped, touching her shoulder. The carpet felt like glue under his feet. "Thanks, I'm fine now. Thanks for helpin' me."

Taking the cooler out of his hand, the maid asked, "What's your full name, Sir? I'm getting the manager! Didn't you call the front desk for help with these things?" She gestured at the large suitcase.

Still straining to catch his breath, he replied, "My name's George Gibson, and yep, I called."

After two men wheeled his luggage through the long hallway, the maid walked him to the reception area.

"Thanks. Thank ya everybody," George said, his heart racing in his chest. He could feel the blood pumping into the arteries of his throat, his arms swelling, his shoulders stinging. He focused on his large overstuffed suitcase filled with promised packages and dabbed sweat off his brow. "If I can get to the—" *Breathe, breathe.* "I just need—" *Inhale, exhale.* "Need help with these suit cases that's all please."

The manager, Aladhar, helped George into the lobby while two strangers wheeled his suitcases into the breakfast area. "Shouldn't we call an ambulance?" the maid whispered to the manager.

Plopping down on a chair next to a breakfast table, George overheard her, and another rush of panic filled him. "No!" He breathed, his hand over his chest. "I'll be okay in a minute…after I take my medicine…after I eat something." He felt a little congestion building in his lungs, and his hands were shaking. How much time he really had left, he didn't know. He never believed that doctor when he told him a few days ago that he had months left to live. He kept sipping cold water that the maids and manager kept putting in front of him. "I'm gonna get myself a little somethin' to eat. Then I'll be fine. And before I know it, I'll be on a bus…restin' and relaxin'." Reaching over his shoulder, he rubbed the back of his neck. "I'll need ya to call me a Taxi in about a half-an-hour. That'll give me enough time to eat, get to the Greyhound station, and

Pete's Crossroad

buy my ticket."

"Sure, Mr. Gibson," the manager said, dashing over to the breakfast table to make another pot of coffee and arrange the breakfast bar. "Angela, you stay with Mr. Gibson for a minute 'til I'm done here. Make sure he's okay. I'll bring him some food." George asked for eggs, toast and coffee.

"Sure Aladhar," the maid said.

"Thanks, Ma'am," George said, looking into her compassionate eyes. He chuckled a little. "You have soft green eyes." He believed he recognized them. "I think those are the same color eyes my granddaughter has." He blinked through the blur around him. "I think I've been seein' those eyes of hers everywhere!" He tried steadying his shaking hands with the warm coffee cup that Aladhar had just given him, until Angela handed him a cool damp cloth. He took it, and wiped his forehead, then quickly swept the cloth over his bald head. He was feeling much better now, and stronger.

"Thanks, Mr. Gibson," she said. "How old is your granddaughter? Too bad she isn't here to help you."

"Sue Beth is—I think—" He scratched his forehead where his bald head met an invisible wrinkle of an old hairline. "Twenty-two." He felt a sudden spurt of energy rise within him. "That's it! Twenty-two. And then there's Andy…lemme see…he's twenty-seven! And Fletch…well, he's twenty-five."

"Wow, what a nice big family," Angela said, peering around as if searching for them to come out of the woodwork.

Setting another sweating glass of cold water on the table in front of George, Aladhar served George his breakfast. "Mr. Gibson, is there anyone I can call to help you? Any family living around here? Any friends?"

George shook his is head. "Nope." He breathed deeply and then began eating. Finally, the fog seemed to be slipping out of his mind so he could think more clearly. "The only family I got is somewhere in Albuquerque. I just quit my part-time job at the Walmart on Crenshaw a few days ago. And the two acquaintances I had there are working now. No friends." He shrugged in embarrassment and ate some more, the food

J.P. Osterman

gradually helping him regain his energy. "I can't call anybody." He laughed as if telling a joke.

Angela frowned and began wringing her fingers. "Oh, I'm sorry to hear that." Glancing around as if she were late for an appointment, she leaned into his face and whispered: "Are you okay now, Mr. Gibson? I gotta get back to my job." Then George heard her tell the manager softly, "That poor old man has only two suitcases to his name. That's it!"

George felt a heavy weight building on his shoulders— needing to see his family. "I'm fine, you two. Just go on and get back to what you were doin' before I bothered ya. Soon, I'll be outta yer hair."

Turning away, Angela called back to him, "No bother, Mr. Gibson." She checked the time on her watch. "I think at lunch I'm gonna call my parents. They live outside of L.A." She peeked out the window, squinting into the distance as if engrossed in a memory. "It's been a while since I've last seem them. I think I'll visit them though this weekend." She asked Aladhar. "Is that okay, Sir?" George saw fright in her eyes.

Aladhar waved at her. "Yeah, sure, Angela. You can switch days with the other girl."

"Ka-ching!" she said, moving her fist as if making money on a bet. "Mom and Dad...here I come!" She began lightly dancing. "Bye, Mr. Gibson, and take care of yourself." Then Angela disappeared down the corridor.

Returning to George who was still eating, Aladhar sat down next to him and leaned into him. He had a look of caution on his face. "Well, Mr. Gibson, you *said* you're okay, but if you aren't breathing better in ten minutes, I have to call an ambulance."

"An ambulance?" George dropped his fork. "No!"

"We could be held liable if something bad happens to you and we let you leave."

George shivered. He saw his suitcases and cooler by the sliding door, and a taxicab at the curb. The green light at the corner looked like a beacon to freedom. If he could just hop

6

into a taxi and the driver rush through a few more intersections, he could be at that Greyhound station. Being carted off to a hospital would spoil all his plans of making amends to Donny and his grandchildren! He breathed, forcing his heart rate to slow down. "Oh, I can't have that now." He rubbed his chest and then patted Aladhar's hand. "I gotta get to my son and my grandchildren." He put his pill case into his jacket pocket. "I took my medicine. I'll be fine in a few minutes." He didn't want to tell the manager he was running out of time, and running out of life.

"Okay, Mr. Gibson. I believe ya." Aladhar returned to the front desk; but now and then, glanced at George who was continuing to take mouse-sized bites of toast and sipping coffee.

After finishing eating, George told him, "I'm fine now, see?" He had to make that bus. He had to be at the station on time. Again, checking his pocket watch, he slapped the face shut. "It's 12:43, Mister—"

The motel manager showed him his name tag. "You can call me Aladhar."

"Aladaar?"

He giggled. "Aladhar. I'm from Bangladesh. I know, the name is not American and hard to say."

"Aladhar." George felt his face burn. "Sorry, Aladhar, can ya please call me a cab now?" The one that had been at the front of the motel had already left. "I gotta get to the Greyhound station. I haveta catch that bus!"

"Sure, Mr. Gibson. The waiting time is usually around ten minutes." Aladhar dialed the number.

"Great." George wiped his lips, set his napkin on the table, and took one final sip of coffee.

Aladhar was behind the counter, finishing checking out two guests, and the breakfast bar was clearing of patrons. Aladhar had a handful of receipts in his hands, and counting them. "That one suitcase of yours look like a treasure chest, Mr. Gibson. It's huge!" He laughed, but his wide brown eyes creased in shock and fright. "Do you have your whole life inside it and that carry-on of yours or what?"

Walking to the counter to pay the bill that Aladhar was handing out to him, George chuckled and signed his name on the credit card. "One o' those has gifts in it," he said proudly, peering over his shoulder at the trunks. "I haven't seen my son Donny in over forty years." He read his shaky signature on the receipt. He felt his eyes sting and the ink blur. "And I've never even seen my grandchildren." He swallowed and coughed. "So I hope the presents I'm bringing for 'em will...ya know...sorta let me get my foot in the door with 'em all...sorta help me break the ice, if ya know what I mean."

The manager had an expression of surprise on his face. "Wow...forty years. That's a long time not to see family." "Where I come from—"

"Where's that again?" George asked as a woman walked into the lobby with her baby.

"Bangladesh," Aladhar replied, ripping the receipt off the machine and handing the copy to George. "Where I come from, we never go so long without seeing family." He smiled, and George saw his gleaming white teeth. "I live with my in-laws, my wife's sister's family, and her grandparents. That's how important family is to us."

"Wow!" George put the receipt in his wrinkled wallet. A sudden deep loss filled him. "Well, I hope these gifts I'm bringing my family will make a difference." He wished they were in front of him so he could kneel down and pray for their forgiveness. "I just *know* they will. They *have* to!" He felt his soul on fire. Under his breath, he whispered as stinging tears filled his eyes. "I hope Donny will forgive me. If I can find him."

"Huh?" Aladhar glanced askance at him. "What did you say, Mr. Gibson?"

George waved off his question. "Ah, nothin'." He felt an ache in his stomach and patted his eyes on his sleeves.

"Where are you traveling to, Mr. Gibson?" Aladhar asked, handing George a copy of the *Los Angeles Times*.

Pete's Crossroad

After reading the date, Wednesday, April 20, 2011, George inhaled the fragrant strong scent of coffee that perked its way through his senses, energizing him. "I'm headin' to Albuquerque, New Mexico." He shuffled a little on the tile floor and snapped his fingers playfully at a baby sitting on his mother's lap at a breakfast table. Waving to the baby as if tickling him, he scooped up his jacket and began walking slowly toward the exit. The mother smiled and the baby giggled. George wondered if his grandchildren had children yet. They were in their twenties, like the woman feeding her baby.

"Have a safe trip, Mr. Gibson," Aladhar called, and then phoned for two men to help George to an outside bench with his luggage.

After sitting down with his luggage pushed close beside him, George began watching cars and buses pulsing by on the busy street as distant waves continued sloshing on the beach in Santa Monica. He slid out his 1943 pocket watch from the inside lining of his jacket pocket. "It's 1:10 p.m." The blue sky had a few clouds that looked like stacked balls of cotton. They appeared like a stairway leading from the rooftops to Heaven. "Most people, when they go to bed at night, believe they'll wake up the next morning." He peered inside the lobby and watched the woman spoon-feed her baby. "Not me. Not anymore."

After the cab driver pulled up next to him and loaded his luggage and cooler, George plopped down into his seat and told the driver where to take him. "To the Greyhound station." It was only minutes away. Making final small talk with the driver, he said: "When I get to Albuquerque, everything'll be all right. I'll start over with my son, Donny." He glanced up into the blue Heaven and breathed in fresh air. Maybe in a few days he might never see, hear, taste or smell, ever again, and he'd also be in desert territory, a big change from coastal living. "I'll finally meet my grandchildren. I'll set things right! It's never too late to start over again…is it?"

The driver replied, "I don't think so." Then he dropped

J.P. Osterman

him off at the station.

At 2:00 p.m., and huffing to the ticket counter, George bought his bus ticket. Pinching the ticket between his fingers, he hailed the porter. "Hey, Mister!"

The man groaned and stopped loading luggage. "Yeah?"

George waved the porter to come toward him. He felt as if he were directing a boat toward a dock. "Can ya be extra careful with that luggage o' mine? I have fragile things in 'em!" His extra-large suitcase was inches away from the man's grip and cockeyed.

The porter wiped sweat on his sleeve and puffed out a breath of exasperation. "Uh-huh. I'll secure it in the center."

"That suitcase contains everything I own," George said, his carry-on rolling behind him and his little cooler in his other hand.

"Yeah, sure, it'll be okay the way I pack it," the porter said, lifting George's carry-on up the stairs of the bus for him.

Pete's Crossroad

Chapter 2 – Passengers on a Bus

Slowly climbing the steep stairs into the narrow aisle, George nodded hello to the driver. "Good afternoon!" He caught his breath and grabbed the rail. "My name's George Gibson, young fella." He shook his hand.

Tipping his blue brimmed hat at George, the driver smiled. "I'm Daryl. Welcome aboard and take a seat." He pointed to the back of the bus and looked at his watch. "We'll be leaving in fifteen minutes. So you still have time to pick up a snack or drink from the station if ya want."

"Thank ya kindly," George said, and then he walked down the aisle. Rocking from side to side as if lead were in his shoes, he spotted a seat. Everything beyond that row appeared full; and feeling a pinching sensation in his chest, he realized he needed to sit down, fast.

"Mind if I sit here?" he asked a young man sitting next to the window.

"Huh?" the man appeared startled. Someone had broken an unspoken rule and talked to him!

"It's a long ride to Albuquerque, and I sure could use this aisle seat young man," George breathed.

The young man had black hair and sunglasses sticking out

of the pocket of his white shirt. Pulling his briefcase next to him, smoothing down the black suit coat on his lap, and scooting close to the window, he said, "Sure, take the seat." Quickly he turned away.

George thought the guy looked like a famous race car driver even though he was dressed like a salesman, but he didn't want to tell him that, at least not yet. Lifting his carry-on like Atlas rolling the world on top of his shoulders, he heaved it into the luggage rack and surveyed the bus. He had bought a little cooler with him, but couldn't see a spot where he could put it.

The bus was nearly full now, but there were still a few vacant seats in the back and one towards the front of the bus. The luggage racks around him were chock full of small carry-ons and packages—one looked like a gift wrapped fishing rod and another like a boxed up body board. George ducked down to sit down, not wanting any one of those falling on him. He had been through enough accidents in the eighty-six years of his life. He shoved his small cooler under the chair in front of him. "*Ahhh*," he exhaled, closing his eyes, feeling his body sag into his chair. Finally, he had made it! He was almost to Albuquerque! And he had made it on time, but still had a long way to go. Remembering Robert Frost's poem, *Stopping by Woods on a Snowy Evening*, he kept inhaling deep gulps of air until the rubbery feeling in his arms disappeared, until he could hear the talk and laughter of people around him.

The bus engine revved and then hissed as the loading platform turned into a maze of scurrying cars and passengers darting in and out of traffic, avoiding collisions. George closed his eyes, took out his white handkerchief and dabbed his forehead. Feeling as if he could melt into his seat, he began listening to all the noises that sounded like cars clover leafing over a freeway.

The sounds triggered memories, and he recalled a time during World War II when he was charging through enemy lines with his .30 caliber M1 Carbine. Then he remembered the grinding noises of his green John Deere tractor when he used to farm his Indiana land from 1946 through 1962. *1992…* He coughed and flinched in his seat. He had to leave his family that year. It was a horrible drought, and he had to search for other employment, he had to stand in long lines in search of any type of work. "Desperate times," he said, burrowing the back of his head into his cushion. "Those were desperate hard times."

"Huh?" the young man sitting next to him asked, his voice sounding terrified.

"*Whew!*" George sighed and set his jacket on top of his blue cooler at the side of his left foot. "Nothin' young man," he said, rubbing his armchair. He laughed as he whipped out a small bottle of water from his cooler and swallowed two pills, his medicine. "I'm not gonna bite ya, young fella. Don't worry."

"*Hmm*, I never thought *that*," the man said. Then he cleared his throat, loosened his tie, and took a sip of water as he returned to watching people scurrying in and out of the station.

George heard a young passenger two rows in front of him say, "Ten minutes until we leave, Hideki. You better hurry!" A Japanese man wearing brown corduroy pants and a red flannel shirt stood up and darted out of the bus.

Slowly lifting his bottle of water to his lips, George chugged down the last of it, pouring some into his white handkerchief and rubbing his stubble face and the backs of his hands. He wanted to stop those flooding memories that for some reason were starting to trouble him. "Why? Why now?" he asked, wiping the handkerchief over his face.

The young man twisted his body toward him. "Is something wrong, Sir?"

George believed he looked as if he were about ready to call the police. "No, young man." He waved off his concern. "Everything's fine." He looked long and hard at the young man sitting next to him. At least *he* could stare out the window. George wished he had the distraction of watching faces too, not just a partial pedestrian view with a rooftop. Wiggling in his seat and pushing the backs of his arms into the cushion to adjust for comfort, he said, "Thank you kindly."

"What?" the young man asked, flinching.

The young man didn't look muscular, but athletic, and maybe even famous as if he had appeared in movies. Wearing a black suit, white shirt, and smelling of expensive aftershave, he definitely to be some type of a salesman. That meant they had something in common.

"My name's George Gibson." Coughing, and feeling a pin-sticking ache in his chest, he covered his mouth. "What's yer name again, young man?" He cupped his arthritic fingers around his ear to try to hear him better. He needed hearing aids, but could never afford them because he never had insurance, and Medicare didn't cover the hardware. "I can't afford the fancy hearing aids they have these days, so I have to keep asking people to speak up." He knew he hadn't asked the young man his name, but he also knew how to extract information from people. His company had named him salesman of the year in 1965 and 1967. He knew how to make someone open their door after closing it in his face.

The man had a perturbed glare in his brown eyes. George interpreted the look as: "I'll tell you one thing, and from now on leave me alone."

"Pete," the young man answered, picking up his briefcase and setting it under his window. "Pete's my name." Then he turned away.

"Please ta meetchya, Pete." George definitely felt the cold shoulder.

The bus door hissed shut, the clutch popped into drive, and all the passengers grew quiet and began looking out the window. The ambience felt soft and calm, and people appeared relieved at finally being able to settle down and let down their guards on their way to their destinations.

Glancing at the two people in front of him, George remembered having to look over people when he had to ride

Pete's Crossroad

Army buses through France and England. He recalled riding on an LCVP boat as it rocked and dashed through tall waves on its approach to Normandy. He believed he was on that boat right now!

Suddenly, the bus bolted, bringing George back into the present. Gasping, he almost said something, but he bit his lip, believing that Pete next to him would think he was nuts or ill. The bus might stop, and the Daryl driver might force him to disembark. No! He couldn't have his life interrupted like that right now!

Relief settled in him when Daryl pulled a microphone down from the console and clicked it on. "Good afternoon folks, I'm Daryl, and I'd like to thank you for this opportunity to travel with Greyhound." He was middle aged, and George thought he sounded like a disc jockey on a radio station. "Our first stop will be a fifteen minute layover in San Bernardino. And we should arrive there at approximately 4:15 p.m. Meanwhile, please enjoy the music on the channels at your sidearm, and feel free to access our wireless internet connection. If you need assistance, please let me know at any time during our journey. ..."

Daryl kept talking facts, but George tuned him out to stare out the window, beyond the terrain where Pete appeared to be deeply contemplating. Another memory popped into his mind: The expression on his wife's face back in 1962 when he left her at a Greyhound station in Chicago for two years to take a job as a salesman in Denver. He recalled her face back then, beautiful, with round features and a long nose like Eva Gardner. His son Donny had that nose. Donny...how old was he back then? Where is he now? Can I find him? When he wondered what he'd do if he *couldn't* find Donny, his thoughts blurred into the telephone poles and cell phone towers whipping by them. "What was that exact date?" he asked, snapping his fingers, straining to remember the details.

"What?" Pete asked, jumping in his seat.

George said: "I'm just trying to remember a date. That's all."

J.P. Osterman

Opening his thermos, Pete poured himself some coffee, sipped it, and said, "Oh." Then he leaned away from George to look out the window.

Smelling Pete's cream-and-sugar scented air, George sank in his seat as a date flashed through his mind: June 7, 1962. It triggered a memory that welled into a full-blown reality, transporting him back into time. He was at a bus station in Chicago. A woman sitting on the bench next to him had her radio turned on and playing "Lonely City." The woman was his wife, Sue Lynn. With a sad expression on her face, but sitting up tall, strong, and proud, she kissed George goodbye. Putting his arms around Sue Lynn, he then kissed his son Donny, goodbye. Donny was a feisty tow-haired boy of five at the time, and a baseball pitcher wannabe. The Chicago bus depot had almost the same exact roof with the same shake shingles as the one George's bus just left at the Los Angeles station. The seats were the same brown benches, and even the people looked the same, except for the style of clothes. He remembered the hate on Sue Lynn's face, and her angry eyes, and her disbelief when he told her, "I'll be back in a few weeks." She cried as George boarded the bus and it left the station. He remembered seeing her figure sink on the horizon of the street as he watched her from the back window of the bus. "I didn't see Donny again until he was ten," George said, swallowing back tears, waving at an empty bench they had just passed, believing he was still seeing Sue Lynn and Donny, and envisioning them waving goodbye back to him.

Pete turned to him and gave him a shocked glare. "What? You talking to me?"

George felt trapped. Beads of sweat hit his forehead. Gulping in a huge draught of oxygen, he said, "Oh, I was just remembering a time I said goodbye to my family. That's all." He sank back into his seat, glanced down at his stiff knees, and began rubbing his pained thighs. He still believed he was hearing the lyrics of "Lonely City." They were curls of vengeance wafting through time until he could make amends to Donny and his grandchildren. Those lyrics and faces would always haunt him until he could receive forgiveness. Now, Albuquerque was becoming more than a final destination, it was morphing into a spiritual force, pulling him to some unknown final calling.

"Nice to meet ya, Pete. I don't think I said that before," George said, imbibing the smell of coffee wafting up from Pete's cup.

"No, you did, Mr. Gibson."

"Call me George, Pete." Again he smelled the air that wafted into the depths of his being. "That sure smells good! Brings back memories of those old Folgers commercials!"

The scent triggered a memory from the fall of 1963. He, Sue Lynn, and five-year-old Donny were finishing eating breakfast in their little farm house kitchen. With her twirling flowered skirt, Sue Lynn looked like a dancer from the 1950s show *American Bandstand*. Donny stood up from the table, kissed his mother on the cheek, and gave George a big high-five goodbye. "I'm gonna miss the school bus, Dad! See ya after school Mom...love ya, Dad!" George believed that every household was playing out that same scenario at that same moment in time. Except they had fallen on hard times. The crops were failing. They were near financial ruin. He had to leave home to find work—to send home money or they'd lose the farm and wind up homeless.

"I caused my family to die!" George cried, dabbing tears.

Passengers in front of him peeked up behind their seats. One man asked, "Is the guy sick?"

"Is he nuts?" another whispered loudly.

Waving them off, George coughed, sniffled, leaned a little into Pete's direction, and said, "*Ahhh*, all those suitcases were so heavy they nearly killed me, that's all!" He had to think of something, or fake an injury, to keep them from believing he was crazy, or tell Daryl to stop the bus.

"What?" Pete asked, straightening up in his seat as if George had just startled him awake. "I'm...um...sorry, Mister if I bumped you or accidentally poked you." Pete scratched his chin. "You're not making much sense though, Mr. Gibson." He craned his neck to see above the head of the passenger in front of him. "Maybe I better call Daryl."

"Oh, no…don't do that! I'm sorry, young man," George said, loosening his collar and sipping water from a cold bottle he had pulled out of his cooler. Straightening up, he pointed toward the bottom of the bus. "Everything I own's in one giant suitcase down there." He laughed. "One hell-of-a-trunk! That's it." He felt proud, until he thought about everything he had owned over the course of the last fifty years. So much, but he had lost it all. He had land when he was in his late twenties, a home on his land by the time he was in his mid-thirties, five cars, and several closets of business suits. Those he believed were the most important things, now gone. His wife, son, and grandchildren, gone. "Everything's gone," he said, staring at the aisle floor to the left of him.

The lines on Pete's face twisted in confusion. "Don't you have a place? A house? An apartment. Something?" Adjusting his elbows on his arm rests, obviously trying to get comfortable, he folded his hands against his starched white shirt and talked to George with the side of his face plastered against the blue-green-red headrest. He crossed his legs. He appeared like a perfect package of protection and a successful salesman.

From all of Pete's quick evasive movements, George gleaned that Pete was uncomfortable talking. Part of him wanted to cut off the conversation too; but when he glanced at Pete's perfectly tailored suit and his richly polished black shoes, he realized that Pete reminded him of himself over fifty years ago, back in 1962, when he had left Sue Lynn, when he had left his little Donny. And with all the memories bubbling up in his mind like water rising and surging in a riverbed, he found himself talking more even though he told himself to shut up and say no more.

"Well, where do you live, George?" Pete asked again in a snappy tone of voice.

Pete's Crossroad

George peered into the brown depth of Pete's eyes. "I had a room in a small house that I shared with a couple o' guys." Groaning, he reached inside the seat pocket in front of him, hoping to find a bag of peanuts or crackers. "But something came up, so I packed up for Albuquerque."

"Oh," Pete said, his lips turning down as he glanced toward the front of the bus. The new hour was merging into afternoon traffic; and now-and-then, the bus lurched as it came to a sudden grinding stop.

The bumper-to-bumper jolts made George hold his stomach and rock in his seat. "*Rrr.*"

"You okay, George?" Pete asked. "'Cause if not, I think there's a barf bag in that seat pocket."

Taking another sip of water but also feeling dizzy, George said, "No...I'm okay, Pete, thanks." He lifted out his white handkerchief and wiped his bald head. "All these sudden movements reminded me of the time I got sea sick while in the LCVP boat heading to Normandy beach." He laughed when the bus finally approached a clearing in the road and began rolling at 55 miles per hour. "Say, where you from, Pete?"

Scratching his sideburns, Pete replied, "Hollywood." He took another swig of his coffee, gulping it down hard. "Actually, more around Los Angeles." His chest was rising and falling, and his hands were gripping the arm rests so tightly that he looked as if he were about to take off in an airplane. "I was sharing a place with a guy I worked with in Los Angeles."

"Wow," George gasped, "it sounds like ya don't quite know exactly where ya live either, Pete." Chuckling, he sat up straight and tall, believing he might be sitting next to a movie star. "Been in any films out there in Hollywood?"

"Uh-uh," Pete replied, shaking his head no, the expression on his face painful as if someone had kicked him in the past and he had learned a hard lesson. Then he adjusted his little round vent high above his head and nuzzled back into his chair, staring wide-eyed into the seat in front of him. Folding his arms again in a gesture of self-protection, he rolled his shoulders into the cushion, obviously trying to burrow into a comfortable niche. When he inhaled deeply, Pete sounded like a person running into the ocean after spending a day out in the scorching sun.

"That's a mighty big city, Hollywood," George said. The sign on the side of the hill flashed through his mind. To him the place stood for people who left their hometown lives to fulfill their dreams of success; however, most people encountered failure instead. He related to the latter. "You don't look like you come from a big city though."

"Not originally," Pete said.

"Oh? Where?"

Pete shrugged. "I don't like talking about it, Mr. Gibson."

"Oh, okay," George said, his head bending a little in rejection. "Ya know…we have that in common."

"What's that?" Pete asked, his brown eyebrows rising.

"It sounds like we've both been wanderin' around for years. We've both been livin' without really knowin' where we're goin'," George replied.

"*Hmm.*" Pete turned away from him.

Suddenly, George thought of the first time he spotted Pete. Laughing, he leaned a bit into his face. "Ya know, when I first saw ya, ya reminded me of a race car driver I once saw on TV. I like watchin' the races, especially stock car races."

"Really!" Pete said, reeling back.

George inspected the features on his face. "The famous race car driver…lemme think—" He snapped his fingers that barely made a sound. "Oh! Tony Stewart. That's him. They nicknamed him Smoke."

Pete shook his head. "Tony Stewart? Never heard of him."

"Well, ya look just like him with your dark hair and athletic build." George moved his forefinger in front of Pete's face as if tracing his features with a charcoal pencil. "Your dark eyes…and ya slick back your hair just like him…and the shape of your face is like his too. And I notice ya like mirrored sunglasses." He winked, elbowed Pete gently in the arm, and

Pete's Crossroad

gestured at the glasses peeking out of his suit coat. "Race car drivers wear *your* type of glasses so they don't wreck their cars in all that sun dazzle."

Pete's lips opened in amazement and he rubbed his chin. "Really."

"He's famous, that Tony Stewart," George said.

"How famous?" Pete asked. "And you're sure I'm his look-a-like?"

"Ya sure do!" Then George gestured like a race car whizzing by on a track. "Tony Stewart won the Winston Cup and the Nextel Cup. *Zoom*! He's a real crackerjack! Don'tcha ever watch auto racin' on TV?"

"Not much," Pete shrugged as he slipped out his cell phone and checked the time. "What about you?" He looked at him askance. "Where are *you* from, George?"

George realized that Pete was changing the subject to get the focus off himself. Inspecting Pete from his knees to his fingertips, he noticed that Pete looked suddenly riveted to his seat. Something bad had happened to him in the past, or was terrifying him now. George decided to go in the direction Pete wanted to take him, hoping to learn more about what was bothering him later on in the future. "Where am I from? Well, I'm a little bit from all over the place."

Breathing a bit more easily, Pete said: "Oh yeah? Where?"

Leaning back and glancing at the young disheveled woman sitting next to him across the aisle, George replied: "I started my life on a little farm in Indiana…Hannah, Indiana. That's about a-hunnert-and-fifty miles southeast o' Chicago. Ever hear of it?"

Pete exhaled a hard "Nope."

George let out a laugh, reached up, and turned on his mini-light on his ceiling panel. Peering outside through Pete's long window, he noticed the day was overcast. The smog had a nesting hazy resting on the foothills, shading all the palm trees and freeway signs. The billboards appeared toasty bronze. He couldn't tell whether it was afternoon or dusk.

J.P. Osterman

Time blurred. He felt in between ocean and desert, sun and moon. The freeway was disorienting like rocketing off Earth, until the word *Albuquerque* flashed through his mind, stabilizing medicine. "You're not alone, Pete," George began. "Most people haven't heard of Hannah, Indiana either."

"Hannah," Pete repeated.

"Last I heard about Hannah, it ain't farm country anymore," George said. "Everything from Schererville to Wanatah is all built up now. All that crop land is now businesses and restaurants."

Pete shook his head in an expression of bewilderment. "Farm country is pretty far from Los Angeles, George. What brought you all the way from Indiana to here?"

The bus engine revved as it picked up speed. Now they were heading away from the big cities on the I-10 freeway. When Pete turned to see the sights, George guessed Pete might never return to Hollywood. For some reason, Pete was making a great escape out of Los Angeles. He felt sorry for him. He wanted to put him further at ease, so he continued to talk about what made him leave Indiana.

"I started out as a farmer, Pete, after World War II," George began, slipping a bag of peanuts out of his jacket pocket. He opened the wrapper, sprinkled a few nuts into the palm of his shaking hand, and then threw them on his tongue. The salt-sharp taste felt gritty—his mouth stinging as the tang seeped past his dentures down his throat. After swallowing, he continued: "Then in 1962, when my crops failed for the third year in a row, I turned to traveling salesman, cowhand, handyman—*anything* for work." Inspecting Pete's face and seeing that he looked interested, George said, "I dressed like you're dressed right now, fancy mostly." He pointed to Pete's silver buttons on his suit coat lying over the arm of his chair beneath the window. "Mostly, I was a Fuller brush salesman. Sometimes, I sold Encyclopedia Britannica." He laughed as he remembered door-upon-door slammed shut in his face. "You name it, Pete…I did it." The bus turned sharply, and George grabbed the edge of the seat in front of him. "But I retired from that line o' work about ten years back. Then I started workin' for Walmart part time." He coughed, choking.

"You okay, George?" Pete asked, thrusting George's bottle of water into his shaking hands.

"Fine," George waved as he coughed through another rasping breath. He remembered what the doctor told him a few days ago: "Mr. Gibson, you need hospice care." Leaving most of his belongings behind for his roommates, he had his friends help him pack up his things, and he ran to the Motel 6 instead. But he didn't want to tell Pete that. Pete might tell Daryl the bus driver, who might make him disembark from the bus at the next stop and call an ambulance. That would put an end to his plans to see Donny and his grandchildren. He couldn't have that. Albuquerque was calling to him like God speaking his name through a megaphone!

George spit into his handkerchief; and when he noticed that the sound had disgusted Pete who reeled back in fear of catching some type of bad illness, he wadded up the dirty cloth, glanced down in red-faced shame, and took out a clean handkerchief from his travel bag, clenching it tightly in his fist. Glancing into Pete's face, he noticed lines of curiosity; and he realized that something he had said had ignited a spark of enthusiasm in Pete.

"So you were a pretty good salesman then huh, George?" Pete looked back and forth from George's handkerchief to his face. "From what you said earlier, you seem like you were a *great* salesman. You won lots of awards!" He appeared to want to learn everything now. "So, George," he whispered, "what *are* the keys to success?"

After his breathing regulated back to normal, George sat back relaxed. "Yep, I sure did win lots of awards…everything from trophies to money." He gobbled down another mouthful of peanuts, and then reached into his bag, whipped out his half-empty bottle of water, gulped down the rest of the beverage, and then stuck the empty bottle into the flap in front of him.

Pete shook his head in an expression of self-confidence. "I sell too."

"Whataya sell?"

"Mannequins," Pete replied, his shoulders and jaw lifting in pride. Reaching down into his shiny black briefcase, he pulled out a folded glossy paper and handed it to George. "Here's a brochure I distribute to my customers." The look on Pete's face was inviting. He was obviously hoping that George might know influential people who might want to place orders. "I was a clothing designer at one point, in L. A. But then I just took this job with Fossil Inc. in Santa Monica about a month ago. That's why I'm going to Albuquerque. To display and sell these models in a booth at the convention center." He pointed to several mannequins on the front flap that were dressed in designer wear. "If I sell my quota, I'm hoping the CEO, Terrence Frapley, will give me a permanent position where he has an immediate opening. He has several available right now, around the world!"

"Maybe New York City?" George asked.

Shrugging, Pete replied: "Maybe…but I don't know. All I know is that I have all my stuff in storage. I need a permanent job with this company. Then I can settle down somewhere."

Bumping Pete jokingly on the arm, George waved the brochure that Pete had given him in the air. "See, Pete! We *do* have something in common. I told ya so."

"What's that?" Pete asked.

"We're both lookin' for permanent places, Pete," George replied.

His head tilting as if he were weighing in on the definition of permanent versus temporary, Pete said, "I guess you could say that, George."

Steadying the brochure in front of his eyes, George squinted to try to read the small print. "My vision's kinda bad, Pete," he said, his nose wrinkling as he held the brochure into the light and then brought the paper to the rim of his sliver framed reading glasses. Unable to make out the words, he still said: "My, yes! Mighty fine brochure, Pete. You did this yourself?"

"All on my own!"

He handed the brochure back to Pete who waved it in the air like a flag. "Oh, you can keep that one, George." He tapped his briefcase. "I have tons of 'em." He shone the confidence of having passed out a million of them.

George grew puzzled. If Pete were really a designer, couldn't he afford to fly? Why take a bus? Biting the inside of his lower lip as if trying to stop from asking the question but still curious, he decided to asked Pete the question anyway, to test the waters of their growing friendship. "So, Pete, what are ya doin' on a bus?" He nodded at Pete's perfectly pressed shirt and expensive shiny suit coat. "A guy like you, dressed nice as ya are, can surely afford to fly."

Pete cleared his throat, unbuttoned the top button of his shirt, and rubbed his neck until blotches appeared. His skin was white. For someone living near the beach, he hadn't hardly spent anytime out in the sun. George almost asked him if he was a workaholic, until Pete began checking his cell phone for messages. Then George realized that Pete was definitely covering up something. Every time he had asked him a personal question, Pete turned away, obviously avoiding him.

"*Ahhh*," Pete groaned.

"What's wrong?" George asked.

"Not one message from my team in Albuquerque. Darn!" he replied.

"Getting an answer otta ya, Pete, is like ironing a patch over a hole in a pair of blue jeans," George chuckled.

"Huh?" Pete grimaced.

"Well…I just wondered why you're not flyin' to Albuquerque, that's all," George said softly, realizing Pete wasn't making any sense, or he was misinterpreting his expressions and body language that appeared evasive and aloof.

J.P. Osterman

"Oh," Pete said, waving off the misunderstanding. "I hate flying. And my sales partner and best friend, Fred, said he'd set up the booth at the convention center and cover for me so I could take the bus instead. So I'm here...on a Greyhound! Who woulda ever guessed!" Rubbing his eyes like a child trying fighting off sleep, he appeared about ready to doze off as a strand of his back hair dropped over his ear. Quickly, he brushed it back. He was the type of person who hated having anything out of place, anything less than perfect.

George thought that if Pete were to grow plastic skin he'd look like one of those mannequins he was selling. "Ya hate flying then, huh?"

"Can't stand it," Pete replied, gripping his armrest as if George's comment had launched him inside a plane. He raised his head toward the little round vent that streamed cold air into his face. Black strands of his gelled hair flickered. Any moment and they might completely come undone. "I can't go back to Santa Monica."

Knowing he had just tapped into a delicate piece of Pete's life, George asked, "Why not?"

Pete eyes looked as if they were scanning the brushy mountains outside their window for a hide out. "That's it. I can't go back." He looked mesmerized. "Maybe I'll head up to Vegas. There's a big bash going on there after the convention. I don't know." Pushing up his sleeve, he checked the time on his Rolex. Then he tapped its face. He appeared agitated and afraid.

"What's wrong in Santa Monica, Pete?" George asked, this time louder than before.

Pete glanced outside and then quickly checked the time on his Rolex as if experiencing a panic attack. "I, uh—"

"Your watch not working, Pete?" George asked, lifting out his watch. "Looks like we've only been gone a half an hour. It's 3:15 p.m."

"Oh my God!" Pete yanked his laptop and ear plugs out of his briefcase.

Pete's Crossroad

"What's wrong?" George gasped, believing that maybe Pete had left something behind at the station.

"The game!" Pete fired up his laptop.

"What game?" George craned to see the screen.

Pete had the eyes of an excited ten-year-old. "Atlanta Braves versus the Dodgers. The game's gonna start any moment." He turned away, diverting all his attention into his laptop.

"Sorry to bother ya," George whispered in his direction, but Pete wasn't listening, and George continued perusing the brochure Pete had shone him. There were one-inch pictures of mannequins on display in several manufacturing companies, but he didn't have a magnifying glass to see their details. There were dwarf-size mannequins, pot-bellied mannequins, mannequins with tiny waists and long arms; pear-shaped, full-hipped, and full-figure mannequins. George strained to read the manufacturer's name. "Where'd ya say ya work, Pete?" he asked. "Who do ya work for?"

Pete whisked the brochure out of his hand. He had a look of embarrassment on his face. "You won't mind if I take this now." He slapped his laptop closed.

"Well, I—"

"I'll put this brochure with the others...and my catalogue. I designed them all myself," Pete said proudly, jamming the brochure deep inside the pocket of the briefcase. He gave out a feigned laugh. "These brochures cost a lot to print you know." One caught on his sleeve, attaching to the material like glue. Pete pried it off against his laptop.

"You look like something just scared ya half to death, Pete," George said, concerned. He had little time left, but Pete appeared to be engaged in his own unique race against time. Something was very wrong, and Pete was being extraordinarily closed lipped.

"Nah, nothing's wrong, just urgent, that's all," Pete said, his hand shaking, a little sweat beading below his small black sideburns.

Could Pete be afraid that I might say something negative

about his brochure? George wondered, gesturing at the laptop he had shuddering like house blinds. "I thought you were going to watch the baseball game."

"It's not on yet," he said, touching the laptop. Obviously he had used the game as a ploy to stop the conversation.

George pointed to a small picture in the brochure that Pete had tried carefully to smooth out and save. He was still trying to salvage the wrinkled brochure, treating it like piece of delicate gold foil. "I knew a lady once who looked like that mannequin right there." All he could really see was a 1950s retro skirt. Still the hoop style reminded him of Sue Lynn. "Beautiful thing she was."

"What happened to her?" Pete asked, sliding his laptop into his briefcase and stuffing his earphones into his pocket.

George laughed excitedly. "I married her!" He recalled the day he met Sue Lynn. He had just taken over the family farm when he spotted her in a long line of women at a Grange dance in May of 1955. "That one moment changed my life."

"Changed your life? One moment can do all that?" Pete asked.

"Sure! I asked Sue Lynn to dance with me, and we married six months later." Rolling up his empty package of peanuts, he shoved it into the little waste bag at the side of his seat. "We live in moments, Pete. Life really happens in seconds." He tapped his armrest to the beat of a second hand on a clock.

Pete shook a little. "Oh, you mean marriage, *mmm*, not *ever* for me! I'm wanting to strike it big in the fashion industry, and make money, millions!"

"I guess *that* could be one o' them kinds a moments," George agreed, remembering so many now flashing through his mind. "Seems like I'm thinking back about all o' my life-changin' moments while yours are all ahead of ya."

Pete nodded in agreement. "I guess you're right, but you'll never catch *me* walking down the aisle."

Chuckling, George said: "Don't talk so fast, Pete. Look

around ya." He gestured at the sleeping woman across the aisle from him. "Anything can happen at any moment that could alter your life for good. Anytime, you could meet yer special person." Feeling a cramp in his leg, he shifted in his seat and moved closer to Pete.

Pete's Adam's apple jiggling as he swallowed hard. He had fear in his eyes…a haunting black terror that appeared in pupils. Did marriage trigger the change, or something terrible in his childhood? Pete clammed up as if he might break out in a sweat. "Oh, yeah, *ahem*, I guess you're right." Then he turned away and looked out the window.

Leaning back in his seat, George suspected he was getting closer to learning the truth about Pete; but in the process, he was also alienating him. Taking the approach of talking to him like father-to-son might reel Pete back to having a conversation. "I have a son who lives twenty-five miles outside of Albuquerque."

"A son?" Pete asked, turning toward George. "Huh!"

"Yep. His name's Donny."

"That's nice," Pete said, folding his arms comfortably.

Trying to remember Donny's birthday, George tapped his forehead. "Donny has three children…my grandchildren!" He laughed. "My gosh, when I was your age and looking into the future, I never thought I'd ever have grandchildren!"

"I sure don't believe I'll ever have any!" Pete exclaimed.

George tapped his armrests like a king perched on a throne. "I might have a great-grandchild too, but I don't know yet until I get there, until I can see Donny face-to-face."

"How long has it been since you've seen son, Donny?" Pete asked, smiling and clasping his fingers.

Pete's grin appeared plastic, and George believed he was now treating him like a prospective customer. Looking askance into the ceiling light, George replied, "Oh, let me see…Sue Lynn died in 1996. So that was the last time I saw Donny."

"Why so long?"

Another memory flashed through George's mind. "Sue

Lynn, my wife, came down with cancer many years before that. She had several rounds of chemotherapy." George couldn't tell Pete that he hadn't been there to comfort her in her last days. He began feeling constricting guilt.

"Sorry about that, George," Pete said.

He shook a bit through the sad memory. "Donny had Sue Lynn's body cremated after she died. When I did finally arrive in Albuquerque, he yelled at me quite a bit for…for not making better funeral arrangements, not being there, but I couldn't…I just couldn't!"

"Oh, wow," Pete said, his face whitening, the father-son conflict obviously affecting him.

George felt a sudden brain fog stopping up his thoughts, and he rubbed his forehead to try to stop it. "Donny told me he never wanted to—to see me again."

"Oh, no," Pete frowned.

Coughing, George said, "Donny broke off all contact with me after that." Again, he cleared his throat that stung as tears filled his eyes. "I wrote him several times…my son!" He felt the words rip something behind his ribs.

"It doesn't make sense that he'd do that, especially since you tried reaching out to him several times," Pete said.

"Yep. Christmas, birthdays…but to Donny, I was already dust," George said.

"*Whew*, sounds like you've spent *years* trying to reach him, but with *no* answer," Pete said, but then he suddenly calmed down. "But luckily, you have, 'cause you're on your way to see your son right now."

George hadn't told him the real truth—quite the opposite. "Remember what I said about a person's life changing in a second?" he asked.

"Yeah?"

He laughed in the realization that he had lived through, and learned from, hard and painful lessons. "Well, regrets and what ifs can do the same thing to ya, Pete," he gasped for air. "Over time, they grow to the point where they cut off yer circulation, like a bad branch diseasing a tree. It dies way too soon, before its time...dies in a heartbeat." He suddenly felt his skip.

"Looks like *you* know that truth as a *fact*," Pete said, fear showing in his eyes.

George shook his warning finger at him in a playful gesture. "Well...now's the time to be thinking about yer own life, Pete." Then he realized he was scaring Pete. Pete's plan was to make money and be successfully famous while his topic of conversation was obviously putting a damper on Pete's vision for his life. "When ya alienate your family, it's really the beginning of your own death." He saw Pete's wide-eyed glare and white cheeks. "Some things, some pains and injuries, *I* caused *myself*...no one to blame but me...myself."

Pete gasped, "Wow! I never thought about life that way."

"You're young, that's understandable," George said, rubbing his fingers over his bald head. He felt a strange pinching in his shoulders. His chest felt suddenly heavy. He unbuttoned the top button of his red and green checkerboard-pattern shirt. "Sure wish I could get some more water." He took out his handkerchief and patted his forehead.

The woman next to George leaned across the aisle. "Hey, Mister, are you all right? I have a cell phone. I can call an ambulance."

"No—I'm, I'm fine, but thank ya kindly," George said. The odd thumps in his heart now fading.

Pete stood up and grabbed the handrail below the baggage rack. "Mr. Gibson needs some water!" Jumping over George, he ran to the back of the bus, to the restroom.

The young woman next to him stood up and walked to the front of the bus. Quickly, she returned with a cold bottle of water. "Daryl told me to give this to you, George."

"Is everything all right back there now?" Daryl called, a piercing expression showing in the reflection in his rear-view mirror. He looked about ready to make an emergency stop.

"I'm giving him some water! Let's give him time before you stop the bus." The young woman gave Daryl the thumbs up signal. With shaking hands, she opened the bottle, put it into George's hands, and then sat down quickly, rubbing her arms. She appeared overly nervous, and engrossed in a deep internal battle. She didn't want the bus delayed either.

George noticed her always in her seat, and either asleep or staring at objects. "Thanks, Ma'am," George said, lifting himself a little off his seat, readjusting his back into the cushion. "I think I'm better now. What's your name?"

When she smiled, her two front teeth appeared coffee stained, and they had a little space between them. She looked like a waitress. George had also smelled a lingering cigarette scent emanating from her. "Sandy. My name is Sandy Walston." Strands of her blond hair slipped off her ears and onto her thin pale cheeks. She shrugged shyly and was sometimes shaking. Maybe she had a drinking problem or drug problem, or perhaps she was leaving L. A. to escape trouble. Her pallid lips began vibrating; and then she sighed deeply, put her head on the headrest, closed her eyes, and seemed to fall asleep immediately. "I'm sure you'll be okay now, George." She yawned. "Let me know if I can help you again." She was out of it!

Pete returned, scooted into his seat, handed George a bundle of wet paper towels, and then increased the air flow on the ceiling vent. "I can let you use my cell phone to call your son, Donny, right now if you want to," he said, showing him his phone.

Listening to the wheezing sounds coming from his chest, George took out his wallet and began rifling through its contents. His fingers were shaking. At one point, he thought he was going to spill everything on the floor. "Donny's number has to be here somewhere." He couldn't find it. "Maybe it's up there, in my carry-on."

"I can get that for you," Pete said, standing.

George shook his head. "No, I think it's in my big suitcase. But that's in the storage compartment."

"Oh." Pete sit down slowly, glancing at the time.

Pete's Crossroad

"Maybe the driver can get the phone number out for you when we stop." He pulled out his bus schedule. "We have a thirty minute layover in Blythe, California. That's about another fifteen minutes away."

"Good, good," George said, feeling a bit better, but he still felt a slight ache when he moved his left shoulder. He wasn't better. He knew it. Some type of rip had occurred deep within him, scaring him. *I haveta make it to Albuquerque. I just haveta!*

"You can get out in Blythe and stretch your legs a bit, George," Pete said, his voice encouraging. "Someone told me the transit center there has a good place to eat. I'm sure once we arrive, you can call your son. I'm sure he'll pick you up, no problem." He looked down at the floor, exhaled, and then ran his fingers through his hair.

George noticed Pete's exaggerated body language that appeared dismal. He really didn't want anything more to do with him. He only wanted to sit back, relax, and finish his bus ride in peace. *I'm complicating his life*, George thought. Another sharp pain struck his chest as if a pin had pushed through it. He put his hand over his heart and sank into his seat. "You look about ready to dive out the window to get away from me 'n my problems, Pete," he laughed. He always believed humor would lighten any situation, maybe even keep him from dying.

Pete quickly turned to him. "George, I—I just can't—"

"You can move to another seat, if you want to, Pete." He gestured at the back of the bus. "Don't mind me. I won't cause no body no more trouble." He patted Pete's hand.

Pete pulled it away and returned to glancing out the window. "No problem, George. Where I'm at is just fine." Still, he scooted close to the window.

Chuckling, George said, "Most people never get to sit next to a dyin' man."

"Huh?!" Pete sat up and turned to him. "Whataya mean, dying?" The black pupils of his eyes were round with fright. "Dying? Right now?"

Two people in front of them peered up over their seats.

J.P. Osterman

After hearing them exchange words with Pete, George felt another bout of brain fog blocking his thoughts. His arms felt numb, his chest heavy, his skin cold one minute but hot the next. He didn't quite know what to do, except for what the doctor had told him before he left, "Get yourself to a hospital the second you have any of these symptoms." He began to believe the worst: he might not make it to Albuquerque. Out the huge front window, he saw the black pavement with its white dividing lines, all outstretching anguish into the distance.

Glancing around, he eyed the people around him. There were two children way in the back eating crackers. In front of them, a group of laughing and texting teenagers. In front of them, a row of college kids—obviously on spring break—who were snickering and passing around beers from a cooler. At the front of the bus, conversing in Japanese, were the tourists. What would happen to everyone, he thought, if I need to stop? He never asked people to go out of their way for him, and he hated asking for favors. The last legacy he wanted to leave behind was being a bother.

Tapping him on the shoulder, Pete asked, "You think your son, Donny, could meet you at the bus station in Albuquerque if Daryl can get a hold of him?" Pete poured another cup of coffee from his thermos. "If you can't find his phone number in your big suitcase, it might be listed in the phone book."

George felt a little better now, after drinking some water and lifting his face into the rushing cold air coming from his ceiling vent. "I suppose so. I'm hoping to settle down in Albuquerque, by Donny and the grandkids. So if I can't find the phone number, I'll just call a Taxi, get a motel, and then wait until I can get a hold of Donny."

"Oh, great! See? Problem solved!" Pete was looking to Heaven, implying that after Albuquerque, he'd be rid of George and finally be able to remain happily alone.

"Maybe Donny, or one o' the grandkids, can find a little space to squeeze me in," George began, "and if they can't,

34

Pete's Crossroad

well, I'll just scrape me up one of those little mobile homes in one of those fancy trailer parks." The dream felt refreshing. "My place'll have a pool, and lots of lantern lights, and a little space out in the back where I can plant some seeds I brought with me right here in my coat pocket." He leaned to the side and tapped his pant pocket, the sounds of mixing seeds comforting him. "I'll grow a few ears-o-corn and some radishes. And if that sand ain't too hard in Albuquerque, maybe I might even try my luck with tomatoes."

"Sounds like a solid goal," Pete said.

"You look like ya don't believe me," George said.

"Oh I do!" Pete leaned away from him.

George shook his finger and furled his eyebrows. "Lemme tell ya about tomatoes."

Pete laughed a little. "Tomatoes?" He gestured out the window. "I don't know where the heck you're intending on planting tomatoes, 'cause Albuquerque is desert territory."

"Tomatoes are delicate things to grow," George said, finally catching his breath. "They're worse than roses." Putting his hand over his stomach, he remembered what the doctor had told him: *We're looking at hospice care for you, Mr. Gibson...soon.* "No, no!"

"What?" Pete asked, concerned, and pointing at George's jacket setting alongside his cooler. "You should check your wallet again...try to find your son's phone number before we get to Blythe." Pete handed him the wet rag that George had flung over his armrest.

George began tapping his forehead and face with it. "Lemme finish my story about tomatoes."

"Well...all right, George, but I think you're wasting time. You should be looking for your son's phone number," Pete said softly. "I normally wouldn't suggest something to a stranger, and I always mind my own business, but—"

"Bugs," George smiled and shuttered. He made creepy crawly expressions with his hands.

"Bugs?" Pete looked perplexed. "Now?"

"Bugs love tomatoes, and worms eat 'em right up, Pete."

J.P. Osterman

Pete sighed. Obviously he was giving into listening to the old man's story. "My dad fished with worms, but I always *hated* fishing. My dad used to wake me up real early in the morning, and I *hated* that 'cause I was always a night person, even as a kid."

After a long pause, George said, "Sounds like you hated your dad."

Pete appeared taken off guard. "Uh, well—"

Seeing him fidget, George realized that what he had just said made him feel uncomfortable. A great distance began spreading between them. "Sorry about that, Pete. I guess I was a bit too blunt."

"Yeah, George, you sure were, whoa," Pete said, his head bowed in obvious shame.

"Lousy worms!" George said, laughing, changing the subject, watching Pete recover from his blunt comment. "I once sprayed five fields with insecticide, but the bugs always came back. Those God awful critters almost took out an entire crop of soybeans." If a bug had been in between his fingers, he would have pinched off its head. "Darn bugs nearly drove me bankrupt." He felt a penetrating sadness creeping through him. "That's one of the reasons I had to leave Sue Lynn and the kids, and get a city job."

"Oh," Pete said as if putting two-and-two together. "I guess sometimes taking the best precautions don't always yield success."

"Yep," George said. "Seems like my entire life has been just that...one precaution after another...one fight after another."

"Naw," Pete said, "that can't be completely true!" He laughed a little.

"I'll tell ya what I did back then...back when those bugs killed my crops," George said.

"What did you do?" Pete asked, now on edge of his seat, his eyes filled with longing for all of life's problems.

"I walked every row and sprayed every plant by hand,"

Pete's Crossroad

George said. "Took me two weeks workin' eighteen hours a day!"

"Wow!" Pete said.

George hit his armrest—a pulse of fight moving into him. "But you know what?"

"What?" Pete asked.

"I got rid of those worms." He tapped his cup holder angrily. "Yes siree, I walloped 'em good." He swung at the air. "Then the rain came and pummeled 'em into the ground into fertilizer! Wouldn't ya know a destructive force turned into a growth hormone!" He huffed out a happy sigh. "I thought everything was all right after that." He saw his hands, rough like alligator skin. "I thought the rain was a good thing and would take me outta the red. I believed we'd all be all right…we'd all be safe and a happy family."

"Well, what happened?!" Pete asked.

George lurched forward in his seat. "One week's worth of rain brought me out of a downward spiral and saved me and my family for a little while."

"Great!" Pete said. "What a story, George. You sure know how to keep a person's interest. What a tall tale!"

"I'm not kiddin', Pete!" George said, stomping his foot a little. "I might be an old geezer, but I've never told a lie."

"Sorry, old man, I didn't mean—"

"Yeah…right…gimme a second here." George put his hand over his chest and drank some more water. He could feel congestion building, hear raspy noises. Soon, if he would be in serious trouble. "People of my generation don't fib, Pete."

"I never said you were lying, George," Pete said softly. Then he turned away. "It's just part of the job guys like us have, you know, stretching stories to close a deal and keeping peoples' attention so they don't walk away from us."

George remembered times like those, especially when his family was near starvation. But he didn't like that evil trait within himself, and he barely used the white-lie strategy to manipulate unsuspecting people. He believed Pete didn't mind lying and manipulating though. He was a man of many secrets.

"Okay, fine." Pete finally said.

George peered around Pete to glance out the window. He saw tall eucalyptus trees, their trunks shedding bark like carrot skins. Workers wrapped in yellow aprons were poking trash with sharp sticks. Oleander bushes were fanning out tall and fat. The bus was streaking past shopping plazas. Hot air over the pavement was wavering in a new type of solar heat. George felt as if the bus were accelerating inside a time warp— and he in a cocoon. He was lifting out of his seat, looking down on the passengers from a small point on the ceiling, so small. One moment, he believed his spirit had lifted out his body; the next moment, he was glancing at Pete, who looked suddenly like Donny. "*Ahhh*!" he shouted.

"What's wrong?" Pete asked, grabbing the back of the seat in front of him. He waved at Daryl the bus driver who was busy turning the big black steering wheel.

George's arms dropped on his lap like weights, his legs felt numb. "My eyes are playin' tricks on me," he said, laughing. "But I'm fine! Just dandy, Pete."

"You don't look fine and dandy to me," Pete said, glancing at George from head to toe. "Even your bald head looks pale, like your cheeks. And you have gray bags under your eyes. I think you need help, old man. Fast." He waved at Daryl, but people were standing up and sitting down in their seats and moving into the aisles. The bus was about to pull off the road, and people were preparing to disembark at Blythe. "How old are you anyway?"

"Eighty-six, Pete." He huffed out a chuckle. "Eighty-six and a half to be exact." Wiping his forehead, he added, "You know, Pete, I lived through the Depression. The *Great* Depression!"

Sitting back down and glancing at his watch, Pete said: "From what I've seen on TV, those were pretty hard times, George. I don't think I could have ever survived that."

"You do survive though," George said. "You make it

Pete's Crossroad

through hard times. You push on even when you don't think you can take the next step." He wanted to pound that toughness into Pete, to instill in him a get-up-and-go attitude that he called Hope. Suddenly, when he looked at Pete, he saw a young version of Donny! And Donny wasn't going away! He was as young as Pete, and almost the same physique and facial features! But he'd never tell Pete that his eyes were playing tricks on his that way—making him see someone who wasn't there. Daryl might pull him off the bus permanently after labeling him "crazy," so he just kept on talking, telling himself: *he looks like Donny, but he's not, he's Pete*!

Donny or Pete, Pete or Donny…they both were the same to George now.

Chapter 3 – Address Unknown

After the bus stopped in Blythe, George and Pete began gently rifling through George's huge suitcase to find Donny's address and phone number. Daryl was patient, but approaching his limit of endurance when George refused to unwrap the gifts.

"You might have accidentally placed the paper with Donny's address and phone number in one of these, George," Pete argued, holding one of the gifts. The box was shoe-sized and wrapped in 1962 newspaper with a bright yellow fraying bow. Pete began gently shaking the gift-wrapped package.

George yanked it away from him. "No!" He pulled the box next to his chest, trying to be as careful as possible not to inflict damage.

He remembered Sue Lynn gently setting the contents inside the box, but he had never asked her what was inside the tissue paper. The box and the yellow ribbon were the last things Sue Lynn had touched. George had to preserve the gift, had to keep the contents special, because then they were still living and breathing Sue Lynn. He had to hand that gift to one of his grandchildren.

"These are all special to me," he said, his breaths heaving as he cradled the gift. "There's no way Donny's address is inside any of these four gifts. I'm tellin' ya. I know I wouldn't do that, 'cause that'd mean I'd haveta unwrap 'em, and I never did that!"

"Okay," Daryl and Pete said simultaneously, backing away from him.

Slowly George calmed when he read a small name tag dangling in the breeze. "What's inside this here box is what I wanna give Sue Beth, my granddaughter. It's from her grandmother direct." He set back the four gift-wrapped packages neatly in his suitcase as Daryl stood glaring at him with his hands on his wide hips. "These were the last things my wife, Sue Lynn touched." He began wiping away tears.

Daryl slapped on his hat and began repacking the luggage compartment, but gave George a little more time to pack up his large suitcase. He was treating every little object as holy. "Obviously, the two suitcases he has and his little cooler are the only things the man has left of his life," he said, "and keeping him going!" he whispered to Pete.

Lifting up George, Pete said, "Okay, okay." He helped George lay all his wrapped gifts back into his suitcase— cushioning the bows as George had done at the motel. Then he fastened the latches on the big suitcase and motioned for Daryl to stick it back into the cargo hold. "Come on, George, let's get back on board. If you don't, the bus can't leave and we can't keep on schedule." He helped George climb back on the bus.

With his hands folded in authority, Daryl asked George, "Now, you sure you don't need a doctor, Mr. Gibson?" He wiped sweat off his forehead. The desert air was hot, the humidity almost nonexistent, the flowers wilting through a water shortage. "From what *I* saw happening back there on the bus about an hour ago, it sure seemed to me like you need a doctor." Daryl was meticulous.

"I'm okay, fine, I told ya, so thanks, and let's get movin' 'cause I know people are waitin' on me, and I don't want 'em angry at me." George said, stepping up the steep three stairs.

"Our next break isn't until Phoenix, Mr. Gibson," Daryl

said, sliding into the driver's seat. He pulled up his sleeve and checked the time. "You have five more minutes to decide, Mr. Gibson. Then this bus leaves. Or if something happens in that time, I call an ambulance."

Waving for passengers to go around him, George said: "I know. I'm all right, Daryl."

People were re-boarding the bus, sidling around George and greeting Daryl. Some passengers were giving George disturbing glances that he interpreted as fear and dread. He wanted to tell them: I'm not a giant dust devil that's gonna overturn the bus in the middle of the desert! Some people, like the Japanese tourists, were kind to him, and offered him help, but he couldn't make out their broken English.

George just kept looking down. Now and then, he bit his lip. He didn't want to say something he might regret, something that might bring the bus to a permanent stop. He had to get to Donny…who was somewhere in Albuquerque. Or was he? That was his last known address…but now, that could be all wrong.

Sandy Walston who had helped him before said, "You okay now, George?" She touched his shoulder, and he felt her compassion. "Did you get enough to eat and drink at the rest stop?" She was shaking and haggard, even though she had slept most of the way from Los Angeles.

Thinking she looked a little like Goldie Hawn dressed in flip-flops and surf clothing, George patted her hand and soaked up some comfort from her kind eyes. "Thanks, I sure did. I'm fine now. Thanks, Sandy. There aren't too many people like you in the world today."

"You're welcome," she said, giggling like a shy child; then she made her way to her seat.

Plopping down half-breathless besides Pete who was busy getting baseball scores off the internet, George tapped him on the shoulder. Instead of jumping in shock as he had done when he first talked to George, Pete pulled out his earplugs and said, "Are you better now?"

Feeling fatherly, he patted Pete's arm. "Yep, thanks."

Pete's Crossroad

Taking the lid off a tall cup of coffee he had bought at the depot, he wiggled into his seat, nuzzling the back of his head into the puffy headrest. "Did I tell ya about the Great Depression, Donny?" His elbow bending from arthritis, he scratched the top of his shiny head.

"Donny?" Pete sat up confused and peered around the bus. "My name's Pete. Remember?"

"Oh yeah," George laughed, feeling embarrassed. "Right! Sorry 'bout that. Donny's been on my mind, that's all." Still, whenever he glanced at Pete, he was continuing to see Donny the way he remembered him the last time he saw him in August of 1996. Hitting his forehead with his finger, he tried snapping out of his hallucination. He knew that Donny was now in his early fifties, and he had no idea how he had changed in those fifteen years, but he was seeing Donny in Pete's face—a thin, blond-haired man with wire-rim glasses who looked like Robert Redford. Then, Donny was a young executive living in Chicago and helping his mother, Sue Beth, with the farm whenever he could.

Elbowing George and handing him a packet of sugar for his coffee, Pete said: "No, George, you didn't tell me about the Depression. You mentioned it though. And I said I didn't think I could have ever made it through those hard times."

George settled back in his seat and began sipping coffee. "In the Depression, we bartered for things. My parents had walnut trees, so we traded walnuts for chickens. And we had all kinds o' potluck meals with people. There were Saturday night dances, Sunday afternoon picnics, hay rides..." He felt suddenly jolted back into the past. He inhaled deeply, imbibing all the sights, smells, and sounds. He continued, "People came through for one another during those times, Pete." He sipped his coffee. "Yes, those were the days. People sure don't care like *that* about other people anymore."

"I can't imagine hard times like those," Pete said. "I grew up in bad neighborhood, in Hollywood, where most people live with steel bars on their doors." Cupping his hands, he blew into them, his breath colliding with the cold air streaming in from the vents. He closed it off. "You have *no* idea what a horrible place my neighborhood was. You survive *only* when you succeed in making people believe you'll fight back! There's no one to help you. No one. And my parents…"

Seeing fear and anger well in him to the point where he couldn't finish his sentence, George said, "You look like someone's about ready to kill ya or something, Pete. What's wrong?" He touched Pete's sleeve, but Pete pulled away. "I know you've been worried about me. I'm sorry I've been such a, well, bother to ya." He leaned over his armchair, trying to catch a glimpse of Pete's face. "But now, I'm worried about you, young fella."

Pete shrugged. "No, no bother." His voice was low, his face expressing tension, his eyes shut tight. "I just don't— well—really want to talk about my past. That's all."

"I understand," George said. "Times always change so quickly, with each generation." Outside it was dark, except for the lights alongside the freeway that appeared to streak alongside the bus like lightning. "Or maybe I'm just so gosh darn old and stuck in the past." He shook his legs to let the blood circulate. "People don't seem to have a clue about what's really important, how to treat people, or who they really are these days."

Pete snapped back, "Do *you*?"

"Huh?" George wiped his stinging tearing eyes.

"Do *you* know who *you* really are? Especially after having lived so long?" Pete asked, louder than before.

"I—well—sort of, *guess* I do," George replied, but also speechless as to how to sum up an entire life with all its lessons in just a few short words. "But what I can tell ya about who I am and what I learned…would be just opinions."

Pete grimaced a little. "That's okay. *Well?*"

George traced Pete's face in the air with his finger. He had done that with Donny—his way of driving a truth into his son. "I learned that sometimes in life, ya gotta take risks…that most times, you have no control over *anything*…like the weather, and worms eatin' all yer crops. I'm guessin' you're the

type of person who likes to control everything." He knew the worm eating scenario was a metaphor, but Pete was getting the application to life. He also wanted to tell Donny how sorry he felt that he couldn't be there for him during those terrible hard times. He'd failed Donny. "Well?"

"Maybe…go on."

Taking another sip of water and then plopping his head against the headrest, he said, "I can tell ya one thing."

"What's that?"

George breathed and then said: "You didn't have a good father. That's one thing I know about myself." Again, he wiped his eyes. "I'm good at readin' people and knowin' what's troubling 'em." He realized the years of neglect he had wrought against Donny.

Pete didn't answer and turned away. George could see the light of his cell phone reflecting off the metal tray in front of him. Pete was obviously trying to call someone.

Trying to get a glimpse of their location on the freeway, George could only see his reflection in the bus's opaque window. He was old, his face worn and leather wrinkly, his white brows thick, his cheeks now stubble. It's not me, he thought, rubbing his chin. That *can't* be me! Leaning back in his seat, he shut his eyes. The sight was unbearable! "Old Jim, one o' my best friends, died in 1972," he began. "Everyone I knew is dead…and I never got to say goodbye to any o' them."

"What?" Pete asked, turning around suddenly.

"Sue Lynn wrote to me when Jim Frakes got sick, but I didn't come home, even after he died, Donny," George said.

Pete looked perturbed. "George, I think I better call Daryl. I think I should tell him to stop and call an ambulance. You don't look well. Really. You're sweating, and you're breathing sounds…different, and—"

"Another friend of mine, Pat Harner, the one I mentioned before, he died right after I took to the road in 1964," George added, his hand pressed firm over his chest.

"You're painting a pretty bleak picture about life, George, so that indicates something's wrong with yours right now,"

J.P. Osterman

Pete said, dialing wildly on his cell phone. "It's getting really depressing. It's making me wanna move, especially if you don't take my advice and get some help." He gathered up a blanket and rolled it into a ball. Under his breath he muttered: "That's why I don't talk to people." He began punching the blanket, making it fit in his grip. "Everything becomes so darn complicated...so out of hand...and I get all sucked up into *their* lives and stuck. Messy! I hate messes!" He grabbed his pillow. "You're like a tornado, George. And I don't have a clue as to what you're saying or talking about most times. And you're calling me Donny all the time. You need help!"

Looking up, George saw an expression of anguish on his face. He appeared confused as to what to do next. "Look, Donny," he began, "I'm your dad. Don't go. Please talk to me. Please!" He grabbed Pete's arm.

Pushing it away, Pete said, "*George*...my name's Pete, Pete Turner. You're hallucinating. Snap out of it!" He sat back down and threw everything on the floor.

The bus bounced a little from hitting a road bump, waking some of the passengers who sat up and glanced out their windows.

Seeing Pete so agitated, George said, "Where's the rest of my family?"

Pete sank into his seat. "Maybe if I tell you about me, Pete Tuner, and about my family, you'll snap out of it. Huh, George?"

"Pete?" George asked, not recognizing him. "No, you're Donny!" He rubbed his eyes.

Pete poured water on a handful of Kleenex and touched George's face with it. "I have a family, George," he began, "I have a sister, Kimberley." He sniffled and cleared his throat. "She's two years older than me."

Sighing as the cold water touched his skin, he focused, and saw Pete, not Donny. "Thanks." He swallowed hard and closed his jacket around his shirt collar. He could feel his lungs straining to imbibe more oxygen. "Sorry about all this, Pete. Go on. I really wanna hear about your family."

Pete's Crossroad

Concentrating on his words and the rhythm of his voice, George felt his chest pain lessen.

Giving George a drink of water, Pete continued: "I was born in Denver. My parents still live in Denver...at least I still think they do...but I really don't know. I left for Hollywood right after I graduated from high school. That was about eight years ago. When I couldn't find an acting job, I got a loading job in L.A. and went to college."

That was a lie! A while ago, Pete had said he had grown up in Hollywood. What was true about Pete? What were the lies? George grew more interested in the mystery sitting next to him. "Why did ya leave home so young?"

Shrugging, Pete replied: "I just split. That's all." His lips turned down as if he had tasted spoiled food. "I couldn't stand being at home anymore." He rubbed his eyes, which were now red and irritating him. "My parents divorced each other and remarried other people."

"Uh-huh," George said.

"What about you?" Pete asked, folding his arms, his previous helpful voice suddenly changing to a vindictive tone. "What happened to Sue Lynn, your wife?"

George gave out a sad *tsk*. "Sue Lynn died of breast cancer." When he glanced into the opaque window, he saw her small figure superimposed there, dancing invitingly toward him. "At least I still have Donny...somewhere in Albuquerque. I can't wait to see 'im."

Pete reeled. "What if you can't find Donny when you get to Albuquerque? Do you know if he's still even living there, George?"

George winced through another chest pain. "I just don't wanna think about that!" He coughed and bent down to inhale more air into his pinching lungs. "I brought Donny and my grandchildren presents. It'll be like Christmas morning when I give 'em all their gifts." Again he coughed.

"They should like your presents," Pete said. "Presents are always icebreakers. I'm sure Donny and your grandchildren will warm up to you after you give them their gifts."

J.P. Osterman

George pointed downward where Daryl had packed his suitcase. "A gift for little Andy, Fletch and Sue Beth. That's their names! I sure hope they like what I'm bringin' 'em."

"I don't see why not," Pete said. "What's in all the presents?"

Feeling exited as he imagined a perfect Christmas morning, George replied: "The Barbie's for Sue Lynn. It's a collector's edition." He giggled and rubbed his hands. "And Donny told me that Andy really likes baseball cards. I bought him a Pete Rose collectible. He can keep that for another century and it'll be worth loads o' money!"

"Now see? *I'd* love something like that," Pete exclaimed. "I just *know* your grandchildren will really appreciate those things."

"Hope so!" George said.

Pete paused. "Didn't you say you have another grandchild?"

"Oh! Fletch!" George laughed. "He's the youngest. He's twenty-five."

With an expression of shock on his face, Pete said: "Twenty-five? But from what you told me, I thought your grandchildren were real young and—"

"I'm giving little Fletch my pocket watch." Sliding the watch out of his vest, George opened the glass face, his fingers lightly trembling. "I've had this Hamilton since 1943…since I was drafted into the War."

"World War II?" Pete asked.

"Yep."

"Wow," Pete said.

Listening to the time ticking the seconds, George watched the second hand. It was moving twice as slow as the speed of his beating heart. The hour hand struck 10 p.m., and the minute hand landed on the number twenty-five. George jumped in his seat.

"You don't look good right now, George," Pete said. "I have to tell Daryl. I don't care what people asked me to do in order for this bus to arrive on time. You're not okay…you're condition is deteriorating, and no amount of water or coffee of food is helping." He stood up, but George grabbed his shirt and pulled him down.

"No, no, I'm all right!" he said, lifting his face into the cool air flowing through the vent. "I gotta get to Albuquerque, Pete. We *can't* stop. We can't!"

Pete sat down slowly. "Okay, George. I understand because I have a schedule to keep myself. And I know how much seeing Donny and your grandchildren mean to you. But if you grimace in pain and put your hand over your heart one more time...and if the medicine you took back at the depot doesn't kick in and start helping you soon, I have to tell Daryl. It's the right thing to do. We have to stop...and call an ambulance. Plans change."

"Ya mean, *my* plans change," George breathed, 'cause after they cart me away, *you* can just move on and get to where yer goin' on time." Trying to steady his heart rate by breathing low and shallow, George gestured for Pete to calm down too. "Just take a look at this watch though, will ya, Pete?" He shoved the thick gold metal into his hands.

Pete turned it gently around in his fingers and then handed the watch back to George. "Yeah, it's real nice! I never got *anything* at all from my dad except—"

"A JC Penny special." Again he unclasped the watch from its chain to showed Pete the ticking hands. He stared at Time steadily pacing, and he began seeing something else.

Tick -- The black lines turned scissor-sized in his mind.

Tick -- The round glass morphed into an hourglass.

"I'm running out of time!" George called.

"Out of what?" Pete asked, glancing around George, obviously thinking he had spilled his water or medication.

George slapped the watch shut, holding it tight against his chest. Glancing outside on the horizon, he saw a bright star. He remembered once standing under the night sky on his farm with Sue Lynn, making wishes. "I hope they'll like what I'm bringing 'em. Please, God...make 'em all like what I'm bringin 'em."

J.P. Osterman

"I don't see why they wouldn't," Pete said, glancing at his Rolex. "We're almost at Phoenix, George. Maybe Daryl, you and me can call Information in Albuquerque and see if we can reach Donny, your son."

"Did I ever tell ya what happened to Donny when he was ten years old?" George felt flooded with anguish when he remembered the horse he had bought for him. He had forced him to ride the stallion even though Donny was terrified of it and had refused. He had always pushed Donny, drove him way too hard.

"No what happened, George?" Pete asked, "but make it quick, because the bus is about ready to pull into that truck stop in about a mile. We're stopping to eat."

George put the lid on his empty Styrofoam cup. "A horse threw him."

Pete gasped. "Was he hurt?"

"The fall nearly killed him." He gripped his armrests. "It was my fault...all my fault!" He believed he could feel the vibration of Donny's body thudding to the ground.

"My God!" Pete exclaimed, a pained expression on his face. "How did that happen? And it was *your* fault?"

George pounded his armrest. Half the ceiling lights on the bus clicked on. "Donny pulled on the reigns too hard, I guess, or maybe Rocket wasn't as tame as I thought he was." He remembered Donny crying after the accident. Every slice of the memory felt like a knife inching its way into his chest. "Donny pleaded with me not to ride that horse. But I didn't listen." George held a wad of Kleenex to his eyes and wiped them. "Rocket threw Donny because I made Donny ride 'im...I forced Donny to ride 'im."

"*Haaa!*" Pete gasped.

George was experiencing the pain of that moment's disaster, now his agony. "I made Donny ride that horse when he begged me not to," he moaned. "I *made* him."

"You *made* him? Forced him? But he was just a boy!" Pete now had an expression of disgust on his face.

The memory of the accident was like a drumbeat.

Pete's Crossroad

Cupping his hands over his face, he said, "I'm sorry, Donny!" He grabbed Pete's shirt and cried into his face, "I'm so sorry, Donny! Please forgive me!"

Passengers began standing up and peeking over one another like rising dominos to catch a glimpse of all the commotion. Some were calling George crazy, some were whispering loudly, "What's going on?"

Pete stood up and stared down at George. "Poor kid! He could have died!" He glanced at the back of the bus. "My dad was the same way. Just like that. Just like *you*! He nearly killed me and my sister a few times! The guy was nuts! And crazy!"

George believed their friendship had just altered in a matter of precious seconds as he watched Pete searched for an empty seat. If the situation were reversed, George believed he'd do the same. "Sue Lynn and I rushed him to the hospital. Donny needed stitches in his lip, and he had a broken leg and arm, but he was okay in a couple o' days."

Backing into the window, Pete kept repeating, "My gosh!"

George began remembering a few other instances when Donny "got hurt." The memories were like the desert sand pummeling the windows, and he couldn't just brush them away—excuse the injuries as being the horse's fault or Donny's clumsy ways. They were his fault. As Donny had always cowered away from him in fright, George now saw that same terror on the face of the man next to him, Donny. "I'm sorry, Donny," he cried, holding his hand over his heart while also trying to grab Pete's sleeve. "I want to tell Donny I'm sorry," he began, "and I keep seein' his scared little face everywhere I go!" He rubbed the top of his bald head. "I'm sorry, Donny." *Breathe.* I'm gonna make it up ta ya!" *Breathe.*

"I'm getting outta here," Pete said, trying to sidle toward the aisle.

Obviously disturbed by all the commotion, Sandy Walston was now wide awake and craning her neck to get answers. "What's wrong? Can I help?" She began glancing around, trying to get the attention of other passengers.

Pete gestured at George. "I don't wanna sit here and

listen to how he abused his child!" He reached over and grabbed his black suit coat. "Sandy's your name, right?"

"Yeah, Sandy Walston. What's going on?"

"Just what I said." Pete reached over George's legs, trying to grab hold of his briefcase. "This old man here abused his kid." His nails scratched his seat as he searched for more of his belongings. "George here nearly killed his kid, Sandy. I want nothing to do with him. I'm outta here!"

Sandy's mouth dropped open. "You're acting as if *George* just slugged *you*. Pete's your name, right? Is George your dad or something? I'm confused. Did he hurt you or something?"

"Uh-uh," Pete snapped, nodding no. "I haven't seen my dad since I left home. George isn't my dad…just…just some guy who sat next to me. Darn! Darn it!"

George could hear Pete's disgust. Sitting with his hands covering his face, he began soaking up the beating. He deserved it…all the anger, the guilt, the shame, the loathing.

"Oh," Sandy said.

"See…*this* is what happens when you talk to people, to strangers," Pete said, still fishing for his belongings in the dark.

"What?" Sandy asked, rubbing her eyes.

"You get too involved…too mixed up in other peoples' wild business," Pete said. "I feel as if my brain's gonna explode any minute!"

"Oh," Sandy said, "but I still feel sorry for the guy," she whispered, nodding at George.

Suddenly, George believed he was floating high above his body where he was hovering steadily, listening to them.

"Now, he looks as if he's out cold now though," Sandy said, "like he's asleep. I don't think you have much to worry about now, Pete." She tapped his arm. "He doesn't look like he's going to bother you. And we're gonna be in Phoenix in a few seconds. Daryl can talk to George and assess his condition."

Pete stood up and glanced down at George. His head was rolling gently with the movements of the bus. "I guess you're right, Sandy," Pete said.

Pete's Crossroad

George felt as if he were fading in and out of existence—on the bus one second, another second hovering above them.

The other passengers began flicking on their overhead lights. A few stood up to discern all the loud racket as the Daryl slowed down the bus and turned on his microphone to speak.

Sandy Walston said: "We're almost at the Phoenix station. Can't you put your differences aside with George until we get there?"

The bus slowed as it approached the off ramp. As the bus lurched when Daryl put on the brakes, George returned to his body and went into tunnel vision. He couldn't see anyone except Donny's face as he stared at Pete. Panting and feeling a ripping sensation emanating from deep within his chest, he said: "Donny, I'm so sorry. I wanna make it up to ya."

Sitting back down, Pete suddenly felt pity for George. He also noticed a white urgency on his face. George had asked for forgiveness, but he was asking the wrong person. He appeared about ready to die. He would die never having been forgiven. What would that mean for eternity?! "It's okay, George. Just calm down."

"Yeah, George," Sandy interrupted, patting his arm. "Drink some water if you can. We're almost at the station. You can get out then…and move around."

"I bought you and the kids gifts, Donny," George said, grabbing at the air, reaching out to hold Donny. He clutched Pete's sleeve, pulling him towards his face. Every breath now felt like it might be his last. "And—I have a—a special gift for my little—little Sue Beth." *Breathe, breathe.* "Straight from—from her grandmother!"

Pete said, "George, I'm not Donny." He grabbed his leathery hands. "I told you, I'm *not* Donny, but we're almost at the Phoenix station…we can try to contact him when we arrive there."

The man sitting directly in front of them popped his head over the seat. Through the outline of his lips in the dark, he appeared about ready to snap at Pete. "Just tell the old man you're Donny! Shut the guy up! I'm having an anxiety attack up here!"

"Quiet, Herbert," the woman next to him ordered. "Let's mind our own business and keep out of this. You want to have to give a statement to the police and stay in Phoenix? Not me!"

Pete whispered hard into George's ear. "You'll have to apologize to Donny yourself, George. Saying I'm sorry to me isn't going to absolve you from almost killing your child."

Gasping, George felt a sharp pain in the center of his chest. "*Ahhh!*"

"What's wrong?"

Not a word.

Pete shook him in his seat a bit.

"Get some water!" Sandy shouted. She opened her bottle of water and began splashing George's face.

George felt his heartbeat thump and then skip a beat. He felt the blood in his brain withdraw into a fog. He couldn't breathe, and he grabbed Pete's wrist. "Help!" he heaved.

The bus ground to a sudden stop, and those standing to look at all the commotion jolted forward.

"The suitcases!" someone cried. Several toppled down and hit passengers.

"*Ahhh!*" one of the Japanese tourists screamed.

The doors hissed open as people began craning over seats to get a glimpse of George.

Someone shouted, "I'm getting outta here!"

Another passenger cried from the back, "What the hell's going on up there? Sounds like someone's dying!"

One woman stood up and called, "That old guy's finally gone crazy, I think."

One of the young Japanese tourists jumped around a few seats to get to them. He leaned over Pete and said, "You okay, Mister Gibson?" He appeared short and thin in the dim ceiling light, and he had wispy short hair that had a downy quality.

A sudden flow of blood hit George's chest. He popped awake, but his skin felt clammy and deathly cold. "Fine," he

Pete's Crossroad

gasped.

"My name's Hideki," he said, "Hideki Toyotama." He bowed, an obvious gesture of respect. "We are all sitting in the front. But you let us know if you need things, Okay?"

Obviously speaking for George, Pete said: "I'll let you know, Hideki. Thanks. Just give us room. I think Daryl called for an ambulance."

Hideki walked back to his seat, now and then peering over his shoulder at George.

George remembered the exact moment thirty years ago when Donny had said: "Old man, get outta my life! Never come around again! I don't *ever* want you around me or my children!" Donny's voice was now loud in his mind. "How can I tell Donny I'm sorry?" he whispered, still trying to catch his breath. "I'm dyin', Pete. I'm not gonna make it to Albuquerque. I know it."

Sandy leaned over the aisle seat. "I just know that Donny will one day see you, Mr. Gibson."

Pete leaned into her ear. "George is really looking for some kind of absolution, or forgiveness from his son and grandchildren. But he has *no* idea what their address is let alone their phone numbers, Sandy."

"Huh?" The lines on her face pinched in confusion. "You mean this old man is traveling all this way…and he doesn't even know his son's phone number?"

"Yep," Pete said, fluffing up a small blue pillow and putting it under George's head. "He doesn't have a clue where his son is in Albuquerque. When we get to the station, with the help of some Greyhound representatives, Daryl's gonna have to try to locate his son Donny."

"And call the police!" Sandy gasped, sitting back down in her seat.

George began staring into the opaque window. He could see the tall streetlights burning outside the station as the bus ground to a halt. Through a slight mist, the bulbs looked like the golden delicious apples he had once picked in Michigan. Their shapes changed, forming round sand dollars he had found on a beach in Oxnard, California. Then he saw angels' wings. "Sue Lynn!" he cried, sitting up, raising his arms to grasp her, needing to touch her white figure.

"Oh my gosh! He's seeing Heaven!" Sandy screamed, leaning into his face.

"George! George!" Pete called, trying to call him back to Earth.

More passengers jumped out of their seats.

"I think he's dying!" a woman cried.

"Seeing angels is a pretty good sign of that," a man called.

"I love your smile, Sue Lynn," George said, crying. "Please forgive me. I'm so sorry, Sue Lynn."

"Let me through everybody!" Daryl called, making his way back from the front of the bus. "I called an ambulance. It should be here any minute." The motor was still running in idle, the bus lightly vibrating.

Sandy whispered as she pointed in the direction of George's stare, "I think he's seeing his dead wife."

"You think so? I don't see anything," Pete said, glancing around the dimly lit aisle while also trying to force George to drink water.

"It's like his wife…what was her name?" Sandy asked.

"Sue Lynn," Pete replied.

"Yeah, he's seeing Sue Lynn. She's probably forgiving him I bet, and maybe even waving at him to join her."

A passenger peeked over the seat. "Wow, I never thought I'd *ever* see something like this! Spirits and angels, like you see on *Touched by an Angel*."

Pete gestured for him to leave. "Give the old guy some breathing room!"

"What's his name?" Another passenger asked. "I'm gonna pray for him right now."

"George," Pete replied, watching George commune with his vision.

"I don't want to keep reliving everything bad that keeps happening again and again, Sue Lynn," George said.

"He's talking to his angel wife!" Sandy said, pushing

passengers out of her line of sight.

Passengers turned quiet, peering in anticipation that something spiritual might at any moment morph into reality so everyone could see it.

Until Daryl voice interrupted the holy moment. "Move it, people! I'm comin' through!"

"Please forgive me, Sue Lynn," George said, now staring into the little ceiling light. "God...I'm sorry." He felt the oxygen cut off at his throat. "Help!" He gasped, clutching his throat.

Pete tore open George's shirt, the buttons popping. "Anyone know CPR?!" Most people had rushed off the bus.

Seeing Pete's eyes as Sandy splashed water on his face, George cried, "I—I can't breathe!"

"Isn't there an oxygen mask or something around here?" Sandy screamed.

"Haaa...haaa..." George felt his skin tingle as he struggled for air. He grabbed at the armrest, trying to prying himself up. "I can't—can't—"

Then he fell limp—his arms falling on his lap.

Sandy gasped and began shaking. "Oh my God...I think he's dead!"

"No!" Pete said, pushing lookie-loos out of his away.

Other passengers tried lifting George into the aisle, but the space was tight. They couldn't pry him out of his seat.

"Is the ambulance here yet?" a passenger shouted.

"I see it!" someone yelled. "It's about two minutes away!"

After five people heaved George out of his seat and laid his lifeless body in the aisle, Pete grabbed water from another passenger and doused George's chest. "Hey George!" He shook his shoulders. "I didn't mean what I said, George! I know you made mistakes. But like you said...you're trying to make up for what you did. I believe that."

"He *is* dead...Isn't he?" Sandy said, drawing out her words, lifting up her purse and clutching it to her chest as more passengers bolted off the bus.

"I don't know," Pete said, kneeling by George.

J.P. Osterman

"Check for a pulse," she said.

"Okay." Pete felt George's wrist. Nothing. "Gosh, I feel like I'm moving, but that I'm standing still. What the heck's wrong with me?" He patted his cheeks and drank some water that she handed to him.

"You're in shock," Sandy replied, taking over where Pete had left off, feeling for a heartbeat in George's wrist. She put her ear to his chest. "I hear slight beats!" She shot up. "Daryl! Where the heck are the paramedics?"

Pete felt stunned as he gazed at George's lifeless gray face that now looked peaceful. He had been in so much distress and turmoil, and laden with overwhelming guilt and regret, most likely, for most of George's life! "I've never seen anyone die before," he said, leaning into George's eyes that were still a bit open. Quickly, he closed them shut with his fingertips. "My God!"

The ambulance finally arrived. Two paramedics dashed onboard, lifted George's body out of the bus, and lay him on a gurney. Everyone disembarked from the bus, many people watching George's progress from far away on the loading platform.

One paramedic began pumping on his chest, performing CPR. "Come on tough guy...you can make it..."

The other paramedic walked toward Daryl, Sandy, and Pete with a portable device he had just powering on, obviously to input information. "Did Mr. Gibson have any family traveling with him?" The paramedic working on George was about to use a defibrillator.

Pete replied: "Not with him, but George has a son, Donny."

"Donny Gibson?" the medic asked, inputting the name.

"Yes, George was on the way to Albuquerque to visit him...no, actually *live* with him. That was the plan...at least in George's mind." Pete bowed his head, trying to fend off powerful tears. "That's what George was hoping for. That's what he wanted...more than anything, to be reunited with his family." The medic continued looking up information in a

58

Pete's Crossroad

data base. "I'll get more information from you later, about what happened on the bus, but you can go now and join George," he said.

Patting Pete's arm, Sandy said, "It's okay. Come on, let's check on him." They watched the two more paramedics applied sticky patches to George's throat. "Maybe George will come back. Maybe he isn't dead."

Before the paramedics rolled the gurney into the ambulance, Pete and Sandy ran to George's side. "You wanna see Donny…right, George?" Pete asked. "Come on…pull through!"

One paramedic asked them to step back as she shocked George's heart with a defibrillator. The whining sound was piercing, but George's vital signs were still flat lines.

Pete called: "George, you're almost to Albuquerque! Hold on!"

Suddenly, inhaling deeply as if a miracle had instilled in him a second chance, George opened his eyes. He could see Pete through the plastic breathing apparatus. Tell—" *Breath.*

The paramedics sighed in relief and began relaying his vital signs to the hospital. "Back away!" one medic shouted to a few inquisitive bystanders.

A Greyhound official ordered Pete and Sandy to retreat to a cordoned off area as Pete strained to hear George's words. "What, George?"

"Pete!" George was seeing light coming from everywhere. "I gotta talk to Pete! Now!" He knew he had only precious seconds.

The paramedic waved to the Greyhound official and then gestured to Pete. "Let that man pass!"

George saw Pete in a halo of yellow when he walked up to him. "I'm sorry." *Breath.*

"Yeah, George," Pete knelt down alongside him.

"Tell Donny I'm—I'm sorry," *ha…ha,* "so sorry."

"Tell Donny you're sorry, George?" Pete asked. "I don't think—"

George's body suddenly relaxed, his fists unclenched, and

his head turned lifelessly to the side. Condensation stopped forming on his respirator.

Pushing Pete aside, the paramedic said, "You have to leave now!"

"Oh my gosh!" Sandy yelled to a crowd, her fingers tapping her lips. "He's dead!"

Standing away from the paramedics, Pete shook his head in utter disappointment. "No man…no way." He rubbed the back of his neck and sat down on the curb. "No way! This can't be happening! Getting to Albuquerque meant *everything* to him." He hadn't realized it, but he was crying, and beyond sad. He glanced around in the brightly-lit loading platform. Some people were giving him their condolences, others simply walked away, and everyone else left him for the Greyhound station. George's near lifeless body was now pointing in the opposite direction of Albuquerque. "Now, it looks like we're gonna be stalled here in Phoenix. And it's hot and dry as hell. If he dies, will his body be stuck here? What the heck's gonna happen now?"

Sandy sat down next to him on the curb. "I don't know what's gonna happen, Pete, but Daryl will figure something out. This is a long stop. We have time. And he's not dead yet. They're still trying to revive him."

"Uh-huh," Pete sighed. The streetlights were burning bright discs of light in circles on the pavement. Staring into one, he thought he saw a faint outline of George. When he blinked, George was gone. "*Whoa*—am I tired or what!" he exclaimed, rubbing his stinging eyes. He noticed his hands shaking. He was watching someone die—*die*! Panic rushed through him. The opposite of death is life—*life*! An hour ago, George was alive! He remembered their conversation about the precious fleeting moments in a person's lifetime. All of George's had run out; and as George had told him, all of his were yet to come.

Greyhound employees rushed out of the station as paramedics inserted another IV into George's arm.

Pete saw Sandy shuddering a little, and he gave her his

Pete's Crossroad

jacket. Wrapping it around her shoulders, she said, "It's April, but this Phoenix air is heavy."

"Yeah," Pete said, wiping his eyes. "Before when we stopped in Blythe, it was hotter than hell! Here, it's like an ocean front squeezed its way into the desert." He pointed to a patch of cacti. "See? They seem to be blooming in front of our eyes." Then he spotted George on the gurney with paramedics working wildly on him. "He's dying—"

"No, he's dead now I think, Pete," Sandy said, craning her neck to get a good look at George's body.

"Dead...but this place is blooming," he sighed. Then he laughed a bit.

"What's so funny?" she asked.

"This whole friggin' game of life and the meaning of it all," he replied, motioning to the ambulance. He felt suddenly empty and lost, as if stopped and staring at a giant fork in the road—a real crossroad—and unable to decide the next course of action. Walking with Sandy to the accordion entrance to the Greyhound station, Pete saw Daryl and stopped him. "Well...how's George?" He knew the answer.

The paramedics lifted George's body into the ambulance. At his feet, he could see a body bag. The hospital was in the opposite direction of Albuquerque. "I know George *never* woulda guessed that something like this could have happened to him to take him so far off his plan when he woke up this morning."

Daryl shook his head in an gesture of disbelief. "We practice for these kinds of scenarios." He gave out a despondent sigh. "But God All Mighty...*never* in my life did I *ever* believe I'd actually be faced with something like this on my own bus." He wiped tears from his eyes. "Someone dying on *my* route."

"I know," Pete said. "I'm trying to figure out what's happening inside that ambulance to George right now. But I can't see through those windows. What do you think?" He'd ask Daryl again, this time, a little more forcefully. "How's George gonna make out?" He watched the medics who were

J.P. Osterman

holding defibrillator paddles. Now and then they were blasting his chest with electrical current. All Pete could hear was the long steady *beeeeeep* of a flatline. "Come on, George…come on," he whispered, clenching his fists, his throat burning.

Thrusting his hands into his pockets, Daryl wiped his sweat-soaked forehead. His blue uniform shirt was half-open as if he had ripped it out of his wrinkled pants and tucked it back in. He checked his phone as the ambulance doors shut. "George didn't make it, Pete." He patted Pete's shoulder as he pointed at the medics who had just shut off the defibrillator. "George is…gone. That's what the front desk just messaged me to tell both you and Sandy." He continued receiving and returning text messages.

Walking up to them with a coffee cup in her hand, Sandy Walston wheezed out a terrified breath. She had heard what Daryl had just told Pete. "He's dead?" She grabbed Pete's arm. "Horrible! Terrible for him and his family!"

"I know!" Pete said.

She looked ready to sink into quick sand. "Just think…all day we were sitting right next to George!"

Pete could see through the window of the ambulance as the paramedics covered George's body with white sheet. His throat stung and he coughed back more tears. "George was almost there. He almost made it to Albuquerque…to Donny and his grandkids." Then he remembered all the gifts locked away in George's large suitcase in the bowels of the bus. "He had gifts for them all! He wanted to make things right with them."

"Yeah," Sandy said, opening her purse as if peeling open a closed flower.

It was an expensive designer purse, not at all matching her other clothes. He knew that. He knew *everything* about the most expensive clothing lines in the most upscale shops and stores. He tried to keep from focusing on it. She was a mystery, with her jittery mannerism and her disheveled appearance. And she appeared agitated most of the time, often changing from tired to energetic on a whim.

62

Pete's Crossroad

"You said that George had been, well, mean to his kid." Rifling through the contents of her purse, she pulled out a stick of gum. "Too bad. I guess he did some pretty bad things that he was just now desperate to make amends for." She put the stick of gum on her tongue and began chewing hard as if the flavor might suddenly fade. Was she quitting smoking?

"Yep, you're right," Pete said, remembering what George had told him about the horse that had thrown Donny. "Some pretty heavy abuse I think."

Daryl sighed in exasperation. "It sounds like the guy suffered most of his life over whatever he did." He coughed and shivered. "Sure the heck is cold here this time o' year." He rolled his blue jacket over his shoulders. "Big lesson to learn in all o' this," he said nodding at the ambulance.

"Yeah," Sandy huffed, "don't have kids. I don't and I never will!"

Walking alongside her, their shoes tapping the sidewalk simultaneously, Pete folded his arms across his chest to keep out the cold. "Sounds like you're on the run maybe?" She stopped chewing her gum and peered up at him quickly. "Or are you ditching someone? Boyfriend or husband?" He laughed, but he was really being serious.

She stopped and put her hand in front of his face. "I'm not going there!" The gum popped between her teeth. "I don't wanna talk about it!"

"Whew, all right, sorry, Sandy," he said, brushing his fingers through his hair.

She exhaled in obvious relief to regroup and regulate her emotions. "Now what, Pete? What about all of George's things? Who's gonna— Who will—"

"Take care of George's body?" he asked, glancing at his Rolex while walking toward the bus station. He had his briefcase held tightly at his side. "I don't know." He smelled coffee, and the light fragrance of fresh-baked cinnamon rolls making his mouth water.

"I can't do anything about it though," Sandy said, her face showing signs of panic.

"No one asked you to," Pete said to her, gently. After a pause, wherein he didn't know whether to ditch her right then and there or keep up with her, he asked, "Where are you heading?"

"I don't wanna talk about it right now," she snapped.

If he'd continue to ask her questions, he realized she'd ditch him. Maybe that's a good thing though, he thought, especially since he felt as if he'd just been through a big earthquake. *Go*! *Please leave*!

He groaned as he watched the ambulance lights circling, their red-and-white reflections pulsing off the windows of the bus station. "I'm gonna grab a drink and then talk to Daryl."

"Maybe I'll see you inside later on, Pete," she said. Then she left…as he wanted her to leave, but he really didn't want her to go. He felt so confused! He'd never felt so shaken up and disoriented, except maybe, when he was a child. Still, he'd always managed to prevent being entrenched in uncomfortable or chaotic situations. He avoided whirlpools and people's problems! He liked being and living detached and off-limits—on the fringe—of peoples' lives. Not now…

Something profound, yet normal, had just happened that was leaving him feeling totally lost and disoriented. But I shouldn't be feeling this way, he thought. People die every second of every day, right? And this guy was a stranger to me! A sudden numbness filled him, and a sense of loss and aloneness in the world as he watched the ambulance leave the station with George's dead body. "I know you never expected *this* to happen when you woke up this morning, George." He felt angry at the little time he knew he had left in life that was really just an illusion of an open ocean. That's how George described life. Now, he was also seeing life as being fragile.

Part II

Pete Turner

J.P. Osterman

Chapter 4 – Hideki Toyotama

Sitting at a booth and taking a swig of beer, Pete watched Daryl as he huddled with several police officers and Greyhound officials in an area next to the ticket booth. As passengers scurried in and out of revolving doorways, Daryl was giving his statement of what had happened to George on the bus. A forensic expert walked up to them with a small black bag in his hand. It had to contain the possessions George had on him when he died. In between taking drinks of beer and eating pretzels, Pete glanced at them every so often. He was waiting for Daryl to call him over, or a time when he could interrupt them, so he could give his account of what had happened to George.

Eighty-six years old. That's how old he was. A nauseating burp hit his throat as he held his hands into the light, inspected them for lines and sags. *Eighty-six. Eighty-six minus twenty-six…hmm, that's sixty. Maybe more…maybe less…time I have left.* When he saw a few blue bulging veins, he hit the table, gulped down his beer, and ordered another.

He began to remember the things he had said to George, hurtful things. Hot guilt rose into a headache. He couldn't take back those words now, even though he had told George

Pete's Crossroad

he hadn't meant them. Pete had his elbows on the table, his head low, and his fingers buried in his hair as he began rubbing his scalp. He began thinking: Tired, I'm so tired, but I can't quit. I just wanna know what to do next! But I can't stay here in Phoenix…I gotta be at a conference in Albuquerque, then me and a few people from work are supposed to hit Vegas for a celebration party. I'm supposed to get a promotion! He believed those plans were now all up in the air if the police might want to detain him for some reason.

Grabbing the beer from the server, he set it down on a white coaster stamped with a picture of a Greyhound bus. It had streaks behind the wheels, giving the message that people can purchase a ticket, pack up, and go anywhere. He felt suddenly grounded—and trapped.

Still, he's dead, a person died right in front of me! Pete took another swig of beer that was beading water down the bottle. *I can't tell him I'm sorry.* "Damn!" he said, pounding the bottle on the table, and then he dabbed cold water on his eyelids. The server slid him a handful of napkins as the sounds of bus engines revved on their way out of the station.

"Wow, Pete. Take it easy!"

When he glanced up, he saw Sandy Walston again. She looked different in the bright light than she had in the dull glow on the bus. "You changed clothes," he said.

Folding her arms across her chest and shaking a bit as if she were cold, she said, "Yeah, I felt like I had death skin on me or something. I had to shower and soap it all off. Thank goodness this place has that accommodation." Her hair was still wet and brushed back as if she had just changed after taking an ocean swim. "What's next?" she asked, sitting down at the booth opposite Pete. She waved and got the server's attention. After asking for a glass of ice water, she said to Pete as she gestured in Daryl's direction, "What do you think's gonna happen to George's body?"

Pete checked the time on his Rolex: 11:15 p.m. "I think the bus is leaving Phoenix on schedule, at 11:40." He pointed to the enlarging crowd of medical professionals standing alongside Daryl. "But I have no idea what's gonna happen with George." He laughed. He felt helpless—out of control. "I had no idea about what to predict right now, and I'm usually pretty good at doing that, managing things, 'cause that's what I do for a living...set things up and design order."

"Ya look completely exasperated, Pete," she huffed. "But I can understand. I don't have a real clue about tomorrow either, and tomorrow's only minutes away!" she laughed.

He sat up quick. "You can say that again!" He glanced at his Rolex as the server returned and set down a sandwich and order of fries in front of him. "All I know is that I have to be in Albuquerque for a sales convention tomorrow afternoon."

"That seems pretty simple," she said.

Chuckling and nodding at all the medical experts still engrossed in writing down information alongside Daryl, he said: "I hope I make it there though. No telling what could happen, but I don't see the police yet."

"Yeah, I guess the bus could stay here for quite some time," she said looking at a long line at the ticket counter. Her eyes shone a sudden fright.

Knowing he wasn't the probing type, he didn't want to chase her away by asking her personal questions, yet he didn't want to be alone either to talk to Daryl. He'd change the subject. "I'm starving," he said, spreading mayonnaise on his bread.

"Me too," she said, eying his sandwich, her mouth appearing to water. Before he could ask her if she'd like to share his sandwich with her, she said: "I just ate one o' my snacks. I'll get something else later."

After taking a bite, Pete swallowed the food that tasted like a lump going down his throat. Everything seemed to be changing now, even his taste buds! "This bread is like leather," he said, flinging the sandwich on his plate. Everything fell apart.

"You're still in shock I bet, Pete," Sandy said, watching him eat. She pulled a pack of crackers out of her purse. "And it's late. And that beer's probably igniting the acid in your stomach into a real fire," she chuckled, her body shuddering lightly, until suddenly she breathed and the deep inhalation appeared to calm her down. One moment she looked lost and frightened; the next second, composed.

Pete realized she was either really sick or really terrified, and trying to hide from someone who might be following the bus. She might need help. But from what had just happened to George, he really didn't have time to help her; and besides, he really didn't want to know the details of Sandy's life. Pushing away his beer, he said: "I Guess I should order some coffee. That's what I really need now." He leaned into the smudge-stained tabletop and ran his fingers through his hair. "You look like you could use a coffee yourself, Sandy." He watched her lips turn a shade of blue as her body vibrated as if a sudden chill swept through the restaurant. Now her manner scared him, and he reeled back at bit. "You look like you're freezing to death!"

She flung a shawl over her shoulders. "Yeah, I'll take a cup of coffee, good suggestion," and then she coughed.

As she peeked inside her designer purse with a lost and worried expression, Pete surmised she couldn't even afford a cup of coffee. "It's on me, Sandy, don't worry about paying," he said, picking up the menu. The server sped by, and he ordered two coffees.

"Thanks, Pete," she sighed. Her hair was beginning to dry, and soft blond strands were falling into her eyes. Quickly, she brushed them away. "It's still pretty scary what happened, huh?" she said softly. "A person dying like that." Her lips quivered as she slowly set her cracker down. She was thin and could use to eat something more substantial than crackers. Her appetite appeared nonexistent too, but not necessary from George's death.

"Yeah," Pete said, handing her a napkin. "You seem like you're taking George's death pretty hard, Sandy." She had on a charm bracelet, and every time she moved her hand, the little silver and gold keepsakes jingled as she drank her coffee.

She wiping her eyes. "It's because I almost died myself,

Pete."

"What?" He sobered up.

Her hands began trembling. "I almost overdosed, Pete," she said, picking up her coffee cup and pressing the Styrofoam with her fingernails. She blushed.

"Wow, I woulda never guessed!"

"But I can't talk about it. I just can't." Her face lowered. Her knuckles were white as she gripped the cup tightly, steadying it to her blue-tinged lips as she continued sipping her coffee. With each sip, she closed her eyes as if completely enjoying the taste and the aroma.

"Fine, I understand," Pete said, clearing his throat, not wanting to pump her for more information. Then again, he didn't really want to know more. Knowing more on the bus had only gotten him into more trouble. He had to change the subject. Besides, shortly, they'd be back on the bus and going their separate ways. In a half-an-hour, he'd never see her again in his entire life. But that reality triggered a panic in him making him want to know more about Sandy! He felt as if he were riding a rollercoaster! "So, how about eating the other half of my turkey and rye sandwich?" He pieced back together the other half of his sandwich, set it down on his napkin, and then pushed his plate in front of her. "This thing's like a kid's puzzle in kindergarten!" he laughed.

Picking up the sandwich with shaking hands, she said: "You have a good sense of humor, Pete. No…a *great* sense of humor. Thanks." She began devouring it.

A small group of Japanese tourists walked up to them. Holding a digital camera in front of Pete and speaking in broken English, one tourist said, "I took pictures of some sites at our last stop." He knelt down next to Pete and began showing him scenes on his camera. "I found this one of you and the man who just died. If you have email, I can send it to you."

"George was his name," Pete said, glancing at the picture of him and George walking out of the rest stop with cups of coffee in their hands. "George Gibson." He searched his pocket, found one of his business cards, and gave it to the him. "Here's my email. Thanks. I'd like the picture."

The Japanese man smiled and bowed, the gesture showing respect. Wanting to fit into the American culture, he told Pete he wanted to introduce himself by his first name instead of his last name, as custom in his culture. "Hideki is my name," he repeated, shaking hands with Pete and Sandy.

"Pleased to meet you, Hideki," Pete said, bowing a little, also trying to return his respectful even though he believed he looked funny. "I remember when you offered George some water, Hideki. That was nice."

Smiling with his white front teeth showing, Hideki said, "Yep, that was me!"

Sliding into the booth beside Pete, Hideki said, "Maybe you could download this picture into a laptop right now if you have one." When Hideki's face lowered, Pete saw sadness in his eyes. "It'll give you something to remember him by. You and old man George were talking quite a bit. You looked like close friends." He appeared uncomfortable and shifted his feet. "You seemed close...even though you had that little argument." He pinched his fingers and added, "Just a *little* argument I'm sure...*hmm*?"

Sandy coughed, looked away, and tapped her finger on the table a few times.

"Yeah, it was a little disagreement, that's all." Feeling as if some of the other people who were on their bus when George had died were looking at him and accusing him of being partly responsible for George's death, Pete remembered his last words with George when he threatened to move to another seat: "George nearly killed his kid. I'm outta here!" The quarrel wasn't little as Hideki had said, but huge, and probably all the passengers would remember it forever, and even blame him for George's heart attack. Maybe that's what they were telling Daryl and the Greyhound reps who were still taking statements. Hot guilt began spreading through him, and he felt a sting of shame burn his cheeks. "Yeah, I have my laptop right here." He pulled it out, set it on top of their table, and

J.P. Osterman

fired it up. "I wanted to get the rest of my belongings out of the luggage rack. Maybe the people at the front desk are going to want us to change busses." He saw their bus pull into another ramp.

"We unloaded our things a few minutes ago," Hideki said, and the five other Japanese tourists who were standing behind him smiled in anticipation of leaving soon.

Sandy gestured at the bus that looked like a boat dead in the water. "You think someone will be questioning us? Asking us details about what happened to George as if we're murderers?"

Pete sighed and connected Hideki's camera cord with his laptop and then initiated the download. "They could, but Daryl's talking to the big shots right now. I think they're discussing what they're going to do next."

"I know they unloaded George's carry-on from the overhead," Hideki said, "but I don't know about the huge suitcase he had in the bottom of the bus." He made the sign of a big box with his hands.

Pete handed Hideki his camera. "Thanks."

Straightening his fanny pack, Hideki tapped the head visor dangling on his arm. Under it was his red watch. "Daryl and those executives better decide what we're going to do and soon," he began, "because we leave in seven minutes." He had a serious look on his face—his thin black eyebrows forking, his straight lips smacking as if he might have a fit should the bus veers off its schedule.

"Let's go talk to Daryl," Sandy said, standing. "I wanna know what's going on. I'm sick of just sitting here and wondering."

Glancing at his black briefcase, Pete remembered his tight schedule. Every moment was like a finely tuned calculation. "Let me think a minute," he began, "maybe I'll come with you." He yawned and rubbed his tired burning eyes.

"Mr. Turner," Hideki said firmly, "you seem really stressed out…exhausted, and tired."

Huffing a little, Pete said, "A month ago, I took a new job

selling mannequins. I'm also a designer. I *could* get a promotion in a few days."

Hideki reeled a little. "Mannequins? *Hmm*, interesting. You look like you sell real estate to movie stars."

His Japanese tourist companion said: "You are dressed like movie star, Mr. Pete. And you walk and talk like you live in Beverly Hills. We took a tour through there."

"Nooo," Pete said, straightening his collar. "I sell mannequins, like you see in display windows. I'm also a fashion designer."

"*Oooo*," they said in unison.

Pete saw their enthusiasm wane as he continued: "And tomorrow afternoon I have a big sales convention in Albuquerque. I have to be there at 1 o'clock, on time. It's a real important event. It's like life-and-death!" He tapped his laptop as if it contained the Declaration of Independence. In it, and his briefcase, were all his presentations and designs, years of hard work.

"Wow!" the Japanese tourists exclaimed.

Slicking back his hair, Pete felt a little important now. He smoothed down his white cuffs and adjusted his silver cufflinks. "After the big convention, my buddy and I are supposed to travel to Las Vegas." He took out his mirror sunglasses, puffed on the lenses, wiped them off with a napkin, and then stuck them back into his jacket pocket.

"*Oooo*, Las Vegas," they said with enthusiastic wide-eyes.

"Uh-huh, it's like…the most important trip and opportunity in my life!" Pete exclaimed.

"*Hmm*," Sandy said, glancing at him askance with her arms folded across her chest. "Most important trip *in your life?*"

"Yeah, yeah," he said forcefully, folding his arms. He was going to defend his plans like a linebacker. He took his sunglasses out of his pocket and shoved them into a flap in his briefcase. Now, everything appeared perfect and in order. Then he straightened his collar. "So I have to get going too." He picked up a crust of bread and began squishing it into a ball. "I can't stick around here in Phoenix, or head off somewhere else. I could lose my job!"

"I see," Sandy said as Hideki turned a little towards him.

Pete pounded the table. "Darn. Why now?!"

"You sure mad, Mr. Pete!" Hideki said, careening back.

"Sorry...I'm just tired," Pete said, gesturing that they didn't have to be afraid of him. The opposite was true. He was fuming inside, and trying every cognitive self-talk trick to keep his emotions bottled up so as to not explode. "You all don't understand."

"Understand what?" Sandy asked.

"George was like...like a complete mess! And none of you saw that, or experienced what I experienced with him." He breathed, trying to calm down as the run felt like it was spinning.

Sandy reached across the table and touched him. "But it's not your mess, Pete."

Shaking his head in disagreement, Pete replied: "I never believed something like this could happen. This could ruin my life!"

"How?" she asked. "No one's asked you to do anything for George...to give up anything." She breathed deeply. "I think you're blowing things outta proportion, Pete." Suddenly, she stopped everything and began patting her lips. She appeared about ready to cry but trying hard not to let go of her emotions. "Unless...maybe you're *really* at fault for what happened." Her voice was slow and soft. "Like, you were a bit too hard on George, and that big argument the two of you had caused his heart attack."

Hideki and his tourist friends grew silent, their eyes wide in shock as they glanced back and forth at one another and then at Pete and Sandy.

Feeling as if the room were closing in and hearing the bus engines idling alongside the curb, Pete jingled his Rolex and put his fingers over his eyes. "I didn't do anything to cause his heart attack. George was taking medications for a heart condition, or maybe cancer...I don't know."

"Oh, I'm sure they know all about that then," Sandy said,

and the tourists appeared to understand as they leaned back in to listen to him. "Look, I feel bad about everything that happened to George. The argument was stupid…and I feel so dumb that I said what I did when he told me what a bad father he'd been to his son Donny."

"Oh," Sandy said, in an expression of understanding.

"Weird how some things trigger other things." He waved at some steam wafting up his nose from his coffee. He plopped the cup down on the table and grimaced at it.

Sandy said: "Well, no sense making trouble for you if someone does question us."

"Thanks," Pete said.

"I mean, we don't know what happened between you and George. None of us were sitting right there in between you and listening to every word, right everyone?"

"Uh-huh," Hideki said, glancing downward.

"Mm-hmm," another agreed.

Pete realized those were placating looks and glances, and he hadn't told them the complete truth about George. Tapping his cup, he said: "George asked me to tell Donny some things. He asked me to deliver a message to his family." He swallowed hard to fight off numbness and tears.

"What?" Hideki asked softly, his eyes intense as if he were gathering tons of information to make a profound revelation.

Sighing and feeling his world grinding to a halt, Pete said: "George asked me to deliver Donny, and his grandchildren, a message…in person. Donny *and* his grandchildren!" Pausing, he sipped his coffee. "God!" He peered up at the florescent light. Closing his eyes, he heard the sounds of bus horns and cars beeping. Inhaling, he smelled French fries and heard them sizzling in a deep fryer. Exhaling, he heard the sounds of shoes clattering across the floor as people laughed in the booth behind him. "God! Why me?" he shouted, gesturing to Heaven.

Sandy sighed and touched his arm. "Look, Pete, let's talk to Daryl. I want to find out too what's going to happen to George's body and his things. He has family though,

J.P. Osterman

somewhere." She was blinking as if terrified someone might ask *her* to do something. "Besides, all of the things you're worried about might already be taken care of. Who knows, maybe George's son's on his way right now to Phoenix!" She began rubbing the palms of her hands as washing away a huge problem. "Maybe you'll be able to tell the son that message soon yourself, at least over a phone."

Hideki said, "Miss Walston has a point, Mr. Turner." He reinserted his camera into its case and zipped the lid. "But then again—" His mouth dropped open, and he peered upward in a gesture of profound spiritual recognition.

"But what, Hideki?" Pete asked, feeling sudden dread spread through his body.

As he shivered, Hideki unwrapped his striped sweater from around his waist and pulled it over his shoulders. He looked scared. "In my country, in Japan, if a person's things are left scattered in many places, and the body *not* put to rest, that person—"

"Like George's pocket watch, luggage, gifts, and body, you mean, right?" Pete asked.

"Like *everything* of George's," Hideki said, emphatically. "They are *all* his identity, and now scattered like puzzle pieces. And he asked *you* to fix his broken world. He wanted *you* to continue his journey to mend his life."

"A life mender? Me? Huh! God, I can't even mend my own life," Pete huffed, scratching his forehead.

"Puzzle pieces that need putting together, *hmm*," Sandy said, deep in thought. She was obviously contemplating her own life.

"Yes…if George's life did not concluded the way he wanted it to end, George *will be* a restless spirit!" He said those words so quickly, he seemed ready to sprint to the bus to outrun a ghost that might pop into existence and attach itself to him forever. He was eying Pete as if he was contagious, and the haunting permanent.

Sipping her steamy coffee, Sandy said, "So Pete…if George asked *you* to deliver a message to someone before he died, then you *must* fulfill George's request. That's what *I'm* getting out of what Hideki just said."

"Oh my God!" Pete sighed, feeling forced into doing a chore. "Let's just hold off on that notion for a bit. That's just a cultural thing...for the Japanese. In America, we don't practice that tradition." When he saw he had offended Hideki, he apologized. "I don't mean to be disrespectful, but I don't have time to be a *life menderer*...or problem fixer...or puzzle master."

"Okay, okay, Mr. Turner," Hideki said, leaning back in his seat. The foreboding tone in his voice was clear as he added, "But I'm just telling you the facts."

Pete paused to think about the stern warning: Help George rest in peace or be haunted forever. He still didn't believe it. "Hmm," he said, wanting to break out laughing but stopping the impulse.

Hideki's companion thrust her face in between them and exclaimed, "Hideki is right, Mr. Turner." She shook her finger at Pete. "George *will* haunt you!"

Pete saw a serious fear widen in her beautifully brown eyes. She was young, and obviously highly intelligent. They all were! He saw from the logos on their jackets and matching visors that they were scientists. Glancing into each of their stunned eyes, Pete suddenly believed that if all of Hideki's friends held on strongly to their beliefs in the afterlife, maybe there was truth to what they were saying.

She continued: "The same thing happened to my cousin. Her friend's spirit attached to her like glue. The ghost kept spilling things on her, poking her, nearly drove her crazy! She couldn't even go to work."

Nodding, Hideki said: "It's true! The attempt to extract that ghost from her failed until her cousin took the ashes to Hawaii, fulfilling the woman's last wishes."

Still waving them off as being silly, Pete said, "Come on!" He laughed. He turned to Sandy. "Let's go talk to Daryl."

After thanking Hideki for the picture and lifting his briefcase that felt like a heavy weight, Pete walked with Sandy

J.P. Osterman

to speak to Daryl. When he reached him, Daryl told Pete he had unloaded Pete's luggage and packed it in the cargo hold of the new bus. He had also set his jacket in the corresponding seat so as to save it for him. The old bus had been relegated to the main depot for deep cleaning. Then Pete said to him, "We're also wondering—well—"

"What's going to happen to George's body," Sandy interrupted, and then she coughed and sniffled. "And his things." She had tears in her eyes, and dabbed them off on her sleeve. "Sorry, this is bringing back some bad memories. I lost my brother, about three months ago."

That startled Pete. Now he realized why she was taking George's death so hard. "I'm sorry, Sandy," he said, glancing at her shaking arms. But that still didn't make sense, because she was acting so fidgety and distracted all the time as if she were on the run, or terrified of someone.

"My condolences, Sandy," Daryl said. Giving out a great sigh and straightening the rim of his blue hat, he pointed at the large counter where officials were busy making phone calls. "George's body is at the county coroner's office. And we're checking our records to notify his next of kin." Two young college students wearing USC jerseys dashed up to Daryl, asking him about the bus's departure. Daryl told them they had eight minutes. Turning back to Pete, he said: "Anything you might be able to tell those clerks at the desk would be a great help, Mr. Turner. You too, Sandy. After all, you two were sitting right next to George Gibson."

"But Pete talked to him most of the time," Sandy said quickly. She had large eyes as she stepped back.

Daryl told the Japanese tourists that they could board the new bus, and then he asked, "Did George give you any specific names of other family members, Mr. Turner?"

Pete squinted into one of the streetlights to try to remember. "Oh yeah! But his wife, Sue Lynn Gibson, is dead. I know he has a son, Donny Gibson, and three grandchildren." Pete felt fatigue move through his mind, dampening all the details. "But I can't think of their names right now." He rubbed his forehead, and it hurt. "I'm just really tired."

Daryl bit his lower lip as he paused in thought. Finally, he said: "You might want to go and tell what you *do* remember to the clerks. They're looking through George's possessions. Any information you can provide will sure speed up this whole notification process, and give closure to the family."

"Great!" Sandy exclaimed. "There *is* a little something you can do to help to put the puzzle pieces of George's life back together, Pete."

Pete wanted to include Sandy into the whole helping endeavor too, but then Daryl said, "Until we can talk to Mr. Gibson's family, and get some addresses and proof of ID, everything belonging to George will be shipped to our main facility and be logged into a secure storage facility." Two men dressed in overalls, obvious maintenance workers, were removing George's large suitcase and setting it, his carry-on, and cooler aside for a future pick up.

"So all his things will be like, in lost and found?" Sandy asked, cramming a few cans of soda into her small cooler. She had the eyes of a fish avoiding a hook.

Daryl walked out the door, and Sandy and Pete followed. Pete continued to look back over his shoulder. Something was pulling him back to the bus terminal.

"You have seven minutes until the new bus leaves," Daryl said. "Maybe I can give you twelve at the most, so you can talk to the clerks. If people complain, I'll tell 'em that I can make up for lost time by adding a little touch of speed to the journey," he giggled; then blushed in the obvious realization that he would be breaking the law, just a smidgeon. "But I've got to keep on schedule, so I can't hold the bus beyond twelve minutes." He pointed to the Greyhound's opaque window. "Everyone's got somewhere to be, and they wanna arrive on time."

"Yeah, me too!" Pete said.

Daryl tugged on his jacket in an expression of pride. "We have to keep the customers happy you know."

"Just hold the bus for me," Pete said, turning around and

dashing into the station.

"I'll honk before I pull out! That'll mean you have a minute, Mr. Turner!" Daryl called.

When Pete made his way inside the turnstile, he glanced back, believing Sandy wasn't far behind him, but she was nowhere. Scanning the windows of the bus, he suddenly spotted her, waving at him, out the doorway. "That's just great!" he huffed, realizing that whatever he was about to do, he'd have to do it alone. Sandy would not be helping him. "Why can't I be like that! Just leave…just take off!"

A stranger overheard him, grimaced at him as if he labeling him crazy, and said, "Take off then, buddy. Don't be a whiner!"

"Sorry," Pete called. Walking to the counter, he mumbled: "Why me? Why the heck me?" He thought of what Hideki had said: That if he didn't deliver George's apology to his family, or George's possessions, or see to it that George's body was properly put to rest, then George *would* haunt him. *Yeah, right. Who would haunt me…wanna be attached permanently to me?* "You really expect me to believe *that?*" he called into the air.

"Believe what, Mister?" an old lady said, wincing at him.

"Nothing."

When he reached the main desk, he said to the female attendant, "I may have information on George Gibson. I sat next to him on the bus." He gave her his name and old address; but when the woman asked him to divulge his current address, Pete said: "I don't have one yet. I just started a new job."

Typing on her computer, she said, "We tried to locate Donald Gibson in Albuquerque, but the sheriff said that he and his family left that city over five years ago."

"Really!" Pete said. "George had nobody? He was heading into a dead end?" Pete hit the counter.

The ticket agent sighed. "We're still searching, Mr. Turner." We have a link with the police in several cities right now. She appeared helpless, but not hopeless.

Pete's Crossroad

Pete felt as if the world stopped turning. "Maybe dying on the bus was the best thing that could have happened to George, rather than arriving in Albuquerque, believing he had family there, and then realizing he was completely lost and alone while searching for them."

The woman dabbed tears out of her eyes. Then she perked up. He remembered a name because the attendant's name tag looked like the one dangling on one of the gifts George had for his family. "How about an Andrew Gibson?" Pete asked. "How about the name, Sue Beth Gibson, Gail?" Pete believed Gail might locate addresses and phone numbers to those names.

Another clerk interrupted. "The Albuquerque sheriff is telling me he has a Donald Gibson on the phone in Amarillo, Texas. I'm transferring the call to you now, Gail."

"Amarillo, Texas?" Pete repeated, trying to figure out the distance between Albuquerque and Amarillo. Had George been confused about the locations. For sure *that city* wouldn't be on anyone's list of top ten destinations.

The receiver gripped tightly in her hand, Gail asked, "Is this Mr. Donald Gibson?"

Pete listened carefully while now and then glancing at the bus idling alongside the curb. Peeking at his Rolex, he didn't have much time before Daryl would have to leave.

"Don Gibson wants to talk to you, Mr. Turner," Gail said, handing Pete the phone.

The receiver looked like an enlarging black rocket. Part of him wanted to sprint toward the revolving door. The other half of him felt sick to his stomach, but he grabbed the phone. "Hello?" His throat dried; the room turned white and silent.

"Mr. Turner?" Don asked.

"Yes, I'm Pete Turner."

"Hi…can I call you Pete?" Don asked.

He had a firm friendly voice that sounded strong, confident, and self-assured. He recognized a bit of George's tone in Don's voice. "Sure." Pete coughed as Gail set a little cup of water in front of him. Sipping it, he felt relieved.

J.P. Osterman

"You're George Gibson's son, Donald Gibson. Right?"

"Yep, sure am," Don replied.

"I sat next to your father…all the way from Los Angeles to Phoenix," Pete said. The conversation went cold, as if they had been cut off. "Hello?"

Don said, "I understand my father died." His voice now sounded raspy as if he needed a cough drop.

Sighing, Pete said, "Yes. He died as the bus pulled into the Phoenix station."

"Oh, uh-huh," Don said. The loss seemed to make no difference to him.

"Two attendants just unloaded his luggage," Pete said, trying to be meticulous about all the details. "They say they're sending them off to their main office until someone claims them." He was hoping Don would tell him he'd take care of everything—from George's body to his possessions. Then he could head to Albuquerque, untethered, and make a clean getaway in a few days to party hard with his best friend and co-worker, Fred, in Las Vegas.

"We live in Amarillo, Texas," Don said.

"Where's *that*?" Pete asked, heartburn flaring into the base of his esophagus. He gulped down some more water.

"In the upper panhandle," Don replied. "Wait a second, Pete." Someone was with Don. It was a woman's voice that had interrupted them. Pete could hear Don covering the receiver, shouting, and then whispering strongly. They were angry, and arguing.

"What's that, Mr. Gibson?" Pete asked, trying to make out their words.

Daryl walked up to the counter and gestured to Pete that he had three minutes until the bus would depart. Pete gave him the thumbs up. "Look, Mr. Gibson, I don't have much time. The bus is about to leave." Still he heard arguing. "I just wanted to tell you that your father was on his way to visit you. He had presents for you. He thought you were living in Albuquerque though." Pete thought Don would take the hint that he was a bit perturbed.

Pete's Crossroad

"Presents?" Don asked. "Huh!"

"What?"

"My dad was a bum, Mr. Turner." Don was breathing hard. "And no good."

Not believing what he just heard, Pete stretched out the phone in front of him, grimaced, and then put it back to his ear. "Don, your dad didn't look like a bum to me." Feeling hot, he cleared his throat. He wasn't used to speaking his mind to people, but for once he had to. "George had everything he owned in his one giant suit case and a carry-on. He said he wanted to buy a little mobile home and live around you guys somewhere." He paused and took a deep breath as he listened to a passenger discuss ticket prices behind him. "It sounded like George wanted to spend his last years with you, Mr. Gibson. He wanted to make up with you."

"Oh," Don said.

"I just want to let you know that before I hang up," Pete said, his eyes stinging, his throat still hot and dry. "Before I take off on the bus for Albuquerque." Pete was hoping the entire ordeal would finally be over—that he could board the bus and finally get some sleep. "So...goodbye—"

"Wait!" Don said.

"Huh?"

"Mr. Turner...Pete," Don began.

"Yes..."

"If—if I tell the clerk to allow you to bring my father's things here...to Texas, would you?" Don asked, softly, slowly.

Not only thinking of the inconvenience but also of George's body at the morgue, Pete replied, "I have a—a convention I have to be at tomorrow! It's my job." He gasped for air as his arms tingled through a panic attack. "I have plans. I've already paid for a Vegas trip. I can't just blow everything off."

"I know, I know, I'm sorry," Don said. "How about after your meetings?"

There was a strong silence over the phone as Pete listened to the voice of an announcer calling out the departure of his bus. He had less than a minute. "I— I—"

Hideki ran into the station and waved for Pete to board the bus.

"Just a second, Hideki! Tell Daryl I'm almost done!" Pete called, waving at Daryl who had reversed the bus so as to make his run easier and faster. Pete's head still ached, his stomach burned, his thoughts colliding. He was a planner, not at all spontaneous.

"We'll reimburse you for any inconvenience, of course, Mr. Turner," Don said. "I think it's only about a five hour bus ride from Albuquerque to Amarillo, Texas."

"Amarillo is quite out of my way, Mr. Gibson," Pete said, thinking of Las Vegas. That's the direction he intended to take with his best friend after the end of the convention.

"Mr. Gibson," Don said, "I can have a ticket waiting for you in Albuquerque. Sue Beth, my daughter, is right here on the computer next to me. She'll book the ticket for you the second you agree. And we'll fly you to Vegas."

"Really?" Pete asked, believing that might work. Again, he heard strong whispers.

"I know this is an inconvenience for you, Pete…and I'm sorry. But please…won't you consider bringing us my dad's luggage instead of the possibility of having them lost somewhere in transit or a big warehouse? Sue Beth can pay for your ticket, right now."

Pete remembered her name, remembered the Barbie doll George had said his wife Sue Lynn had boxed up for her, at least that's what he said was in it. "Sue Beth?"

"Yes, my daughter," Don said, "and my son, Andy, is in the next room, on the phone with the morgue. I'm considering shipping my dad's body here, to Amarillo instead of allowing the morgue to just bury him there in Phoenix. I don't know." There was another long pause. He was muffling all the noise on his end.

"Hello?" Pete asked, feeling uneasy. When he first began talking to Don, he didn't seem to care anything about George. Maybe that's what all the background arguing was all about.

Pete's Crossroad

Perhaps Sue Beth and Andy were fighting with their father over a proper burial for George.

"Pete," Don said, pleadingly, "if you can escort my dad's things from Phoenix to Amarillo, we can at least make sure they'll get here. There could be important documents, and maybe photos in his suitcases." His tone was sharp. Don was still very angry with his dad. "Could you do that, Pete? Bring my dad's things home to us?"

Whew, Pete exhaled, wiping his forehead. "I—I suppose, Mr. Gibson." But that might mean no Las Vegas trip with Fred, or at the most, a shorter vacation. Still, after the convention in Albuquerque, if he could make his quota in sales, he could ask his new boss, Terrence Frapley, for a permanent job. That would mean, finally, a permanent home. He could always hit Vegas in the future. Unlike George, he had the rest of his life before him.

"All right, Mr. Gibson," he said, acquiescing. He felt like he had just signed a contract in blood!

"Great! And Pete, *please* call me Don," he said.

Pete felt a skittish about the possibility of having to dole out money he didn't have. "Don, you'll have a bus ticket waiting for me in Albuquerque though, right? I mean, I have limited funds. I'm sorry, but—"

"No, no," Don began, "definitely you'll have *that ticket*. And me, and maybe Sue Beth, will meet you at the Greyhound station in Amarillo."

"Fine," Pete said.

"For now, we can say goodbye; and on my end, we'll continue to discuss what we're going to do with my dad," Don said. Don had to be an executive or business owner because he sounded comfortable with making transactions.

"Okay," Pete said, feeling glad Don couldn't see his face because he would have seen "you're imposing on me" written all over it.

Don said, "Pete, let me talk to the clerk—I think Gail's her name—and I'll tell her to repack my dad's luggage. She needs confirmation from me that I won't hold Greyhound or

J.P. Osterman

you responsible for anything lost or stolen."

Pete felt suddenly accused. "I assure you, Don, I haven't taken *anything* from *any* of George's belongings."

"Oh, I didn't mean to blame you for doing that, I'm just the cautious type I suppose," he giggled. After a pause, they exchanged email addresses, so Don could coordinate times and receive personal information to make reservations.

"Bye, Pete," Don said. "How about letting me talk to Gail now."

Scowling a bit, Pete handed the phone back Gail.

"My God," Pete whispered.

"What's wrong?" another ticket agent asked.

Feeling that Don had just skillfully manipulate him, Pete said, "The guy sounds like a jerk."

Her lips straightening in surprise, the ticket agent said: "Then, *why* are you doing this, Mr. Turner? *Why* don'tcha just take off?" She waved as if shooing a fly.

He thought about Hideki's ghost prediction that scared him a bit. "Well...I don't know...but I'm gonna figure out why, 'cause if I don't, I can see that my life's going be a *complete* mess if I keep getting mixed up in peoples' lives."

She laughed. "I can relate!"

Turning around to leave, he came face-to-face with breathless Daryl. "You ready?"

Yawning, Pete picked up his heavy briefcase containing his laptop. He felt he had aged five years in the past six hours. "You bet."

Gail handed Daryl a small stack of colored forms and said: "Repack the dead guy's stuff. Oh, and make sure you include that black bag containing all of Mr. Gibson's personal effects that were on his body when he died. Just stuff it in one of his suitcases. Mr. Turner here is taking Mr. Gibson's possessions to his family in Amarillo." She emphasized each word, obviously protecting herself from a lawsuit.

"Got it," Daryl said, reeling in surprise, his belly round over his belt. "So you're in charge of George's luggage now, huh?" Pete gave him all the details of his phone conversation

Pete's Crossroad

with Don as they walked out the revolving door and onto the boarding platform. Daryl repeated Gail's orders as he rifled through the forms in triplicate with the maintenance men.

Pete stopped at the foot of the steps. "This is crazy!" He kicked the first step. "I mean, why the heck am I doing this? This is stupid!" Rubbing his eyes and feeling dizzy from lack of sleep, he wanted to run back to the ticket counter and back out of his commitment to escort George's things to Amarillo. Gail could just phone Don. She could let him off the hook, and he could go about the rest of his life.

Suddenly, he spotted George's extra-large worn out suitcase that appeared to have traveled with George for decades. It was leathery black, and peeling, with a few stickers, but a monument to George's life—to a World War II veteran and a man who had survived much conflict, strife, and regret. As a maintenance man thrust the small black bag containing George's possessions into the front compartment of the suitcase, Pete realized it had to contain George's wallet and antique pocket watch that George had painstakingly pulled out and shown him along the trip. He remembered George's arthritic fingers, white knuckles, wrinkled hands and strong lines on his face. George could barely move most times! And he always wore a grimace on his face in between smiles. He had to have *always* been experiencing excruciating pain! All to see Donny. He could have just forgotten about Donny and his grandchildren. He probably could have just stayed in L.A. and right now be resting peacefully instead of having a heart attack and dying. But no, George was determined to change, to make restitution, and to beg Donny to forgive him for all the terrible mistakes he'd made. Then he remembered the last moments he had spent with George. George believed he was seeing Donny and not Pete; and he said right before he died, "Donny, I'm so sorry…please forgive me."

Pete felt tears sting his eyes, and his father's face flashed into his mind. Wishful thinking if *he* could receive the same type of apology, given the reality that he didn't know where his father was living or if he was even alive—all buried questions now bubbling to the surface of his awareness as he watched that maintenance worker pack George's suitcases in the cargo hold. He thought, really, can't I just leave? Leave! He remembered George telling him through a pained dying expression, "Tell—tell, Donny, I'm so sorry."

Staring at George's suitcases, he remembered when the bus had stopped in Blythe where George and he had rummaged through it to locate Donny's address and phone number. George was traveling to Albuquerque blind—not even knowing if Donny was still living there! Now, Pete believed he could see every sock, tie, shirt, and piece of underwear in that suitcase. He then recalled the most important contents, the gifts George was determined to give Donny and his grandchildren—George's second motivation to see his estranged family. He said his dead wife, Sue Lynn, was the one who had wrapped the special gifts with that kiddy wrapping paper over fifteen years ago. All those years, George had been keeping the special gifts undisturbed, and packed them delicately in a row.

Pete kicked the bus step again. "Darn! Darn it! I gotta go!" George was in him.

Hideki, the Japanese tourist, ran to the front of the bus and thrust a cup of coffee in front of Pete's face. "Here, thought you might like this, Mr. Pete, 'cause you been up so long…working so hard for Mr. Gibson," he said.

Feeling surprised and touched, Pete said, "Wow, thanks, Hideki, I can sure use it." He never expected a complete stranger to hand him something that cost money.

Taking a sip as he boarded the bus, Pete heard the cargo hold snap shut. That was it…George's luggage was all holed up. Turning to Hideki who was sitting a row behind Daryl with his other tourist friends, Pete said, "Well…looks like I can't back out now. I'm going to Amarillo after I finish my work in Albuquerque."

Hideki replied with excited eyes and a smile, "Mr. Pete is taking on George's quest!"

Pete felt numb at that statement as Daryl stomped up the

Pete's Crossroad

stairs and slid into his seat. But Pete didn't want to sit down just yet. He leaned down and peered through the bay window, watching the rumbling buses in front of them roll away from the depot. Glancing over his shoulder to the back of the bus, he noticed that most of the passengers had turned off their little ceiling lights and had fallen asleep. It was almost midnight. He spotted the place where George once sat on the old bus, the place where he had had his heart attack. He felt shaky, and grabbed the steel bar to keep from faltering.

"So, why did ya do it?" Daryl asked, pushing the gearstick into drive.

"Do what?" Pete asked. The bus lurched, and Pete lunged a bit.

"Agree to take Mr. Gibson's things to Amarillo," Daryl asked, his body tilting as he steered.

Pulling his briefcase close to him, Pete replied, "I don't know." Then he laughed. "Heck, I don't know really why I do a quarter of the things I do."

Daryl chuckled. "Yep, sometimes I feel that way myself."

Glancing back again, he sipped his coffee and spotted Sandy. She had changed to a different seat, and was fast asleep with her blond hair blowing lightly over her eyes. Why did she do that? Had he done or said something wrong? Did she want to get away from him? He felt small, and abandoned. Taking a hard sip of strong coffee, he tried to douse those thoughts out of his mind. He only wished he had brought his beer.

"Greyhound woulda shipped George's things for free, you know," Daryl said, driving onto the freeway.

"Yeah, yeah, I know," Pete began, "going out of my way seems stupid."

Daryl laughed, but Hideki tapped Pete on the shoulder interrupting them. "Hey, I think you are doing a *good* thing."

Pete gave him a surprised glare. "How's giving up a trip to Las Vegas ever a good thing?" He felt like sending Don anonymous hate mail.

"You are doing this to find peace yourself you know,"

Hideki said, handing Pete a little bag of potato chips.

"No I don't know," Pete scoffed.

"It's a quest...wow, a real journey!" Hideki said.

"Thanks for these," Pete said, lifted the coffee and bag of potato chips in the air in a show of gratitude and staring into Hideki's awe-filled eyes. He and his Japanese companions had probably chipped in and bought them for him.

Daryl leaned a little into the aisle and said, "The guy's got a point."

"What's the point?" Pete asked, plopping down in the front seat. Looking down, he saw his scruffy shoes and began dusting them off with a white napkin Hideki handed him.

"Going to Amarillo, a new city, *will* be a bit of an adventure; and besides, not too many people would do what you're doing...that's for sure," Daryl said.

"I agree, Mr. Pete," Hideki said.

Feeling perturbed, he gave out a feigned laugh. "Hideki, you don't have to keep treating me like I'm some sort of important person or hero," he shrugged. "I appreciate the chips, and the coffee—" He smiled at the other Japanese tourists who were brimming with smiles at him. "Please, just call me Pete, okay?"

"Pete," Hideki said firmly, as if he had become their spokesperson.

The back of his head hitting the cushion, Pete said, "I don't know, Daryl. Call me a sucker, but I guess George deserves someone to be his ambassador, even if he's dead." He yawned. "Now I'm tired, and need some sleep."

Daryl stepped on the gas as the bus merged with another freeway. "Well, we have a long drive a head of us."

"Ten hours," Hideki whispered loudly.

Pete looking beyond Hideki and spotted the place where he had sat next to George on the other bus. The two buses looked the same, down to the color of the seats and headrests. He felt a knot hit the top of stomach.

"What's wrong?" Hideki asked.

Rubbing his nose, Pete said: "I don't know if I can go

back to where I was sitting…the spot where George got sick, but that's where Daryl said he put my jacket." There was no one sitting in that entire row of seats. People had avoided them, even Sandy.

"I know what you mean. I understand, Pete," Hideki said softly.

Suddenly, Pete remembered Hideki's earlier words. "What did you mean when you talked to me about taking over George' quest? Does it have to do with George's family not having his things, but then when they *do* receive them, they'll be happy or have good luck or something?" Pete whispered, leaning back, making sure Hideki could hear him. "Do you *really* think that George's spirit is restless? That he might be here, inside this bus, *right now*? "'Cause that's what you were implying." Hideki was listening as if he were mentally taking down every word for later perusal. "Maybe George *will* haunt me because he has unfinished business?" He felt scared and trembled as he peeked back and looked at George's empty seat. For a flash-of-a-second, he thought he saw George sitting there, waving at him. "*Ahhh!*" he cried, crunching down into his seat, putting his fingers over his face. People around him gasped, began mumbling, but then returned to sleep when Pete told them he had spilled coffee on his pants.

"You look terrified," Hideki whispered, touching Pete's arm, obviously trying to calm him down. "I just know George will be smiling down at you for taking his belongings to his resting place," he said, bowing, again showing Pete respect. "That's what we do all the time for our dead in Japan. And because George had no one, no friends, family…you seem to be the only one who can find eternal peace for him. *That* is the quest."

"George's spirit smiling at *me*? Huh!" Pete panted. "Well, I tell ya what, Hideki."

"What?" Hideki asked, his eyes wide and white.

"If George's ghost does haunt me," Pete began.

"Yeah?" Hideki leaned into him eagerly, as did several of his friends. Hideki was now glancing around, ghost hunting.

J.P. Osterman

"I'll tell George's ghost, or spirit, that I'm carrying all of his things back to his family," Pete concluded.

"That's right," Hideki said, snapping his fingers. "That's a clear conscience, Mr. Pete." He turned serious. "Don't ever forget that. You're doing the right thing. *You* know it! And you don't realize it right now, but some day, you'll be rewarded."

Coughing, Daryl interrupted them. "All right you two." He had a chastising voice. The bus was barreling through the crisp desert air at sixty miles per hour, on a long stretch of road with only streetlights and trucks. "Take your seats. Get some sleep. We've all got a long day ahead of us." Daryl's shoulders pitched toward the aisle as he reached for his tall coffee thermos, and then he snuggled down into a special cushion he had on his chieftain's chair.

Walking toward the back of the bus while staring at his old seat—the window seat next to George's aisle seat—Pete heard the sounds of his shoes squishing on the rubber floor mat. He felt the pump of blood into his chest, his sinuses suddenly stung, and everything in front of him blurred, except for George's empty seat when he reached it. It wasn't their exact seats, but they might have been because he felt suspended in two places—the past and present. He paused in the aisle.

Some of George's words began echoing through his mind: "I'm sorry Donny! Forgive me! Pete, tell him that. Tell Donny—"

Pete shut his eyes. For a moment, he believed he might collapse.

Then he felt a calm tap on his shoulder. "Sandy!" he said, looking into her warm eyes and breathing in relief. He was surprised she had approached him. He thought she had purposely distanced herself from him because of something he had done or said. He believed he had that effect on people. They always seem to run away from him, especially women, always breaking up with him.

"How ya holding up, Pete?" she asked, adjusting her

Pete's Crossroad

sweater around her waist.

Sighing, he strained to see her whole face. "Well, okay." He glanced down at George's empty seat, setting his hand on top of it, until fear gripped his stomach and he put his hands into his pockets. But he still needed his jacket. It was over by the window and contained vital contact information. His briefcase containing his laptop was getting heavy. That window seat would be a throne if he could just get past George's seat and sit down in it.

"Listen" she whispered, "you can come back and sit with me if you want to."

"Yeah, I, um, noticed you moved," he said, pumping up his shoulders.

"Yeah, even though it's a difference bus, it's still the same place, and I just couldn't sit across the aisle from...where George sat," she said, and burst out crying.

He grabbed her shoulders. "Hey, it's all right, Sandy. I feel the same way too!"

She began wiping her tears on her sweater. "Sorry, I just feel so bad," she cried, inhaling, her face showing pain in the burst of sudden light that a few passengers had switched on. "George never had a chance to say goodbye to his family. I can't imagine...heading to a strange place, not even knowing their addresses or phone numbers." She sniffled, and Pete handed her a Kleenex that a passenger thrust in front of his face. Taking it, she blew her nose as she continued to come up for air. "Poor George." Her throat stretched as she inhaled, *ha, ha*... "He died without saying he was sorry. It's so terrible! Without ever making peace with his family." Sobbing and lightly rocking, she had her arms folded in obvious protective mode. "I can't—"

"*Shhhh*!" a passenger whispered.

"Sorry," Sandy snapped.

"Hey, Mister," Pete said, defensively, "a guy died, right here, in this spot we're standing in." He tapped the top of George's seat. "The lady's feeling sad about it. Cut her some slack!"

J.P. Osterman

The disturbed passenger said, "Yeah, right," and then he turned around and burrowed into his seat.

Still standing in the aisle, Pete whispered in Sandy's ear, "Did you hear about what's going to happen to George and his things?"

Drying her eyes and yawning, Sandy replied: "Yeah, Hideki and his group told everybody. You're going to make sure that George's family gets all his things. I'm so proud of you, Pete. Gosh…you're like, awesome." In a little disc of light emanating at her from the back of the bus, she appeared haloed like an angel. "I couldn't do what you're doing. Never." The sound of shame was in her voice.

Trying to be humble even though he realized he could use his kindness as a way of getting close to her, he said, "Well, it's nothing, but then, I guess it's a good thing too."

"Not for me," she said as she walked back to her new seat. There was an empty one next to it, so Pete followed her. "I've been through enough for one day," she said.

When she sat down and brushed back her bangs, in the bright ceiling light, he noticed the wrinkles on her forehead, gray hairs, and crisscrossing lines around her eyes. Now, in *this* light, Sandy looked fifteen years older than when he had seen her in the station. He reeled as if waking up from a nightmare. His eyes had played tricks on him! She was so much older than he had believed her to be, and unattractive! How could he have not noticed that hours and hours ago? "I'm gonna go back to my seat, Sandy" he said, chuckling, stepping away from her. She looked almost as old as his mother, and he was about to hit on her. He rubbed his eyes, hoping she might change back into the attractive woman he believed her to be, or else, he was gone. All the chaos surrounding George, and his heart attack, and his confusing situation must have played tricks on all his senses.

"There's no way I could go outta my way for someone, Pete," she called to him. Then she covered up, and flicked off the ceiling light. Now, she looked like a long sack of potatoes!

"Yeah, I understand," Pete whispered loudly, feeling glad

Pete's Crossroad

she was excusing herself from any future responsibilities. That way, he wouldn't have to think of reasons to reject her. Sliding in front of George's old seat, with memories of George's sick and pale face blaring through his mind, Pete yawned and then whispered, "Gosh, I almost asked her out on a date!" Plopping down in his window seat, he set his briefcase on top of George's old seat and rolled his jacket over his arms. He imagined George laughing along with him. "Sandy's gotta be about my mom's age. Gosh, what was I thinking! You should have seen that, George, noticed that and told me," he laughed, and then yawned deeply.

He believed he heard George's voice: "It's because ya never really let go o' your mother, that's why. You're constantly seein' yer ma in all the women you're pickin, Pete."

"Huh? What?!" He glanced at George's seat. All he could see was a checkerboard-patterned material and his laptop that had slipped out of his large briefcase. Clicking on the overhead light, he stood up and yanked out a blanket from the overhead compartment. The couple in front of him groaned, and he clicked it off quickly. Covered himself and nuzzling close to the window, he said jokingly—not believing that George's ghost could really be sitting next to him: "Go away, George. I'm tired. I need some sleep." He swatted the air, and then poked the space where he believed George was now speaking psychobabble. "And when I'm done returning all your things, leave me alone. Okay?"

Hideki crept up and poked Pete.

"Huh?" Pete cried, jumping.

"He's really here, isn't he, Pete? George is still here!"

"Hideki?" Pete sat up straight. "Cripe! You terrified me!" His blanket hit the ceiling as he uncovered himself. Then a cold shiver ran through him. "Do you see him? See George?" he whispered.

He shook his head no, his thin, black, hair shining like silk under the light. "Nah, I not see him, but like I tried to tell you earlier—"

"Tell me what?"

J.P. Osterman

"*Aaaa*," Hideki sighed in frustration, "Japanese tradition says that only when a person reaches his or her final destination and resting place will his spirit find peace and leave this Earth."

Pete slapped his forehead in an expression of fatigue and frustration. "So what happens if I can't get each of George's things into the hands of those they belong to? Then there's the guy's funeral, and—"

"You must," Hideki said, "because George's objects contain all of his wishes and desires to seek forgiveness. He wanted to leave his family love."

"Huh?" Pete sighed, not fully understanding what Hideki was telling him. "But why me? Couldn't the Greyhound employees have done the same thing? I mean, I'm totally giving up my time here…completely going out of my way!"

Shaking his head firmly, Hideki said, "You were the last person George spoke to. The person he told his deepest secrets to. George picked *you*."

There was a big pause until Pete said, "So?"

"You have George's picture in your laptop," Hideki said with a serious expression on his face, pointing to Pete's computer as if a ghost had paid a visit to him in the past.

Pete countered, "But you have George's picture in *your* camera."

Shhh, a passenger behind them whispered.

"Sorry, Sir," Hideki said, and then craned his neck up to Pete. "I deleted it."

"*Ahhh!*" Pete said. Suddenly, he sniffed the air, believing he had inhaled a whiff of George's Listerine scent.

"When you return George's things…the objects he loved…to his family, and see that George is buried, you'll be free of George," Hideki said, staring with fearful eyes at the seat in which George had begun to take his last breaths.

Pete grimaced. "This is nonsense! Sheer malarkey!"

Hideki knelt down and motioned to George's seat. "Then what's that magazine doing there?"

A tractor magazine was lying next to his laptop. Pete

Pete's Crossroad

believed someone was playing a bad trick on him now. "What? Did you put that here?" He remembered that George had told him he had been a farmer in Indiana.

"No," Hideki counter.

"Well, someone put it there on purpose, to make me feel responsible for George's death, or to get back at me for holding up the bus or something." Pete leaned as close to Hideki as he could until his armrest stopped him.

"There aren't any tractor magazines anywhere on this bus," Hideki said touching the picture of the old John Deere on the front cover. "And look at the date."

Rolling over and looking closely at the cover, Pete felt a burst of cold air hit him from the open vent on the ceiling. "June 7, 1962! No way! This was George's! How did it get here?"

Hideki stood up and backed away. "Told you so, Pete. It's George."

"Let's see if there's a logical explanation." Pete stood up and checked the overhead compartment. There, in the center of the rack, with nothing around it, was George's carry-on. Obviously, when the attendant was gathering George's things, he mistakenly took another carry-on. "But still, now did the magazine get from the carry-on to the seat?"

"Good question," Hideki said.

"The magazine couldn't have just materialized out of nothing!" The magazine grew two sizes in his eyes as Pete slid his laptop off George's vacant seat. "It probably slipped out the carry-on when the attendant slid out the other carry-on."

"But how did the magazine just get *that* way just *now?*" Hideki asked, rubbing his face that dimmed as he stepped backward toward the front of the bus. He suddenly stopped. "Did George ever mention that date that's on the cover?"

"Hmm, June 7, 1962." Pete recalled the date. "Yeah, he said that was the day he had left Sue Lynn. That's why he kept the magazine. He said it was an inspiration for him to become successful so he'd never have to leave his family and farm again." The print had faded, the ink unlike anything modern.

J.P. Osterman

"He said he regretted this day more than any other. I think that's why George changed into different person with his family."

"Makes sense," Hideki said.

Pete picked up the magazine. The tractor on the front cover seemed to expand as if it were in 3D. Throwing it down, he rubbed his stinging eyes, trying to adjust his vision in the darkness.

"You must fix whatever George Gibson left unfinished," Hideki said. "Now, I'm more certain of than ever that George's spirit is with you."

"Just great!" Pete huffed, almost agreeing with him.

"Once finished, you will be free...*free.*"

Pete realized that to be free of George might mean losing his job, and perhaps cost him his savings, especially if he'd have to offer Donny to bring George's body to Amarillo and bury him there. "Darn!" he said, plopping down in his window seat. When he glanced at the tractor magazine, it was open to the centerfold depicting an advertisement of John Leyton performing in New York City. Beneath his name and a bar of musical notes, Pete saw the title of the song, which must have been a hit at the time, "Lonely City."

"Why me," Pete huffed, slapping the magazine closed. Yawning, he rolled his head over his billowy cushion. "Why me, George? I could lose everything...my job...money. And what about a motel and paying for a car after I arrive in Amarillo? I'm supposed to be focusing on making my sales quota tomorrow at the convention. And my Vegas trip's most likely shot. Darn! My life feels like someone's shooting it to hell in a hand basket!" Those were the words his mother had always said from the moment he could remember to the moment he left home in Denver. He kept repeating those hypnotizing words until he fell asleep.

Pete's Crossroad

Chapter 5 – Sandy Walston

Hideki shook him. "Hey, Mr. Pete…Pete, wake up."

"Huh?" Pete popped up in his seat. "What's up, Hideki?" Daylight was streaming in dimly from the bus windows. Outside, the terrain was different from Phoenix. The rolling Albuquerque land was high desert at the base of the Sandia Mountains. The high desert air was sage and piñon scented. The bus was passing through the desert grassland and savanna covered with a mixed piñon-juniper-evergreen and the occasional black twisting oak tree. They were at the western base of the mountains, now covered with numerous prickly pear cacti and peaks dotted with snow.

"It's morning, Pete. We're almost in Albuquerque," Hideki said.

Daryl's voice suddenly resounded on the loudspeaker. He approximated the Albuquerque temperature at ten in the morning: forty degrees, and rising to fifty degrees by eleven a.m. "There's been a steady stream of snow for the past few days," Daryl said, "but yesterday and today, the snow's begun to melt. I hope you brought boots," he chuckled.

Pete didn't think that was too funny as he glanced down at his black Florsheim shoes. "It's gonna be cold, Hideki. I think we're over a mile high here." He shivered, grabbed his jacket, and stuffed it into his carry-on so he could quickly access it. "God, I'm not used to this! I'm used to ocean breeze and fog in the morning...Santa Monica. In the distance, he could see dark patches that looked like silver strips of ice water. "Anything stranded out there will die!" He swallowed hard, believing he might either freeze at night or bake during the day.

Hideki said, "Die and never be found until an explorer searches the land."

Thinking the coldness capable of penetrating the glass, Pete stood to move over to George's seat.

Hideki held him back. "That seat's taken," he whispered.

Exhaling in exasperation, Pete said, "I still think this ghost and spirit stuff is nonsense."

His eyesight fixed on George's armrest as if watching someone moving, Hideki said: "But didn't you see him, Pete? You *said* you saw George."

Pete still believed that Hideki was so engrossed in his own traditional burial beliefs that he was hallucinating George. "Well, I was tired. I dunno. I was probably just reacting to that tractor magazine that the attendant dropped." He didn't tell Hideki that the magazine had unfolded to the center after he had returned to his seat. He didn't tell him he had heard George's voice either.

After glancing at his watch, Hideki smiled. "It's almost ten, Pete. The bus is almost at the Albuquerque station. I just wanted to wish you luck with your life."

Nodding, Pete replied, "Well, same to you, and all your friends." Craning his neck over the head of the man in front of him, Pete waved at the other Japanese tourists who were beaming wide smiles back at him, bowing in respect, and packing up their things.

"Just remember, Pete," Hideki said in a warning tone of voice, "make sure you give all of George's things to his family." He whispered sternly, "Make sure George's body has a proper burial. That's very important...most important!"

Pete's Crossroad

"Yeah, sure, I'll try," Pete huffed, tired of being lectured, annoyed at hearing superstitions. "George's body is in Phoenix, at the morgue. From what Donny said, the State of Arizona will bury him for free."

Hideki shook his forefinger. "No, no! You can't let that happen!"

"Ah come on, Hideki," Pete said, feeling weighted. "You're asking me to do the impossible."

"Well, I don't know about that, but *I* do know that if your motives are pure and your intentions right, spiritual entities will help you…even *send* you help in various ways on your quest to help George," Hideki said in a tone of voice that made Pete believe he was used to a lifestyle of spiritual living.

Pete had no real awareness about a spiritual world except what he'd heard in church, off-and-on when he was a small child. God? He remembered saying the name as an explicative! Now Hideki was telling him that he would receive help on his quest, assistance from a higher invisible power…an intelligent designer? Yeah, right!

Stretching out his legs and covering them with his jacket because of the cold, Pete said: "I know that George's son, Don, is checking into shipping George's body to Amarillo. But he was undecided, and I can't *force* someone to ship a body across two states." Frustration burned in his stomach as he heaved in breaths of oxygen, trying to grasp on to some sense of control. "Don and his family have to *want* George buried near them. And *they* should have to pay for it! I can't pay for a body transport and burial. I can barely pay for myself!" He shoved down his sleeves, covering his Rolex, hoping Hideki wouldn't see his expensive possession. If all else failed, in an emergency, he could get five grand for it!

Hideki looked down at George's empty seat as the bus lurched into a lower gear in preparation to stop. They were about to exit the freeway and pull into the Albuquerque station. "Then George will never leave you alone, Pete." His head bowed and he pointed outside. "So beware of vultures, snakes, and spiders if you decide not to help a wandering spirit, 'cause a mad spirit can bite you at a time you least expect it."

"Come on!"

"Bad luck *will* follow you, Pete," Hideki maintained, almost teary eyed. "A vengeful spirit is never good to have at your side and on your back." He was obviously quoting an ancient Japanese saying.

"From the look on your face, Hideki, you're totally convinced that you're right, and I'm wrong," Pete said.

Hideki shrugged and sighed. "That's my culture, Pete. I'm just telling you how over one hundred million people living in Japan believe. That's all."

Pete felt a rush of shame hit his cheeks. By not acknowledging Hideki's cultural practices, he had been insulting him. "Well, maybe I can convince Donny to either ship his dad's body to Amarillo, or at least have his cremated remains shipped to Amarillo." He watched for Hideki's approval. "There is no difference between being buried or cremated, right?" he asked, hoping Hideki would say yes.

"Probably not," Hideki snapped, "but I don't know. Only George will know when he appears to you and tells you.

"*Ahhhh*!" Pete exclaimed, yanking his laptop onto his lap.

Hideki bent down low alongside George's empty seat and continued: "The point is…George wanted to be by his family. There were important things he left unfinished, and now you are the deliverer of all of George's things and memories he desperately needed to take to his son and grandchildren.

Pete tossed his empty coffee cup into the little trash compartment in front of him and swept up the tractor magazine. "Can I ditch this thing? Throw this away too?" He had no use for anything agricultural whatsoever.

Hideki stopped him. "I wouldn't. Everything George owned is important. Keep everything you find of his until you reach his family. Give the magazine…every small thing…to them."

Pete thrust the magazine into his briefcase and grabbed his coat just as the bus ground to a halt at the bustling station. "Okay, all right," he said, glancing at the floor, scanning all the

Pete's Crossroad

nooks and crannies, making sure he had picked up and packed everything—everything of his own and George's He had to rush out and tell the baggage handler the mistake that was made fast! When he spotted George's empty cellophane peanut container, he groaned, whisked it up, flattened it out, and thrust it into a side pocket of his briefcase.

"Good job, Pete, now you're getting it," Hideki said, waving to his Japanese companions who were motioning for him to hurry back to his seat and pack his things. "You never know what George is going to do to help you on your way, now *your* quest."

"Uh-huh, right," Pete said, still disbelieving him.

Motioning to his companions that he was almost finished talking to Pete, Hideki continued: "Help George make peace with *his* family." With the wise expression on his face, he looked like a master of some sort of ancient religion.

Pete began to believe that he had better not mess with the beliefs Hideki was trying to instill in him. "So, you think George's spirit will be around to help me when I need help, do you?" He stood up, grabbed his briefcase, and pulled down his carry-on and George's carry-on off the rack. He and Hideki began walking toward the front of the bus.

Hideki met up with his Japanese friends who began greeting Pete. After they exited the bus—the frosty desert wind wafting in their faces and whipping their hair—Hideki said, "George will be around if you look for him, Pete."

"Gee, thanks," Pete said, rolling his jacket around his shoulders. "As if I'm really going to stand right out in the open and talk to George," he laughed. "People will think I'm nuts!"

"See you, Pete!" Before dashing away, Hideki handed Pete a bookmark he took out of his pocket containing writing. Breathless as if terrified that his companions might leave him, he said, "I forgot to give this to you." He pointed at the writings that were hand-painted.

"Wow, this is beautiful!" Pete gently glided his finger over the gilded edges. "This looks like a medieval manuscript!"

J.P. Osterman

"My friend wrote these Buddhist sayings in Japanese for you," Hideki said, pushing his collar up to his ears. He looked almost frostbit as his hot breath curled into the coldness. "They're powerful words."

"Thanks!" Pete called, waving and smiling at the young woman with Hideki. She was the one whose cousin had the ghost attached to her until the woman fulfilled the spirit's wishes. He guessed the bookmark was her idea to help him with his quest should he become discouraged or distracted. But then again, if what they were telling him was true, and with the little evidence he had seen, George's ghost should be materializing in some way or another to prod him on to fulfilling his wishes. "What's this all say, Hideki? Can you quickly translate?"

Hideki was backing away as he said: "One quote reads, 'Fall seven times and standup eight'." Hideki suddenly tripped on a black silicon burp in the cement but regained his balance. "The other Buddhist saying is, 'A flower falls, even though we love it; and a weed grows, even though we do not love it'."

"Ha! Wow!" Pete said, flipping over the bookmark several times. "I guess I'll have to think of these often, especially the metaphors." He slipped the ornate bookmark into his briefcase, but when he looked up to talk to Hideki, he could barely make out his face through the powerful morning sunshine. "Hey! I'll never see ya again! Too bad!" he called out, feeling suddenly alone again. This was starting to happen a bit too much—overwhelming emotions of feeling isolated in spite of being around so many people. He was hating it! Another bus pulled up, and Hideki and his friends boarded it. Pete let loose of his carry-on and waved frantically to Hideki. "Thanks! Bye!" After the hems of Hideki's brown corduroy pants and red flannel shirt disappeared into the idling bus, Pete lifted his heavy briefcase and began wheeling his carry-on down the frosty sidewalk toward the station. Quickly, he turned away from Hideki's departing bus, feeling as if he had lost something, or left something on Daryl's bus even though he knew he hadn't. *I'll never see any of those people again...and it's*

Pete's Crossroad

bothering me…darn it…why? People pass by people every day…and who cares…nobody 'cause that's just life…we can't connect to everyone…not everyone can make a difference in each person's life! His eyes were stinging in the new coldness—no longer ocean breezes and big city congestion with corporate buildings and apartment structures.

The desert marigold flowers were encrusted with a bit of snow. And the Englemann—as the sign said—prickly-pear cacti around the entryway gave a golden hue to the building. But as he approached the revolving door, he noticed the deadly prickly pear pins. They could be disabling should he accidentally get stabbed by one. Suddenly, he felt terrified to touch anything, and he rushed inside the station.

In front of several kiosks, Daryl caught up with him and told him that the maintenance crew would be unpacking George's things for storage. He informed Daryl about the mix-up in carry-ons, and he handed George's carry-on to him, telling him to make sure he unloaded his own carry-on from the cargo hold. The ticket clerk had Pete's ticket to Amarillo ready at the booth, and they needed to give it to him another baggage claim so they could entrust George's belongings to him on a 3:50 a.m. bus that was scheduled to leave the station after his convention.

After waiting for the crew to inspect his ticket and after he claimed his carry-on, Pete freshened up and changed his shirt in the restroom. He still had to look perfect and professional for the convention that would begin in just a few hours. After picking up the ticket Don had reserved for him, and securing George's luggage for the trip to Amarillo, he stopped everything when he spotted Sandy Walston in the sky-lighted dining section. Sitting and staring out a booth window, and wearing a pair of shorts, flowered t-shirt, and flip-flops, she looked dressed for a trip to Hawaii. Her outfit was entirely out of place in the frigid air of Albuquerque, but it did make her look younger, especially her designer purse.

Pete glanced from the exit, to the other side of the station, to the dining area. Should he go say hi, or avoid her?

J.P. Osterman

Taking one-step forward and then three-steps to the side, he was about to head to the vending machines until his black briefcase knocked him on his leg.

"What the heck!" he cried, lifting it up, inspecting it.

It swung at him again, hitting him in the chest.

"Ouch!" He began fighting with it.

Two elderly women stopped in front of him. One asked, "Sonny, are ye bein' robbed?"

The other said, "Mary, call the police!"

Pete calmed them down. "No one took anything from me, ladies. This thing's just heavy and weighted down wrong." As they walked away with puzzled expressions on their faces, he added, "Thanks anyway." He recalled what Hideki had said: That George would communicate with him along the way. George would be helping him. He didn't he'd be hitting him though. "Darn thing! Stop it...stop it now," he whispered to his briefcase containing his laptop. "Helping me? This stupid thing's gonna killing me!"

A little boy stopped and scowled at him. "Mommy, that man just called me stupid."

The boy's mother walked up to Pete and showed him her fist. "Get yourself to a shrink, idiot!" She grabbed her son by the arm and rushed away with him.

Pete felt red-faced humiliation. "I didn't mean anything, ma'am, honest!" He waved at the little boy and smiled. "Sorry!" Then he whispered down toward his briefcase, "George! It's you, isn't it? Whataya want darn it? I wish you'd just appear and tell me. Light up the sky with words or something!" He remembered Hideki saying that George's picture was now in his laptop. Maybe the laptop might unleash George's spirit if he'd open it. Pete was beginning to believe Hideki now. And when he realized his briefcase was bumping toward Sandy, he guessed that George was guiding him to talk to her. Why? Hideki had also said that whatever George would lead him to do would be for his own good ultimately— and to help him on his quest. "Okay, I'm going...I'll talk to her," he whispered to his briefcase.

Pete's Crossroad

Walking toward Sandy, he noticed she looked better now, all rested up. He set his hulking briefcase down and wheeled his carry-on beside her. "Hi, Sandy, mind if I join you?"

Jumping a little, she appeared startled out of a daydream and then gestured for him to sit down opposite her. "Oh, Pete, hi!" She coughed, smiled, and then brushed back her hair with her fingers. She had on silver dangling earrings that matched her charm bracelet that kept jingling every time she moved her right arm. Her face had the wrinkled expression of someone who was close to retirement. He couldn't believe he had mistook her for being so young yesterday, that he almost had asked her out of a date. Then she sipped her water as she glanced everywhere. She appeared afraid of being recognized.

"Thanks," Pete said, folding his arms, sitting back, watching to see what she might do next. Following her anxious gaze, he noticed that everyone in the station was preoccupied with purchasing tickets, meeting people, picking up luggage, or ordering and picking up fast food. No one was looking at them, but obviously Sandy was keenly aware of every detail.

Then, he recalled George saying something to him about Sandy in a dream after Sandy and he had parted company and after he noticed her real age. "Sandy looks a lot like yer mother, Pete. You know where she's at right now? Ya got unfinished business with her from yer childhood, Pete. Ya gotta find yer ma!" He woke up.

Now, with Sandy sitting right in front of him, and seeing that she definitely resembled his mother, George's words must have come from George for sure! George knew things he'd never told him! Yes, Sandy definitely did resemble a younger version of his mother. His mother was a nervous person too, but she had to be because the last time he saw her, when he left home after graduation, she was living with his abusive alcoholic father. His mother really hated her life and never could escape her bad situation. Had she by now? Where was she? George was making him thing about that, and he hated it!

"How ya doing, Pete?" Sandy's hair was windblown, her

face void of makeup.

"Fine, I have a little time, so I thought I'd come and say hi to you," he replied. He didn't have time, but ten minutes or so with her wouldn't hurt and should be enough time to figure out why George wanted him to talk to her. He ordered a coffee. Pete surmised that ten years ago she must have been the object of attraction, but she also carried herself as if she had endured a horrible catastrophe, or survived the consequences of some type of suffering. George had really told him: "Many of the mistakes I made were my own bad choices." Sandy's wide-blue eyes were showing consequences in their repetitive shocked and startled expressions. She was afraid of people, always sitting away from crowds, always distancing herself to be alone, by a window, staring blankly into the sky and terrain. He was wondering why on Earth George would want him to spend time with Sandy—and what Sandy could do to help him on his quest.

After talking about how each of them had slept on the bus, Hideki's departure for another tourist destination, and the chilly Albuquerque weather, Pete said, "I have to fire up my laptop." He opened it up, turned it on, and then took a bite of a breakfast burrito he had ordered. He was hoping to find George's spirit in it, show the proof to Sandy, and then exonerate himself from being crazy. Or maybe, just maybe, if Sandy could see George's spirit, maybe George might have something encouraging or helpful to say to her.

"Pete, didn't you say you have a business meeting in Albuquerque?" Sandy asked, glancing around him to the ticket counter. The loudspeaker called out her number, and a server delivered Sandy her breakfast: a toasted bagel and condiments.

Pete pulled out his cell phone. "Yeah, I'm calling for a car now. My sales meetings are all at the Albuquerque convention center. There's a design show this afternoon and my company has a booth there. I have to be there by one o'clock."

Ripping open her sugar, she said, "Selling mannequins, right?"

Pete's Crossroad

"That's it, and presenting some of my clothing designs," he replied, punching out the phone number of the limo his company had reserved for him. He confirmed the pick-up time as icons on his laptop popped up, ready for him to access his picture file. "So what's next with you, Sandy? Where you headed?"

Her lips quivered under her straight nose and her blue eyes watered. "I think Florida." Then she clammed up and drank some water.

Pete felt suddenly uncomfortable. He was a salesman, but didn't know how to talk to her! "Oh, nice." She remained silent, different from how she had been on the bus. "Did something happen, Sandy? You seem upset, like you talked to someone who said something that ticked you off."

Blotting the sides of her eyelids, she said: "I found out that I'm not getting some money that I was expecting." Her body language stiffened. She was holding back anger. "I just found out I got gypped though." She huffed, bit her lip, and sneered as she stared out the window. "Jerk! Life's so friggin' unfair!"

Suddenly, George's picture flashed onscreen. Pete saw the old man moving, walking in place, the sun shining on his bald, melon-colored head. George shot him a friendly wave and a grin. "Hello, Pete Turner," he said. He had pearly white teeth and a halo around his body that shone in rays coming from Heaven's gate. "Wow, it's mighty beautiful here!"

Pete gasped, feeling as if he was sitting at the top of a roller coaster and about to drop. "See this?" He whipped around the laptop screen so Sandy could see it.

Her lips straightened. She looked more terrified of Pete than of what Pete was showing her. "Yeah, that's a picture of George. Did you take it?" She squinted into the image, breathed hard, and folded her arms as if protecting herself. Then she turned away, her neck muscles stretching like taffy.

"You didn't hear him then…hear George say something to you?" he asked, standing up, peering at the screen until he caught a glimpse of George's picture. It was different from the one Hideki had taken of the two of them together, standing in line waiting to board the bus with cups of coffee in their hands. George was now standing alone in front of the bus. George could manipulate images in his computer! He wiped his eyes and ran his fingers through his hair. "Wow...I can't believe this!"

"You all right?" she asked. "I mean, it's been one heck of a long trip...and this desert is terrible!" She touched her arm, motioning at the dryness.

He felt perturbed that George had left him so alone; and now, would make him appear crazy to anyone who he'd try to convince that he was seeing a ghost. "I'm fine...nothing's wrong." He pulled the laptop back in front of him.

George's face popped back on the screen. He looked a bit like an animated cartoon. "Ask her what's wrong, Pete. Something's really bothering 'er."

"*Ahh!*" Pete said, putting his hands over his face.

"Haven't you ever felt that way, Pete?" George asked. "Like ya never had a friend?"

Nearly tipping over her coffee, Sandy stood and dashed over to him. "What do you see?" she asked, sitting down.

Pete inhaled and slapped the table. "You'll never believed me," he began, "and you'll say I'm crazy." He dumped some water on a napkin and wiped his face, the cold liquid feeling good on his skin.

He then told her what had happened—from the moment George died, to Hideki telling him that George's spirit was now inside his laptop. "I don't have a choice but to deliver George's things to his family, and I have to make sure that George's body is interred properly."

"*Hmm,*" Sandy said, "and I thought *I* had it bad."

He laughing in agreement. "From what Hideki says, I have to do all those things or I'll have bad luck for the rest of my life...*and* George's spirit will haunt me as a poltergeist!"

She glancing back and forth from the laptop to Pete's face. "Yeah, I remember Hideki and his friends talking about ghosts and spirits. And from what you said is happening to you, maybe he's right." She appeared calmer now, more settled and less afraid.

Pete finished eating his breakfast burrito and wiped his lips. "Ya think so? You think there might be something to this whole Japanese tradition of helping dead people make peace with their families?" He felt dread, wondering how he was ever going to make it through important sales meetings at the convention center with a ghost haunting him.

Sandy's eyebrows lifted in curiosity. "You never know. A lot of people believed in spirits, angels and demons." Wiping a spot of coffee off the table, she rubbed her eyes as if having been stung by a desert allergy. "I know that's why I'm going to Florida."

Pete straightened up. "Really?"

"Yeah," she began, looking at the time and craning to get a better view of the busses arriving and departing outside the frosty window. "I told you last night that I had just been to a funeral."

"Uh-huh," Pete said.

"My brother died...over three months ago," she said, sniffling.

"Yeah...sad," Pete said, believing there was more she wasn't telling him. He kept peering at his laptop screen to see if George's face might pop up at him again.

"Well, my family's having a big Easter gathering," she said, pulling her small purse next to her. "We're going to scatter his ashes. He was my twin." Her hands began shaking. "God, I feel so lost without him." She looked as if she might break out crying again.

"Oh," Pete said. "At least you don't have to go through it alone though. You have family."

She exhaled in disgust. "Family! Right! They're taking all his money even though I have his will right here in my purse!" Her face reddened in anger. "Holidays and family don't mix. Hasn't anybody ever told you that?" She sipped her coffee but grimaced at the taste. "Gosh...I've gotten myself into horrible spots...awful states. Drugs, detox, marriages...all because of sicko family members!" She began crying again, dabbing her eyes in between coughs and pants.

Turning his plastic fork, Pete said, "I can relate." He bit his lip and closed his eyes, remembering his own family gatherings when he was a young child. "My father was a drunk. Still is as far as I know even though I haven't seen him or my mother in years. And my mother was always yelling at him, or crying. My sister and me would huddle in secret crawl spaces until they were through arguing. The place was hell...the house a fright ride." His plastic fork squished on the table. "Gosh, what's happening to me here? For a split second, I musta blacked out or something. Completely not like me!"

She waved, implying *no big deal.* Then she said, "It sounds like everyone in your family was about as miserable as everyone in mine, Pete."

Feeling a brain fog slip into his mind, he said, rubbing his temples, "Yeah."

"Making matters worse, I left my husband two weeks ago." Her face paled; her eyes shone fear.

"Really?" Pete said, leaning into the table.

Looking around as if her husband might materialize, grab her, and yank her out of the bus station, she said, "I'm starting over. *After* I make a little stop to say goodbye to my family, for good, although they really don't know that yet." She inhaled, obviously trying to calm down further. "Maybe, like that laptop advertisement I read on your computer said, I could get a good settlement. I memorized that attorney's number that popped up on the screen. He's supposed to be the best in that area as a probate lawyer, and there's also a divorce attorney in the group." She whispered: "I have over twenty thousand dollars in an account. I don't want *him* touching it."

"Oh," Pete said, wondering how such a website could have activated on his laptop since he hadn't connected to Wi-Fi. That had to have occurred the little time she had the laptop in front of her while he was busy eating. As she continued to talk about her predicament, he realized she was in the process

Pete's Crossroad

of ditching a bad life—her entire past. Now, her paranoia made sense to him! "I tell you what, Sandy, I wish *my* mom would have done the same thing you're doing." He brushed the shattered plastic fork on his Styrofoam plate. "She was miserable living with my dad. That's why I left home."

While Sandy grabbed his wrist in an empathetic gesture, he remembered a time when he was five years old, when his father hit his mother, and then in a drunken rage, turned around and slapped him.

"No relationship has worked out for me, Pete," she said.

He wanted to tell her: *Me either…they always leave.* Instead, he said, "I have to go." He felt his heart palpitate. *I gotta get outta here!* he thought.

Sandy looked surprised. "Okay, sure Pete, yeah." Pulling back in a gesture of embarrassment, she began wringing her fingers. "I understand."

Pete hoisted his briefcase off the floor and then tugged on his white cuffs. He realized his sudden departure from her had hurt her feelings. Making sure his cufflinks were secure, he said: "It's not you, it's me, Sandy. Talking about things in the past like that gets me…well—"

"I'm sorry I said too much, Pete."

When he peeked into her eyes, he saw they were blue pools of pink-tinged water. "I have to go. My limo *has* to be out there." He glanced at his Rolex. "The driver's probably waiting for me."

Standing, Sandy helped him pick up his breakfast garbage by sweeping some wrappers on her tray. "I'll get this, Pete. Sorry, I didn't mean to scare you 'cause you look like I just terrified you by what I said." She gave out a feigned laugh. "Remember when George said you looked like that race car driver, Tony Steward?"

He stopped everything. "Yeah? I finally found the guy's picture on the internet."

"George was right, that Tony Steward is cute!" she said softy in a conciliatory expression.

He continued quietly packing up his things as if slipping

away from a woman in the middle of the night. When it came to closing his laptop, the lid flicked back at him. "What's wrong with this darn thing!"

"You're gonna break it, Pete," she said, steadying the top of it. "Wait."

He was heaving in a panic, believing he was going to be late for the limo and now seeing stars. Peering quickly out the window into the crowd, he thought he saw his mother standing by the loading zone, smiling at him with beckoning arms, motioning for him to run to her and hug her. "*Ahh!*" he said, plopping back down in his seat.

"What's wrong?" Sandy asked, giving him water.

"I feel dizzy!" Closing his eyes, he believed the dining section was spinning.

"It'll be all right, Pete, you'll see," she said, patting his arm.

He hugged her. "Sorry, Sandy. I don't know what's happening to me. It's like…I'm seeing people." Wrapping his arms tightly around her shoulders, he smelled her flower-scented conditioner. "Gosh, you even smell like my mom."

She laughed. "I'm forty-eight, Pete, so I probably *could* pass as your mom."

For a moment, he believed he was touching his mother, and he cried a bit. "I don't even know where she's at," he said, rubbing off his tears, pulling away from Sandy in embarrassment. "The last time I talked to her was four years ago. She was still living in Denver. But I haven't seen her in about eight years."

"And?" Sandy asked.

He slid his palm under his chin in thinking mode. "I told her I wanted nothing to do with her anymore."

"Sad," Sandy said. "Wow, the ultimate rejection."

Finally able to close the lid on his laptop, he said, "I didn't mean to say that thought. I was just angry, awful angry."

Her voice rising, she said, "Sounds like you've been angry all your life, like me, Pete." Suddenly, she motioned to the curb. "Could *that* be your ride?"

Pete's Crossroad

"Huh?" Pete let go of her hand and turned around. On the curb, he spotted a tall, muscular, Native American Indian man wearing baggy beige pants, holding a sign, and standing in front of a shiny stretch limousine. Then he saw his name written inside the turquoise-and-red framed whiteboard. Pete grabbed his briefcase and his carry-on. "Yep, that's my driver!" He had never seen anyone dressed like him but driving a limo. He had on moccasins and a pointed cowboy hat with a colorful feather sticking out of the right side.

Sighing, he realized he had to say goodbye to Sandy. Looking her in the eye, he said, "Well, this is it. We finally go our separate ways and on with our lives. We gotta say goodbye." For once, he felt glad to have known her as he remembered the time just a short while ago when he wanted to run away from her. Now, he was beginning to feel a little sad that he'd never see her again. He wondered where she'd be a year from now, ten years, fifty years. Glancing around the bustling station, he realized that about everyone. He didn't have a camera, but he did have an iPhone. "Can I take your picture?" he asked.

With a shy expression on her face, she swept her hair behind her ears and said, "Yeah, sure."

Sliding his iPhone out of his black suit coat, he turned it on and said, "Say cheese." He would always remember her smile and her laugh. He'd also remember her agitation and fear about taking on responsibility. She had lots of money coming to her, but could she manage it. He hoped she'd make it okay, on her own.

Click. He snapped her picture and then slipped his phone into his pocket. Swiping up his briefcase and picking up the black handle of his carry-on, he walked to the revolving door.

"Take care of yourself, Pete!" she called.

"You too," he called, waving to the man who looked nothing like a limousine driver. He believed the man was about to get back into his limousine and take off without him. He began running to the curb, the cold desert air hitting his face, nipping his eyeballs, stinging his sinuses. The man had heard him and waved in acknowledgement.

"Have a good life, Pete!" Sandy yelled.

"You too!" He noticed she had a happy bounce about her as if infused with hope.

"Wait!" Running toward him, she had something in her hand. Breathless, she reached him. "George said he had a granddaughter, right?"

Pete was distracted by a sudden commotion at the loading platform. People were pushing and shoving to check in their luggage that looked like a tall brick road, blocking his passageway to the limo. "Yeah, her name's Sue Beth."

Grabbing his hand, she put a charm into his palm. "Give this to her for me, will you?" She looked like a shy school girl as she refastened her bracelet onto her wrist. "I had that skate charm for thirty-five years. My mom gave it to me, and I'd like to pass it on to someone." Her voice was soft and low, as if the silver skate charm meant the world to her. "I don't have any children. Sue Beth will like it."

As he inspected the charm, he imagined Sandy roller-skating in a rink as a child. Probably, not many of them still existed. The rink was like the farmland George had once owned, probably bulldozed to make room for an expanding city. "I'll be glad to give this to Sue Beth when I meet her," Pete said. "I'm sure she'll treasure it." Putting the skate charm into his white shirt pocket, he watched as she began running back inside the station. With his carry-on tight beside him and his bulky briefcase tucked under his arm, he jumped over luggage to get to the limo, and almost tripped and hit the driver's sign. He stopped, catching his breath.

"Mr. Turner?" the man asked, bouncing lightly to keep warm, his breath puffing clouds of steam in the crisp air. He had deep brown skin with a face that looked like images he'd seen of Aztec Indians.

"That's me," Pete replied, handing him his briefcase.

"Hi, I'm Chuck," he said, tipping his transparent sunglasses at Pete. He opened the door for him and then slid Pete's small suitcase and briefcase on the carpeted floor.

Pete's Crossroad

"You're going to the convention center, right, Mr. Turner?"

"Yes, please, Chuck, and please call me Pete." Pete handed him his reservation information the company had given him.

"Sure thing, Pete," Chuck said, matching his information with Pete's and confirming it with his iPad.

Relieved at finally being able to head to the convention center, Pete nestled down into the soft leather seat; but just as the limo was about to drive away, he noticed Sandy running at him, flagging him down.

"Wait, Chuck!" Pete said, sliding down the window, and the limo jolted to a stop. "Is everything all right, Sandy?"

She had the shock-eyes of a deer blinded by lights. "I saw him, Pete!" She was breathless and cold, her cheeks and nose red as she brushed back her blond hair.

"Saw who?" He glanced around her, about ready to have her jump into the limo if someone was after her.

"I saw George! George talked to me through your laptop," she said firmly but softly. "I'm sorry. I didn't want you thinking I was nuts. Heck, sometimes I doubt my *own* sanity...but it's true, and Hideki was right, George is alive, in spirit, and I *did* see him."

"You saw a ghost?" Chuck asked.

After motioning for Chuck to give him a second, Pete wondered why she hadn't told him that sooner so they could have really talked about George and his quest. "It's okay, Sandy, and I believe you, so that's makes us both crazy then, he laughed."

"Life's so hard, Pete," she said, "and I have no idea where the heck I'm going...where I'm gonna end up." She began crying again. "But at least you're on the right track...you can make it, Pete...so go and conquer the world!"

Seeing that she might lose her composure, he wanted to stall for just a little more time to make sure she was all right. "You saw George?"

She put her fingers on the window glass. "George smiled at me in that picture you showed me of the two of you

J.P. Osterman

standing together. Then the information about that group of attorneys popped up on the screen." She wrapped her sweater around her cold throat. "I wrote it down on a napkin." She show it to him. "George helped me, Pete! He helped me! Isn't that amazing! He's not a bad ghost…he's a good one!"

Chuck turned around after honking at a bus that nearly rammed them. "We have to go, Mr. Turner."

Waving, Sandy called through cupped fingers, "I just wanted to let you know that George told me to go on. That I might fall down seven times, but I need to stand up eight!" Her voice was sounding shallow. She was disappearing in their distance. "Bye Pete…"

The limo was now far away from the curb as Pete stuck his head out the window. "George gave you hope, Sandy, never let go of it!" he yelled. The cold air made him snap back into his seat. He could only see her doll-sized figure through the rear window and lines of pedestrians.

Sandy hollered: "I'm free!" She had her hands high in the air. "I'm freeee!"

Sandy Walston was gone.

Pete's Crossroad

Chapter 6 – The Crossroad

"I'm dropping you off at the convention center, right?" Chuck asked, doffing his hat with the feather in it. He had smooth black hair tied in a short ponytail.

Pete thought that if Chuck were to wear his hair down and put on a ceremonial headdress, he'd look like a young Black Elk whom he'd seen a picture of while taking a college course on cultural diversity. "Yep, thanks, to the convention center, please," Pete said, glancing at the time: 10:45 a.m., and he had to be there by eleven. His schedule for the day was hectic. Sales booths, customers, schmoozing, breaking down the booth, and calling corporate in Santa Monica would be eating up all of his time. "How far is the convention center, Chuck?" He was tapping his feet so hard, his knees were knocking, and his blood pressure felt like one hundred fifty over a hundred! He thought the stress of enduring George's death was bad, but this stress felt near heart attack level; and he recalled George's heart attack. Quickly, he worked to calm himself down and breath steadily in the air conditioned car.

"You can grab a water out of that mini-frig," Chuck said, his brown eyes reflecting in the rearview mirror.

"Thanks," Pete said, whipping out a cold bottle of water,

unscrewing the lid, taking a deep swig that felt like ice melting down his throat. "Ahhh, this is great!"

Chuck turned a bit so he could talk to Pete through a long frame holding a sliding glass door. "The convention center is about five miles from here. We'll be there in about fifteen minutes. Traffic!" He stirred the limo in between a line of cars preparing to make a right turn. "And I hope you have a coat. It's cold here in March."

"Nope, just this jacket, but I'll buy one after the convention is over." Seeing that the snow had stopped, Pete took out his laptop to check his email. It was always the normal thing to do, but this time it felt like an eerie experience as he imagined George popping up and talking to him. After he punched *send* to confirm his arrival in Albuquerque to his boss, Terrence Frapley, the email icon faded, and George appeared on-screen in the picture Hideki had given him: A living 3D image, smiling, and waving.

Dressed in overalls with a John Deere cap on his head and his hands in his pockets, George said, "And what if that company doesn't have a job for ya after the convention, Pete?" He had an expression on his face as if knowing something Pete didn't know—information from a higher source. "Whatcha gonna do then, Pete? 'Cause that's what yer hopin' for, isn't it?"

Pete felt as if his morning sausage lurched into his esophagus. "Oh God! Not again!" He slapped down the lid on his laptop and cupped his hands over his face.

Chuck glanced quickly back and said, "Did something bad just happen?"

Pete didn't know how he was going to make it through the day. He had to worry not only about sales, but also how to avoid being perceived as nuts if he should see George while on the job. "You'll never believe it if I told you," he said, exasperated.

"Oh, I wouldn't be so sure of that," Chuck said, "'cause I've seen some pretty strange things in my life."

Sliding against the window and looking outside, Pete

Pete's Crossroad

spotted stucco shops, souvenir stores, and art studios. The edges of bus benches and street signs were painted with turquoise, reds and greens. In the late morning chill, people were moving like slow-walking ghosts. The pace of the world had slowed way down to the half the beats of a ticking clock, quite opposite of the highly-powered, pressurized punctuality he was accustomed to in Los Angeles. Noticing the deepness of the warm colors everywhere around him, he sighed repeatedly, and then realized that his headache had stopped. The deep blues, oranges and greens felt inviting, like a cool shower after a long hot day.

Suddenly, he remembered he didn't have a place to live in anymore, that his future was hinging on today's sales. The pressure returned and felt constricting. He'd have to produce, sell, make a great impression, and be ready with quick retorts to lure customers to his booth and keep them there should they scoff off his sale's pitch, toss down his brochures, or back away from his presentations. Adding to the pressure, he realized times were tough. People were losing jobs every day. He couldn't afford to lose his! He couldn't afford to be stranded in Albuquerque with a modest amount in his checking account and that mediocre amount in his savings account. Everything he had was in a storage facility in Santa Monica. He still had that payment to make soon.

"You'd be surprised at the stories I've heard, Mr. Turner," Chuck said abruptly, obviously making small talk. He was like a bartender—a sounding board and advisor for his customers.

Pete sipped his water and held up his laptop so Chuck could get a good glimpse of the screen in his rear-view mirror. "Have you ever had someone die, and then talk to you afterwards?" He almost let the laptop drop out of his hands he felt so frustrated with George and all his probing questions.

Chuck's head bobbed. "So you have a spirit hanging on to you. A ghost."

Startled that he believed him, Pete said: "Yeah, you bet I do!" Then he had an idea. "Hey, maybe if you could see this guy too, you wouldn't think I'm crazy."

J.P. Osterman

"What's his name?" Chuck asked, turning left at a signal.

"George," Pete groaned.

Nodding at the passenger's seat, Chuck asked, "Is George, the ghost, sitting next to me right now?"

"Uh-uh," Pete said, shaking his head no. "It's a long story." He felt foolish about telling it.

"Tell me," Chuck said. He had a tone of voice expressing confidence. Chuck might have answers!

"Basically, I met George Gibson on a bus in L.A. He was an eighty-six year old man who sat next to me all the way to Phoenix. Then he died, just like that."

"Wow," Chuck said.

"Right after we pulled into the Phoenix bus station!" Pete almost believed that George's death was happening all over again until he remembered his ghost in his laptop.

The limo tire bumped the edge of a curb, and the laptop slid against the door and popped wide open. George as a ghost was there again. "Ahhh!" Pete gasped, catching the laptop before it crashed to the floor. At least this time he didn't scream at the apparition. He was getting used to George's impromptu appearances.

"Anyone else see the Spirit of George?" Chuck asked.

"That woman who was flagging us down at the depot," Pete replied. "Her name was Sandy."

"Oh yeah!"

"She yelled that George had told her to move on with her life." Pete felt his face redden in embarrassment. This entire thing still had to be crazy, and he felt completely ashamed that he was beginning to buy into the fact that George was alive, and in Limbo, and gleaning information on his computer.

"That's a wise spirit then," Chuck said.

"Wise?" Pete asked, shifting in his seat. "Don't you think the wise thing for a spirit to do would be to leave this place?" He pulled up his collar. "Life's hard, man. If I were a ghost, I'd want to be in Heaven, or flying around the galaxy or something," he laughed. Snow was scattered in parcels on the sidewalks and streets that looked covered with shiny broken

Pete's Crossroad

eggshells. Bustling in and out of shops, people had on thick coats and down jackets, their collars high over their ears, their gloves and hats thickly pelted.

Chuck laughed. "My father often tells me an Indian prayer that might help you figure out why this ghost—"

"George," Pete said, gesturing at his laptop.

"Why *George* might be latching on to you," Chuck said.

Pete's eyes met Chuck's brown pupils in the rear-view mirror. "Okay, what prayer is that? Hey, if it helps, I'm all ears!"

Making another turn, Chuck's said: "And while I stood there, I saw more than I can tell, and I understood more than I saw; for I was seeing in a sacred manner, the shapes of things in the spirit, and the shape of all shapes as they must live together like one being."

Pete remembered it. "That's Black Elk! I've heard that prayer."

"Uh-huh," Chuck said, smiling. He looked five years older than Pete, but he sounded wise and knowledgeable. He had obviously learned deep lessons in life.

Pete wanted to know more and to learn those lessons before he'd have to live them himself, so he said, "What's the difference between a wise spirit and a dumb spirit?"

Chuck moved his fingers on the steering wheel to see his speed. "An unwise spirit is mean, a jokester. Those aren't good." He shook his head in dread. "But a wise spirit remains caught between two worlds to complete unfinished business. But when the issue, or deep trauma, is resolved, swoosh…the spirit is gone."

"That's it then!" Pete felt energized. "He, George, the ghost…wants *me* to take all his possessions to his children. He wants me to tell his son, Don, that he's sorry for some bad things he did to him when he was a child." He leaned toward Chuck and sat on the edge of his seat. "I've got to complete George's journey home to his family. I've also got to convince his Don to bury George, or cremate him and inter him, somewhere around his family. That's what a Japanese tourist,

J.P. Osterman

Hideki, told me on the bus. I have to give George's family his things, and make sure George's remains are buried." He laughed and gestured in frustration. "But that sounds downright nuts, doesn't it, Chuck? That sounds impossible for me to do, especially the burying part!"

About ready to pull into the convention center decorated like a gigantic fan opening in the sky, Chuck said, "My ancestors do that all the time. Most cultures do, Mr. Turner."

"What?" Pete asked, noticing a small chain with an arrowhead dangling down from the rear-view mirror. Cultural icons surrounded Chuck, including the long feather on his hat. Pete surmised they all meant something very special to him.

"That's our way of life, Pete," Chuck began, "to pass what we know down through the generations. And when our old people die, we bury them with our ancestors. We respect and honor their souls. There *is* an afterlife."

Pete felt he might have insulted him. "Sorry, Chuck, you're American Indian." He knocked his forehead in a gesture of stupidity. "Like the Japanese tourists I met on the bus who told me about George's ghost in the first place, you have a whole different way of living from us—"

"White people?" Chuck said, laughing.

"Sorry," Pete said.

Chuck's eyes peeked up into the rear-view mirror. "It's okay, Pete," he said, his voice calm and accepting. "I once experienced a big identity crisis in my life, when I was about your age, but it, well, resolved when I accepted culture and yours and began learning to live with our differences." His voice turned wary. "And from the fidgety look I saw on your face when you were talking about your high-powered job, and everything you have to do today...*whew*...I think I'll take my culture over yours *any* day."

Pete shuddered and nodded in agreement.

"And you look scared to death to follow through with that dead man's request," Chuck added. "That's natural for us. We do that kinda stuff all the time." He put his limo into park gear and began gathering paperwork.

124

Pete's Crossroad

They were now among a line of cars at the convention center with people dressed in formal wear disembarking from cars, taxis, and limousines. The fast pace of life turned suffocating. His eyes stinging, Pete put his hand over his heart as he watched all the bustling traffic. Glancing out the window opposite him, he gasped when George appeared on the seat, looking around the limo with amazement in his eyes. "There he is! He's here!"

Chuck dropped the forms and quickly turned around. "Where?"

"George is sitting right next to me!" Pete said, unbuckling his seat belt. But before he could grab George's transparent arm, he jumped back into the laptop, but was still visible on the screen.

"Never been in one of *these* things before, Pete. What a ride!" George said, tipping his green-and-white John Deere hat at him. Then he looked askance at Chuck. "Thanks for the ride, young man."

"Did you hear that?" Pete asked, whipping up his laptop and holding it into Chuck's line of sight.

Pulling up the limo a bit so he could stay in the same parking spot a little longer, Chuck asked, "Hear what?"

"George just thanked you for the ride," Pete replied, pointing frantically to his laptop screen. "He said he'd never been in a limo before."

Chuck leaned back and said, "Well, thank you, George."

As the limo revved in idle, the laptop flicked off. "The battery just died, darn!" Pete said, sliding the laptop over his thighs and shaking it a bit.

"So George is gone?" Chuck asked, turning back around to his paperwork.

"I don't know. I guess I have to plug it in around my booth somewhere, charge it, and then wait and see." Pete could finally get a good look at Chuck. Without his wide-brim hat and the light not obstructing his face, he had high cheeks bones, a and a broad forehead. His nose was long and a bit curved, and his complexion a light-burnt smooth sienna.

J.P. Osterman

"George is gone at least for now," Pete said, sighing in disappointment. "I just wish I could get rid of him permanently." He glanced at the time. "I'm almost late." He really was late, but he believed he had a good explanation if his boss, Terrence Frapley, should ask him.

Chuck shot him a serious expression as he pointed at Pete's laptop. "Maybe I can help you."

"How?" Pete asked, pulling his carry-on next to him and shoving his laptop into the sturdy side pocket of his briefcase.

"I know an elder at the kiva," Chuck began. "He specializes in strange occurrences and phenomena that can't be explained by science." He pulled out a form and handed it to Pete for a signature.

"Is he like, a medicine men?" Pete was skeptical. He believed medicine men just huddled together around campfires, chanting, smoking peyote, and experiencing drug-induced hallucination. He signed the form and returned it to Chuck.

"No, way, Pete!" Chuck said firmly. He had a startled look on his face expressing a great belief in the elder's practices. "Walks-With-Dreams is his name. He's given me much guidance. He helps people interpret what's happening around them." He glanced outside, keeping close eye on the traffic.

"Really?" Pete asked, lifting his briefcase, half-wanting to stay and listen to Chuck even if that might mean Terrence Frapley firing him. But that possibility made his heart skip.

"Look, Mr. Turner, Walks-With-Dreams I'm sure will meet with you if I arrange it." Chuck's voice was calm and reassuring. "You just have to let me know now so that when I pick you up at 5:30, I can take you to him." He put his arm over his seat, and a piece of his woodie-patterned shirt draped over it. He was obviously needing an immediate answer, waiting for Pete to decide what to do.

"So this man, Walks-With-Dreams, might be able to make George tell me exactly what he wants, and what kind of a burial he wants? And if I can't make that happen, when

Pete's Crossroad

George will detach from me?" Pete asked, gesturing in exasperation. "Cause I feel so weighted down by all this…like I have ten thousand pounds of pressures on me right now!" He glanced at people dashing into the giant convention center. Their breaths looked like streams of hot steam in the frosty air. He felt so small as he burped, tasted acid, and put his hand over his heart.

"I can't guarantee answers to all those questions," Chuck replied, "but I can tell you that Walks-With-Dreams might be able to communicate with George, and make his transition easier out of that computer of yours." He pointed at Pete's briefcase. "If anything else, he'll definitely be able to give you insights as to how to help the restless spirit." Chuck's face took on the expression of a very serious nature. The world might come to an end if Pete didn't believe him! "Walks-With-Dreams is my grandfather. He's one of the spiritual guides on my reservation…a shaman," he whispered cautiously as if his grandfather might appear.

"Shaman?" Pete repeated, reeling back from Chuck's terrorized expression.

Outside, the traffic was intensifying—cars honking, tires screeching to sudden stops in the slush. "Haven't you ever heard of a shaman?"

"Oh yeah!" Pete said respectfully.

Chuck rolled his eyes. "*Tsk*, let me try explain how they work a little to you." He answered his cell phone, and then quickly input numbers into his GPS. Turning back, he said, "You know how if you put vinegar and baking soda together in a crucible, you get—"

"A volcanic explosion," Pete said. "Yeah?"

"Well, my grandfather's like the crucible…the place where the two opposites exchange or interact," Chuck said, waving at a security guard who had walked toward the limo, motioning for Chuck to move. "Shamans help people mend their souls."

Pete folded his arms. "I don't need mending," he said. But when he glanced at the laptop inside his briefcase, he realized that if he'd tell anybody about seeing a ghost, they'd hospitalize him for being psychotic. Chuck as the only one with him right now who believed him. Chuck was all he had to help him. "Hmm, maybe I do, need mending," he finally said.

"I think you're out of balance, Mr. Turner," Chuck said. He obviously had a different perspective on life, on reality, on people. And he spoke with conviction, convinced that his grandfather could help Pete, or help George's ghost, or at least help Pete deal and manage George's spontaneous appearances.

"Out of balance, hmm," Pete said, almost believing Chuck one hundred percent. "But how? How can *I* be out of balance?"

The security guard was back, this time showing a little more anger as he tapped Chuck's window, giving him the signal to move. "I don't have much time," Chuck said.

"Call me, Pete." Pete jerked up the handle of his carry-on and clasped his briefcase.

"Okay, Pete." Watched the disgruntled guard, Chuck said, "Usually people get out of balance after something bad happens. Or they do something they know isn't right."

"A crisis then," Pete said, donning his jacket.

"Yeah, that's pretty much right," Chuck replied. "Or there's something that you're ignoring, but your soul is screaming for you to pay attention."

"Ignoring," Pete repeated, wondering what in the world he could be in denial.

"I know my grandfather can help you, if you have time for it," Chuck said.

Pete thought hard and glanced at the time. He was now definitely late for work. He had to decide quickly. "I don't see any harm in meeting with your grandfather after this is all over, Chuck, thanks, make the arrangements." He opened the door to leave, the cold air streaming into his face.

Chuck looked at him askance with a joking expression. "Do you have a little Native American Indian in ya, Pete?"

"In me?" Pete asked, shocked. He believed that if he'd say no, Chuck might take back the invitation. But he didn't want to lie. If he did, George might overhear it and tear into

Pete's Crossroad

him later! And from Chuck had already said, maybe George was not only a ghost, but also his conscience. "I really don't believe I have Native American blood in me."

"Huh," he said, "usually these paranormal things only happen to people who are in tune with the spirit world."

Glancing at the blue sky without even a cloud in sight, Pete said, "Nope, and I don't have any priests, nuns, or pastors in my family either. I'm just you're average guy," he laughed. "Actually, I was hoping to go to Vegas after working today. Me and another salesman had the whole five-day trip planned out." He felt cheated as he held his briefcase. "Now that plan's all shot to heck."

Chuck shrugged and said: "Plans sometimes don't work out the way we expect them to, Pete. That's why I'm driving this limo." He patted the headrest in front of Pete. "Walks-With-Dreams told me that I'd have a very interesting life filled with meeting new people if I'd take up driving a limo," he chuckled. "See? I met you. I guess we were meant to meet, and I to help you."

"I guess you're right," Pete said. He was beginning to feel powerless against the cold winter, and insignificant among the throng of executives hustling into the convention center.

"And someday, you might also help me," Chuck added, tracing a sphere in the air with his finger. "Everything's like a wheel, a circle. Everything's connected, and one deed always comes back to you in one form or another."

"Whew," Pete breathed. "Okay, Chuck, I believe you." He swallowed hard in the bitter breeze and pinched down his collar to keep out the wintry air. "I'll see ya at 5:30." He lifted his carry-on and briefcase out of the limo. The sidewalk was arctic. He could feel the chill bleeding through his shoes, stinging his toes. He felt so cold, as if his black suit might turn into frost and encrusting him in ice! Blowing into his fingers for warmth, he said, "Please tell Mr. Walks-With-Dreams that I look forward to talking to him." Glimpsing around the limo, he felt lost and alone. He thought George might have felt the same way when he left L.A. for Albuquerque. This is the place

J.P. Osterman

George desperately wanted to be but never arrived.
    "See ya at 5:30, Pete." Chuck's limo left the curb.

Pete's Crossroad

Chapter 7 – You're Fired!

The domed convention center was like a steel-girted version of Grand Central Station in New York City. Pete had been there twice after accepting two prestigious sales awards. Grabbing a cold frosty water glass from a server dressed in hip-hop designer clothes, he stopped everything and let go of his carry-on that cracked as it hit the shiny waxed floor He felt like a compass needle! He needed directions! The booth…the mannequin booth. That's what he needed to find. But giant booths, cubicles, and long tables were converging and diverging into giant labyrinths. He was completely lost; and if he couldn't find his way to the Fossil Inc. booth, he'd have to call his sales pal Fred. He texted him, *I'll be there in five minutes.*

Walking over to a booth selling candies, he bought a pack of chocolate covered tarts and began devouring them. He was hungry. Announcers were calling on the loud speakers about exciting events and advertisements. As he peeked through crowds and jumped to look over their heads, people were bumping into him, knocking his arms without apologizing. He felt like a careening shopper the day on Black Friday.

Then he spotted the sections selling designer fashions. One hallway contained a row of mirrors and dressing rooms.

J.P. Osterman

After making his way through that crowded walkway, he noticed a large booth with naked mannequins lined up on stands and platforms. A blue neon sign flashing Fossil Inc. stood at the entryway with small mannequins dancing by way of mechanical pulleys to programmed music—from rap and hip-hop, to country and rock. Pete remembered the dimension of their entire area: 50 x 85, with a several entrances to lure customers and sell, sell, sell!

To the side of one of the displays, he saw one of his colleagues, Tina Bowlett, a black woman in her early twenties. She was busy dressing a dwarf mannequin in a snowstorm exhibit that Pete had designed a week ago. Vibrant, short, and model thin, Tina had her hair spiked shiny purple. She had on skinny jeans, a peasant blouse, and a beaded necklace with dangling earrings. She often dressed half Goth and half 1950s! Once she had confided in him that she wanted to be a model; but because of her height, no agency would hire her. But Tina always had a positive attitude and never gave any indication that she felt rejected or victimized by the industry.

When she spotted Pete, she waved him over and handed him his tool kit. "Pete, you're so late!" She was out of breath but fiery as she continued dressing the mannequin.

"Traffic was terrible," he said, helping her, "and I didn't fly, remember? I took the Greyhound." After they exchanged pleasantries about their trips, he put away his tools, plugged in his laptop, fired it up so he could present a PowerPoint presentation if needed, and then he took out all his brochures and set them in a decorative container at the front of the booth. Every now and then, he glanced at the icons on his laptop screen. He didn't want George popping up on him again, and he decided to slide it behind a mannequin and drape it over with a piece of cloth that looked like snow material under a Christmas village.

Turning on the chill-fan in the snow booth wherein she had dressed mannequins for a ski party, Tina asked: "You ready for Easter, Pete? Today's Thursday. You only have two days to get home to make it home to spend time with family."

Pete's Crossroad

He remembered decorating Easter eggs when he was a child, but nothing more than that. No church, no family gatherings, Easter was just another ordinary day to him. "Nope," he said, as he greeted a prospective customer and handed her a brochure. "All our mannequins come porcelain finished," he told the customer, "but we can design each one to the measurements you give us when you place your order."

Opening his brochure, a woman was straining to see the pictures he had created on the company's software. He remembered that George had the same expression when he showed him his brochure as well. At the time, he believed the problem was with George's poor eyesight. Now, he was feeling concerned. He opened one up. The brochure wasn't at all the one he had designed and okayed for the printers! Someone had made a terrible mistake, and on purpose! No one would copy hideous and small images! "Who did this?" he asked, looking around at a few sales clerk. There were three he couldn't recognize, but they were selling fashions, designs, and clothing lines; but he couldn't make a sale if customers couldn't see the mannequins! He recalled that his old boss had okayed the brochure a week ago. His old boss told him they were great, and he didn't see any problem! Pete felt suddenly confused and shocked. "What went wrong with these?"

No one heard him through the commotion as more customers passed the booth. When they picked up his brochure, he tried to describe the images, but people appeared repelled by them. He pulled Tina aside when she dashed busily behind him. "My gosh! My brochures are awful and I have no idea how this happened!"

"I think I have an old catalogue for you that I brought just in case," she said, running to a box and then bringing back an outdated catalogue. She began raking in customers with her fashion designs.

Seeing her closing sales, and during a lull, he said to her, "I don't know what's going on, Tina, but when I showed my brochure around at Fossil everyone said they were great. These are crap!" He picked up a handful of them that customers had left behind and threw them into the trash. If I'da had the one I designed, I would have succeeded here today." He was now failing to get his quota and felt suddenly sick. "Something bad is going on, Tina. I'm telling you, something isn't right!" He scratched his scalp and then quickly, self-consciously, smoothed back his hair. "I've never messed up…never!" Now he was trying to come up with another plan—one he could implement, fast.

"I'll look at your brochure later, Pete," she said, "but the brochures corporate gave me before I flew here are doing well." When Tina had another small gap in traffic, she said, "So what are you going to do this weekend?"

He glanced around, looking for Fred Aspon, his close colleague. He wouldn't be hard to spot. Fred was gregarious, and a jokester. He had an effeminate walk and talk, and was astute at communicating with people. He treated each person as a close friend or intimate relative. Maybe that's why he got along with Fred so well, he once speculated. He had always admired that quality in him. He always wanted to be naturally gregarious and at ease with people. How the heck he ever managed to make it this far in sales he had no idea!

"Fred and I were supposed to lose ourselves in Vegas this weekend after the convention," Pete told Tina. "But I can't go. He's gonna be disappointed." After talking to a customer who slid a brochure into his pocket, winked at him, and then sauntered away, he asked Tina, "What's Fred wearing today?"

After signing her name to a receipt, she said, "A pin-striped suit with the most expensive white shirt I've ever seen…and gold cuff links! He's dazzling today!"

"Where is he?" Pete asked. He walked outside the booth, into traffic, and began almost throwing his brochures into peoples' hands.

"Fred's picking up lunch for us. I just received a text from him," Tina said, as she unlatched a mannequin's leg and began dressing it. She had a wig under one arm and bust pads under the other. "This is so cool, don'tcha think, Pete? I've made eighty thousand dollars for Fossil so far, selling reps

Pete's Crossroad

from Target and Macys two fashion labels."

Watching her, he felt suddenly dejected that Fossil's line of new ornate mannequins were not selling at all. He had designs to show people, an entire lines of clothing he'd worked hard on for months. He was hoping to make his quota in sales and then present his designs to the new boss. "I don't know about cool, but it's a job, and I hope I can save the rest of the day and sell a whole slew of mannequins!" He had to. He believed his life was on the line.

Tina stopped what she was doing and smiled. Her teeth were like slivers of white gum. "Well, I gotta be happy doing what I'm doin'," she said. "No sense being miserable at your job, 'cause misery just breeds more misery. I gotta have a good attitude no matter what."

"What a mantra!" Pete said, peering around at the marble-eyed mannequins. Back at his small office, he dressed them, sold them, and took phone orders while waiting for seamstresses to finishing sewing clothes. "Tina," he began, "sometimes I talk to these things like they're people. I actually hold conversations with them!"

She laughed. "I can relate! I practice what I'm going to say to customers on these mannequins. I arrange them in various imaginative settings, and then I role play." She hit her head in a self-deprecating gesture. "They've become my world, I work so hard and so much overtime."

Disappointed when another potential customer dropped his brochure into a trash can, Pete called, "jerk!" Through the noisy crowd, he didn't hear him.

Reaching back, Tina tossed some fake snow onto the display platform. "Aren't you happy selling these, Pete? I mean, you have a pretty cushy job. And next year if the Fossil continues to do well, the company will expand to Europe, and some of us might be picked to open a store there." She continued to talk about all the benefits and opportunities.

Pete wasn't listening. Happy? Looking at the variety of sizes and shapes of the various mannequins, he thought that if he'd just put on some of their outfits and stand completely still, he'd look just like them…get lost among them. "Tina, I'm just counting down the time to 5:30, when I can get out of here." Suddenly, he felt a tap on his shoulder.

"Hey, Guy!"

Turning around and looking into green eyes, Pete saw Fred Aspon. He grabbed his shoulders. "Finally!"

"How ya doin', pal?" Fred asked, slapping Pete lightly on the side of his head. Fred was George Hamilton tan, and a dynamo fueled by energy drinks.

"Great, pal!" Pete said. They shook hands wildly.

"Ya ready for Vegas, Pete?" He raised his eyebrows in mischief and rubbed his hands together as if prepared for a naughty nightlife. "Ya ready to drive outta here tonight?" He pulled Pete away from Tina. "I gotta get laid, and very drunk," he said slowly.

With a disgusted look on her face, Tina grimaced and shouted, "Oh, come on Fred! I heard that." She shook her finger at him. "One of these days, some husband or boyfriend is gonna pound you for stealing his woman." She quickly turned away and handed a brochure to a customer. "Don't come calling me when you're in the hospital or a morgue, 'cause I'll tell ya I told you so."

"Party pooper," Fred called. Then he winked at Pete and said, "She was great in the sack though!"

"Gosh, Fred," Pete said, his stomach sick, "I can't believe you just said that!" He liked Tina, respected her for her old-fashioned qualities. Fred had obviously told her a lie to make her believe he loved her. He was commitment phobic to the max, but never this cold and callous. Poor Tina. Now, the day were taking a terrible turn. This wasn't the Fred he knew. What the heck had changed him in the last week?

Tina had heard Fred's comment. She snapped around and shot him an embarrassed and angry glance, but her entire aspect shone hurt and pain. From now on, working with Fred would be hard on her.

"Hey, I never say forever," Fred said.

"Take it easy on her, man!" Pete said, knocking him and

Pete's Crossroad

then pulling Fred closer to him. "Come on, man. That's not cool. She's our friend. What's wrong with you!"

Fred laughed, and then suddenly groaned in pain as he stared angrily at his shiny shoes. "Something hit me…damn! Your laptop *hit* me! It scuffed up my shoes!" He was about to kick Pete's laptop that was half-jutting out an exhibit.

Pete karate chopped his leg. "That's mine, and no way could it have hit you. That's crazy! *You* kicked *it*!" Pete slid his laptop under the table.

Fred looked seething. "This is a five hundred dollar pair of shoes!"

Pete knew who had done it: George. But Fred would never believe his story. Then again, he'd never tell Fred about George the way he was acting so strange and inhumane! "Come on, a computer didn't just jump up and hit you, Fred." He returned back to looking through the brochures setting in fanned shapes on the white felt tablecloth. Perhaps some might be all right; however, thus far, all of them were trash.

"Five hundred dollar shoes," Fred kept repeating. "Ruined, and I think there are gashes in 'em." After smoothing back his hair, Fred handed a brochure to another customer who Tina pulled aside and began giving a sales pitch. "You're paying for my shoes since that's your computer, Pete."

"No way," Pete said, astounded at Fred's audacity. "And what's this?" Glancing at Fred's brochure, he noticed the pictures were large, bright, and printed on expensive shiny paper that had to have cost the company two dollars apiece.

"The company had me completely redo *your* brochure, Pete," Fred said, crossing his arms while tapping his shoe. He had a retaliatory scowl on his face as if getting even with Pete who had done something terrible to him.

"What?" Swallowing a knot of saliva, Pete felt his heart sink. *Did someone turn Fred against me? Today is definitely spiraling!*

"Corporate is revamping your sales pitch," Fred said, motioning for a customer to sign Fossil Inc.'s guest list. "The managers are heading the company into an entirely different direction." He seemed indifferent that Pete might be perceived as being inferior to him. "But, hey! I just sold seven of our newest models to reps today." He danced in place and shoved his fists into the air in victory. "That's seven hundred dollars in commission. And the day's still young. By tomorrow, I just know I'll be way over my quota." He patted the sales book filled with receipts. "Party! Party!"

Pete stepped aside and began waved old brochures at anyone who'd look at him. "Give me a few hours and I'll catch up to ya, Fred." He worked hard at trying to distribute the old catalogue pamphlets to anyone approachable. They declined after glancing at them.

Tina sidled up to Pete and said, "I just sold five hundred orders of new pant outfits!"

Glancing down, he wondered if someone had jinxed him. "What's going on?" he asked Fred.

"Whataya mean?" Fred replied. Then he pointed to a small group of business executives moving toward their booth. "Uh-oh."

"What are *they* doing here?" Pete asked, nodding in their direction.

Fred dropped his pen, and Tina nearly knocked over a mannequin as she peered around to get a good look at them. "Corporate," Fred said, picking up his pen, groping for the knot in his tie and adjusting it. "That's the new guy, our boss, the VP of Sales, Terrence Frapley who's with them all."

"He looks like Donald Trump, but without the toupee," whispered Tina, giggling.

Pete brushed back his hair and smoothed down his jacket. "Do I look all right?" he asked Fred, wanting to make a great first impression. "I've never met him."

"Yeah, sure, fine," Fred replied, brushing him aside, sliding his brochures at the front of the table.

"Hey, what are ya doing!" Pete felt lightning anger course through his body. Fred was obviously trying to get a solid edge over him. Fred was bucking for *his* job! He remembered the last business meeting a week ago.

Fossil Inc. had to lay off two sales reps, twenty

Pete's Crossroad

employees, and shutter a store in Chicago. They were struggling to find low-paid workers so they could manufacture quickly and ship more product. That mass firing was a warning to everyone.

Before Pete could move Fred out of the way, Terrence Frapley was in front of him, picking up his awful brochures off the table and inspecting them. From the stern look on his face, Pete realized he was in trouble. He remembered watching a TV episode in which Donald Trump pointed at an employee and proclaimed, "You're fired!"

Backing away in an abandoning gesture, Fred shrugged and waved goodbye to Pete.

"Best friend, huh!" Pete mouthed at him. Could the rest of the day get any worse?

Before Pete could call Fred a traitor, Terrence said, "Mr. Turner? Pete Turner?"

Pete swallowed hard. Frapley's face was enlarging. "Yes, Mr. Frapley. I've never met you, Sir, but I'm glad—"

"I want a private word with you, Mr. Turner. Follow me." Terrence straightened his expensive jacket and began walking out of their booth.

Pete felt as if he were adrift in a boat and heading toward rocks. "Yes Sir, Mr. Frapley." Glancing at Tina as the remaining executives walked into the booth, Pete noticed her frown. Her sad eyes followed him until he couldn't see her any longer. Obviously, she was disturbed, and realized what was happening but couldn't intervene.

Pete followed Terrence, nearly stepping on his heels at times. With each maneuver through a crowd, he felt as if the floor tiles might explode! He remembered what George had said: "People live life in moments, in seconds." This was one of those times, and something awful was about to happen. Blood thumped in his chest. People were talking, laughing, and cutting great deals. All he could hear was his breath Everything slowed down in motion.

Realizing he was in trouble, he began thinking about his resume and all its details. He had had this job at Fossil Inc. for one month; and the job before this at Fashion Diva for three years. He had a specialty degree, and a Liberal Arts degree. *Still*, he thought, *what am I gonna do?*

Suddenly, Terrence motioned for Pete to enter a small meeting room next to a concession stand. Inside, Pete found himself among shelves of corn, green beans, mustard, and ketchup. Sitting down, he thought that if George could be there with him, he would say something completely off kilter, like how funny Terrence would look with a raccoon pelt on top of his head instead of a toupee. He laughed.

"What?" his boss asked, grimacing.

"Oh, nothing, sorry, Mr. Frapley," Pete replied.

After sitting down, Frapley said, "Where were you this morning, Mr. Turner?"

"At the Greyhound station, Mr. Frapley," he began, "but I'd like to introduce myself—"

"Bus station, huh?" He was perturbed, no, *overly* perturbed and hateful. Pete couldn't understand why. "You should have flown to Albuquerque, like Tina Bowlett and Fred Aspon, Terrence said. "You could have been here when the doors opened to fix those brochures of yours." He slapped one down in front of Pete. "You call this professional?" The hit made the paper tear. "Mr. Aspon said three companies broke off their contracts with us because of *this* half-rate brochure of yours."

Stunned, Pete inhaled. "Mr. Frapley, the other vice president, who took the job a few days ago, approved this brochure." He began nodding no. "Look, I'm don't know how this mistake happened, and I'm sorry—"

"We have to let you go, Mr. Turner," Terrence said.

"Oh, come on, Mr. Frapley!" Pete pushed off from the table. "The VP before you approved my bus trip! Clarence approved the brochure. He even helped me design it!" Everything was going horribly sideways, and Pete was fighting to fix it.

Folding his arms and posing as a god of war, Terrence said, "We're keeping you on payroll until Monday, but that's it.

Pete's Crossroad

You're fired."

Pete remembered his possessions—what little he had—sitting in a storage facility outside of Hollywood. "What aobut my things at the office, and—"

Glancing at his Tag Heuer watch, Terrence said, "I'm giving you two week's severance pay and medical benefits until the end of the month." He stood up, and Pete felt the man's condescension waft over him. "No hard feelings though, Mr. Turner." He slid a folder out of his jacket and held it like a prayer book in front of him. He handed Pete the termination package. "Send us your address, and we'll mail you the items you have at work. No problem."

Pete opened the folder and scanned the paperwork. "A check for $3,221.19?" He laughed. "I don't have an address! And I don't have a place to live! I was told by your predecessor that you were going to promote me. I moved out of my place before I left L.A. I was *due* a promotion, Mr. Frapley. I don't get what happened and why you're letting me go." He told him he was hoping for an opening in one of Fossil Inc.'s designer stores so he could have a permanent job.

"Mr. Turner, we have to let you go," Terrence said. "It's At-Will employment. Nothing personal."

Clenching his fist, Pete realized he had to stop talking or else he'd say something he'd really regret. He had always believed it best not to burn bridges no matter the situation. Someone wanting to hire him might call Terrence, so he'd better bow down gracefully now. Terrence had power.

"Okay, Mr. Frapley," Pete said, opening the folder. Quickly, he signed the papers and shoved his check and termination forms into his briefcase.

"Be sure to send us your address and a phone number where you're staying, Mr. Turner," he said, emphatically, his voice also sounding urgent. He appear closed off and shielded. "That's important...that we know where you're at in the next few days."

Pete thought Terrence's body language was odd for the situation. Terrence looked fearful, not angry at how he'd traveled to Albuquerque or the poor quality brochures. *My past has been spotless. I can easily make up sales in the next city like I've done before. The entire situation is surreal—a nightmare!* He said to him, "I'll email you my address and phone number later, Mr. Frapley, most likely from a motel; and when I do, please send me medical forms and all the other documents I might need so I can apply for unemployment!"

Chapter 8 – Tina's Gift

Leaving the room, shutting the door, and then walking toward the booth, Pete felt a bit relieved. "Who needs all these fake lights, exhibits, show rooms, and mannequins anyway?" he muttered. "That guy's a total jerk! I don't know why, and I don't understand what's happening, but this entire day is so surreal...like George's death!" Anger hit him like a punch in the arm. He breathed in and out, hoping at some moment he'd stop feeling like looser and a failure. Outside the crowded booth, he saw Tina with sad downturned eyes.

She had his jacket over her shoulders, his briefcase, and was pulling his carry-on. "I thought it would be best for me to bring you your things," she said. "I packed your laptop, and here's your suit coat. Fred said the limo driver called. He's waiting for you in the foyer. His name is Chuck."

"Yeah, I know him, Thanks, Tina," Pete said, walking toward the exit. "I feel totally humiliated, Tina. Getting fired took me *completely* off guard. I thought I was doing so well...great sales, great—"

"I don't know *what's* going on, Pete," she said, whispering. "It's strange, like this company's turned upside out in a matter of days. Something's wrong, and maybe I'll be next to get fired." Patting his arm, she added: "I'm so sorry, Pete. Believe me, I would have warned you if I would have known."

"It's okay, Tina, really." He checked the side of his briefcase to make sure his laptop was there. He couldn't wait to see George's face and do a little research on the company.

Tina pointed to his suitcase with tear-filled eyes. "I bought you a sandwich and put it in your carry-on pocket."

Her sudden smile reminded him of Sandy Walston when they had parted ways. "Thanks," he said. "You just take care of yourself. Watch your back." He wiped the lines of tears off her cheeks. "I can't stand to see ya cry."

She gave him three business cards. "Pete, you can count on me being a good reference. Write me later on."

"Thanks, but you know what's bothering me the most?" he asked as they walked through a labyrinth of booths and aisles to the exit sign.

"What?"

"I lost my best friend, just like that," he said, snapping his fingers. "I thought Fred was my best friend—huh!"

"Well, life as you once knew it is obviously gone, Pete," she said.

He knew he didn't have much time before she would have to leave and return to the booth. "Yeah, gone. I guess you never know what life has in store, huh?"

"Nope. I'm sure learning *that* lesson," she exclaimed. "So, do you know what you're gonna do now, Pete?"

He didn't want to tell her about his plan to visit Chuck's reservation, and his homeless situation, and his limited funds; but he did want to leave her with a hopeful impression of his future. "I'm heading to Amarillo. The bus leaves at three-fifty a.m."

Tina reeled in surprise. "Amarillo! There's nothing there, is there?"

He shrugged. "It's a long story, but I have something to do there."

"A job?" she asked, excitedly.

Pete's Crossroad

He had to lie. "Maybe, but I don't know. I'll write you."

"Okay," she whispered, stopping and then glancing at the booth. "Do you think Terrence Frapley let you go because of what happened on your last job?"

He didn't think *anyone* knew about that bad incident, except for Fred. Now she knew, but what had happened at Fashion Diva couldn't have got him fired at his Fossil! He felt more confused than ever. Peering at all the merging crowds heading toward the exit, he exhaled. He didn't want to battle those old memories he believed he had left behind at Fashion Diva. "I don't know. Maybe. But that means that Fred must have planted some bad seeds that got me fired." He started burning with anger. He wanted to punch Fred.

"I'll see if I can discover something, Pete." Tina pulled a small crucifix out of her pocket and put it inside Pete's white shirt. It jingled against the silver skate charm that Sandy had given him. "I don't know if you're religious or not, but pray."

Pete let go of his carry-on and patted his shirt pocket. "I never had much time to think about religion or faith, but I guess now's a good time to start asking for some divine intervention," he said, chuckling.

Tiny motioned at his pocket. "It's Easter on Sunday."

"Oh yeah!" He remembered her reminding him of that.

"Easter's different," she said, a hopeful light reflecting in her eyes. "People might have been lost all year long, or have had bad things happen to them, but I believe Easter is a time for new beginnings, a day when people can begin to walk down a new pathway in their life."

"Crossroads, huh?" He took out the cross. The silver arms were like street signs. He was definitely standing at a crossroad right now!

Folding his fingers over the cross, she said: "I pray that God will lead you in a right path toward a great future." She reached up and kissed him on the cheek.

He felt the same emotion he experienced when Chuck told him about his grandfather, the visionary Walks-With-Dreams, who was supposed to mediate between this world and

J.P. Osterman

George's world. Given what Sandy just said, shouldn't God be resolving George's unfinished business? He definitely didn't want to tell her all the mysterious supernatural problems plaguing him because she might want to join him and start a quest to find God! He didn't have time for that! "Thanks, Tina. I'll keep in touch." Setting the cross in his pocket, he knew he'd email her, but he also knew he'd never see her again.

She suddenly perked up. She was obviously forcing a good attitude so that she could go back and work at the booth. "When you get to Amarillo, put me down as a reference."

"Okay!" Then she disappeared in the crowd. Trying to catch a last glimpse of her, he could see only winter props and mannequins. One of them he had posed and dressed just two days ago. He then saw Terrence Frapley conversing happily with Fred. He was about to call out, *cut throats*, until he felt a tap on the shoulder.

"Hey, Pete!"

He turned around. "Chuck, *you're* a *sight* for *sore eyes*!"

"I heard ya got some bad news," Chuck said, shaking his head. "Tina told me. She was worried about you. Too bad, Pete. Sorry."

"Yeah, and I wish I could enact revenge!"

"But then you'd go to jail, Pete," Chuck began, "*tsk tsk*, ya don't want that."

Picking up his carry-on and lifting his briefcase, Pete said, "Look, Chuck, I just lost my best friend over there who's now schmoozing it up with the boss! Jerk!" They began walking toward the exit but approaching a giant food court. "Fred helped me get this sales job with Fossil over a month ago. But after what just happened, it seems Fred sabotaged me." He felt light headed. "Darn...I never saw *that* coming." Chuck steadied him. "The new boss just fired me."

"You look dehydrated, Pete, and you're probably exhausted," Chuck said, grabbing Pete's carry-on.

After thanking him, Pete said: "Nothing makes sense, Chuck. Before I left, the head boss approved my bus trip *and* my brochures. I never looked at them because I believed they

Pete's Crossroad

were perfect the way I and the boss approved them." That boss left the company right before I left L.A. But here's the thing: Terrence Frapley fired me because the brochures were bad—even though they *shouldn't* have been bad, and he also fired me for taking the bus here instead of flying. I think I was set up…or sabotaged."

"Wow, crazy!" Chuck had an expression of bewilderment on his face.

"I know it's sounds like I'm being paranoid," he said.

"No, go on."

"But shouldn't the guy who left before Frapley took over have told Frapley what he'd done and how I was traveling here?" Pete asked. They were now at a giant food court. Pete had hours to kill.

"Something does sound out of synch at that Fossil company, Pete." He took out the invoice for his limo. "They paid me though, so your boss had to have approved your method of travel."

"Yes!" Pete exclaimed. "See?!"

Maybe if you step back from the situation and wait a couple of days, you'll get a clear perspective and be able to put all the pieces together," Chuck said. "You're too close to what happened right now. You gotta a case of myopia."

Pete covered his mouth when someone passed by him and sneezed. "What's myopia? I can't afford to get sick."

Gesturing to a bar and veering toward it, Chuck replied, "Myopia is where you can't see the big picture because you're emotional about all the little events."

"That makes sense," Pete said, scratching his cheek.

Chuck stopped and said: "Wanna beer before we go visit my grandfather, Pete? Come on, ya need a break. It's the cure for myopia." Again he laughed.

Chuck could flow with life; and from what he'd said earlier, he had learned not to take each disappointment as a deathblow or failure. Wishing he could be more spontaneous and less serious as well, Pete was drawn to him. He had calm mannerisms and an inherent honesty in his voice and words.

J.P. Osterman

Peering at the direction of the Fossil booth, he wanted to run there and slug Fred and Terrence before leaving. *No, that would just land me in jail!* But that's what his father did whenever he got fired after drinking on the job or going in late to work. He'd go to the office, rage, and punch the boss.

Breathing to calm down, Pete turned away from the booth, thrust his briefcase under his arm, and said: "Sure, Chuck, let's get a drink. I'm off work now, permanently, and totally dispensable in the world, so what the hell!" He was laughing when they reached the counter, plopped down on a barstool, and Chuck put a bottle of cold beer in front of him.

"We're all replaceable, Pete," Chuck said after sipping his beer.

Pete saw a power in him, a strength he didn't understand. "Knowing you're dispensable and replaceable doesn't bother you?" he asked, feeling a sudden rush of loneliness followed by fear. He felt reality shifting, and a sense of falling. Everything was changing. He didn't know into what. "How can you say something that cold and stay so calm, Chuck?" Looking at him from head to toe, Pete traced Chuck's tall outline. He a had survived a big battle, not a cowboy and Indian war, but a crisis, a tragedy, a struggle.

Looking Pete in the eye, Chuck said, "I have my family and my community. And I have faith that no matter what happens, I'll be all right and survive. I'm not in charge." He pointed to Heaven. "There's a Higher Power in charge and who has a plan and a purpose for me...for everybody."

Pete felt disoriented. *Failure* kept repeating in his mind. He remembered trying so hard to climb a rope in gym class, but he could never touch the ceiling. "I don't know what's next for me, Chuck. And as for a purpose...well, I thought I had one already...*my* dream...selling my designs. I was almost there...until all *this* happened. I just don't know what went so wrong?"

Pete's Crossroad

Chapter 9 – The Kiva

After finishing their beers and getting into Chuck's limo, Pete donned his Polaroid-mirrored sunglasses, popular in California and standard for law enforcement.

Chuck scoffed a little and said, "Some sun cheaters ya 'got on there, Pete."

Pete interpreted that as, *what are you hiding?* "Cool though, huh?" He tapped the rims like tipping a hat.

As he began driving away from the convention center, Chuck said, "When you enter the kiva though, Pete, make sure you take those things off. We enter the kiva as transparent as we can make ourselves." Then he chuckled, "Some people even get naked." Pete shivered a bit. "But you don't have to."

"Whew—thanks!" Pete said, taking his glasses off.

"My grandfather thinks sun cheaters hide a person's identity." Chuck turned up the air conditioning. "He won't talk to you wearing those things because he can't see your eyes, just his own reflection in the lenses. The eyes are the seat of a person's soul." He tapped the area over his heart.

"Oh, sure, I understand," Pete said, sitting back, the words of his ex-boss still echoing through his mind: "We have to let you go, you're fired."

J.P. Osterman

"You want to get to the truth of what's going on inside your laptop still, right?" Chuck said as the limo entered an freeway on ramp.

"Definitely," Pete replied, his stomach sick until the convention center went out of his line of sight. "But to tell you the truth, Chuck, right now I'm more worried about all my things I have in storage in Santa Monica and my Sebring convertible in the park-and-ride in L.A."

Chuck shifted in his seat a little. "I'd be concerned about that too."

Popping a breath mint, Pete said, "I feel like I've been on a Ferris wheel ride that stalled at the top."

Chuck called back laughing, "Oh, and don't forget...the seat is rocking and you're prayin' to touch ground."

As the limo raced down the freeway, passing buildings, the terrain yielding to gently rolling ground, Pete noticed the drastic change from city to desert country. It was a typical Albuquerque spring day, windy and almost frost-cold. Still, he felt the sting of failure burning his eyes—tearful irritations he wiped off his lids. As they sped past the last clump of green trees to head into dust-deviling beige sand of the upper edges of the Chihuahua Desert, he muttered, "What am I gonna do now?" Resting his chin on the armrest, he stared out the window. Blocking the horizon, the snow-capped peaks of the Sandia Mountains towered high and beckoning. He could get lost up there.

Chuck said simply, "Maybe my grandfather will help you with that, Pete."

The drive to the kiva was long and far from Greyhound station. The sun blared high in the sky, heating mounds of snowy sand to the nougat color of a 3 Musketeer's bar. The thick cacti jutting out of the desert landscape looked like vertical piles of green prickly stalks, and the tumbleweeds appeared to shimmer as they rolled across the pavement of phantom water. Winter was meeting springtime in Albuquerque, usually the driest part of the year in the area where the wind sometimes blusters at 20 to 30 mph, and

Pete's Crossroad

afternoon gusts can produce periods of blowing sand and dust. One mirage after another, the terrain appeared dappled with alluring puddles; but with no bird or person in sight, Pete knew that rattlesnakes and scorpions were lurking in the endless crisscrossing bars of green brush and snow covered sand.

Chuck said: "If ya like snow, Pete, get a good look at it now, 'cause before the end of the day, all of it'll be gone. And this is the last you'll be seeing of it for a long time. Summer's coming. It's gonna get *real hot* here in Albuquerque."

Believing Chuck might be suggesting that he look for a job in Albuquerque, Pete said, "I don't think I'll come back here, even though I have no idea what I'm going do or where I'm going to go after I finish what George wants me to do for him in Amarillo."

The drive was smooth to Chuck's home area, but the tires cycling on the pavement sounded like melting rubber. He hoped they weren't! If the limo would stall, he and Chuck would be stuck in the boondocks, alone. Feeling panic, he wondered whether he could trust Chuck if something bad happened. After all, his life was now in Chuck's hands, and he was in hostile territory.

"You look scared," Chuck said, as if reading Pete's mind.

"There's not a car in sight," Pete said, wringing his fingers, craning to meet Chuck's eyes in the rearview mirror. "I hope this limo's in good condition."

Chuck laughed as the limo wound through a little mountain pass and made a left turn into the Pueblo of Sandia reservation where Chuck's tribe had lived since around 1300 AD. "No fear," he said as the car bounced lightly down a long driveway. "The company checks the car." His voice was reassuring as Pete took in a relieving breath of air. "I'll getchya back to the Greyhound station way ahead of schedule."

Pete glanced at his Rolex. "The bus leaves for Amarillo at 3:50 a.m. It's 3:30 p.m." Leaning back, he spotted a few black tree trunks that were in reality toppled telephone poles. Electric lines appeared to be absent, but there were water tanks and transformer kiosks dotting the landscape. People living

151

here had to be expert sowers, reapers and managers of the unforgiving land—frontier land he imagined as cowboy and Indian territory where wagon wheel trains must have broken down as people migrated west. He inhaled air-conditioned oxygen that cooled his face, bringing back the memory of Fossil Inc.'s mannequins poised in fake snow exhibits. He couldn't get the image out of his mind. Their porcelain faces were perfectly sculpted—preserved probably longer than he'd be alive. The reality of death suddenly petrified him again.

"Here we are," Chuck said suddenly, pulling into a small sandy parking lot of a large circular building. "This kiva is built above ground. But ancient kivas were built below ground and could only be accessed with a ladder." He put the car into park, the arrowhead on its chain wavering as if it were pointing them to the direction of wisdom, the kiva. "My family's part of the Kiowa-Sandia people," he began, "members of the pre-Columbian Tiwa language group. Their lineage can be traced all the way back to the Aztecs."

No one was around, not even a car, only bright sun, pockets of green brush, mounds of snow-covered sand, and the sounds of a few rustling tumbleweeds. Stepping outside with his briefcase tucked under his arm, Pete began shaking off specks of dry mud that had splattered the edges of his black suit pants brown. The dry cold wind whistled as it whipped across his face and raised the hair on his head. A dash of sand hit his mouth, and he spit out the grit. "It sure is quiet out here," Pete said, trying to be positive, "and awfully isolated."

Like the gusting wind, fear wafted into his bones and he clenched his collar against his throat. Was Chuck for real? Maybe he had pulled some kind of trick on him, or maybe he was planning to rob him, or murder him! He was used to L.A., and like most people living in that area, cautious about his safety, worried about being mugged or killed by a stray bullet, and always looking over his shoulder.

After Chuck took the lead toward the white kiva dome, he said, "Pete, I think you've developed some type of paranoid social gene. But I can't blame ya. You need it to live and

Pete's Crossroad

survive in that corporate world that just fired ya."

Pete accidentally stepped on an ant hill in the middle of a paved sidewalk, and the disturbed critters scattered wildly. "Yeah, trust never did come easy for me, not even as a kid. I can just imagine what I'm like now at twenty-six! If I were someone else, meeting me for the first time, I might not like Pete Turner." He felt disoriented again.

Pushing his collar up past his ears, Chuck suddenly stopped, his cheeks almost red from cold. "Don't say that, Pete." He whipped off his sunglasses. "We all have the next moment...and as many seconds as there are to this life, we can all choose to change *if* what you say is really true, that you don't like what you've become. Just do something else!"

Panting to stay warm, Pete felt speechless as he stood facing him, the wind now blowing grains of sharp dust between them. He felt as if they were waiting to draw pistols in a desert gunfight.

"I don't think that what you said is true though, Pete," Chuck continued firmly, "'cause I met you, I like you. You're an okay guy. I just see that some bad things have happened to ya, that's all." Then he turned around, waving for Pete to follow him into the kiva.

Clearing his throat in the uncomfortable encounter, Pete asked, "Is anyone at home in there?" When he looked back at the limo, it appeared as a black waving rectangle in a mirage.

"My grandfather's inside," Chuck replied, standing at the kiva door, gesturing for him to enter. "We all take turns dropping him off and picking him up here."

Fine sand sprayed Pete's shoes, and he tried shaking it off, but everything appeared sticky and permanent.

Chuck laughed. "You look like you're doin' the *Hokey Pokey*," he said. "It's no use cleanin' your shoes anyway. They're ruined. Sorry...shoulda warned ya."

When Pete remembered that he didn't need them anymore anyway because he didn't have a job, he changed from perturbed to indifferent. "Yeah, so what," he said, entering the warm kiva and brushing off his heavy briefcase.

J.P. Osterman

He could hear the dry wind whip around the outside walls as he transitioned from swirling dust clouds to the holy place.

"Grandfather?" Chuck called, walking toward a great fire pit in the center of the room. He turned to Pete and whispered, "Please keep your voice very low…like the volume where you can hear the wind over everything else. This is a holy place. Sunlight, wind, rain, and earth speak over everything else." The walls were crests of shadows, and Pete couldn't see beyond fifteen feet, but the ambience was calm and peaceful with brick insulation as a natural air conditioner.

"Sure, Chuck," Pete whispered as he tried to imitate Chuck's solemn calm movements.

"Hacho, Grandfather," Chuck called out in his native greeting. Chuck was proud of the fact the his grandfather was one of only 144 native Kiowa that still spoke the Southern Tiwa-Sandia dialect, known as Kiowa-Tanoan. Chuck had told him he was working to learn as much of the language as he could from his grandfather while he could. He was getting old, and might not live many more years. Stepping boldly beyond the fire pit, Chuck sounded like a child looking for his parent. Calling out his grandfather's name again and speaking more of his language, Chuck appeared to have a lowly but special place in his family.

When Pete heard the sound of a man singing, he stopped. His heart beat rapidly, but then calmed. Chuck told him the song was a preparation, a solitary song of transcendence from this physical world to the spiritual world. Pete remained outside of the stone-paved circle surrounding the fire pit and set down his briefcase gently next to one of several thick cushions also surrounding the circle. The old man's melody was a low soft song, making Pete suddenly sleepy, with the realization that no one would harm him. Glancing around the smooth white walls decorated with tapestries, dream catchers, and rows of pictures that had to be tribal elders, Pete began wondering what kind of answers Chuck's grandfather would have concerning George.

Then, an old man stepped out of a shadow at the back of

Pete's Crossroad

the kiva. Chuck's grandfather had to be well over a hundred! As he lumbered toward the circle with Chuck's assistance, he appeared to have a perpetual backache. He didn't have on any special type of head dress, or costume, or war paint as TV shows often tend to portray Native American Indians. Pete believed that if he had met Walks-With-Dreams on a street in L.A., he would have perceived the elderly man to be just another human being, not a visionary legend Chuck had hailed him to be—a medicine man with special abilities, a shaman.

"Pete, this is my grandfather, Walks-With-Dreams," Chuck said after sitting down next to his grandfather and gesturing for Pete to sit down on the other side of his grandfather.

"Nice to meet you, Sir," Pete said.

"Grandfather, this is the man I told you about, Pete Turner," Chuck said.

The old man nodded, and Chuck stood, retrieved a piece of large wood, carefully set it into the fire pit, and then lit the fire. A spicy smell began circling through the room.

"So this is the man who was just fired?" the man asked.

"Yes, Grandfather," Chuck said.

He glanced at Pete with inspecting brown eyes and then pointed at his face. "You are Ghost Man."

"Ghost Man?" Pete repeated. He felt every line on his face twist in confusion. "But I'm not dead. I'm not a spirit."

Walks-With-Dreams fanned the little wavering flame in the fire pit. "Ghost Man's life has changed. Ghost Man…you have a *big* problem."

Smelling the air, Pete surmised the scent was at its peak at for summoning spirits. He wanted to get down to business. "There's a man, no a ghost, in my laptop computer, Mister Walks-With-Dreams. That's my problem." Saying the man's name sounded strange as he lifted his laptop out of his briefcase and set it up on a cushion in front of them. More pops and cracks hissed in the fire. "His name is George Gibson." He opened the screen, the laptop turned on, and an icon to an Imaging program initiated. "See! I didn't do anything except charge the battery." He pushed the screen in front of Walks-With Dreams so that Chuck could see it as well.

Walks-With-Dreams placed his palms face up on his crossed legs and began humming a faint tune. Then he stopped. "You're wanting me to explain what is happening to you with facts. That way, I will believe you and not call you what the world would call you, crazy."

"You bet," Pete said firmly, "yes, thanks, please! Give me some advice about what to do." He knew he was begging.

The old man pointed to the black screen that began filling with more icons. "George is a guide spirit," he said. He closed his eyes, sighed, and said, inhaling as if taking in George's invisible words, "They are not dead who live in the hearts they leave behind." He waved in the air, spreading around little strands of incense he motioned for Chuck to disperse into the air. "I learned those words from the Tuscarora tribe." He pointed at Pete his warning finger. "Ghost Man, you must keep Spirit George alive until his family can come to know him."

Chuck gestured at the laptop. "I don't see George's face right now, but I know he is trapped inside the technical device, Grandfather."

"I knew it!" Pete snapped. "But how do you know if you didn't see him?"

Chuck rubbed his hands together. "The customer I had after I dropped off Pete said she felt a cold spot when she got into the car. The arrowhead compass dangling on my rearview mirror spun several times, and several objects I touched zapped me with static electricity."

"Spirit George *definitely* wants his presence known, and to leave the device at will," Walks-With-Dreams said.

Pete tapped the picture file and brought up George's image. "This is what George looked like before he died," he began, "but when the Japanese tourist took our picture, it was of us together, walking toward the bus with coffee in our hands." With his forefinger, he followed George's shape. "Now this shows George alone. And whenever I bring up his

Pete's Crossroad

picture, he's wearing something different, and his stubble grows just a tiny bit more each time I see him." He felt a knot of a headache, and began rubbing the center of his left brow. "I just want to know for a fact what's going on here. I thought that maybe you could see George, and give me a clue as to what exactly he expects me to do, and what'll happen to me if I can't do everything." He cleared his throat. "After all, from what I've always watched in movies and—"

"On TV?" Walks-With-Dreams said facetiously, as if sick of psychics and writers who know nothing about the Native American ways.

Pete's body sagged. "Sorry."

The old man showed him his palm in a gesture of forgiveness. "What else can you expect, except to believe what you've been programmed to believe on that tube?"

Remembering that George couldn't stand technology either, Pete continued: "But isn't it true that Native Americans are supposed to be highly spiritual and able to sense and connect with forces in nature and energies?"

Chuck laughed and Walks-With-Dreams said: "Yes, we do have a deep respect for nature, but I don't think you've come here to talk about religion and philosophy."

"No I haven't," Pete said, feeling embarrassed.

The old man nodded in understanding. "You came here to know more about a complete stranger."

"Spirit George," Chuck interrupted, stoking the fire.

"And why George has attached himself like glue to you," the elder said.

Pete reeled in fright. "Attached like glue?" He thought of the words "attached to the hip" and imagined Siamese twins. For a split second he believed George might always be with him. "God no!"

Walks-With-Dreams hummed as he motioned for Pete to calm down. "Spirit George had only hours to live when you met him. He was breathing his last breaths while sitting next to you." He spoke softly, slowly, but deliberately, his voice wavering. His long years and vast experiences had taken a hard

157

toll on his vocal chords.

Chuck had an expression of awe on his face. "You don't think it was just coincidence that put you on that bus with George beside you, do you, Pete?"

Pete snickered. "Coincidences happen all the time though. Coincidences *are* life, Chuck." Breathing deeply and feeling defensive, he added: "Just go outside and stand there. The Earth's revolving, and it's in a perfect green zone, rotating in precision with a moon we need for our survival." He kept thinking: *coincidences happen all the time; no big deal.*

"No big deal." The old man's torso moved gently as he rocked.

"Huh?" Pete gasped. "Did you read my mind? Chuck! You're grandfather just read my mind! I swear!"

Before Chuck answered, Walks-With-Dreams said, "You just go on believing that everything is *coincidence*, Ghost Man," he said, his tone of voice challenging. "But here this, when you arrive at your next destination, look for things either falling into place, or opportunities falling apart." He stretched out his arms and then brought them close together again. "That's how you'll know your truth path."

"What's all *that* supposed to mean?" Pete asked, believing that a tree could fall on him tomorrow.

"People, places and opportunities that align at just the right time and place are *not* coincidences," the old man began, "but are compass needles, directing us."

Chuck perked up. "Don't forget to add intuition, Grandpa," he said, sternly. Obviously, he didn't listen to a gut emotion, made a bad decision, and then regretted his mistake. "Discernment is like a muscle. You have to work at it and the gift will help you do right from wrong."

Pete scratched his head and felt more confused than ever. "Whew," he began, clearing his throat. He also felt defeated by that awful firing. "Well, I sure could use a compass now," he began, "because I have no idea where the heck I'm going."

For moments, they sat and watched the picture of George who had a smile on his round, wrinkled weathered face. He

Pete's Crossroad

had on a brown fedora hat pinched a little above his brow, and was wearing a brown suit, white shirt, and sun-yellow tie that appeared brightly ignited by glow rays from Heaven.

"He looks dressed for Sunday church," Pete said, "and I bet those clothes are in his large suitcase. But I can tell you for certain, that's *not* what he was wearing on the bus."

Walks-With-Dreams said: "You want answers about George, but really George has brought you here, to me, to find answers about yourself."

Pete thought his tone of voice was like a drill. "Answers? For me?" He almost wanted to grab his socks and shoes and run out of the kiva. Then he remembered what the elder had told him when he first entered: "You have a big problem."

Suddenly, like an echo ricocheting around the kiva, Pete heard: "Go to Amarillo, Pete." It was George.

"Here that?" Pete said, jumping, the laptop nearly falling on a rug. "George told me that I need to go to Amarillo."

"Nope, I didn't," Chuck said, folding his arms. "But I believe you." The light from the fire pit wavering across Chuck's face, made Pete believe he was sitting among an entire group of Pueblo Indians in the background.

"We don't have to see George," Walks-With-Dreams said. "The main thing is, *you* see George." He pointed at Pete. "But will you listen to George?"

He was feeling agitated as he glanced into the fire. "A picture is causing me to look like I'm insane! I can't believe it!" Pete said, closing his eyes. Again he heard George whisper. Could Walks-With-Dreams have succeeded in freeing George from the laptop so he could finally appear at will? The entire room seemed to be in a spiritual battle between freeing George and imprisoning him in the laptop.

Walks-With-Dreams sat up straight. "In Brazil, a woman *died* after a photographer took her picture. She believed the camera stole her soul."

Chuck's brown eyes widened. "That's true! Grandpa showed me the article." He sat up until his back appeared perfectly straight. "And Crazy Horse never allowed anyone to take his picture for the same reason. Many tribes believe that if someone takes their picture, they're stealing that person's face, that person's power, that person's soul."

Walks-With-Dreams began tapping the air as if playing a rhythm on a drum. "A picture is a deeply personal and spiritual connection to the person taking it and the people looking at it afterwards," he said. "The Dakota people have a saying: 'We will be known forever by the tracks we leave.' You, Ghost Man, are making those tracks for Spirit George."

Chuck leaned into the fire and gestured at his grandfather. "My grandfather is leaving his imprint on me; and I in turn, am leaving that imprint on my children," he said with certainty.

Walks-With-Dreams showed his palms again in a unmistakable gesture of authority. "The *real* question you ought to be asking *yourself*, Mr. Turner, is: In what direction is George leading *me*? Me…personally?" Walks-With-Dreams began to rock in place ever so slightly. Chuck whispered that a spirit was moving through him! "George is trying to tell you something about yourself. You need to listen." He pointed at Pete's heart. "Something that can change your life."

"But I'm trying to help *him*," Pete said, now more confused than ever.

Nodding, the old man said: "But really, in helping George you are helping yourself. You are changing *your* life."

Heaving in exasperation, Pete said: "But how is going to Amarillo and delivering George's things helping me? It's actually a—well—a hardship for me." Then it occurred to him that he might be sounding selfish—concerned about his own wellbeing. Chuck and Walks-With-Dreams were quite opposite, living their entire lives for their community. Their worldviews were completely different, but Chuck's worldview was working for him, making him a contented person with the ability to leave a positive mark in the lives of others.

"If you think about all the little details you've encountered on your quest thus far, Mr. Turner," Walks-With-Dreams began, "you should notice that some things about you *are* changing all ready."

Pete's Crossroad

Pete scratched his chin and began nodding no; but then he glanced into the blue of the fire pit. He had been fired—and now these two people alongside him were exposing him to a different kind of firing, in a place he'd never imagined himself to be, a desert, and feeling powerless over forces he couldn't understand—George and Terrence Frapley.

Chuck uncrossed his legs and folded his hands. "I know one thing about you that's changed just in the past few hours."

"What?" Pete asked.

"You were just fired," Chuck said frankly.

"Yeah," Pete huffed, "and a guy I thought was my friend betrayed me. And the people I was working for sound crazy! And the company sounds so mysterious now." He felt anger rolling though him.

"Situations are not as they appear, and people are not as they show themselves to be," the old man said. "Those are things you've learned on this road to delivering George's things." He stood and began walking around the fire pit.

Pete couldn't stop staring at Walks-With-Dreams. "I think I understand now," he said, sighing, recalling Fred's new brochure, the one that made him look bad.

"There's more as well," the old man said.

"What's that?" Pete asked.

Facing him, the old man said: "Forgiveness comes with deliverance."

"But I can't stand that guy!" He clenched his fists. "He got me fired! I just know it! Either that, or the company is dirty somehow…but I can't believe that." Pete felt anger burn in his cheeks.

The old man grinned and gave Pete a sly look out of the corner of his eye. "There is something you must do, Pete, and then you can forgive yourself."

"Huh?" Pete asked.

Cutting the air with his hands as if blessing Pete, he said, "Do what must be done, and then forgive yourself."

Pete felt as if he were fully conscious, but falling asleep hypnotized. He began seeing a scene from his past that occurred just a few months ago before getting his job at Fossil.

Hot air came blasting up from the fire pit, hitting him in the face, cocooning his body like a caterpillar. He wanted free of the vision, but his eyes fixed on the blue flame.

Suddenly, he felt transported back to 2008. He was a clothing designer in Hollywood at Fashion Diva. The boss ordered him to pick up another load of clothes from a downtown Los Angeles warehouse. When he walked into the dimly-lit, dilapidated, five-story building; he spotted an entire crew of young oriental seamstresses hunched over churning sewing machines. The entire building sounded like a saw mill that never quit! Their terror-filled eyes were constantly glued to the material spewing out clothes. The hot room made him gag for oxygen, and the sharp ozone scent reminded him of a bad electrical job someone had done on his home when he was a boy that nearly brought the house down in flames.

He saw the same women several times when his boss had ordered him to bring up a big load. Some looked as young as thirteen. His gut told him that Fashion Diva might be involved in the slave trade, or human trafficking. In secret while waiting for a load of clothes once, he took out his Sony Cyber-shot and clicked a few pictures, but he never emailed those pictures for fear of losing his job. He hated causing trouble, or the possibility of having to testify in court, or getting fired! As far as he knew, Fashion Diva was still in operation, and raking in millions by exploiting those young girls and women who were probably kidnapped, or lured into America with a promise of a better life. Little did those people know they'd be slaving for the rest of their lives so that high-end clothing shops could make a fortune. Then he saw their drained and tired faces. He heard the sounds of their sewing machines grinding and revving twenty-four-seven. The vision suddenly faded, and when he glanced up, he was standing at the far side of the kiva, having walked several yards from the inner circle. He saw Walks-With-Dreams and Chuck standing behind him, ready to catch him should he fall.

"Ahhh!" he cried, kneeling.

Pete's Crossroad

"You okay?" Chuck asked, helping him to his cushion.

Panting as if he had just exited a rollercoaster, Pete gripped the seam of the cushion, holding on for dear life. He wiped sweat off his temples and neck when Chuck handed him a cold rag. The kiva felt unbearably hot—as those women probably felt slaving in that warehouse factory 24/7.

"You saw a demon!" Walks-With-Dreams exclaimed, now sitting directly opposite him on the fire pit.

"I guess so," Pete said, gasping for air as Chuck handed him a bottle of water. He knew then that George was also part of his own conscience crying out for him to do the right thing. He had forgotten those women so long ago. They were someone else's problems.

"Here, drink this," Chuck directed, handing him an old engraved bowl.

It was spicy, but invigorating as he sipped it, telling them what had happened and that the occurrence was his vision. Then he said: "I talked to the manager of Fashion Diva about what I saw, and he said that if I told anybody about it, he'd have me blackballed from the industry." He pounded the edge of his seat. "Darn!" He sipped more of the energizing potion. "I just quit then, disappeared, and went to work at another company, Fossil Inc., a few cities away. Fred said was an opening there selling mannequins. They didn't seem to have anything to do with the clothing industry. I thought I was safe working there, and could continue drawing my designs and sell them later, but given everything that happened to me today, maybe I'm not so safe."

"No one is safe when bad things are going on," the old man said, his head turning in disapproval.

"Tell me about it!" Pete said. "I bet some of those mannequins at the booth were wearing clothes made by those women who were brought here illegally."

"Ah-ha!" Walks-With-Dreams said, his body lifting. "That's what you're discovering about yourself."

George's voice came through the flame: "You have to do something to stop them, Pete."

J.P. Osterman

Pete stood and pointed at the fire pit. "Did you hear that! George is talking to me again!"

Walks-With-Dreams handed Pete his laptop. The screen was completely dark. "No, but *you* heard him."

George gestured at Pete with a serious pleading expression. "Everything *will* change for you in Amarillo, Pete. Just wait." Now George was walking on a cloud. He winked. "And I'll change too when we get there."

"Yes, everything will change for the both of us, I hope," Pete said, hypnotized. He closed his computer and slipped it back into the side of his briefcase. "I have to go."

Chuck squinted at him. "Is that what George told you?"

Pete felt the fear of ten bad dreams. "Amarillo, Chuck." Sighing and closing his eyes, he said, "I hope nothing like this ever happens to you, Chuck. This ain't fun...ain't a picnic."

Walks-With-Dreams said in a serious voice: "Pete, I was here when Chuck experienced something like what you're going through right now. He had me, and friends."

Pete felt dislodged in time with no friends. "I just want this to be all over." He felt fatigue move through his body that a good sleep might ease. "I feel like I'm going through some kind of physical fitness test but I don't know what I'm being tested for!" He believed he was going to lose his mind, and he put his hands over his ears as if the Emergency Broadcast Signal was blaring.

Chuck patted him on the back. "We're here."

"And you'll meet others who will help you as you continue George's quest," Walks-With-Dreams said. "But you need to be watching for help. Be on the lookout for all the little things that seem to align themselves just right."

Glancing up into a light curl of smoke rolling to the ceiling, Pete said: "I guess when I get to Amarillo, I'll find out what I have to do next."

After putting on their shoes, Pete glanced at the time. It was 6:30 p.m. He had hours ahead of him before catching the bus to Amarillo. When Chuck opened the door for him to leave, he believed he was leaving the past behind and heading

Pete's Crossroad

into an entirely different world.

Walks-With-Dreams rubbed his stomach. "We go out for steaks. I'm hungry!"

Chuck laughed. "Okay, Grandfather."

As they walked to the limo, Pete said: "It'll be my treat. But not somewhere really expensive. And stop at a Bank of America on the way, will ya, Chuck? I have to deposit my last check." That was new for him—paying for the dinners of strangers.

Chuck gave him a friendly slap on the shoulder. "Sure, Pete. Then I'll drop ya at the station."

He told them about not having anywhere to call home and about all his things in storage. Driving back to Albuquerque, Walks-With-Dreams pulled Pete close to him, leaned into him, and whispered, "George tipped me his fedora hat and told me to tell you that *things* can be replaced."

Pete gasped in amazement. "You did see George then!"

The old man shook his index finger into Pete's face, winked—just like George's habit—and said: "You sure bet I did!" He even had George's mannerism as if George had transferred a bit of his personality directly into him! Then Walks-With-Dreams took out an arrowhead, clasped to a chain, and put it over Pete's head.

"What's this for?" Pete asked, perusing the ancient arrowhead. Now, it was at its final resting place, over his heart.

Like a father, Walks-With-Dreams patted Pete's arm. "The arrowhead is so you'll never forget what happened here today. Never forget us, and we will always remember you." They exchanged phone numbers and emails, and Pete shook their hands in a farewell gesture.

After dinner and spending an hour on a Greyhound bench waiting, Pete boarded the bus in the black of night with the discs of zapping streetlights bending like coat hanger hooks above the long line of revving bus engines. Yawning as he glanced at his watch, he read: 3:45. But the time was Anti Meridiem. He would be in Amarillo in five hours and fifty minutes. *Then I can give everything to George's son, Donny, and split.*

J.P. Osterman

Then George will leave me alone, and I can get on with my life.

Suddenly, out of nowhere, sitting right next to him in an empty seat, George appeared in an outline of yellow. "My body, Pete! You forgot to photoshop my body correctly!"

After George's ghost puffed into nothingness, Pete took out his laptop and began modifying George into several solid images. George was appearing and disappearing alongside him at the back of the empty bus.

"We've got a whole string of things to do when we get to Amarillo besides seeing Donny and burying my body, Pete."

"Oh yeah, what?"

"You know…those poor girls. Ya gotta do something! Fast!" Now he had a terrified expression on his face—like someone being hunted.

"Fine," Pete huffed. He remembered the vision he just experienced and rubbed his eyelids. He was beginning to dread the future—having to send those incriminating photos to someone. "I have to get some sleep, George, or I won't be good for anything," he yawned. Then he muttered in a whisper: "What do I do next? I've got no home, no job, darn!" Cold air purged the ceiling vent and he wrapped his collar over above his ears. "I'm frigging lost!"

Pete's Crossroad

Chapter 10 – Don Gibson

The bus lurched to a stop, the noise of the screeching brakes jolting him awake. Glancing outside, he believed at first he was back in California. But when he didn't see any eucalyptus trees, men wearing business suits, or woman carrying designer purses, he realized he had arrived at Amarillo. Peering everywhere, he was on the lookout for George's son, Don, who was probably standing somewhere on the platform searching for him. He grabbed his jacket, laptop, and carry-on, and then stepped down onto the yellow-lined boarding area.

A chilly humidity hung like a heavy rain cloud, making his skin feel sticky. Amarillo wasn't Albuquerque. The sun looked like a dime-sized pancake through the dense 10:00 a.m. fog. Definitely, Amarillo was not L.A. either! Still, everywhere he looked he spotted Native American architecture and design, and men were wearing cowboy boots and cowboy hats. They had a powerful walk, depicting direction and purpose. Glancing down at his dirty business suit, he felt out of place. He set down his briefcase, let go of his carry-on, and pulled out the tails of his dirty white shirt, hoping some fresh air might waft on his skin and wake him up. "Whew," he sniffed, noticing all the wrinkles. He couldn't wait to find a motel, take

J.P. Osterman

a bath, eat a good meal, and watch some sports on TV.

"You Pete Turner?"

Turning around, Pete saw a bearded man wearing rimless glasses and dressed in a casual shirt and blue jeans. "Yes," he said, shaking his hand. "You must be Donald Gibson, George Gibson's son."

Baggage handlers were unloading the bus, the hinges of the baggage compartment creaking, and the suitcases making thudding sounds as they hit the cement.

"I understand my dad had two suitcases," Don said, nodding at the bus.

He had broad shoulders and was about a foot taller and much thinner than George. As Don folded his arms, waiting for his Dad's luggage, Pete noticed smudges on his fingers. He had been working with dirt somewhere, but taken time off work to pick him up at the station. He had the look of an outdoorsman, with salt and pepper hair touching the edge of his collar, rimless glasses, straight white teeth, and a squint in his eyes. Pete couldn't see their color just yet. The fog was dispersing, the sunlight breaking through dense clouds.

"Yes, he had two suitcases, one real large, the other an overstuffed carry-on," Pete said. "Your dad said everything he owned was in those two suitcases. And they're heavy."

Don sighed, frowned, and glanced down. "I guess the old man finally died," he said. "I was expecting it for years, but not on a bus, oh well." Then he chuckled. "Huh!"

Pete thought that response was out of character from what George had told him. George had painted Don as a hero, but Don was happy that George had died. Then Pete remembered leaving home, sloughing off his alcoholic abusive father. Maybe he couldn't blame Don too much for the distain that was seeping out of his every gesture. George had been a bad father. He hated his father as well.

Pete believed that if George was alive and listening in on their conversation, George might have a heart attack. Then he thought of his laptop. Maybe George was right there with them, but as a ghost. He'd sure find out later when he'd turn on his computer and check his email. Peeking down at his briefcase, he began dreading the moment he'd have to open the lid and start job hunting.

As the baggage attendant rolled George's extra-large suitcase down the walkway along with the one carry-on, Pete said, "Have you made arrangements to ship your father's body here yet?" He knew that would be one step closer to being set free of George's ghost.

Nodding as if the entire process were drudgery Don said, "It's coming next Thursday. At least that's what the coroner told me in Phoenix."

"Uh-huh," Pete replied, feeling half-way home to freedom. "Good!" It was Friday, so next Thursday wasn't far off to freedom.

"Where ya headed?" Don asked as they made their way inside the station.

The sun broke through thick clouds, giving the sky a yellow-blue glow. In spots, it still looked as if there might be a downpour as Pete spied a rainbow on the horizon, above a deep yellow strand of desert sand. A pigeon flew under the eaves, and two doves cooed.

"I'm not sure yet, Pete said, walking beside Don to the baggage counter, trying to keep up with him. Then he heard the sound of paper hitting the floor; and when he looked down at the colorful pamphlet—his brochure from Fossil Inc.—he began trying to catch it. But each time he was about to grab it, the brochure slipped out of his fingers as if an invisible hand had tugged it away from him. He felt like a kid chasing a downed kite in the breeze! He had to appear silly to everyone watching him! When he finally clutched the ruffled paper, he noticed the splotch marks and shoe prints. But he remembered canning *all* of them at the bus station in Albuquerque. He was certain of it.

Staring in misbelief at the front cover, he noticed they were smeared beyond recognition as if someone had doused the brochure with a bottle of water. George again. But why? "*Wheew*," he said, sitting down and tearing up the brochure. "I can't believe this."

"What's that?' Don asked, obviously shocked.

Pete laughed as he lifted the pieces into the front of his face. "I lost my job," he said, pulling out the tickets he had been carrying for George's luggage. He handed them to Don.

"I'm sorry to hear that," Don said, fanning out George's tickets. "I know you said you were heading to Las Vegas after you delivered my dad's stuff to me."

"Well, those plans are off now," Pete said, standing up. He walked over to the trash can and chucked the shredded brochure into the garbage.

A tower clock struck 10:30 a.m., and the black-paved streets filled with glistening drizzle as people opened their umbrellas or lifted newspapers over their heads to shield them from the rain. Everyone seemed on their way to work, to their jobs. It was Friday, and he didn't have one. Pete felt his blood pressure rise and an irritation intensify like an inflating balloon. What would he do now that he didn't have a 9-to-5 that was really a 7-to-9 job? He felt as if he were at in the middle of a 6.5 magnitude earthquake, diving under a chair to avoid shattering glass.

Don thrust his hands in his pockets and pointed to vending machines. "Come on, Pete, I'll buy ya a cup of coffee. It's the least I can do to thank you for bringing my dad's things to Amarillo," Don said.

"Sure," he said. "Extra cream and sugar please. Thanks."

Exhaling from the bottom of his lungs, Pete watched the drizzle from a large picture window. He was feeling hopeless, and stranded. But he had cash. Enough to keep him holed up somewhere without worrying about utter homelessness for a few months. But where? He never thought in his entire life that he would find himself wandering into a place like Amarillo. It sounded like armadillo! And he'd never been south of Tennessee in his entire life. Europe once, Canada twice, but he never thought he'd ever lay his eyes on a real cowboy and spend time in a real desert. Glancing at the welcome sign framed in American Indian artwork, he read:

Pete's Crossroad

Amarillo – The Yellow Rose of Texas!

Don folded his legs as he handed Pete his coffee. "What are ya gonna do, Pete?"

Pete's briefcase slipped down the side of his chair but he caught it before it could hit the ground. He had to be extra gentle with it, especially now that George was eavesdropping in on them. He knew it! "Oh, I forgot about something I want to show you."

Don peered around. "What?"

Pete remembered the picture Hideki had taken. "I have a picture of your dad."

Don looked stunned. "Really? You took a picture?"

Pete shook his head. "No, someone took one of George—I mean your dad and me together after we came out of a depot to buy snacks." He lifted his briefcase and tapped the side pocket containing his laptop.

"Wow," Don said with excited eyes that changed to an expression of apathy. "Huh."

"Do you have a flash drive on you?" Pete asked, wanting to show him the picture, hoping that if Don could see his father's image it might ignite some deep spark of curiosity in him to get to know more about him. "I could download your dad's picture so you could have it." He remembered he had no extra flash drive. "Or I could email the picture to you if you have an email address."

Don had a distasteful expression on his face. "I don't do much with computers. I've learned a little, from my daughter Sue Beth, but I don't handle 'em much myself." He took another sip of coffee and turned a little more toward Pete. "Sue Beth is supposed to come over tonight after class. She's in her last year at West Texas A&M University."

Pete recalled George mentioning her. "What's she studying?"

"Music. She wants to teach music to kids." His voice turned optimistic. "And she's a fiddler!"

"She plays the fiddle?" Pete asked, impressed.

"Along with Andy, her brother." Don sipped his coffee

and stared out the giant picture window. People were rushing inside the station and dashing to the ticket counter, the sounds of umbrellas popping open and sliding shut. Don seemed in tune to their rapid movements as if he were bottling up intense feelings. "Did my dad ask about them? His grandchildren?" Swallowing hard as his throat reddened, he looked into his white paper cup and swirled the coffee.

Pete felt confused. Don didn't want to see his father, and he had told his him that he couldn't see his grandchildren, ever. But now, he wanted to know if George had asked about his grandchildren. Pete believed he was cutting into very private territory, into years of Don's turmoil and anger—Don's thick grudge which had obviously become a stronghold. Pete said: "Your dad has gifts in that giant suitcase. They meant the world to him." Pete coughed and cleared his throat as he watched Don's fingers begin to shake. "Your dad wanted to make things right with everyone before he—"

"*Ahem*, died." Don swallowed hard, his neck blotchy, his eyes red with watery tears. He waved his hand in front of his face, and the coffee cup almost slipped out of his fingers. "Listen, Pete." Suddenly, his pain quickly vanished. "I'll call Sue Beth and tell her to bring one of those, those—"

"Flash drives," Pete said, trying not to appear as a know-it-all. As he glanced around Don at the baggage handlers, he realized that he had had conversations with George that probably Don had never had with him—George, his own father. If Don were to really want to know about his dad, he'd have to go through Pete to acquire the knowledge. That was *one* thing Walks-With-Dreams said Pete needed to do: To let Don and his family come to know George. How could he do that at a bus station? Pete needed to download George's picture from his laptop and present it to his family. Maybe that might satisfy George's restless spirit because everyone would have a picture of him. He also remembered George's words: "Everything will change for you in Amarillo." He wondered when and how.

"Pete," Don said, forcefully, "it looks like you hit on hard times."

"Hard times? Well, I guess so, yeah." He felt stunned. He and Don were just talking about flash drives. Boy, does Don know how to change a subject quickly, he thought. Pete admired that ability though. It showed that Don was a fast thinker in emotionally-charged situations. It showed a steady personality and strong disposition. He called those rapid changes in conversations "lightning strike diversions" that allowed the expert rhetorician to have control in a heated sales pitch. He had learned to be that way as a child. His mom had often used many defensive maneuvers to avoid his tornado-twisting alcoholic dad.

"Losing your job is definitely falling on hard times, Pete." Don said, gulping down his last bit of coffee.

Turning his head in agreement, Pete said, "You can say that!" But he didn't want Don feeling sorry for him, or feeling obligated to help him. He had always solved his own problems without assistance from anyone. And he never asked for anything from anyone. He would do the same now. "But it's all right. No big deal," he shrugged. But he still felt like a kid who striking out at the last inner of a baseball game and losing for his team.

Don glanced at Pete over his rimless glasses. "Pete, you sure are taking losing your job pretty soft." He pushed his glasses up the bridge of his nose and ran his fingers through his salt-and-pepper colored beard. "I was a mess when that happened to me many years back." He gave out a painful chuckle. "I wouldn't wanna wish that on my worst enemy!"

"Whew," Pete sighed, "I don't know what to say." He rubbed the back of his neck, a painful spot. "Looks like you recovered though, Mr. Gibson." He peered at him from head-to-toe. "Looks like you're doing well in business now."

Don laughed. "So, so," he shrugged. "You can call me Don, and we can talk about how I recovered later." After a minute's pause, he added, "You *could* stay in town awhile longer, if you want."

Knowing he had to stay but not wanting to tell Don

about his father's ghost, Pete continued staring out the window. It was beginning to get hot outside. Water was evaporating off a red metal roof across the street, causing the air to waver. His skin felt dry, his mouth parched. He had no idea how he'd ever survive for a day out there in this new type of desert, but now he felt forced to linger in Amarillo for a while. "Well, I don't know." He checked his Rolex: 10:54 a.m. "I could stick around until you bury your dad. I assume that's going to happen Thursday or a few days after you transfer George's body here to Amarillo." Outside, behind him, a bus with a sign *Rocky Mountain Express* came screeching to a halt. Pete thought, next week...I'll be on that bus.

Don stood up fast and his body seemed to light up with energy. "My oldest boy is making funeral arrangements this morning." He appeared emotionally unfazed.

"Good," Pete said, feeling relieved.

That meant just a week—maybe a week and a day—in Amarillo, and then goodbye armadillo! Mnemonics. He couldn't separate the two, Amarillo and armadillo. Armadillos have ridges for skin. Amarillo is a desert full of ridges! Don had his arms folded as if preparing for a hunt. He seemed bulletproof. Even long after he'd leave this town, he'd always remember Don, and George, as shielded individuals—friendly to strangers, but enemies to each other.

"So...why not come to my place a stay for a little while, Pete?" Don asked.

"What?" Pete returned. Don had a look on his face implying he wouldn't take no for answer. "Well—"

"Being that you lost your job and all, come on down to my place...my ranch," Don said proudly, bouncing lightly on the balls of his feet. He was wearing beige work boots and khaki pants with pockets.

"Oh, I couldn't, Don, but thanks! I'll just get a motel and rent a car."

"I have a ranch, Pete, with plenty of room, and I own a home-and-garden store."

"I can't!" Pete protested as they began walking to baggage

Pete's Crossroad

claim to pick up all the luggage, then make their way through the parking lot. "My younger son is gone," Don said bluntly, his sad gaze fixed at the floor. "Fletch is his name. He used to stay in the little addition I have at the back of the house." He looked grief stricken. "I have five acres of land and plenty o' room. Please, I won't take no for an answer, and from what I've heard anyway, how close you were to my dad, even if only for a brief time, he'd want you to stick around until his burial."

"Oh, I don't know, Mr. Gibson," Pete said, realizing that something terrible must have happened between Don and his son, Fletch. The bad cycle seemed to repeating itself.

"Please call me Don." He had red cheeks showing a slight embarrassment.

After telling Don that George's carry-on contained a black bag containing George's personal possessions, Pete said, "George mentioned Fletch. He has something in the large suitcase for him.

That news energized Don. "Really? What?"

Pete remembered a few of the items, but he wasn't sure which objects belong to whom; and besides, he didn't want to spoil George's surprise by even guessing. "I don't know, but your dad said your grandmother wrapped them herself." His briefcase slipped out of his grasp, and he quickly caught it. "There's something for each of you inside that big suitcase."

"Really?" Don stopped in the middle of the parking lot, his expression pressing.

"I tell you what, Don," Pete began, "I'll take you up on your offer. I'll stay with you for a few days—"

"Until *after* the burial," Don demanded with large blue-gray eyes. Clouds and parted, and the blue sky was pure blue behind them, the air chilly but fresh. In the sunshine, Don looked like a taller version of John Denver!

After he made that resemblance known to Don, he said, "Did anyone ever tell you that?"

Don laughed and glanced at a few people walking to their cars. "Yeah, I get that John Denver look-a-like question sometimes, he laughed.

J.P. Osterman

"Okay," Pete said, sighing, "I'll stay with you, and when you open the gifts, I'll tell you what your dad told me when he showed them to me. I'm sure seeing them again will jostle my memory." He wanted to blurt out what Walks-With-Dreams had told him—that he had to dispense the gifts himself anyway to put to rest George's spirit. But that would mean telling Don that George's soul was in his laptop. No way would he tell that to Don! To hear something that bizarre coming from a stranger, Don might run right over to the counter and buy him a ticket out of Amarillo.

"Great!" Don said, shaking Pete's hand. Don had to be a man who sealed deals with a handshake, someone trustworthy and honest. "I'll take ya to my place then."

He helped Don load George's suitcases into his silver Ford F-350 Super Duty. Then Don closed the tailgate, leaned against it, and began staring at George's extra-large suitcase that looked more like a treasure chest. He began tapped his fingertips in a drum roll, his eyes bulging with anger.

Rolling his carry-on to the back after putting his briefcase in the car, Pete said, "You look mad, Don."

In a gesture of disappointment, Don said, "I know he tried to contact me…several times." Don's chest heaved as he huffed in frustration. "You just met him on a bus ride, Pete, but I knew the man much longer than that." He rubbed his head as if trying to stop the blood flowing out of a deep gash. "You don't know what happened. You weren't there. You—"

"Hey! I have my own family baggage, Mr. Gibson," Pete said, walking toward the door. He wanted them to get inside, start driving, stop talking. Don took the hint.

As Don maneuvered out of the station, a feeling of claustrophobia wafted through him. He had no car, and staying at Don's place meant he'd have no privacy, and he couldn't come and go as he pleased. They were approaching the small downtown area of Amarillo buzzing with late morning traffic and people beginning their morning shopping.

"Any Enterprise rental offices around here, Don?" he asked, glancing around the hometown street that had R-66

Pete's Crossroad

signs beneath almost every stop sign. He noticed a Bank of America. Later he could return and withdraw money. He watched Don make every turn, tried to remember the street signs, 6th Avenue, the Ambassador Hotel.

"Sure," Don said, "but how about some breakfast first?" They were just passing an old-fashioned restaurant, Stan's Drive-In. "This is our favorite breakfast place to eat."

Pete was hungry, his stomach growling. When he spotted the Ambassador Hotel, the growling sounds worsened. The hotel reminded him of his financial reserves: $3,221.19 in severance pay and $1,573.57 in his saving's account. He coughed, choking on the numbers. He had a storage bill of $375.00 a month and everything he owned was in California, 1,080 miles away. Wherever he'd end up, he'd have to ship everything, or let everything he owned go to auction. He remembered a few precious items he did have in that storage facility: a few things that had belonged to his dad, and Christmas gifts from years past. He couldn't just let someone else take them! He had to find work, soon.

"You all right?" Don asked with concerned eyes.

"Fine," Pete said, pushing his briefcase up to his knee cap. He added up the figures. $4,794.76. That's it. That sum might look like a lot, but he knew that in these economic hard times he'd roll through that cash like a roller-pin pressing out dough. He needed his laptop open and his resume, as soon as possible. He needed to be looking for a job, somewhere—anywhere—in the United States. "You said you own a garden store, Don?"

"Yep," Don said.

"How's business doing in this economy?" he asked, glancing up and down the busy main street where Don's truck rumbled over railroad ties. "Times are hard everywhere. Companies are laying off." He saw a store with a sales rack out front with a few women rifling through dresses. If Amarillo had a relatively low level of employment than other cities around the United States companies would be hiring.

Don pulled into the Stan's Drive-In and parked, and Pete

peered around the inside of his truck. It looked immaculately clean. Don had to be a neat freak! "I had a successful spurt last month that pulled my business out of near bankruptcy," he said cheerfully. "The business I had in Albuquerque failed two years ago, so I moved here." Then he turned suddenly sullen. "Andrew and Sue Beth packed up and came with me." He didn't mention Fletch, and Pete didn't want to ask him, yet. Fletch was a mystery, a topic thus far to avoid; but the longer the avoidance, the more Pete's curiosity intensified.

"You're pretty successful then, huh?" Pete asked, getting out of the truck, remembering all his mannequin brochures that were probably in some landfill. Someday, he'd like to own a business too.

Rolling up his window, Don said, "Yeah, I'd say I'm on the way up again."

"And businesses are doing well here?" Pete asked over the bed of his truck. Don appeared to be a model for success after surviving a terrible set back. He was the entrepreneur type who had a green thumb when it came to creating and growing a company and not just nurturing a garden.

Don shrugged as a skeptical look appeared on his face. "Well," he began, gesturing at the parking lot only dotted with cars, "today's Good Friday, so business will probably be pretty slow around town." As they walked toward the restaurant, Don stopped to greet people. He also smiled and waved to people who were acknowledging him on the street. He seemed to know every person in Amarillo! "A lot of people are probably attending church services today too." He glanced at his watch as the eleven o'clock bells began tolling. "Mass is at noon, so most Catholics will be heading to church."

Pete looked back to the main street and saw rows of what Don had told him were cedar trees. The sound of the wind moving through their branches was like the sound of ocean waves hitting the beach in Santa Monica. He heard birdcalls he'd never heard before—flute and piccolo tones. The smell of pancakes drifted through the air as a family walked out of the restaurant. The father was wearing a tall cowboy hat with a

Pete's Crossroad

toothpick bobbing out of the corner of his mouth. Another man waved for Don to stop. After introducing him to Pete, Don shook the man's hand, and he and Don began talking about brown canker fungus, powdery mildew, and the various pesticides available to eradicate diseases that were killing one of the man's rose bushes. People trusted Don, and they depended on him for solutions to their problems. Don had many friends.

Thanking Don with a smile on his face, and telling Don he'd be in his shop on Monday, the man gestured at Pete and asked, "Is this one of your new hires, Don?" He gave Pete a light slap on the arm. Pete felt dumbfounded. For the first time in a long time, he felt a desire to fit in. He felt as if he was walking on eggshells! *I have to say the right things…not mess up.* He brushed smudges off his black suit coat. Don appeared to approve of him. He liked that! And he breathed in the fresh air, hoping that approval wouldn't change.

Chapter 11 - Amarillo

After breakfast, they began the short journey to Don's ranch. Five miles north of 6th Avenue, he turned down a long tree-lined road with an ornate wrought-iron sign on an gate: Coral Ridge. "This is my ranch," Don said, proudly.

Pete marveled at its quaintness and great expanse. "I've only seen places like these, but never been to one…way out in the countryside." He breathed in the crisp air through his open window. "Every tree, blade of grass and that blue sky is so pure in color!"

Don laughed, "Whataya mean?"

Pete replied: "In the L.A. area, we have a lot of smog, usually every day." He glanced around. "Everything here just looks clean and crisp—"

"Beautiful," Don added, his rimless glasses reflecting a little cloud in the center of the sky.

The rain had stopped long ago, the gray-fringed clouds were turning cirrus wisps, and slips of cool air were streaming through the window as Don approached his beige stucco house on top of a giant mound. As the truck came to a stop in the driveway, dust drifted up around the windows. Two big cawing blackbirds with purple eyes swooped down on the

Pete's Crossroad

truck and then flew off and landed on the limb of a tall black tree that looked half dead from blight or smoke inhalation.

"Grackles," Don said in disgust, shutting the door, motioning Pete toward the house.

Smelling the scent of flowers from a large garden, Pete said, "They're pests, huh?" With his briefcase tucked under his arm, he helped Don lift George's large suitcase out of the truck bed and then he rolled the two carry-ons to a small stairway leading up to a giant covered front porch. There was a white swing there, and he imagined people swinging on it after dinner and on lazy Sundays. "Say, what happened to that tree?" The grackles were cawing restlessly on a giant barren limb. He motioned toward a dry patch of land surrounded by a picket fence with a four-story oak tree at its center. The huge tree looked like it had taken a hit by a meteor!

"Lightning hit it," Don said, his body leaning along with his dad's wobbling suitcase. "Right after Fletch left." Then he opened the front door and stepped inside, waving for Pete to follow him.

That was the first time he had said what had happened to his son Fletch. "Left for where?" Pete asked, delicately.

Don pulled the trunk inside and pushed it along the tile floor where it landed securely in front of an antique armoire that appeared to have been handed down to him by either George or Sue Lynn. "*Ahh*h," he moaned, stretching, bending back in a gesture to ease a sudden ache. "Fletch enlisted in the Army three years ago. He's in Iraq."

Setting his briefcase next to the George's suitcase, Pete could tell there was more to the story when Don left to retrieve George's carry-on. He was getting to know some of Don's tendencies, especially when Don wanted to avoid certain topics, so he changed the discussion. On the porch, he called to him. "You said your daughter, Sue Beth, might be over later?" He then remembered that Sue Beth was supposed to meet him at the station. She didn't. She was becoming a fascinating mystery. He wanted to meet her. "If Sue Beth brings over a flash drive or DVD, I can download your dad's picture for you."

Don glanced at his Timex. "Sue Beth should be out of school in about an hour. I'll call her while you settle in and tell her to come over and meet you."

"Great!" Pete said. Peering towards Don's ranch-style home while squinting through the brightness, he noticed the sun had crept higher into the blue sky. It was still early, and from what Don had told him, the temperature would remain on the cool side for the rest of the day. Flowers were in bloom around the front porch and the side garden, and Don had several gnomes and garden angels dotting the spaces in between some tall blue flowers and patches of yellow-and-white daisies. The yard was photo-perfect, deserving of an award, but there was one striking feature that he noticed right away—a six-foot angel carved out of a tree stump, the black roots jutting out of the grassy ground.

"Did you do this?" Pete asked marveling at the angel statue beyond the porch. It was in perfect view of the swing.

Don had a sentimental expression. "The same storm that knocked the life outta that oak tree over there—" He pointed at the lone oak whose branches forked out like black tributaries on an aerial map. "Killed this sycamore tree too, but I didn't wanna pull it. My oldest son Andy and I carved the angel ourselves using chain saws." He laughed, engrossed in the memory. "I tried to model the face after my mother's face, but I think I was a little off." He coughed, obviously to clear up an embarrassment.

Running his fingers over a shiny wing, Pete inspected the wooden sculpture that had a few ants scurrying through its folds, and a few lines of algae where the sun rarely shone. "It's nice, Don, real nice," he began. "I'm a designer, and I minored in art in college, but I couldn't do something like this!"

"Thanks," Don said, lifting a carry-on up the porch.

"Where is Andy?" Pete asked, stepping inside the house again. He stopped suddenly when he noticed his briefcase had toppled to the floor. Quickly, he whipped it up. George! George was there with them, and he had no idea *how* he'd

Pete's Crossroad

make his presence known in Don's house! He felt on guard and vigilant. Anything could happen since Walks-With-Dreams had freed him from the laptop and since he had photoshopped George into several clothing styles and settings, empowering him with real 3D qualities.

Don slid his dad's suitcases next to the white staircase. "Andy is watching the store for me so I could pick you up," he said, "but he's coming over around noon for lunch while my store manager watches the shop."

Pete grabbed his briefcase and lifted up his carry-on. "So where can I put these things?" he asked. "It's about eleven thirty, and if I can set up in that room you told me about, I can start emailing companies and look for a job."

Don gave Pete the first-floor tour. The spice-scented kitchen was cream-colored and spacious with a giant granite island, and the towering grandfather clock next to the entry way struck 11:35 a.m. "Your home looks professionally decorated in traditional western style, Mr. Gibson. Wow—I'd love a place like this someday!"

Don removed his work boots. "All I really care about is the fifty-two-inch TV in the living room, Pete. Where I watch sports," he laughed.

Nearly salivating, Pete couldn't wait to get his hands on the remote control. "Maybe there's a basketball game on tonight," he said, glanced into the dining room where he spied a long wide table that appeared hand-built out of several types of trees. The glossy table could easily seat twelve. And Don had two hutches containing china and crystal. Pictures of his family were set in perfect unison among the knickknacks. The entire home resonated with the happiness of a close-knit family. But that perception was an illusion. There were mysteries about each one of George Gibson's descendants, and Pete felt compelled to get at the heart of them. Maybe realizing their deficiencies would help him fulfill his dream of having a home and family someday. As Walks-With-Dreams said, he definitely could use some help in the dating arena, 'cause he had problems!

J.P. Osterman

"There might be a game, but I believe Sue Beth has something planned for tonight. I won't be home," Don said. As they walked through a small enclosed breezeway to a room addition at the back of the house, Don paused before a door and stopped, his hand tight on the door knob. He appeared fearful of what he might find on the other side. "I haven't opened this door since February, 2008." The air in the breezeway turned heavy, and Don was breathing hard.

Pete remembered George's difficulty breathing. Being that Don was his son, perhaps he had inherited some type of undiagnosed heart problem. Panicking a bit, Pete asked, "You okay, Mr. Gibson? I can get you a glass of water. Let's go back to the kitchen—"

"No, I'm fine." He stepped away from the door, hypnotized by it.

When Pete returned with a glass of water, and Don thanked him, he noticed that Don sounded like George. He couldn't wait to open up his laptop and discover what George's ghost might say about finally being in Don's house—his son's home.

"February 23, 2008," Don said, finally managing to turn the doorknob. "That's the last time I saw Fletch."

Pete felt as if he were imposing on Don's hospitality. "Mr. Gibson, I can get a motel room. I—I don't want to put you out. I—"

"No," Don said sharply, "I have to open up this room eventually. It might as well be now." He tapped on a light switch, and the breezeway skylight on the ceiling opened, and light began streaming in.

Pete had to ask the hard question. "Did something happen to Fletch, Don?"

Through hard breaths and a long pause, Don said, staring out a small window in the breezeway, "We're just waiting for Fletch to finish his tour in Iraq. But the day before he left, a little over three years ago, we had a bit argument." The giant, half-dead, Texas oak tree was there in the distance, a reminder of their relationship. He was gazing into the charred branches

Pete's Crossroad

that lightning had struck. "Fletch was sort of a wild kid. He got into a bit of trouble, and then enlisted to get out of it." He shook his head in disapproval. "I told Fletch that was no way to solve problems…to put his life on the line. But he was determined to go against me…determined to fight me every step of the way!" Don clenched his fist and shook his head in an attempt to slough off painful overwhelming memories.

Pete said, "I had some of the same issues with my own dad." He watched Don adjusted the window blinds, his hand shaking. "I left when I was young myself. I don't even know where my dad is. Haven't talked to him in, well, probably close to eight years. I don't know where my mom is either."

"Wow," Don said, his face expressing the inability to imagine such a distance. Suddenly, he opened the door to Fletch's room, and he motioned for Pete to walked inside. After Pete entered, he slowly stepped over the threshold. "Well, this is the room," Don said, stepping off to the side. He closed his eyes and breathed, the smells and memories were moving through him and almost intolerable as he planted his back against the wall next to a small window.

Pete realized that if not for him, Don would not have ever entered the room. "It's stuffy in here," Pete said, and Don turned on the thermostat. Cool air began circulating. There was a bed under a window, two dressers alongside another window, and a desk with a small light, its lampshade patterned with basketballs and hoops. On two small bookcase shelves set little toy soldiers, tanks, a few model airplanes and three basketball trophies. But what really stuck out was a two-foot long taxidermy catfish that Fletch must have caught and Don mounted on the wall above the bed. Everything in the room appeared to scream out the once close relationship between father and son. That Don had locked up the room the moment Fletch left was a strong indication that what had happened between George and Don was now also a full-blown rift between Don and Fletch. This was a pattern, that if left unchanged, would most likely play out for generations!

Don began staring at each item. "Wow, all these sure

bring back memories." When Pete saw him touch the tail on the catfish, he believed Don might bust out crying.

Feeling ill-equipped to handle the tension, Pete said, "When is Fletch's tour of duty over?" Calling attention to that future event might give Don hope to make up with his son. "Time heals everything, so the saying goes," he added as he set down his briefcase. It was vibrating! George's spirit was either wanting out, or wanting Pete to say something. Obvious his "time heals" statement triggered the sudden activity because time *didn't* heal Don and George. *He* was supposed to help the two of them reconcile, but to divulge George's paranormal form right now might add fuel to Don's existing anger, and he hadn't cemented a close enough bond with Don to convince him of his dad's metamorphosis. He needed more time.

Don patted the blue bedspread with pictures of white basketballs. He looked like he wanted to tuck Fletch into bed again. "In two months his tour of duty is over," Don said, perking up. Sue Beth and Andy write to him all the time."

Pete wanted to ask, *Why don't you write too?* Then he remembered George. George had a real fear of making up with Don. That's why he had left L.A.—to surprise Don by showing up on his doorstep. That seemed to be their faulty communication pattern—holding in grievances instead of talking about them.

"There's a little bathroom over there," Don said, pointing to a door beside a closet. "But you might have to live outta your suitcase because Fletch's things are still in the dresser." He had a slight look of embarrassment on his face.

Pete wanted to reassure him that he'd treat everything with kid gloves. "I won't touch a thing, Mr. Gibson," he said, setting his carry-on on the bed. "I'm in and out of here...and will be gone next Friday after your dad's funeral."

Wide-eyed and with a calm look on his face, Don said, "I appreciate your bringing my dad's luggage, Pete." His voice had a prayerful thanksgiving quality. "Otherwise, I'da had to go to Albuquerque myself to fetch those things." He glanced around the room with his hands deep in his pockets and then

Pete's Crossroad

walked over to the window. There was a road beyond the blackened Texas oak tree. Don seemed to be tracing the long line as if trying to spot Fletch.

"You're welcome, Mr. Gibson," Pete said, lifting his laptop out of his briefcase and setting it on Fletch's desk. The lid popped open. Pete slapped it down.

"Is something wrong?" Don asked, before leaving.

Holding down the lid, Pete replied, "No, Sir, not at all."

Don suddenly stood there solemnly. "I'm glad you're staying here, Pete." He ran his forefinger over the doorknob. "You were the last person to see my dad, *ahem*. I'd like to, well, hear about him when you have some time." He seemed to be holding back tears.

"Sure!" Pete said.

"After ya settle in," Don said. "And later on, I can drive you down to Enterprise so you can rent a car."

"Thanks," Pete said, untangling his laptop cord and plugging it into the wall socket.

Before Don closed the door, he said, "I'll come knocking when Sue Beth and Andy get here."

Pete couldn't wait to meet them. "Yes, please let me know, Sir, and thanks." Don shut the door as Pete fired up his laptop. He had to see what George would have to say about everything he had overheard!

Chapter 12 – Fashion Diva's Scheme

George popped up instantly on the screen in 3D. He was still bald-headed and heavy-set, with a few beige age spots on his cheeks and forehead, but this time he was cleanly shaven and dressed up in a black suit and tie. Moving at random around the screen, he was a two-inch version of his body when he was alive, and dressed like he was expecting to attend a formal occasion. "I'm back, Pete." Glancing around the room happily with his arms folded, he said, "I *finally* made it. I'm almost at the end of the road...home!"

Pete sighed a sorrowful tone as he leaned in to talk to him. "You're not in Albuquerque, George, but Amarillo." He wondered if George knew that Don had moved out of Albuquerque over two years ago—that Don never intended on seeing his father again.

"Still, I'm with Don now!" he exclaimed in excitement. "And I'll finally be able to see my grandkids." Suddenly, he turned determined. "Pete, ya gotta do something...something important that's gonna save lives." He sounded as if a bomb might go off somewhere if Pete didn't instantly comply.

Pete felt his stomach sicken. "What?"

Pete's Crossroad

Photographs popped up from the warehouse where Pete had once picked up clothes for Fashion Diva in Los Angeles. Scanning all the people and objects in the snapshots, Pete realized that the factory was really a sweatshop and a major hub for oriental slave trafficking in the garment industry. Five more pictures appeared on his screen. If the district attorney could acquire those pictures, the D.A. could prosecute Fashion Diva, bust up the illegal ring, and save hundreds of lives.

"So the vision I had in Albuquerque was right," he said, shaking his head in disgust. "Maybe you're a little bit of my conscience too, George, like the shaman said." Tapping a few pictures, he added, "Maybe this is why life's been so hellish lately. Maybe Fashion Diva is somehow connected to Fossil Inc." He took a long hard pause and then finally said, "Maybe these pictures are the reasons Fossil Inc. fired me." Pulling out his water from the side of his carry-on, he took a deep gulp as he listened to the springtime birds chirping on the bushes outside and the wind whistling across the windowpanes. Time was moving forward, but time was also at a standstill for all the overworked girls stuck inside those pictures—their pained images demanding retribution and justice. Most likely, they were still at Fashion Diva, slaving away for greedy bosses. They were prisoners, either still at Fashion Diva, or brokered out to other sweat shops around the U.S.A.

As if it were a second hand inside a clock, George's arthritic finger pointed to each picture that was sliding across the screen. "You can make a difference here, Pete. Turn in these pictures!"

The air in the room heating up, Pete felt a sudden surge of sweat on his skin, and he unbuttoned his shirt. Shoving his elbows on the desk, he rubbed his eyes after staring long and hard at the pictures. "George, maybe the district attorney will come after me too. Did you think of that?"

"Maybe you'll get a reward, Pete! Did ya think o' that?" George countered, his finger showing him every picture. He was pointing at the painful expressions on the faces of overworked young girls and women. Fashion Diva—or whoever had brought them to America in the first place might be sexually exploiting them as well!

At that thought, Pete ran to the toilet and threw up. Leaning over the bowl, he grabbed paper and wiped off his mouth. "What do I do?" he asked, standing up but feel dizzy. Walking back to the desk, he plopped down in front of his laptop. "I *know* I have to do something about this, George. I *know* I have to send these by email to the D.A. in Los Angeles." Breathing hard, he cupped in hands over his face. "But if I do…maybe they'll prosecute me too. Maybe I'll face some *real* jail time! I've never been in any kinda trouble, ever!"

When he peered into his laptop, he noticed that the pictures had multiplied twofold—cropped and enlarged to show each pained and overworked face. Shocked, Pete grimaced, "God! This is awful…terrible!" He remembered the same feeling on Sandy Walston's face when she was crying over how George had no family.

"How would *you* like to live like this, Pete?" George's voice said pleadingly.

Pete still felt the butter from the morning's toast burning his stomach. "You know I wouldn't like it, George, but…" He imagined the police busting in, handcuffing him, and then carting him off to jail.

"But nothing!" George said. "Just do it. Email these pictures. Report all this abuse, Pete. Have some faith that if ya do the right things, the right things'll happen back to ya."

Remembering that those were some of the same words that Walks-With-Dreams had told him, Pete said, "You don't understand. You're dead No one can jail *you*!" He leaned back, also realizing he was drilling that fact into ghost. "No cop is going to storm this house and haul you off to jail." He plugged in his iPhone for recharging and set his car keys on the desk, remembering he'd have to contact someone soon to pick up his Sebring from the park-n-ride and pay another storage facility bill. But he didn't have a spare set of keys! Pacing around the room, he tried to think of solutions. He felt pulled out of existence—overwhelmed, full of dread. "What do I do?

Pete's Crossroad

What do I do?"

He slid out his shiny-mirrored sunglasses from his pants pocket; and as he gave them a quick cleaning, he remembered what Chuck had called the glasses after Terrence Frapley fired him from Fossil Inc.: "Sun cheaters." Plopping down on Fletch's twin-sized bed he heard a small still voice well into his consciousness. The words sounding as if Walks-With-Dreams was in the room with him. "Innocent people are being offered a better life, but someone is cheating them, betraying them, and abusing them. Do something."

Pete felt half-terrified. "Okay, George." His fingers felt numb as he opened up his email. "All right! If I *don't* do what you tell me to do, I'll never hear the end of it, and I'll never forgive myself anyway. So here goes..." He opened the webpage to the Los Angeles District Attorney's office.

"When are you going to leave me alone, George?" He clicked on the Contact icon and typed in his information, striking the keys hard.

"When will you let *me* live in peace and *you* rest in peace?" He said as he typed in the subject header: "A real sweat shop!" He typed the date: April, 22, 2011, and he wrote the following:

Dear District Attorney:

My name is Pete Turner. While working for Fashion Diva in Santa Monica from January, 2009 to February of this year, I believe I accidentally discovered a sweat shop that is violating labor laws. I also encountered managers who might be involved in the trafficking of slave laborers. I am attaching photos I took as an employee while working for Fashion Diva. As you can see, these photographs are digital and time stamped. I quit the company instead of reporting what I had seen. I feared for my life. Currently, I believe I am being black balled from the industry because of what I had witnessed. I am temporarily in Amarillo, Texas, about to bury a man who died next to me on a Greyhound bus. My previous employer was Fossil, Inc., located in Santa Monica. I worked there only a month, from March until yesterday, April, 21, when Terrence Frapley, the V.P. of Sales and Marketing for Fossil, Inc. fired me. Please forgive me for not sending these sooner.

Sincerely, Pete Turner."

J.P. Osterman

He then attached several picture files. When he was done, he stopped, took a deep breath, and clasped his fingers.

After tapping *Send*, there would be no turning back! He would have to face whatever the D.A. would throw at him. He imagined a cavalry of armed marshals storming Don's door to arrest him, or a court order mandating that he surrender to the Amarillo police for questioning! He felt breathless with panic. He hadn't a clue what could happen, and hated being so out of control and powerless over the results. Before pushing *Send* icon, he peered at the Texas oak tree's skeletal canopy.

"No apartment," he said, realizing George was listening. "No job, no car." His head ached; his eyes burned. Now, he wanted to sleep.

George said, "Everything's going to change for you, Pete."

"Yeah, right, George," he huffed, hitting the *Send* icon. He sat there, staring out the window at the blue sky, at the evidence of a strong gust of wind whipping the green grass. When the screen changed to a message that read, *Your message has been received, and we will reply within the next twelve hours*, Pete knew his letter and pictures didn't bounce. Someone now had them, and it was just a matter of time—and waiting on the edge of his seat—before the D.A. would take action. When he saw that all the Fashion Diva pictures were stored safely back in their files, he sighed and exclaimed, "Finally, this nightmare will soon be over!" Going to the bed and sitting down, he picked through his suitcase and lifted out a pair of jeans, Nike tennis shoes, and a polo shirt.

"Now, don'tcha feel relieved, Pete?" George asked, his ghost body sagging as if he had experienced a catharsis. He was now sitting on the chair in front of Fletch's desk, his body transparent with a light-gold aura all around him.

"Relieved?" Pete took off his Rolex and tossed it on the bed. "I feel like I've swallowed gum and it's sticking to my tonsils." He rubbed his throat. His skin felt dry; his mouth tasted like sourdough bread. "George, you're going to be resting in peace by next Friday." He lunged at him a bit. "But

Pete's Crossroad

I might be in jail." He closed his suitcase, slid it to the carpet, and lay down on to Fletch's bed. The past few days felt like a series of slugs and slaps. "I'm so tired. I gotta sleep."

"The gifts, Pete!" George said excitedly, waving as if he were watching his favorite team winning on TV. Now, he was standing right next to Pete.

"What!? Right now?" Pete gasped as he shot up from Fletch's bed. Dashing over the bathroom, he shoved his clothes on the sink and splashed his face with water. Realizing his voice might sound a bit too loud, that Don might overhear him and accuse him of being schizophrenic or psychotic, he whispered, "George, you gotta quit startling me, especially when I need some rest." He imagined a lifetime of this intrusion, and wished for the day when George would disappear from his life for good."

George was almost dancing while pointing at the door: "The gifts, Pete. Ya gotta give 'em what I brought to them!" He had the face of a father thrilled to wake up on Christmas morning.

"Okay, George. Just let me take a shower, first, okay?" He closed the door, but that wouldn't stop George. "And give me some privacy! Gosh darn it…how am I ever going to make it through the rest of the day?!"

After taking a shower, dressing, and then lying down on Fletch's bed, Pete still couldn't get the images of those women out of his mind, or that Fossil Inc. had fired him, and the connection between Fossil and his old company, Fashion Diva. He was also worried about his car still stuck in the park-n-ride at the L.A. Greyhound station and his things in storage. He reached in his wallet, pulled out Tina Bowlett's card, and called her. She was his ex-sales associate at Fossil Inc. who had told him to phone her if he needed anything. She had given him the silver cross that she said represented his crossroad in life, and that one day he'd find his true calling and purpose. After she agreed to pick up his Sebring convertible at the station, he told her he'd FedEx her the key so she could drive it to Fossil's parking lot—at least until he could secure an apartment somewhere in the United States. Then he called the station to make sure they wouldn't tow away his car and charge him exorbitant fees. Then he phoned the PR representative at Fossil who said the company would allow him to park his car there for 30 days. When he talked to the manager at the storage facility in Santa Monica, she said she only needed to receive a check in the next five business days.

"Whew," Pete sighed. "Problem solved, at least for now."

"You were frettin' and stewin' over nothin', Pete," George began, "but see? Everything worked out fine. You're a natural-born worrier, Pete. That's your problem. You gotta learn to deal with the stresses in life or they'll kill ya!"

Waving in exasperation, Pete said, "That's because life *is* stressful, George." But having staved off at least a few stressors, Pete sighed, until he heard the sounds of car doors opening and closing. "That must be your grandchildren, Andy and Sue Beth." He couldn't see them out of Fletch's little bedroom window, just the black Texas oak. "Don't surprise me by popping up in my face while I'm talking to them, will you, George?" Pete saw George walking toward the door that began glowing with wavering light.

As George moved through the door, he said, "I'm with ya all the way, Pete. Don't worry." He sounded like a coach.

Pete's Crossroad

Chapter 13 – The Meeting

After George's departed, Pete left Fletch's room and walked through the breezeway. When he reached the kitchen door, he heard a commotion. Gently opening the door and stepping into the kitchen, he paused next to a large wooden pantry with his back against a wall and began eavesdropping.

Don said, "Pete's a pretty nice guy, Andy." Don was obviously trying to convince his son who believed the contrary. "Pete just fell on hard times, that's all. He's only gonna be staying here for a week."

"Uh-huh, *right* Dad, you're so gullible! The guy could be a scam artist!" Andy's tone of voice was judgmental and angry.

"You've been there yourself, Andrew," Don began, softy, "and I've fallen on hard times as well. I think you should give Pete a chance."

"I see your point too, Dad." It was a woman's voice— the same voice he had heard in Phoenix when he had talked to Don about his father's death. It was Sue Beth!

Andy replied: "This guy's from California, Dad. He could be a gang banger, or one of those grifters who gains your confidence then takes you for every last dime." He was sounding breathlessly terrified. "Or—or—a drifter, or dope smuggler you see in those *Most Wanted* shows." Andy was obviously a protector, and hopelessly deadlock in a fight against Don who was adamant about not needing protection. "Those people in sharp business suits can be white-collar criminals, dad!"

"Andy, come on…I think you're getting too carried away," Sue Beth said.

"Uh-uh, we'll see who's right!" Andy said. "Where do you think Hollywood producers and come up with those scum-bag criminal characters?"

Sue Beth's voice lowered. "Shhh, Andy, he'll hear you!"

After a pause, Andy said sternly: "Fine…but you *should* think twice about having a stranger in the house. You might wake up one morning and this guy will have car-jacked your truck, or discovered the safe and cleaned it out."

"Andy!" Don chided, "I don't see Pete—"

"Just wait," Andy replied in a warning tone of voice. "You'll see…don't complain when something's gone or stolen, 'cause I'll tell ya I told ya so!"

Pete could hear the stomping of boots on the tile floor. Andy was walking out of the kitchen. Sue Beth said, "Andy, give Pete a chance. He was there when our grandpa died. He obviously got to know him." Her voice was wavering. She had to be fighting back tears. "Don't you want to hear what Pete—a complete stranger, who knew more about our grandpa than our dad ever told us—"

"I was just trying to protect you kids from him. That's all." Don said defensively.

She sniffled, and Pete heard sobbing.

"But we had a right to talk to grandpa, dad," Sue Beth began, "but *you* kept him from us…*you* kept him away. We *never* got to know him." She was stammering through her sobs. Obviously, she was not used to expressing anger to her father. "Protect us from what, Dad? Huh? You never told us!"

There was a long pause until Andy said, "Sue Beth—"

"Let me finish!" she said, her father, Don, not saying a word.

Pete's Crossroad

Pete could hear the sound of wood gliding across the tile floor as if Don or Andy were moving one of George's suitcases. "I told you a little about what my dad did to my mother and me," Don said, his voice vindictive. "He left her alone while she died of cancer." Don's breath was intensifying. He was having difficulty moving George's heavy suitcase.

Andy was in the entryway on the hardwood floor. "Here, Dad, lemme help ya with these."

"I know grandpa left her, Dad," Sue Beth began, "but wasn't that because he was on the road working?"

Don scoffed a hard, "Huh—that's no excuse!"

Sue Beth replied, "I'm just trying to under—"

"I told you a little about what my dad did to me…when I was a kid, Sue Beth!" Don said, interrupting her.

Pete remembered his own childhood. He too had penned up and buried all the harsh abuse from his father.

"My dad, well, just wasn't there," Don said, "and when he was, well, he could be, well, downright nasty, mean—" He stopped.

"I'd like to see Grandpa's pictures," Sue Beth said in a gentle tone of voice. "You said Pete has them on his laptop."

Pete looked back at Fletch's room. Part of him wanted to run there, pack up, and leave. Stopping him were George's last words: "I'm sorry. I'm gonna make it up to ya—"

Pete knew George was about to say, "Donny." He had to stay. He continued to overhead their conversation:

"You're so darn judgmental, Andy," Sue Beth blared.

It sounded as if Andy whipped off a hat and hit it on his leg. "And you don't learn your lessons until it's too late!" Andy argued.

Seconds passed until Don intervened and said, laughing a little, "Fletch would just go knock on the door, get Pete, and drag him out for a beer."

They all laughed. The following silence felt like the air in church prior to a pastor beginning a eulogy.

"Yeah," Sue Beth said, "Fletch was always so easy going…so friendly. Without him, we're all so suspicious and closed off." She sighed. "Fletch was such a free spirit. I hope that war in Iraq doesn't change him."

Pete had had enough. Moving like an agent infiltrating a target, he tiptoed back to Fletch's room and grabbed his laptop. Trying not to make any tapping sounds on the breezeway tile or creaking noises as the door hinges moved, he re-entered the kitchen. The three of them were still talking. He shut the door loudly and coughed, trying to make Don and his family aware that he was now in the kitchen.

"*Shhh*," he heard someone whisper, followed by, "Pete! Is that you?" It was Don's voice.

"Yes, Mr. Gibson," he replied, walking through the kitchen. Don had given him permission to call him by his first name although now Pete wanted to address him in the formal sense to make the best impression on Andy and Sue Beth. After what he had just heard, he knew he'd have to be extra nice and polite—walking on eggshells to get them to trust him, especially Andy.

They were gathered in the living room and standing all together. The first thing Pete noticed was Andy. He was clad in jeans, a checkered shirt, and cowboy boots. His dad Don looked like John Denver, but Andy resembled a young John Wayne. Sue Beth was petite, and didn't seem to share their DNA. She had short brown hair and large brown eyes. She could pass as a twin for a youthful Sally Field. She had on a white blouse with embossed little red roses and green stems. It was a peasant blouse, matching her A-line skirt. She radiated springtime and soft smells in her every movement and expression. Pete felt suddenly mesmerized by her, could hardly say hi to her. Wanting to break the tense atmosphere, he shook Sue Beth's hand first. "Hi, I'm Pete."

She smiled. Her grip was firm. "I'm Sue Beth."

Then he turned to stern Andy. Pete straightened up, waiting for Don to say something. "This is my son, Andy Gibson, Pete," he finally said, and Andy shook Pete's hand. It was a challenging grip, his stare like bull's eyes.

Pete motioned to George's luggage. "I'm sorry for your

loss."

Sue Beth's eyes were watery, and her little shoulders sulked. "Thanks, I never really knew my grandpa, just my grandma."

"Yeah, nice to meetcha, Pete," Andy said, grimacing a bit. Coughing in an obvious gesture to hide his uncomfortable emotions, he added, "Thanks for seein' that my grandpa's things made it to us safely." When he smiled, his lips on one side of his face curved up, showing his white teeth. It made him look as if he had an invisible toothpick perched between them. He had the deep tan of a rancher, with strong muscles like a rodeo bronco buster.

Sue Beth was opposite her brother. She had a sincere, gentle, and trusting personality—qualities Pete felt attracted to, along with her blushing cheeks, perfect smile, and the way she tossed her head a little to swoosh away her wispy brown bangs from her warm round eyes.

Pete pointed at George's large suitcase. "Well, have you looked inside it yet?"

Don sat down on the sofa. Everyone followed his move. "Not yet."

Sue Beth gave him an impatient look. "When can we open it, Dad?"

Sitting with one leg perched on on his other knee, Andy said, "I hope you won't wait until Christmas, Dad." He turned to Pete and gave out a hard chuckle. "My dad likes to put off things now and then."

"Except for his business," Sue Beth said, leaning over and tapping her dad's arm affectionately.

"I called Fletch," Don said. "Actually, the Red Cross."

"You did?" Sue Beth asked, Andy's mouth opening in shock as well.

"I left Fletch a message that his grandfather passed on," Don replied, looking down at the carpet, his fingers clasped.

Andy's head hit the cushion of his leather chair. "Pa, you finally did it!" he exclaimed, the tips of his short blond mustache curling as he smiled.

J.P. Osterman

"He should know about his grandfather's death, I guess," Don said.

Sue Beth glanced at Pete, winked, and said, "Dad, I *knew* you'd finally cave in and forgive Fletch."

Pete said, "Sometimes, unfortunately, it takes going through a hard time for people to, well, mend fences, as the old saying goes," he chuckled.

Andy's planted his feet firmly on the carpeted. "Now it's just a wait-and-see to find out if Fletch will answer."

Sue Beth whispered to Pete, "Grudges! What can I say." As she lowered her head, sadness flowed over her body.

"I'd like to open those suitcases on Friday," Don said, tapping his fingers on the sofa armrest. "It just seems fitting to bury him first though, before I go taking out all his things and looking through them."

"Oh, Dad," Sue Beth began, "you're putting the cart before the horse, don't you think?"

"Whataya mean?" Don asked, feeling his salt-and-pepper beard and then pushing up his rimless glasses.

"I think you should consider opening Grandpa's things before the funeral, Dad," Andy said, slowly. He had his hands firmly folded across his chest. "That way we'll have an idea who Grandpa really was…what he's been doing all these years. We can then say something about him at his gravesite." He inhaled from the bottom of his lungs, obviously wanting to know George, but also trying to protect his father's feelings.

"Don'tcha wanna know, Dad?" Sue Beth asked softly. Turning to Pete, she asked, "Did you see what my grandpa had inside his luggage?"

Her little chin and small delicate face made it hard for Pete to think let alone answer her! "Yes, but not up close," Pete replied. "I suppose you *do* want something to say when you give the eulogy though, and seeing George's things will give you information."

"See, Dad? Pete has a good point," Sue Beth said, her body lightly bouncing. She seemed brimming with energy, positive, and upbeat.

Pete's Crossroad

"I think he does too, Dad," Andy agreed, his lower lip puckering. Pete thought he might sometimes chew tobacco or smoke cigars. He had a rugged look about him.

Sitting straight up, Don said, "Give me the day to think about it. Tomorrow's Saturday. I'll make a decision then."

"Great!" Sue Beth said.

Pete pulled out his laptop that had sunk inside the fold of his chair. "Oh, Sue Beth, did you bring a flash drive?"

"Right here," she said, pulling one out of her pocket.

Pete lifted the laptop in front of him and smiled at her. This close to her, he was beginning to feel lost in her presence and having difficulty concentrating. "I can download these pictures right for you," Pete said.

"Come on with me into the kitchen," she said, motioning for him to follow.

Don followed them, "If you're gonna set up that computer, I'd better make room on my desk." He scurried out of the living room. Obviously, he really wanted to see those pictures of his father but didn't want to admit it.

But before Pete entered the kitchen with Sue Beth, Andy donned his black cowboy hat and said, "Pete, hold on a second." His voice boomed as he smirked at him from under the brim of his hat. He bounced on the balls of his feet—a fighter about to pounce on his contestant.

"Okaaay," Pete said.

Andy had his thumbs through his belt loops, his black cowboy hat tipped forward, shadowing his brow, and his mustache was twitching a little.

Pete gleaned the message, "Be careful what you do around here." He looked like a cavalry general. He also had the tendency to part his legs wide when he was standing still as if he were above everyone, directing them. He had a tough square chin, bristle for a moustache, tiny slits as eyes, and a scowl that could shoot down the enemy. Swallowing hard and taking a step back, Pete realized he was an enemy to Andy. He thought, how am I *ever* gonna win *him* over!

"Andy, stop it," Sue Beth said, walking back into the

living room. "Come on. Pete's a visitor. Our guest."

Pete realized that Andy had judged him a long time ago, mostly likely, after his dad told him that he had just been fired. Then Pete thought of a much bigger cloud looming over him. He might be facing *big* trouble for not reporting all the criminal activities at Fashion Diva. He wasn't in the mood for playing games. Remembering Chuck's honest demeanor, and hoping that an approachable attitude might yield softer results, he said, "Andy, what's going on?" He stepped back—in no way would he allow Andy to intimidate him. He just kept telling himself: I can leave anytime…pack up and get out. Then in the archway between the living and dining room, he spotted George as a yellow-haloed ghost gesturing for him to stay put.

"I'm watching you," Andy said. He tipped his black cowboy hat at him, picked up his jacket, shot a toothpick between his lips, and stared Pete down hard.

Pete stepped next to Sue Beth. "Look, Andy, it seems that you and I are opposites." Andy's eyes widened. "I don't want to tangle with you or cut in on your family. I'm just here because your dad invited me to stay until after your grandfather's funeral. I knew him. That's all. I'm only trying to help." When he looked toward the dining room, he saw smiling excited George giving him the thumbs up signal.

"Uh-huh," Andy said in a skeptical tone.

"I think you judged me long before I walked in here," Pete said, glancing around the house, trying to give the message to Andy that he was not casing the place.

"We'll see," Andy replied.

There was a mirror above the couch and Pete glanced into their two reflections. They stood face-to-face like two gunslingers about to draw their pistols in a fight, with Sue Beth on the side—the damsel needing protection. Pete did a once over assessment. Dressed in California casual, he was a white-collar worker with a college education. Yes, George was right. He looked like Tony Stewart, the race car driver! Andy, the John Wayne look-a-like, had a high-school education and obviously worked or managed Don's huge ranch, and most

Pete's Crossroad

likely worked at his home and garden store. But he didn't ask him what he did for a living just yet. He didn't want to flame an already flaming fire.

Sue Beth opened the door leading out to the front porch. The white wrought iron swing was gently rocking. A breeze had picked up, and a few purple and white flower pedals drifted inside the house. "Andy, aren't you supposed to be at Dad's shop taking over for him today?" She shifted her feet in show of irritation and brushed back her bangs.

Approaching the door with his boots pounding the floor as he walked, Andy said, "See ya later on tonight, Sis. I'll pick up lunch at Burger Barn." He didn't take his eyes off Pete.

Pete stepped back and stuck out his hand to shake Andy's, but Andy pointed two fingers at his own eyes and then pointed at Pete, his way of saying: I'm watching you. He didn't return the hand shake but instead called, "See ya tonight at the round up, Dad." Then he kissed Sue Beth on top of her head. "Make sure your fiddle is polished, Sis. We've gotta win that contest tonight if we want to go to Fiddler's Frolics."

Hugging him, she said, "*You* just be there." Andy left.

Pete asked, "What's Fiddler's Frolics?"

Waving Pete into the kitchen, she replied, "It's an annual contest for fiddlers. Andy, Fletch and I always try to qualify."

"So you're pretty good at playing the fiddle, huh?" He'd never met a musician before. He picked up his laptop, and they walked into the kitchen. Next to the sliding glass door was a long desk Don had cleared off for him.

She peered up at him shyly. "I don't know. I try."

The phone rang, and Don answered it. In the back yard was another huge garden, behind it the Texas oak, and beyond that, cattle dotting the rolling landscape. "You can set up your laptop there, Pete, on my desk." He left briefly to talk in private with someone. Pete felt suddenly nervous, anxious about who could be on the other end of the line. Since he'd sent that report, the everything ordinary, like the phone ringing, felt suspicious.

Sue Beth shouted: "Dad! If it's Fletch, I wanna talk to

him!" They were expecting the call but didn't know Fletch's availability being that he was on a delicate mission.

As Pete set up his laptop, Sue Beth glanced to where her father was talking in the family room beyond the living room. "What was my grandpa like, Pete?" She had her hands clasped nervously.

Looking down into her eyes, he noticed they were big and brown and full, like those of an innocent doe. She had a deep longing in everything about her, as if she loved nature, and picking flowers, and caring for horses, and taking in homeless or injured animals. She was a kind person in every way, and that touched Pete, who thought, *I gotta get outta here*! The longer he was around her, the more he wanted to leave…and the tension between the two extremes began gnawing at him. Sue Beth was perfect for him!

Then George appeared in ghost form right next to him. "Tell her, Pete," he said. He had a white face—cold and lifeless—with lines of pain and creases from crying. George had suddenly changed. He was now serious, not at all excited. "Tell her about me."

Pete realized this narration would be the first of many of George's apologies. "Your grandpa really wanted to meet you," he began. "He was sick though. That's why he left L.A." The laptop whirred with energy as he stretched out his hand for Sue Beth to give him the flash drive. Briefly, he touched her.

"That's why my dad said the coroner in Phoenix didn't perform an autopsy," Sue Beth said, waiting for the flash drive to initiate into Pete's laptop. "My dad said the coroner called a doctor's number he had found in my dad's wallet." Her voice was low and soft as she lifted a small picture off the desk and stared into it. "I guess my grandpa must have realized that he didn't have much—time."

"I know," Pete said as her head gently hit the middle of his arm. "I'm so sorry this had to happen. It's sad that all of you couldn't have met a long time ago and worked out your differences." She was crying, and he didn't know whether to put his arm around her and comfort her, or just let her alone. He didn't know at all how to just touch someone and be present for them—be a shoulder to cry on and an encouraging person.

"Yeah, I know," she cried. The picture she was holding slipped out of her hand and fell on the desk face up. She stroked the glass. "This was my grandma with my dad." She set the picture back up on the desk.

Peering at the photo of George's wife with Don, Pete said: "Your grandpa told me she died of cancer. Sue Lynn was her name."

"Uh-huh."

"I think she died in 1996," Pete added, tapping the laptop screen, and up popped the picture folder.

Sue Beth bit her lower lip and wiped her cheeks with the back of her hand. Her skin had a pale transparency like a vein in a leaf. "I was almost eight at the time. I really miss her."

Pete said, "I don't mean to sound uncaring or anything, Sue Beth, but at least you got to know her for a while. I never met my grandparents."

"Really?" she asked, glancing into his eyes, inspecting them as if searching for caring.

"Honest," Pete began, "my grandparents lived on the east coast, and my parents moved away from there before I was born."

"Oh," she said, as if feeling his loss herself.

"But I can say one thing about your grandfather," he said firmly, taking her by the arms.

"What's that?" she asked.

"He loved you even though he never met you," Pete said, and when they both looked at the laptop screen, there was the picture Hideki had taken of George and Pete at the rest stop. He'd never opened that one up; George did. "Those are cups of coffee in our hands. We were walking to the bus in Blythe, California."

Gasping when she saw the picture, she lifted up the laptop as if she might kiss the screen. "This is him?" She glanced at the picture of her grandmother, obviously trying to decide if they matched each other as soul mates. "My dad looks like him!"

Pete leaned around to peek at it. "Yeah, I guess he does."

"Does what?" Don asked as he came around the corner and hung up the phone. The kitchen turned quiet.

"Dad! This is a picture of Grandpa Gibson!" she said, turning the laptop so he could see it.

As Don perused the picture, Pete saw his beard change shape a little as his jaw tightened. Don put his hands behind his back and puffed out his chest. He was definitely trying to control his feelings. "Nice," he said, quickly turning away.

"I'll print Grandpa's picture from this flash drive later, Dad," she said as she set down the laptop. She didn't take her eyes off of George's image. She looked like she'd just been reunited with a lost pet. Now she had closure, even though she had no idea of all the details missing from her grandfather's lost years.

"Good, you do that," Don snapped as Pete pulled out Sue Beth's flash drive and handed it to her.

Pete believed he had to say something now. The more he was around Don's anger, the more he just didn't understand it. "Mr. Gibson, I—"

"Don," he said flatly.

"Sorry, *Don*, but I have to tell you what your dad told me," Pete said.

Sue Beth smiled widely. "Go on, Pete," she coaxed.

Don thrust his hands in his pockets and gave him a skeptical glower. "*Yeees*," he said, apprehensively.

Pete breathed and said, "George said for me to tell you— I mean, your dad said for me to tell you that he's sorry for what happened to you when you were a child."

Tears welled in Don's eyes as he leaned against the kitchen counter.

"Hear that, Dad?" Sue Beth asked, touching his arm tenderly.

Don remained speechless.

Pete's Crossroad

"He wanted to try to make everything up to you, Mr. Gibson," Pete continued. This time Don didn't correct him but kept on listening. "He was genuinely sorry, Sir. I think whatever happened between the two of you years ago was ripping him a part inside. He lived all those years with regret, and afraid to face what he had done, so he just kept selling things on the road."

"Uh-huh," Don said, wiping his eyes, turning away. His head was bent low, his arms tight across his chest.

Pete could see that Don was a man who rarely cried. Then again, he never did either. Sue Beth grabbed her father's arm and held on tight as if she were a little girl.

Pete moved the arrow on the screen to shut down mode. "That's really why I came here, Don…to tell you what your dad said before he died…not just to deliver all his suitcases in there." He waved at them as if they contained junk.

Sue Beth lifted her head off her father's shoulder. "You came here, all this way, to deliver that message then Pete, right?" she asked with surprise in her eyes.

Nodding, Pete replied, "Yes."

She walked over to him and looked straight up into his eyes. "You could have just taken off in Phoenix. You didn't have to come here."

Now Pete was feeling a little embarrassed. He really didn't know how to handle someone thanking him. "Well, no…I didn't have to come here, but I did." He glanced around the kitchen. There in a dark corner, standing under the door frame was George in spirit form, smiling approvingly, and casting a white outline on the floor. He didn't dare tell Sue Beth and Don, at least not yet, that George was the one who made him take the long trip to make peace with his family.

Suddenly, Don turned around and rubbed his beard. "Thanks, Pete." He reached around Sue Beth's shoulders and put his arm around her. "We really appreciate what you've done…coming here like this." He was obviously struggling to say the words.

Pete peered at the little picture of George's dead wife, Sue

Lynn, on the desk. "Your dad was really trying to make up with you," he said as he slid his laptop into the side of his briefcase. "Mine never did, and I don't even have a clue where the guy is, but I guess, if he were to apologize like I'm apologizing for George, I'd feel better...my life would be less full of baggage, and I'd be able to relate to people better." Now, he felt very embarrassed...out of control as if he'd given up some type of leverage to become vulnerable.

"That's too bad, Pete," Don said, picking up his jacket.

"Wow, you have no idea where your dad lives at all?" Sue Beth asked. She swept up her purse off the floor and inserted the flash drive into it.

Scratching the back of his neck, Pete said, "Nope, my mom either." He laughed as he added, "Or my sister!"

Stopping dead in her tracks with her eyes showing loss, she said, "It sounds like you've never really had a family, Pete. Right?" She had a look suggesting that she'd be bringing up the subject again. She seemed to be that kind of a person, one who delves into the deepest parts of people to know them.

Pete's mouth dropped open. He had to really think about that for a moment. "Well...I guess you're right." A deep sadness churned in his stomach. Glancing around the kitchen containing almost every modern appliance, he realized he had missed out on something grand: a home, a connection, and belonging to family. She had all these things, and she noticed he didn't. She was becoming like a ground wire to him!

Just as Sue Beth was about to ask another question, Don said, "I have to get to my store, you two." He picked up his keys and Sue Beth followed him. "You want a ride to the Enterprise rental car shop, Pete?" he asked, feeling around the corner for his jacket hanging on a coat tree.

"Oh, sure, Don," Pete replied.

"Is something wrong at Gibby's, Dad?" Sue Beth asked. "You look hurried, and worried."

Don shook his head in disappointment. "It looks like Tom's out sick for the week."

"My gosh, no!" she said, implying her father's store would

Pete's Crossroad

be lost without Tom. "Is Tom all right though?"

Putting on his coat, he replied: "I don't know how serious it is. It could be a bad case of the flu. It's been goin' around." He pointed to Sue Beth's bare neck. "So keep yourself covered up when you go outside, ya hear?"

"Sure, Dad," she said, folding her arms.

Huffing, Don said, "Tom was supposed to be watching my shop this afternoon, but now he says he's gotta leave in twenty minutes. Doctor's appointment."

Pete didn't know whether he wanted to come home to an empty house after renting a car or offer to help Don. Following Don and Sue Beth down a long hall to the garage, he noticed an entire line of pictures, all of one person. Each picture was a progression in age from baby to young adulthood. "Who's this?" he asked Sue Beth.

Her shoulders drooped. "That's Fletch. My dad would never say it, but he really misses him," she whispered. Both sides of the wall were filled with Fletch's pictures.

Pete said, "I don't get it."

"Get what?" she asked, rolling her jacket around her shoulders.

Pete glanced down into her wide eyes that had recovered from their sadness. "It's just strange how your brother's gone, but he's really here, everywhere around you."

Her head jerked back a little in surprise, "Yeah, I guess that's true."

He saw Fletch's soccer picture when he was eight years old and then spotted another that showed him smiling with the dead catfish draped over his arms. With long hair usually down below his earlobes, Fletch was short, and obviously a good runner from all the baseball and basketball pictures dotting the wall. And the person taking his pictures always snapped them when Fletch was in action. Don had been to every game and every event.

Sue Beth said: "Fletch is sort of wild. And he likes doing a lot of things, but he doesn't like asking first, or thinking about how his actions might affect other." She had a look of longing in her eyes. "I think that's one of Fletch's problems."

"What's that?" Pete asked.

"*Ahhh*, that he tends to be impulsive, and stubborn," she said. Then she gave Pete a questioning glance. "But don't you think most everyone is like that sometimes?"

Pete didn't really know what to say. She was asking existential questions that he hadn't ever thought about, so he said, "I guess. The guy's young though." He peered at her from the bottom of her skirt to the curve of her shoulders. "Fletch is a little bit older than you, right?" he asked, glancing at another picture of Fletch when he was sixteen.

"About three years older," she said as she straightened one crooked picture. She touched the frame with care and caution, obviously just as she had treated her brother.

Pete huffed a little. "He's not like drugs and alcohol wild, right?"

Shaking her head, she said, "My gosh no! Fletch just didn't listen a whole lot." She shrugged almost as if trying to excuse him. "And he's always on the go, like he has ounces of adrenaline pumping through him all the time." She giggled a little, caught up in a funny memory of her brother.

Don opened the door and poked his head inside the hallway. "You two comin'?" He was in a hurry.

Sue Beth began walking toward him. "Yeah, Dad, I'm just showing Pete pictures of Fletch. That's all."

Don's eyebrows were forking. "I haveta get to Gibby's fast, or Tom's gonna haveta close up my store! We'll lose the opportunity for a lot of business this afternoon. People like to buy dirt and supplies for yard work before Easter."

"Dad, I invited Pete to the roundup tonight," she said.

"Good," Don said. "Now come on, Sue Beth."

Pete careened back in surprise. "You did?"

Sue Beth smiled and bounced like a sprite. "Sure! You're coming, Pete."

Giving out a surprise laugh , he said, "I guess. All right." A jolt of fear suddenly hit him. "I don't know if you're brother's gonna like me at this roundup though. Don't you

Pete's Crossroad

think you should ask him first?" He remembered Andy's two fingers pointing straight at his eyes, giving him the "I'm watching you" glare."

Sue Beth waved off his concern. "*Ahhh*, Andy won't mind. Don't worry about him. I'll call him later. He's all bark but no bite, really." She laughed.

"All right," Pete said, feeling skeptical. "But let me know if he doesn't want me there, 'cause I don't want to cause any trouble between you, and I could spend those hours job searching."

Don had heard that as he hung up from a phone call with someone at his store. "No trouble, Pete. All most everybody attends things like these." He nodded at both sides of the street. "This is a home town, Pete. People come out and support one another."

"Great," Pete said, remembering the people on Main Street talking and laughing. Amarillo was nothing like L. A. or Santa Monica where most people joined crowds on purpose for protection. "What does a person wear at a roundup?" He pinched the fabric of his polo shirt, feeling poorly dressed and uneasy about fitting in at a country roundup. The event sounded like it would take place in a large bar where people listen to music and dance to a live band.

"A shop's around the corner from my store, Pete. You can buy jeans there…that is, if you don't have a pair on ya," Don said, waving them into the truck.

"Fine," Pete said, motioning for Sue Beth to go ahead of him. "Is there a post office near your store, Don? I have to FedEx something, fast," he asked, remembering he had to mail his car key to Tina Bowlett, and a check to the storage facility.

"A block down from Gibby's," Don replied, starting the truck.

"I hope nothing's wrong, Pete," Sue Beth said, giving him a curious squint out of the corner of her eye.

Pete believed she was trying to pry into his life. "No, nothing's wrong," he said, clasping his seatbelt.

On the way downtown, Pete told them about Terrence

J.P. Osterman

Frapley firing him right in the middle of the sale's convention, and that he needed to send his car key to Tina Bowlett to drive his Sebring convertible to Fossil Inc.'s parking lot until he could return to Santa Monica to pick up his stranded automobile.

"Oh," Sue Beth whispered, her shoulders hunching in disappointment. "When do you have to leave, Pete?" She appeared to be lose a good friend.

Pete swallowed hard, cleared his throat and shrugged. For the first time in a long, long time he felt his stomach sink, sink hard and sick, over a woman. A fog hit his head; and when he rubbed his neck, the skin feeling numb. Glancing out the window, he saw Texas oak trees on both sides of the road. Two people were riding horses. A man tipped his cowboy hat at Don, and an entire family waved as Don waved back. The little countryside turned into a hometown city with flower baskets hanging from antique streetlights.

"You think you're gonna go pretty soon then, huh Pete?" she asked again. "Even before my grandpa's funeral?"

He folded his arms and looked at her askance at the opposite side of their back seat. "I'm staying for George's funeral. That's a given," Pete said, unable to take his eyes off Sue Beth. Each time he peeked at her, he couldn't look away from her. More and more he felt locked onto her gaze. Then he felt stupid, like he was glaring at her, and he quickly looked away. He felt like a teenager on a first date! She giggled a little, turned away, and he thought, as he craned to see her brown eyes: *What the heck's going on here? I don't want this!*

Behind Sue Beth and outside the window, he saw an old brick clock tower, Terry's ice cream parlor on the corner of 6th and Sycamore, Haskel's Nickel and Dime, and big signs pointing to the Amarillo City Library and City Hall.

Suddenly, he remembered that time again when he was a freshman in high school gym class. He was half-way in the middle of a sixty-foot long rope, half-way to the ceiling, stalled in midair, gasping for breath, trying to self-glue his eyes shut for fear of looking down, and completely numb. For a good

Pete's Crossroad

grade, he had to hit the red wood bar nailed to the ceiling. He didn't know how. The kids below him were moaning and groaning, and hollering and whistling—bored of watching him and tired of waiting. He felt trapped, with his palms stinging, the skin between his legs burning, his knuckles numb-white, and his arm and neck muscles cramping. He believed he was fighting for every ounce of his life as breath-after-breath he inched his way to the ceiling. All the while, all he could hear was the bristly rope scratching and gnawing on the rubber of his tennis shoes.

Quickly, glancing away from Sue Beth while rubbing his eyes, he wondered why he was remembering that hideous, God-awful time. He had absolutely no idea what any portion of that horrible and out of control slice-of-life memory had to do with him riding in a truck with Sue Beth and Don, mailing a key to someone, and attending a funeral. Absolutely no idea!

Then, as they turned the corner and pulled into Don's home and garden store, Gibby's, Pete spotted a white silhouette waving at him and smiling. The closer they arrived, the stronger the figure appeared. George…again! He was standing at the door, marveling at shovels, tapping rakes, smelling flowers, and perusing shrubs. He had a happy expression on his face at being on a grand excursion.

J.P. Osterman

Chapter 14 – Sue Beth Gibson

That night, Pete sprawled out a map on the passenger's seat of his rental car and made his way from Don's ranch to a large bar on the outskirts of Amarillo. The parking lot was full, the air cool, tropical, and humid, like silk running over his face and arms. Don had told him that the Texas panhandle was experiencing an unusual Gulf Stream current. He also said there was an expression to Texas weather: "Drought, flood, blizzard, or twister. Take your pick."

"Oh my God," Pete mumbled; "Oh my God what have I gotten myself into?!"

After shutting off the engine, he waited in his car with the window open, his elbow on the frame. He felt stuck—really, jammed into a corner—out in the sticks—nowhere—with no direction, no purpose. "Oh God," he gasped, again, as if under the load of a two-hundred pound barbell he couldn't bench press. He stared up into a white neon sign with red lettering zapping out the name of the place—The Vapors. It looked like a billboard, taking up the entire length of the entryway that had four sets of large wooden doors. People appeared to be in a mad rush to get inside. Men were dressed in cowboy hats and boots, the women's boots clattering on the

Pete's Crossroad

pavement. A real Texas stampede, Pete thought. He could hear music that sounded like an orchestra of fiddles, so loud they were probably blaring across the desert.

Swatting a fly, he wondered if he was doing the right thing, or the wrong thing. He really needed to get back to Don's place to open up his email and job hunt, but he also knew Sue Beth was going to be performing. The more he sew her, the more he wanted to be with her. The Vapors was drawing him in like a love potion. Besides, her father had said this was her big night, a huge contest to see whether she would qualify for Fiddler's Follies in Hallettsville, Texas, where ever that is. But Andy her brother was a *big* problem between them.

Once inside The Vapors, he glanced around the huge bar with sawdust on the floor, round wooden tables, a long center stage for performers and customers eating and drinking beer. Down a long row of tables he spotted Don sitting alongside Andy toward the front of the stage. They were all dressed up in country clothes. He'd never seen anything like this before, except for on TV show or in a move. The only thing missing was the mechanical bull. No, wait, it was in another room with a line to ride it running out the door!

Don waved him over. Andy was sitting next to him with his hands clasped behind his neck and his legs parted as if he owned the place.

"Hey California!" Andy said so everyone within a two-table radius could hear.

Pete felt insulted and shot him a fake smile. If they were in elementary school, he'd slug him. Strange, he thought, how growing up hinders all my impulses…too bad.

Don stuck a beer on the table and said, "Hi, Pete, take a seat." After greeting him, Pete sat down next to Andy who straightened up and glanced at the empty stage, his eyes filled with anticipation.

"You look changed, Pete. You found a clothing shop, huh?" Don asked. Don had on a flannel shirt, dark blue jeans, and a shiny pair of black cowboy boots. Pete had on jeans and a Ralph Lauren polo shirt. Pete believed Don must own five or six pairs as must Andy, who had on a new pair from earlier in the day.

Glancing quickly around the bar, Pete said, "I didn't buy a cowboy hat, at least not yet, but I did find a shop a few blocks away from your store." Then he peeked down at his clothes, wondering if he fit in with the Country-Western look. "I hope I picked out the right things." He brushed his fingers to slick back his hair.

Andy shot him a derogatory expression and a laugh. "Where'dya shop? Kmart?"

Pete felt his cheeks turn hot. "No, Murray's, on the corner of 3rd Street." He'd spent two hundred dollars there!

Don sipped his beer as an announcer walked on stage. "Murray's sells great stuff." He looked over. "You fit in just fine, Pete." Then he scowled at Andy, but Andy didn't see the cross expression. His attention was on the dark stage, obviously believing Sue Beth might be performing next.

Pete felt relieved that Don approved. "Thanks, Mr. Gibson," he said, sipping his beer. Suddenly, he heard the sounds of someone plucking strings from back stage—the notes changing from dissonant to resonance.

Don scooted in closer to the table. "Sue Beth is next!"

After the announcer introduced her, Sue Beth walked on stage and smiled to the crowd. She introduced herself, and whistling resounded in echoes, and clapping! She had her fiddle and bow in her left hand while waving to the supportive audience with her right. She was wearing a flowered dress with a row of white lace below the knees, and her hair was brown and shiny, and pulled up high in a gold flowered barrette. Pete remembered the times when she had tossed her head cutely, and coyly bushed back her bangs with her slender fingers so as to keep strands of it from falling into her smooth face.

Giving a quick nod and smile to Don and Andy, she then winked at Pete, who grinned, and then she set the fiddle between her chin and shoulder. The audience clapped; Andy whistled, and Don gesture in encouragement to her.

As Sue Beth played, the crowd clapped in time to her

music. Don said, "That's a *Sally Ann* song. There are a lot of variations on it, but I think Sue Anne has a pretty good chance of winning with this one."

Andy tapped Pete lightly on the arm. "The hard part of the song is coming up. She had a tough time with this set of notes for the longest time."

Pete kept smiling at her as she played the song in perfect sequence. She had her eyes closed in deep concentration moving the melody, in harmony with each musical note. When she began playing a detailed and complicated refrain, the crowd stopped clapping as the room echoed with each elegant tone. Her fiddle rolled gently under her chin, and the bow bobbed up and down as she gracefully completed her song. Finally done, she shot the bow away from her fiddle, dropped the fiddle down to her waist, and bowed to a standing ovation.

"*Tweeeet*," Andy whistled, "Woooow!" he cried as he bolted up and clapped until Pete felt ringing in his ears.

Pete was applauding hard. "Great job, Sue Beth!"

She took a second bow and waved. "Thank you! Thank you so much!" She walked gracefully off the stage in her shiny brown boots that came up to the bottom of her calves.

"Ain't she something'!" Don cried through watery eyes. "Just beautiful! Great!"

Pete felt her music still echoing in his ears—imprinting in his memory. No matter where he'd go after George's burial, he knew he'd always carry Sue Beth's rendition of that *Sally Ann* song with him. "She *was* great, Don!"

The announcer told the audience, "Judges will have their votes in an hour, so stick around, eat some food, and have a drink or two here at The Vapors to find out which one of our finalists will be going to Fiddler's Follies."

The crowd applauded, the lights went on, and Sue Beth walked up to them and stood next to Andy.

With a beaming smile on her face, she said, "Whew!" When she sighed, Pete felt his heart skip in his chest. "That's over! Finally!" she said, blowing out a relieving breath.

Don stood up and kissed her on the cheek. "You were

great, honey," he said. "Great! I'm so proud of ya."

Andy told her the same things, and after she sat down, he slid a glass of beer in front her.

Pete said, "That was fantastic, Sue Beth." He wanted to make sure she heard him, and he reached over and touched her hand that was still lightly trembling from her performance.

Sue Beth's cheeks blushed when he touched her, and she gave him a shy nod as she glanced down at her glass. "Thanks Andy," she said, "I'm really ready for a beer. My throat is parched!"

"Now, we have to wait for the judges," Andy said, staring at the black stage.

Country music from a jukebox was playing softly in the background, and a waitress came over to their table and took their orders for dinner.

Sue Beth sat back in her chair and said, "How's business at the store, Dad?"

Don blew out a breath of air as his back hit the chair. "Tom's gonna be out sick this whole week. I don't know what I'm gonna do." He rubbed his bearded chin and flicked off a stray hair as if motioning that he would be losing money.

Andy had shock eyes. "I gotta work at the ranch all week, Dad. A lot o' our crew are going on vacation 'cause of Easter. I can't help ya at the store."

With a worried glare beaming in her brown eyes, Sue Beth asked, "Whataya gonna do Dad?" She unfolded her napkin and set it delicately on her lap. The waitress had arrived and began serving them. "I have classes all week. Spring break was two weeks ago." Her shoulders sagged in helplessness.

Andy leaned over and told Pete: "She had to take almost a week off of school at the beginning of the semester. The flu."

As he watched sadness spread between them, Pete felt sick. He had always been a real problem-solver whenever a big sale was on the verge of collapsing, but this situation was new. "How about an employment agency?" he asked.

Don tipped his beer bottle. He seemed to be reading the label but his body language was one of frustration. "I called

Pete's Crossroad

'em. They're working on it. but like Andy said, so many people are leaving town 'cause of Easter, or staying at home with their kids who are out of school this week." He sighed, picked up his fork and poked at a potato fry on his plate. "This week's gonna be really busy…and planting season is at our doorstep."

Sue Beth glanced at Pete and her face lit up as if she had discovered treasure. "Pete, *you're* in town for the week. You could take Tom's place!"

Pete sucked in his breath. "Uh…" Everything began streaming through his mind: job hunting, his car, his things, updating his resume, the district attorney, or suddenly having to leave Amarillo to appear in court. "Well…"

Don perked up. "Sue Beth, you can't ask Pete to do that!" He had a look of embarrassment on his face. "Sorry, Pete, she just kind of says things sometimes without thinking."

Pete saw Sue Beth's eyes turn down in distinct humiliation. She had the face of a scolded child.

Wanting to save her, Pete said: "That's okay, Don. I would have thought the same way…said the same thing." He cut a chunk of his steak and took a bite. He wanted to make sure Don knew that Sue Beth's comment was no big deal, but he also didn't want to commit to working for Don. He didn't want to tell them about all of his concerns—everything that could happen to him because of emailing those pictures.

Sue Beth smiled at Pete in a show of thanks as Andy said, "Maybe I can ask around the ranch, Dad, or a few of my buddies might have a day off or two. They might be able to help ya."

Pete felt that he was standing at that crossroad Tina had spoken about. He thought of the time. This was Friday night. He was planning to leave next Friday after George's funeral. Maybe he could help out Don during the day, and at nights barricade himself in Fletch's room and dive into all the employment sites on the internet. As far as the district attorney was concerned, maybe nothing would happen. Maybe his fear of being arrested or served with court papers was unwarranted. He might be panicking and vigilant for nothing!

Putting down his fork, he said, "What would the hours be, Don?"

The three of them dropped their utensils, obviously stunned.

"I knew it!" Sue Beth said, reaching across the table and touched Pete's hand. Her eyes widened as if she had just received a great gift. But she looked that way thus far since Pete had met her. She loved life, lived each moment to the fullest, and never let obstacles defeat her. *Such a strong personality, and intelligent person, with such a delicate body*, he noticed. He kept thinking, *wow*.

Showing an imposing expression, Don said, "Ah, Pete, that's okay, I know ya got a ton o' work to do…bein' that you're looking for a job and all—"

"And *leaving* on Friday," Andy said emphatically, peering at his beer bottle.

Sue Beth said, "But that's next Friday, Andy." She folded her fingers under her chin and stuck her elbows on the table. "Come on, Pete. Convince my dad you can handle Tom's job as a store manager." She craned her neck in a coaxing gesture. "That's what you told my dad you did in Hollywood, or Santa Monica, right?"

Inhaling, Pete felt challenged, and he liked challenges. "I designed clothes at Fashion Diva in Hollywood for three years. The position was very artistically oriented." The photographs he sent to the D.A. suddenly popped into his mind, and he swallowed hard. He needed to divert the conversation away from those dreadful years. "But well, before that, I did manage a little crew and have experience as a clerk and cashier."

Sue Beth beamed with excitement. "See Dad? Pete could help design flower arrangements, or—or maybe landscapes."

Pete laughed a little. "I could try." He ate some green beans and said, "I made it through four years of college, and I'm a quick learner."

"A designer is an artist, Dad," Sue Beth said. She had the gift of seeing the possible in the impossible.

Pete felt pumped up that she seemed proud of him. "I

Pete's Crossroad

think I'm pretty good at sales," he said, trying to convince Don. "Last month I won an in-house award."

Andy straightened up tall and said, "Give my dad a resume, Pete, so he can contact your previous employers in good-ole California and check ya out."

Pete's chest tightened. He felt frozen to his seat. Pete thought, *You would have to suggest that, darn*! Andy was definitely proving to be his worst enemy.

Pete panted in relief when Don suddenly waved off that idea. "*Naaah*," Don said, "I trust ya, Pete. And the manager's job's only temporary, only for a week." His voice was light. Pete heard that the job would be easy.

Andy chimed in, "And it ends Friday, when you leave, right?"

"Andy!" Don said angrily.

Andy took a bite of his steak and began chomping. "Yeah, Pop, yeah. "But at least Pete here could give ya a resume. Most potential employees do that Dad, to make sure their hires are on the up-n-up and for record keeping."

Pete was about to say yes to the job until he remembered the faces of those enslaved women at Fashion Diva. The chunk of steak stuck in his windpipe, almost choking him. Panic set in and he coughed. What if the D.A. were to show up at Don's shop, Gibby's, to arrest him?

"What's wrong, Pete? You look like ya just spotted a ghost!" Sue Beth exclaimed.

Pete wheezed as his throat cleared, and he gulped down water. "Excuse me for a minute," he said, wiping his lips, "I have to use the rest room." He believed he rushed away from the table so fast he could have pulled off the tablecloth and left all the plates intact!

Once inside, he felt terror stricken, and he splashed cold water on his face. Staring into his reflection, he slicked back his hair with a streams of water. "Tony Stewart, huh?" he whispered to his reflection. "Well, I bet *he's* got more courage than me when it comes to fighting back." He peeked at his Rolex: 8:12 p.m. He felt so out of place at Gibby's, and Don's ranch, and The Vapors. Then again, he realized he felt out of place anywhere he'd ever been and most likely would feel out of place where ever he'd go! He splashed more water on his face. Could he really say yes to working for Don? Suddenly, he realized why he was so upset—no, terrified. Saying yes for one week might lead to saying yes for a much longer time. No…uh-uh…not Amarillo…not in the desert…never!

A man walked in, scanned him from head to toe, and reeled back a little. He said, "howdy," and then disappeared behind a stall.

Wiping off his face, Pete suddenly thought of worse things that could happen.

Now that he had emailed incriminating photos to the D.A. in Los Angeles, maybe some powerful people might be upset that he had blown the whistle on them—that he had reported and exposed their L.A. slave trafficking ring and sweat shop. Maybe someone would want to keep possibly testifying against Fashion Diva or Fossil Inc. What he had discovered could bring down billions of dollars in illegal profits. He hadn't really thought of that before. He was trying to do the right thing, like George had encouraged him to do. And Walks-With-Dreams had encouraged him to look for open doors and listen to his gut instincts. But now, all he could do was sweat, panic, and spend every minute peering over his shoulder like someone might nab him at any instant.

Danger! Looking up, he noticed that even the blaring and zapping florescent light appeared red. Maybe he would be putting Don, Andy, and Sue Beth in serious jeopardy by working at the store! He didn't know whether he should run back to the table and lay out everything that had happened to him on the previous jobs—like the references Andy seemed so desperate to get his hands on—or just wait, hoping nothing terrible will happen, until after George's burial and then leave Amarillo on Friday morning. Everything was becoming more complicated, more out of control, and harder to manage. He felt trapped under a hundred secrets.

"Hey partner, you okay?" the man asked, washing his

Pete's Crossroad

hands. He was leaning around, trying to see Pete's face.

Drying his hands, Pete bandied back, "I'm okay, thanks."

The man asked, "You work over at the D-Bar ranch or Heston's Crossing?"

Pete had no idea what he was talking about. "Neither."

The man scoffed a little and scratched his sideburn. "I thought ya looked familiar. Sorry." Then he walked out.

Pete felt a bit vindicated. He didn't believe he fit into the Country-Western atmosphere, but there was one guy who obviously believed he did! His perception was all wrong! Maybe he really *could* fit in, at least for a while. Maybe if the D.A. from Los Angeles or police were to try and hunt him down, they only had his email address and cell phone number. Surely no one would be able to locate him simply on that information alone. And he could ditch his cell phone if he had to. He ran his fingers over his smooth tan face. He had a solution to fitting in: Grow a beard, not cutting his hair, and buy clothes more Country Western clothes that would make him appear more like an Amarillo resident.

Walking back into his seat, he began noticing each passing person—their eyes, hair, their clothes, their talk. He felt light headed, on edge, almost paranoid.

"Dance with me, Pete," Sue Beth said, suddenly appearing in front of him. She had her hands behind her back and a confident glow on her face, and the gentle flirtatious twist of her body made him forget all the dangers he believed were lurking around him.

"Okay…but I can't dance like that," he said, nodding at people on the dance floor who were dancing the two-step.

"I'll teach you," she said, dragging him onto the dance floor. Quickly, they became lost in a twirling crowd.

The fiddle music sounded lively. Blue Grass. He missed her toes twice while gazing into her brown eyes. Looking at her smooth arm, he noticed a charm bracelet on her wrist. It reminded him of Sandy Walston, the strange woman he'd met on the bus. "You didn't have that on while you were playing."

Jingling the bracelet, the silver and gold charms tinkling,

she said, "I've been collecting them since my grandma gave this to me when I was three."

"Nice," he said as he twirled her around. Then he remembered the charm that Sandy had given him at the Greyhound station in Albuquerque. He had put it in his wallet! She'd like it now. Sandy had told him to give it to her anyway. Now was the perfect time. He stop in the middle of the dance floor. "I have something you can to add to your bracelet."

"What?" she asked, looking at him intensely. She was definitely using the opportunity to know him in detail.

Pulling out his wallet, he lifted out the little skate charm and put it gently into her hand. "A lady gave this to me to give to you. She met George on the bus too, and that he had grandchildren."

Her mouth dropped open in surprise, her lips glistened from a shiny balm. "Thanks, this skate charm is beautiful." She took off her bracelet and began working at the clasp to add it to the rest of her collection.

Pete laughed. The charm wasn't really beautiful, but that Sue Beth saw everything in an innocent pure light was beautiful.

"Thanks, Pete, and if you have her address, I'd like to write and thank her," she said, holding up the bracelet with the little skate charm now jingling among the others in the light.

Pete touched her shoulder as dancers around them began laughing and clapping to a light musical tune. "Sandy Walston gave me that charm after your grandpa died. She felt bad about his death, and I think she just wanted to leave something positive of herself behind, not just disappear like we all do after we meet people casually." He emphasized, *casually*, because he didn't want her to think he had romantic feelings for Sandy.

Sue Beth's face reddened, and tears welled in her eyes. Softly, she repeated, "Oh my gosh." She touched the charm as tenderly. "Thanks, Pete. I'll always treasure it, even after you're gone."

Her last words rolled through him like a deep-sounding gong. One day, he might never see Sue Beth ever again. He

Pete's Crossroad

slicked back his hair, feeling suddenly overwhelmed.

She slipped the bracelet around her dove-white wrist. "Thanks, Pete." She hugged him, re-fastening the clasp.

Watching her, Pete said, "It's important that you know that everybody on that bus took your grandpa's death hard."

"Yes," she said, wiping away her tears with her fingertips, obviously not wanting to smear her mascara.

Pete lifted her chin so he could see directly into her eyes. "There was even that Japanese tourist who took the picture."

She laughed and blushed as he pulled her a little closer. "Hideki you said."

"His whole group almost followed me here to Amarillo," he laughed, feeling her breath on his face. He was now that close to her.

"Really?" she asked softly, her brown eyes beckoning him to kiss her.

He touched her lips to his. "Really." He now felt lost, and all his fears dissipated into the arms of Sue Beth, only her.

Suddenly, he felt a tap on his shoulder that startled him, and he pushed her gently away.

"Hey, Pete," Andy interrupted. He had fire-angry eyes of a towering gargantuan.

Sue Beth gasped and stepped back. "Andy!"

Folding his arms and parting his legs in a show of strength, Andy said, "The waitress is wonderin' if y'all are done eating." He glanced at Sue Beth and then at Pete.

Pete didn't leave Sue Beth's side as they walked back to the round table. "Nope, Andy, I'm not finished eating yet." He stood as tall as he could next to Andy who kept giving him the steely eye. Again, Pete saw the words, *"I'm watching you,"* written on Andy's grimacing face.

Sue Beth tucked her dress under her thighs and sat down. "The judges haven't announced the winner yet, huh?" She cleared her voice nervously. Obviously, she had just broken an unspeakable rule, kissed Pete in public, and was hoping her father hadn't noticed, even though Andy had.

"Almost," Don replied as the stage lit up; and glancing at

Pete, he added, "I've been thinking about the job at my store, Pete." He rubbed his lips with the side of his forefinger. "I'd like to offer it to ya on a temporary basis."

"Okay," Pete said, every now-and-then peering at Sue Beth who was shyly grinning at him.

"How's $15.50 an hour sound?"

Swallowing after eating a French fry, Pete realized that if he'd say yes, he'd be staying for sure for the rest of the week— no sudden escape out of town. "I can start tomorrow, Don." He shook his hand, sealing the deal.

Sue Beth said a snappy, "Great!"

Andy tapped Pete on the shoulder to where it hurt. "I'd like a word with ya, Pete. Over there." He jerked his head toward the bar, motioning for Pete to following him. "Excuse us you two," he said to his dad and Sue Beth. He had his cowboy hat low—perched to where it set at the edge of his hairline. When Andy walked in his cowboy boots, his steps thundered, like the heavy-leaded soles of a police officer. It was impossible to see his eyes.

Sue Beth stood up, obviously to intervene, but Andy motioned for her to stay seated as Don began shaking hands with several people who had walked up to him, congratulating him and Sue Beth. Don was oblivious to Andy's anger and irritation.

Pete sat down at a barstool, and Andy leaned on the counter as he ordered a beer. He thought about just walking out of The Vapors and driving back to Don's ranch, but then he spotted George! George sitting at the other side of the bar, and glowing. He was motioning for Pete to stay put. Peeking at his Rolex and feeling uneasy, Pete noticed the time: 8:43 p.m. "Andy, I have things to do and I don't have time—"

Andy place a beer on the bar in front of him with a thud. "Whatchya doin', Pete?" It wasn't really a question, but a warning with dagger eyes.

Pete glanced at the female bartender who backed off. "What do you mean, Andy?" he asked, taking a sip of beer, toying with the band on his Rolex.

Pete's Crossroad

"My sister, dude," he replied. "I saw what happened out there on the dance floor…and I gotta say, Pete, I don't like it." His lips puckered, his mustache twitched, and his knuckles looked red like he had just finished punching something.

Pete glanced back at Sue Beth who was smiling at him as if she had just had a first date. One of Don's female friends hugged her, and she put her arms around the woman's neck like a child would embrace a mother. It was Sue Beth's kindness and care for others that he was seeing now. Not many people have that quality, he thought.

"I like Sue Beth," Pete said, sipping his beer.

Andy exhaled so loudly that half the patrons at the bar left. "She's my sister…my sister!" He pointed at Pete's chest.

"Well…" Pete believed he was peering down the barrel of a gun.

"And you're leaving next Friday," Andy said, his expression a pronouncement of a deadline.

Pete knew where the conversation was headed. Andy had a point. "I see," he said, "I understand." Peering into their reflection in the mirror behind bottles of liquor, Pete realized he had two options, and Andy was making him choose: Stay in Amarillo or leave. His real message was obvious: Don't hurt my sister, or else!

Andy tapped the brown shiny counter with his knuckles. "Leave her alone, Pete." He leaned down by his ear and whispered, "If you hurt my sister…I got friends." He dragged that word out into five seconds.

"I don't intend to hurt *your sister*," Pete countered, punching out each word. Turning his beer bottle on the counter, he wasn't sure yet what he wanted to do or where he wanted to go. And since emailing those pictures to the D.A., he really had no clue what might happen. Everything was in chaos, one giant mess. He was beginning to have feelings for Sue Beth, but enough "feelings" to make him want to stay…to make him want to spend the rest of his life with one woman, and in Amarillo? Uh-uh, not yet! He remembered the words of a woman he dated eight months ago when he worked at

J.P. Osterman

Fashion Diva: "You're commitment-phobic!" she screamed at him, and then broke up with him in public at a club.

As the Master of Ceremonies ran on stage to announce the winners of the contest, Andy tapped Pete's shoulder hard. "Do we have an understanding, Cal-i-forn-ia?" The loud question incited two more people to bolt from their barstools.

Wanting to charge him and fight, Pete breathed, the beer souring on his tongue. Gripping the edge of his barstool, he felt his eyes sting. He couldn't hit him. That would make things worse. "Sure, I understand you, Andy." Andy walked back to his seat, but Pete didn't leave.

The announcer was on stage and suddenly proclaimed, "And second place goes to…Sue Beth Gibson for her rendition of *Sally Ann*!"

Sue Beth jumped out of her seat, and the crowd applauded. Running up the stairs and on-stage, she reached the microphone, stopped, and stared at the audience with a look of gratitude and grace. "Thank y'all so much!" She had tears in her eyes. "Thank you, Dad and Andy! I love you!" The Master of Ceremonies gave her a trophy with a gilded fiddle at the center. "This is for my brother Fletch. You all remember him, I'm up here and won this for him!" She kissed it and held it into the air as the audience clapped ever harder than before. Others knew Fletch quite well, and obviously were missing him.

From the back of the bar, Pete saw Sue Beth glancing around. She was looking for him. After seconds, her shoulders hunched in disappointed, but he didn't want to be at The Vapors anymore. He began walking toward the side door.

Just as he was about to hit the doors leading out into the parking lot, he paused. He inhaled a deep breath of humid air while gazing into the busy blackness of the desert moonlight that was making him want to leave while at the same time pushing him back to the bar. "God!" he muttered at a sliver of a moon, kicking the threshold. "God!" He turned back, walked to his chair, sat down, smiled, and said, "Hey, sorry I was away so long, but I had a call." When he met Andy's gaze, he fixed on it and folded his arms in determination. He believed they were almost in a gun slinging position! All someone needed to call out was, "Draw!" He felt a little changed. He didn't leave, but did as George had told him, and he felt a bit relieved at the consequence!

Still on stage and in a line with the other contestants, Sue Beth ran to microphone, and said, "Oh, I forgot one thing, I'd like to dedicate this prize to my grandfather." She held her ribbon and little trophy of a fiddle in front of her. The crowd stopped clapping. The bar turned quiet. "I never knew my grandfather, *ahem*." She was sounding as if she was swallowing her words. "He died a few days ago."

His face low as if he were experiencing shame, Don was staring into his beer. Andy was squinting at her as if trying to discern her next move.

"But we had a total stranger walk into our lives," she continued in a solemn tone, "a stranger who brought my family comfort and caring." When she nodded and smiled at Pete, he believed she was the only one in the world who gave a darn about him. "Thanks, Pete Turner."

He felt embarrassed when people began clapping for him. Blushing, he waved at Sue Beth as she walked off the stage and back to their table. Don and Andy stood and kissed her on the cheek as Pete cut a slice of his steak and began eating again. This time, it tasted good…so good he could eat two! He was also trying to forget the threatening conversation with Andy, who now-and-then shot him a grimacing smirk. He noticed Sue Beth jostle her charm bracelet, treating it with gentle respect. "What time do you open your shop tomorrow, Don?"

Yawning and checking the time, he replied, "7:30 a.m. on Saturdays."

Sue Beth's face radiated happiness. "And you're closed this Sunday, Dad. Thank God for Easter!" She had a Coca Cola in her hand, delicately sipping it through a straw.

Eating the last bite of his steak, Pete said, "What time do you leave for your store, Don?"

"Set your alarm for 6:30, and I'll take ya to breakfast

before we open the store," he replied.

Staring at her prize with eyes that captured all her hard work and long hours, Sue Beth said, "This is so exciting." She grabbed her father's arm, put her cheek on his flannel shirt, and said, "I'm going to Fiddler's Follies this year!"

Pete thought of the date: April 22, 2011. The days were gliding by so quickly! Last week, he was at Fossil, believing he'd be working for the company for a long time. Last year he was at Fashion Diva, a designer and store manager. Four years before that, he graduated college. Next year? Where would he be? When he turned to see who had slid into the empty seat next to him, he saw a halo of George. George had to have been sitting among them for the entire evening! George had to have seen Sue Beth perform, and win.

He glanced at his Rolex: 9:33 p.m. As he shifted in his seat, he felt pinching in the backs of his thighs. He wasn't used to blue jeans. He wasn't used to Country Western music or ways of living. Could he get used to them? He gave a fleeting glance at the red-headed bartender and The Vapors wall decorations. He smelled the A-1 sauce lingering in the dregs of beef and potato on his plate. He rubbed the soles of his shoes into the sawdust beneath his feet. Time was happening in precious seconds, the way George and Walks-With-Dreams had said. Life! He saw Sue Beth laughing, beaming, full of giggles, and talking up an enthusiastic storm of words. She was so positive and able to draw a crowd just with her presence. He wondered where he'd be on April 22, 2012 at 9:33 p.m.

Pete's Crossroad

Chapter 15 - Attack

Pete punched the alarm on his iPhone off, yawned, rubbed his eyes that stung through a layer of grit from an allergy, and ran his fingers through his hair that felt scruffy but was definitely getting longer since his last haircut. Looking outside into the dawn, he could see a long, thick, black, tentacle-of-a-branch of the Texas oak tree moving in the wind like an old man walking. It was overcast everywhere out there in the Texas panhandle—the clouds low, gray, and bellowing up high in the atmosphere. A downpour could open up at any moment. Unhinging the window, he lifted it, inhaled crisp air, heard the loud squawking of Texas grackles, and smelled coffee wafting from the kitchen.

He had his laptop open and pushed the Start key to fire it up while he dressed for his first day at Gibby's, Don's home and garden shop. While shaving, he heard George's voice, and he peeked around the corner, noticing George inquisitively sizing up the room again.

George said, "You're gonna be a farmer today, huh, Pete?" He had a prideful expression on his face. "I knew I taught ya a little about agriculture on the bus."

Pete laughed and said, "I haven't a clue what I'll be doing, George." He began brushing his teeth, making sure he always had one eye yellow-glowing George.

"Ya considering stayin' on and workin' for my son?" George asked. He was sitting on the bed, his transparent hands propping up his body.

"Ah!" Pete cried, nicking himself a bit, the mirror steaming up. "George, you look like the weirdest cartoon character I've ever seen!" He had on blue jean overalls with a white linen shirt, dressed for working at Gibby's too! "Whataya trying to do…shock me into staying in Amarillo?" Pete stuck his finger in the cut and then glanced at the blood. "What do you want now, George?" he asked, tapping the razor on the side on the sink.

"Nice duds, Pete," George said, bouncing on the balls of his feet as he perused Pete's choice of clothing.

"Thanks," Pete said, glancing down at his outfit. "I hope this is okay for working there." He noticed George's round belly jiggle a little as if George were a living Santa Claus. Pete remembered the way George looked when he was alive. "You seem like you can move around better as a ghost. When you were living—" *Ahem*, he coughed. He knew he was talking about something that could potentially make George mad or sad. He watched for signs of sudden change in George's reactions because he might have to change the topic of conversation fast. He didn't want a ghost mad at him or retaliating against him! He threw the towel on the rack. "When I met you, George, you had trouble bending your arms. And you could barely stir your coffee." He touched his elbow. "Gosh, you were in such pain. Now you're moving around so much easier."

"That's right!" George smiled, showed Pete his muscles, jumped up and down, and then turned around as if he had the athletic abilities of a teenager.

"Great!" Pete said. "I guess the afterlife is being good to you…you know, like relieving you of all your ailments."

Turning suddenly serious, George said, "But I'm not in Heaven yet, Pete." He made a 360° turn and threw up his hands in frustration. "I'm like that ghost in *It's a Wonderful Life*, waiting to see where I'll land in the afterlife."

Holding his stomach, Pete said, "Gosh, that would make me sick all the time if I have to wonder all the time where I'm going when I die!" He plopped down on the chair in front of his laptop but still kept his eyes on George's aqua-clear eyes. "Still, I'm beginning to get used to you, George." He was also hoping that after George's burial on Thursday, George would disappear and finally find Heaven, at least that's what Walks-With-Dreams and Hideki had told him.

Pete unplugged his iPhone and stuck it into his pocket. "I'm working for Don only until next Thursday or Friday, George." He had to be insistent, and he tossed another towel into the bathroom that landed on the tub. "Then that's it." He picked up his jacket and brushed his hair. "I have to get a real job somewhere."

George was right next to him now.

When Pete felt his cold wind-of-a-touch brush up against his arm, he jumped back, startled.

George said, "Right, Pete."

"Hey," Pete said, "all the scary things you're doing to me, George are aging me ten years! Whataya mean, *right?*"

"Model homes, Pete," George said. "A model home's gonna save ya today."

Pete knew that meant trouble. "What do *you* know that I don't know, George, huh? What's going to happen to me?" He stepped sideways and entering George's white halo.

George shook his head and gave him an *I don't know* shrug. "I'm just tellin' ya what I was told to tell ya, that's all."

Pete knew he didn't have money for a house! "You talk as if I'm going to be buying a home ...or that I'm going to go house hunting." He stared into George's happy eyes. They looked bright and alive, but he knew George's body was somewhere between Albuquerque and Amarillo. Again George shrugged, and Pete shifted his feet, pointed at George's transparent glowing body, and said, "What's all this model home stuff about? Out with it!" he asked, again.

Folding his arms, George appeared insistent. "Just think

model homes." He lifted his arms high and looked at the ceiling. "Those are the orders." Then he ascended and disappeared.

Pete began pacing the floor. George seemed to be telling him that he might die today if he didn't follow his instructions. "Was that model home business a message from God?" he asked, stopping, and glancing toward Heaven. Knowing that Don was about to knock on the breezeway door any minute, he quickly combed his hair and then picked up his jacket. "This really has to mean something bad is going to happen," Pete said to himself. "But what?"

He noticed the email icon on his laptop suddenly light up. He had a message! It was outlined in red, which meant it had a special secure connection. When he opened the email, he felt his heart race as he read the subject line: Office of the District Attorney, Los Angeles.

His mouth dried. He swallowed so hard he thought his tonsils disappeared! Scrolling down, he read the letter:

Mr. Turner:

We have received your photographs and agents from many government offices have been undercover investigating criminal activity in the garment district. We have turned the case over to the FBI based in Los Angeles. An agent should be contacting you today, along with local law enforcement: April 23, 2011. Please expect phone calls from Agent Sidney Armon and Agent Leslie Boseby. The FBI will be offering you special protection to secure your testimony.

Sincerely,

Pierce Halston, A. D. A., Los Angeles.

After quickly jotting down the agents' names, Pete slapped down the lid. Special protection? To secure my testimony? What the heck does *this* mean?

Hunt-and-chase scenes from a *Mission Impossible* movie came to mind. He wondered: If the wrong people—criminals—knew that I could put them in prison, could they come after me? Kill me?! Shoving his chair under the desk, he felt adrenaline shoot through his veins, and he jerked the curtains closed and yanked out the plug to his laptop.

Pete's Crossroad

Don knocked at the door: "Pete? Ya ready?"

"Sure!" he replied, half-terrified, winding up the electrical cord and thrusting his flash drive into his pocket. "I'll be out in a minute, Don," he called, shivering.

Don's breathing was audible through the crack in the door. "I placed an order with Stan's Drive-In. They'll have our breakfast waiting for us when we get there."

"Another minute, Don," he said, making sure his iPhone had the maximum bars. Now that the D.A. had contacted him, he couldn't afford to be without it.

"You okay, Pete?" Don asked.

He chuckled a bit. "Yeah, I'm okay. I had to check email, that's all."

Don didn't seem to believe him because there was a long pause, until he finally said: "Okay, but we're runnin' outta time, Pete. We gotta get to Gibby's. Andy and Sue Beth are gonna meet us at Stan's for breakfast too."

"Great!" Pete snapped.

He could hear Don's footsteps retreating through the breezeway leading into the house. When everything grew quiet, he sighed in relief.

Still, he wondered what to do next. The laptop still had the photos on it, and the district attorney wrote, "special protection." Could someone other than those FBI agents come after him? *Nah*, he thought. No one knows my cell phone number or address other than the district attorney. I'm just being paranoid. He slipped his laptop into his briefcase and held it next to him if it contained gold in a Brink's truck. He followed Don in his own car to the restaurant.

Fifteen minutes later, at Stan's Drive-In, Andy and Sue Beth showed up. Sue Beth slipped into the booth beside her father while Andy sat next to Pete. Stan's Drive-In was right out of the 1950s. There were red-swivel bar stools lined up under a long white counter, speckled-scoffed linoleum, and little jukeboxes mounted on tables under a long window that stretched out the entire length of the restaurant. Don told Pete that Stan still owned the place.

J.P. Osterman

Greeting Andy and Sue Beth, Pete shoved his briefcase up against the booth and kept glancing at people in the diner. Feeling suspicious and vulnerable, he asked Andy, "I guess you know most people in here, huh?"

Andy appeared confused. "Of course!" He gestured at two old men sipping coffee at the counter. "Trent and Hunter over there are my dad's neighbors." He waved at their elderly waitress, and she waved back after grabbing a coffee carafe.

"Oh, good," Pete said, gobbling down a fork full of scrambled eggs.

Don's coffee cup clanked on its saucer. "You really seem on edge this mornin', Pete. Is something wrong?"

"No, nothing," he replied quickly and curtly.

Sue Beth gave Pete a sad glance as she looked at her toast. "You didn't even say hi to me, Pete" she said, and then she peeked at her watch as if avoiding rejection but anticipating it. "I have a group project for school, so I have to leave right away after I eat breakfast."

"Sorry…I didn't mean to ignore you, I just have things on my mind, that's all," he said, eating fast.

The man at the far end of the counter, another of Don's neighbors who looked like the elderly Fess Parker from the old *Daniel Boone and Davey Crocket* TV series said, "Hey, Don, my German shepherd was barkin' up a storm last night." He poured cream into his coffee.

Don quickly twisted around and faced him. "Oh yeah, Greg?"

"Yeah!" Greg snapped back, the deep wrinkles above his cheeks and on his brow creasing in complete bafflement. "Old Bailey nearly broke off his chain wantin' to make a mad run to your place. He was like, rabid! Somethin' really ticked him off at your place." The man grimaced. "Any trouble up at your ranch? I haven't heard o' any break-ins in the neighborhood."

After introducing Pete to Greg, Don said: " Nope, and I didn't hear anything unusual. I can't imagine why Bailey acted crazy like that, but thanks, I'll keep a look out for trespassers on my property." Then Don went back to eating his toast.

Pete's Crossroad

Inhaling the kitchen smells, Pete felt suddenly claustrophobic as he drank his orange juice. Something was wrong. A dog barking wildly at Don's place wasn't normal. He glanced outside into the sunlight. Bright rays were hitting the morning clouds, turning them into gold medallions. Cars were turning out of a HEB parking lot across the street. Nothing looked out of place there. A couple of teenagers were walking out of a McDonald's, and an elderly couple had just entered a Walgreen's. Nothing seemed unnatural, and he couldn't spot anybody who looked as if they were concealing a gun, so he kept drumming into himself: *Cut it out. Stop being so gosh darn paranoid!*

Suddenly, Don's cell phone rang and he lifted it out of his blue denim jacket. His eyes shone surprise behind his rimless as he said, "Fletch!"

"Oh my gosh, Fletch!" Sue Beth exclaimed, scooting close to him and peeking at the cell phone screen as Andy slapped his palms on the table in excitement.

Pushing away his plate, Don talked while staring out the window. "Where are ya, son?"

"Where's he at?" Sue Beth whispered, her ear close to the phone.

"Is he okay?" Andy asked, leaning across the table.

Don kept nodding as he whispered, "He's in Afghanistan." He repeated, "Uh-huh," and said to Sue Beth, "He's waiting to catch a hop from a military base over there."

"And? And" Sue Beth asked. She finally craned her neck and said: "Hi, Fletch! I love you!"

Don smiled at her askance and said, "He loves y'all too."

Andy motioned for his dad to give him the cell phone. "Hey bud, it's been a long time. I miss ya."

There was a pause as Pete could here bits and pieces of conversation. He felt like an outsider as Andy said, "We can't wait to see ya, Fletch. I'll pick ya up. Just call when ya arrive."

Andy handed the phone back to his dad who was busy wiping tears out of his eyes. Quickly Don turned away as if embarrassed to have people see him crying. Flushed, Don coughed and said, "I'm sorry, Fletch." His panted out breaths. "I know we…I didn't part with ya on good terms. I'm sorry. Will ya forgive an old stubborn fart like me?" He had a pained expression on his face as he rubbed his cheek, and then his forehead, and finally his red eyes. "Thank ya, son…un-huh…love ya too, Fletch."

Whatever the argument that had occurred between them over the past three years was being resolved and put to rest.

Don said, "So maybe we'll be seein' ya soon, huh, son?" Don held up his forefinger to Sue Beth, gesturing that he'd give her the phone in a minute. He said, "Yeah, we've been watching clips of the war on TV." He put his hand over his chest in a show of terror. "You just take care of yourself, ya hear, Fletch? Bring yourself home safe and sound…ya hear?" Then he drew his napkin to his red and watery eyes as he told Fletch about the death of his grandfather. "We'll be burying him next Thursday, or the latest on Friday. I'll call the Red Cross when I have all the details. They told me they'll get my messages through to ya."

Sue Beth said to Pete before she took hold of the phone, "Every night when we watch the news, we see the names and faces of dead soldiers who die in that war." She began crying. "We pray to God we never see Fletch's name on the screen. It's a terrible way to become famous."

"I love ya, son," Don said, his eyes meeting dim rays of morning sunlight beaming in through the blinds. "We all love ya here at home."

As they continued to talk and exchange the cell phone several times, Pete watched them and remembered George. George had tried to make the jaunt from Los Angeles to Albuquerque so he could make amends to everyone sitting around Pete right now. Pete thought of the irony. He was there, instead of George, communicating with George's loved ones. George would have gone to any length to sit where he was sitting right now and to tell Don he was sorry. At least Don could make peace with Fletch in a different better way. Don's time on Earth wasn't over, as was George's. Don was

Pete's Crossroad

preventing a terrible progressive intergenerational catastrophe by killing his grudge right now.

After hanging up with Fletch, Pete told them, "At least all of you are making up now…and not waiting until—"

"Until after one of us dies," Don said somberly. "I'm just hopin' eveything'll go find when I see Fletch face-to-face."

Through the excitement, Sue Beth asked, "Pete, so do you ever plan on searching for *your* father?"

Pete wondered what made her bring that up all of a sudden as he watched Don wipe his eyes and Andy begin to stare at him with a curious expression on his face. Pete replied, "I don't know." Before he would have snapped back at someone prying into his business and walked away for good. But after having observed Don's cathartic emotions, he began to speculate that maybe making peace with his own family might change him in a positive way. As the waitress picked up his empty plate, he said, "Maybe I'll try to locate my dad, mom, and sister when I find a job somewhere, and settle down."

Giving a slight nod of encouragement, Sue Beth said, "That's great, Pete!"

Andy said, "Yeah…I wish you the best." He still had that look in his eye that signaled he wanted Pete out of town, fast.

Standing up from his seat at the counter, Greg, Don's neighbor, picked up his hat, walked up to their booth and pointed out the window. "Hey, Don, there are people lookin' around your car. You know 'em? They aren't dressed like any of us around here!"

Everyone turned to peer outside. Two men had writing pads open, inspecting all the cars, quickly homing in on Don's truck, as if they were checking license numbers. They had on black, oilskin duster coats with their collars pulled up around their throats, black boots, and thick sunglasses. Pete remembered characters from *The Matrix*. Those people poking around Don's car resembled those suited characters. He sucked in his breath, pulled his laptop off the floor, and plopped it on his lap.

"They're not from around here," Greg said. "You

recognize 'em?'"

"Nope," Don, Sue Beth, and Andy said simultaneously.

Suddenly, the wind whipped back the front flap of one of the men's long coats and a reflective flash flickered off his gun.

"What the heck is that?!" Don said, standing up.

Sue Beth inhaled shots of panic as she let him out of the booth. "They have guns, Dad, don't go out there!"

"They look dressed to kill!" Andy cried.

"Wait!" Pete ordered, holding up his hand. He didn't want any of them marching out of the restaurant and possibly getting shot. Squinting, he tried to get a better look. "Could they be FBI agents or the police?"

Sue Beth stammered, "I— I don't know…but they didn't look like FBI, or CIA, or police officers of any kind, Pete…that is unless law enforcement's changed their dress code to allow employees to wear trench coats."

Andy said, "From their haircuts, and from what I can see of their faces, they look oriental."

Pete gasped. Maybe the two men were searching for him! Maybe they had followed them from Don's place to Stan's!

Don paused like a startled victim about to be robbed. "What's wrong, Pete?"

Greg bent low toward the windowsill and said, "By God! Now they're lookin' at *that* car."

Pete had rented a silver Honda Accord.

"That's the car *you're* driving, Pete," Andy said.

"Yeah, it is," Pete said, watching the oriental men walking around his rental car.

"I've seen men like that on martial arts movies," Greg said, his nose lifting as he studied them. He called to the cook behind a heat lamp in the kitchen: "Lester, call the sheriff!" Fear stricken, he said to Don, "Those men look mighty dangerous. We need the sheriff, now."

Don ordered the waitress: "Get Stan and his sons on the phone! Then scat!" She raced toward the back of the restaurant.

"Get outta my way, Pete," Andy ordered, shoving Pete

out of the booth. "Something's really wrong here!" He pushed up his sleeves as if preparing for a good fight. "I'll show 'em if they try pulling something with us."

Don pressed his glasses up his nose. "Now Andy, we don't know for sure—"

"Nobody messes with us here in Texas!" Andy said, slapping on his cowboy hat. "I'll show 'em—"

"Just stop!" Pete exclaimed.

They began searching him with shocked eyes and bated breaths. Pete had to tell them the truth. "Stop everything!" he ordered, watching the oriental men glance from his car to the restaurant. He ducked. "Can people see inside here?"

Through a terrified expression, Sue Beth said, "Pete, what's going on?"

The oriental, trench-coated men donned their mirrored sunglasses, pulled up their black gloves, and began walking powerfully towards the door.

Andy walked to her side and stood eye-to-eye with Pete. "You better let us in on what's happening, Mr. Cal-e-fornia!" He tapped Pete's chest. "Now!"

The oriental men were halfway to the diner.

Watching their steps, Don told Greg and his other neighbors Trent and Hunter: "Can you guys stall 'em at the door?"

"Sure Don," they replied, and they dashed to the glass entryway. "I'll tell 'em how Amarillo's a friendly town, Greg began, "'cause I'm on the Welcome Wagon committee."

Now the two oriental men were so close to the door that Pete could hear their steps. They paused there and huddled, obviously discussing their next plan. Pulling his briefcase to his waist, he glanced from Andy to Sue Beth and to Don, and quickly stammered out a very short version his story, ending it with, "I have pictures in here that prove there's a big slave trafficking ring in L.A."

"Gosh!" Sue Beth said, putting her fingers to her lips. "Those men are after *you* then?!"

Andy had a bewildering expression on his face. "Human

trafficking? As in smugglers bringing boys and girls into this country by promising 'em a better life but then selling 'em? Damn! Disgusting!" He was madder than ever!

"Yes," Pete said, noticing an exit beyond the restroom. "I worked in the garment district in L.A., remember? It turns out the company I worked for owned and operated a sweatshop. And what else, I don't know. Maybe much more terrible things were going on there as well," he shivered.

"So those men could be after you...trying to find and destroy evidence," Don said, taking out his keys to his truck.

"How about trying to kill him!" Sue Beth said, peeking under the table as if trying to decide whether to run or hide.

Don stopped, his senses suddenly sharpening. "I don't hear the sheriff's siren yet," he said, "but we better get moving." The four of them were now concealed behind a decorative partition toward the back of the diner, the area where waitresses brew coffee, when the oriental men walked in with powerful struts. After Greg, Trent, and Hunter welcomed them, Pete could hear broken English responses. All the other employees had run away.

They watched as Don's neighbors continued to make chitchat with the men who were peering around the restaurant, obviously searching for Pete. The two steely strangers had their arms at their sides—their hands pressing into their trench coats—as if they were outlaws ready to draw guns. They were maintaining icy, face-to-face contact with Don's neighbors.

Seeming more frightened for Pete's safety than for her own, Sue Beth grabbed Pete's arm, and Pete took her hand. The back door was yards away down a short corridor. "You have information that can put criminals in jail then, Pete?"

The oriental men had stepped outside. Mostly likely Don's neighbors managed to convince them that Pete was no longer there after eating breakfast but had left his cars in Stan's parking lot.

"That's right," he answered, patting his briefcase. "I sent them all to the District Attorney yesterday."

"Aren't the police supposed to be contacting you?" Andy

asked. The cook had crawled over to them under a few tables and handed Andy a shotgun. "I thought you had gone...go!" Andy whispered to him. Then the cook gave him a thumbs-up signal and belly scampered back to the kitchen.

"That's what I read this morning when I opened up my email," Pete said. "The district attorney told me FBI agents and marshals would contact me to take my statement."

Don swiped his fingers through his gray hair as Andy cocked the shotgun. The oriental men had heard that! They slugged Greg in the stomach and punched Don's other neighbors in the face. The three old men took off running as the oriental men began running back to the restaurant, whipping open their jackets, and reaching for their handguns.

Don grabbed Sue Beth and ordered, "Get out the back door now and wait!"

Seeing the men rotate the cylinders of their handguns, priming them for action, Sue Beth ran to the exit door and gently opened it. By now, the men were again at the front entryway, but the door was locked.

"Greg musta locked it up 'cause Stan gave him a key to help him out sometimes," Don said, breathing in relief at their small break.

"Yeah, but it won't be long before they blast their way inside!" Pete said.

Andy ducked down low and aimed the shotgun at the men as Don pulled Pete under a table.

"Get ready to move out," Andy said, still low behind a booth. He threw several cups at the entrance. "There's a side door to a meeting room over there. They might leave the main entrance and try that one," he whispered. "Dad, when I fire, you get to the truck, pull it around back, and wait for me. We need to head straight to the sheriff's office."

Pete peeked over the booth to get a better view of the attackers. They had taken Andy's bait and were slinking around the other side of the diner. "I think Sue Beth's getting the car. She had out the keys."

"No!" Andy said, peeking up, trying to see her so he

J.P. Osterman

could deter the men somehow if need be.

Don gasped and said, "What's takin' the sheriff so long?" He glanced at his watch. "They should be here by now!"

Pete sulked. "Maybe these are powerful people I'm dealing with, who can hack into phones or interfere with emergency communications...or maybe they intercepted the call, or have someone here in Amarillo working for them."

"Maybe that's how they tracked you to Amarillo," Don added, "through your call, or email."

Pete turned back, and when he saw Sue Beth standing in the open doorway, he said, "Maybe someone at the D.A.'s office in L.A. leaked my location. I don't know."

"Damn!" Andy yelled.

Two loud shots rang out at the front door. Don pulled Pete under a booth. Pete could hear them cock their guns again, ready to fire.

"Stop!" Andy shouted, aiming at them.

One man aimed at Andy, but Andy shot him in the chest, the power hurling him against the cash register in a banging explosive collision. Coins rippled across the floor, and an echo of a groan.

"Give up!" Andy shouted as the other man ducked behind a booth. Andy's arm slipped on a splash of coffee on the table, his quick aim faltering, as the other attacker shot his gun, missed Andy, and hit the wall behind Pete.

"Come on!" Sue Beth called from a crack in the door.

"Get back!" Andy ordered, again firing. This time, the blast blew apart a booth. Glass shattered, cotton stuffing flew, and wooden splinters pierced the dusty air.

A pinging sound vibrating in his ears after hearing yet another powerful shotgun blast cracking out another shot, Pete saw the tabletop heave. "The guy's trapped, and trying to push the granite slab off of him!"

Don ran up to the mess scattered along the linoleum, but Andy called: "Dad! Get back!"

"Grab his gun, quick! " Don cried.

Running behind Don, Andy and Pete pried the granite

Pete's Crossroad

tabletop off the oriental man. Don found the gun and held it cocked in the man's face. Finally, a crowd had gathered outside as siren sounds blared in the parking lot, but they weren't at all approaching the restaurant!

Almost Breathless, Don asked: "Who are you and who sent you?"

The oriental man's glasses were still on his eyes, and blood was running down his forehead and cheeks as Andy yanked off the glasses to get a good look at him. He was young and muscular.

"This guy looks trained to do this kind of stuff…hunt down people," Pete said.

"Yah!" The man said in an broken English accent, his eyes wide and intensely focused on Pete. He couldn't even say the word "you". He obviously was new to America. "Yah are a dead mahn." He exhaled, his breath labored as he coughed, and blood oozed out of his mouth.

"Dead?" Pete gasped, glancing out a broken window. A florescent light fixture fell onto a pastry holder and plumes of dust beat the air.

"More come…now…kill you, now!" the dying man said, and then his body sighed in lifeless perusal with the floor.

"He's dead," Don moaned, standing up. He grabbed his thighs and panted as he heaved in mouthfuls of air.

Pete knelt down by the body, inspecting the dead man's graying cheeks. "We better gather as much info as we can about these guys," he said, and then he gestured at the parking lot. "I see squad car lights reflecting off the clouds they're so close. The cops will never let us near any of this evidence once they get inside."

Andy stood like a barrier between them and a piece of glass that shattered onto a booth. Ducking, he cried, "More of these types of guys will be coming after you, Pete. You heard this one tell ya that." They all glanced at the two dead oriental men, their bodies covered with rubble. Pete remained with one of them while Andy tiptoed over broken glass to the other corpse, the soles of his cowboy boots crackling and crunching on silverware, broken plates, and pieces of plastic glasses.

Closing the man's eyes and then noticing colors beneath his t-shirt, Pete said, "Yeah, I know. I'm trying to figure out who they are."

The shot-gunned air still smelling sharp and pungent, Andy said solemnly, "I think it's best for you to be gettin' back to California now, Pete." After uncovering the man he shot who lay buried under a blanket of dry wall, Andy patted down his leather jacket. "God, this is awful!" he grimaced. Standing, he bent over as if he might vomit.

"Take it easy, son," Don said as Andy regained his composure. "Any ID on him?" Don then turned around and ordered, "Pete, reach into that guy's jacket and see if you can find something." His eyes widened. "Oh, and make sure whatever ya touch, ya put back the way ya find it. I don't wanna be accused of evidence tampering. No Sir!"

"Right, Don," Pete said. Tapping the dead man's pant pocket, Pete extracted a wallet and opened it. "I can't read this. It's all in Japanese...or Chinese...I don't know."

"I found a passport," Andy said, opening up a glossy brown folder and drawing it close to his eyes. "Robert Smith. Toledo, Ohio." Tossing the ID on the dead man's body, he straightened up tall and shook his head in alarm. "That guy doesn't look like he's from Ohio."

"He has a lot of people who helped him get this far then!" Don exclaimed.

Pete noticed the colorful tattoo on the man's neck and said, "You ever see anything like this?" He took out his iPhone and snapped a picture of the tattoo as Andy crunched his way back through a trail of glass

Kneeling down to get a better look, Andy traced a triangular blue-ink line that framed a head of a snake. "This guy's definitely a member of some kind of secret society or gang. Do you see a tattoo on that guy, Dad?"

Pulling down the other dead man's collar and lifting up his black t-shirt, Don peeked at his chest and said, "Tattoos are all over this guy's body." Anxiety seemed to spread over

Pete's Crossroad

Don's shaking hands. "My hunch is that you're right. These guys belong to a sophisticated gang...and probably have cutting-edge technology that can wirelessly tap into computers, cell phones and telephones." He stood tall, gave out a fretful sigh at Pete's briefcase, and breathed as his entire body lifted and his shoulders sagged—his way of demonstrating that Pete's life, and maybe all their lives, might be in terrible danger. "Snap a picture of this tattoo, Pete," he said, "maybe Sue Beth can look it up on the internet...see what we're dealing with."

Pete felt the pain of an unbearable headache. Pressing his palms to his forehead, he said, "I can't believe this is happening." A small 2-by-4 crashed down from the ceiling, generating a large burst of dust as it hit the floor. He coughed, fanning the particles out of his face.

Finally, the sheriff thundered into the restaurant with his gun pointing in all directions. "Everyone! Stay put!"

J.P. Osterman

Chapter 16 - Trackers

The sheriff stopped targeting objects and put down his gun when he spotted Don and Andy. "Where's Sue Beth?"

Opening the door, she dashed inside yelling, "Dad! Andy!" She raced to Don who grabbed and hugged her. She had kept all the people outside away from the restaurant and directed the sheriff inside. Then she asked Pete, "You okay?"

Blaming himself a bit for the attack but feeling glad they had all survived it, he exhaled in relieved and replied, "Yeah."

She pointed at the alley. "I drove the truck to the back. The engine's idling." She gasped when she spotted the two dead men. One was still bleeding out from the chest wound.

"I think ya better go and turn off the truck," Don said, looking around for a clean booth. "We haveta tell Clay here what happened." Then he said to Pete, "He's Sheriff Clay, but everyone just calls him Clay."

After wading through glass and dry wall, Clay ordered: "Don't touch a thing. It's evidence. We don't want any contamination." He pointed firmly to booths, gesturing for everyone to sit down.

Before Sue Beth left, Pete stopped her. He felt responsible that he had put her in danger, and he wanted to

Pete's Crossroad

make her feel better. "I'm so sorry," he said, holding her, comforting her. Watching Clay peer down at the bodies, he never believed he could ever be involved in a real live shootout. He felt dizzy, the room appearing to spin on an axis. His mouth tasted sour and dry.

"It's okay, Pete," she said. She had a little smile on her face and brushed back a wisp of a bang. "This wasn't your fault. You did the right thing, but unfortunately, the right thing is back firing on you right now. Soon though, I'm sure Clay will straighten it all out, let's hope." She peered at a sparkling jukebox, a light bulb zapping and then popping. After patting his arm, she left for the truck as more sheriffs rushed out of their squad cars, drew their guns, and charged the restaurant.

Don seemed to fold in two as he plopped down in a round clean booth on the far side of the restaurant. "Wow," he said, waving for Andy to sit down beside him. "Some mess we're in, huh?"

Clay gave orders to two incoming officers, walked over to Pete, Andy, and Don, sat down and said, "Okay, y'all, let's go over what happened here." Pete thought Sheriff Clay looked a bit like Donald Trump, having the exact same color toupee, except Sheriff Clay had prominent cheekbones, pock marks on his face, and was a bit heavier than the Donald.

Andy asked Sue Beth to open up the photo app on her iPhone. "Sure, Clay. We even took a few pictures. Maybe they can help us identify these men, and give us clues as to where they came from." He gave him his iPhone so he could see the images.

Sue Beth added, "And if they're after Pete, maybe we can discover who hired them."

After a long pause as the sheriff began examining their photos, a man who looked like a thin Dom DeLuise came running into the restaurant. When he saw a plank partially covering a dead man's body and the interior of the diner half-destroyed, he yelled, "What the hell happened?" He kicked a board as the sheriff ordered him to leave. "But this is my place!" he shouted.

Don stood in a gesture to try and calm him down. "This is terrible, Stan. I don't know what to say...I'm sorry—"

"What the hell happened?" Stan cried, making a 360° turn while raising his arms in the air. "Don? Don!" He began kicking debris and rubble as another sheriff ushered him out the shattered front door.

Sue Beth brought over a pitcher of ice water from behind the counter and set it along with some glasses on the table. "Are you all right, Andy? Dad?"

Andy held up his hand in front of her as if telling her to wait a moment. "Just sit down, Sue Beth," he said, and Don reached around him to grab her hand.

Clay lifted his iPad out of his brown jacket. "Okay, let's get started." He also clicked on a small tape recorder, and said to Don, "Oh, I think it best you call your store, Don and tell someone to close up for a while."

Whew, Don sighed as he dialed. "I'll have the security company put a sign on the door."

Sue Beth said, "Gosh darn that this had to happen. Today's one of our busiest days of the year."

"Closing the shop's gonna take a giant chunk outta Dad's sales this month," Andy said, his face buried in his hands. "Dad, just tell the security company you might open at ten. It's only seven fifty-three a.m."

Don turned around and asked Clay, "How long ya think we'll be here answering questions?"

"Dunno," Clay replied, lifting his arm off the table and glancing at his sleeve, cautious as to not to get anything on the starch-pressed material.

Pulling up a chair at the end of the booth, Sue Beth asked, "Are you all right, Andy? After all, you shot two people." This time her voice was demanding an answer.

"Andy slapped his cowboy hat on his arm. "Not really." He nodded at the dead men whom the coroner was inspecting. "I have to figure out how to live with this."

Don grabbed a little bit of Andy's cuff. "You had to

Pete's Crossroad

shoot, son. They were about to kill us. Ya had no choice."

Andy rubbed the back of his neck. "I'm gonna remember this for the rest of my life." The wrinkles on his face creased in dejection and his mustache twitched in anguish.

Clay typed in that information while the coroner wheeled out the bodies. Outside the crowd was in turmoil. Some people were crying, pointing frantically into shards of glass and mounds of splintered wood. TV newscasters had already stationed cameras at the broken front door, and two more patrol cars were speeding and flashing their sirens into the parking lot. Clay spoke through his microphone attached to his collar, telling sheriffs outside to clear away the crowd. Then he said to them through his microphone: "We have no idea yet just who we're dealing with. Pedestrians could be hurt, so keep 'em all back by the street. And call Homeland Security. This could be a terrorist attack. We have to take the utmost precautions." He had a slight lisp, but his voice was brusque and certain.

"Let's see what we have here." Clay sent the pictures Andy had shown him through an encrypted internet connection for identification. While they waited for a response, he asked Pete, "Why were these men after you?"

After Pete told Clay about his previous jobs at Fashion Diva and Fossil Inc., he said, "Back in Albuquerque, my boss, Terrence Frapley, fired me from Fossil right there at the convention center."

"Terrence Frapley," Clay repeated, typing the name into his iPad. "Go on."

Outside, little circles of spectators and witnesses began exiting the parking lot as sheriffs began cordoning off the crime scene with yellow tape. A Farmers insurance agent stepped out of her car, and Stan ran to her with his hands on top of his head as if he were about to pull out his hair. Inside the restaurant, a detective extracted a slug from the wall where one of the oriental men had shot at Andy but missed. Another detective began taking pictures of all the damages.

Pete glanced at Sue Beth's fingers now on top of his

hand. As he held them, he felt a jolt of encouragement. "I think the fashion industry might have blackballed me because I discovered some evidence of a human trafficking ring."

"Did you report that?" Clay asked matter-of-factly.

Pete felt ashamed. "I guess I didn't think much of what I had seen at the time." Faces of young girls popped into his mind, together with long lines of churning sewing machines that seemed to stretch into eternity. "I snapped some pictures when I had to get close-ups of various fabrics, designs and time tables."

"Uh-huh," Clay said. "You worked for two clothing and design companies then."

Sue Beth added, "Pete said he uncovered a slave trafficking ring and a sweat shop ring."

"Uh-huh," Clay said, still typing intently.

Pete gave a touch of support and said, "Yeah, she's right. I worked at Fashion Diva for three years, and Fossil Inc. for about a month."

Clay stopped typing. "It's common practice for these types of criminals to close one shop when they're discovered and open up a new one right across the street. You might have quit, but all the while they still had their eyes on you."

Pete remembered that happening. "My God! Maybe that's what happened! Fashion Diva went out of business but merged with Fossil, and I didn't know it!" He drank water as panic rushed through him. "But I never thought they'd pick up and move across town. Do you really think Fashion Diva re-opened as Fossil Inc.?"

"Most likely," Clay said.

"Oh God! I coulda been killed *way* before this!" Pete hit the table, the room appearing to spin again.

Andy gave out a sigh of disgust. "So if that Fossil Inc. was blackballing ya, and you had proof of all their criminal activities, that would explain why that guy fired ya like he did, and way out in the dessert."

"Sure does," Pete huffed.

"Maybe my grandpa saved *your* life when my dad diverted

ya off course to Amarillo," Andy said.

"Could very well be the case," Clay began, "'cause it's hard to find a body in the desert. Then he lifted his eyebrows toward a damaged section of the restaurant. "People put out a hit on ya, Mr. Turner, obviously wanting to silence you so they can continue on with their dirty business, and killing you is right-on with their plans," he added, slowly and eerily.

Believing he saw accusation in Clay's eyes, he exclaimed, "You don't think I was involved, do you?!" No way! I swear!"

Clay inhaled and stopped typing. "Hmm."

Pete leaned as far across the table as he could until his chest ached. "No way! I sent photos exposing the sweatshop. I'm sure you can access the D.A. in L.A. through proper channels to prove I'm tellin' ya the truth!"

"You heard back from the D.A. then?" Clay asked, typing into his iPad again.

"Yeah," Pete began, swallowing hard and then drinking more water. "The D.A. there said I should be expecting a call from two agents." He lifted out his wallet and pulled out the note onto which he had scratched their names.

"They are?" Clay asked, motioning for Pete to give him the note.

"Agents Armon and Boseby," Pete replied, giving him the letter.

Clay held the note close to his eyes and read it. "We never received word to pick you up or anything." He bit his thick lower lip that appeared half-baked by tobacco chew. "Our office never received an order with these names on it." He began typing again and said, "Strange."

"You mean terrifying!" Sue Beth added, clenching Pete's hand, her eyes full and wild.

Pete shook his head in disagreement. "Not really strange, Sheriff. If those two guys were foreign hit men, or members of a sophisticated gang here in America, they could have high-tech equipment that intercepted the D.A.'s message to me, or the one I sent to the D.A. in the first place."

"They could have received those photos and your email

and discovered you're here in Amarillo," Don said.

Sue Beth added, "Or they could have someone working inside the D.A.'s office!"

"Oh my God," Don said, his voice rising in panic. "We don't know who we can trust, Clay, and one o' the guy said before he died that more people will be coming after Pete."

"And maybe us because we're his friends and know about the photos," Andy said.

Clay waved over two sheriffs. "Call the Los Angeles District Attorney's office quick," he ordered. "I want to know right now what's going on…what they want us to do with this man who is supposed to be their witness." He turned to Pete as they left and said, "What's your full name again?" He continued typing into his iPad.

"Peter Robert Turner," he said, watching Clay type.

Her eyes filling with sudden astonishment, Sue Beth said, "Turner's your last name?"

Pete nodded. "Yeah, why?"

Waving as if she had made a silly connection, Sue Beth said, "Oh, I could be wrong…I guess Turner is a pretty common name—"

"What?" Pete asked.

"Something more I should know Sue Beth so I can add the information here?" Clay asked, clicking the Send icon that began relaying almost every word Pete had told him and photos Andy had shone him. They began waiting for a response.

Don prodded Sue Beth to speak more as he said, "Well, out with it, Sue Beth. What were you just thinking about the name Turner?"

"My history professor's name is Dr. Turner, that's all," she said.

Pete sat up astounded. "Do you know her first name?" He felt as if the dust in the room suddenly stopped floating.

Sue Beth had an expression of deep concentration on her face. "Oh, Kimberley Turner I think. That's it! Dr. Kimberley Turner."

Pete's Crossroad

"It's her!" Pete gasped, sitting up straight.

Clay pulled him down as he peeked cautiously outside.

Andy and Don asked simultaneously, "What's wrong?"

Pete felt on the verge of tears. "Kimberley Turner is my sister's name! Could she be my sister? Could she be here?!"

"You got a sister?" Clay asked with a shocked expression. "We need to check this out right away and contact her. She could be in trouble too if your mad bosses find out." He typed in more information into his iPad and then suddenly stopped. "I have an email that just came through. I'm opening it."

Sue Beth had a smile of excitement on her face. "Your sister, Pete…right here, in Amarillo! Wow!"

Andy gave Pete a nauseated glance. "I think you need to leave town, Pete." He nodded at Clay who was still reading the message. "Whataya think, Sheriff? Shouldn't ya just escort Pete back to L.A., if need be?"

Leaning back, Clay set his iPad on the tabletop, pinched his fingers between his brow, and began shaking his head as if he were feeling hopeless about what to do next. "It ain't gonna be that easy."

"Huh?" Pete said, scoffing in disbelief. He remembered George telling him that his life would change in Amarillo. He never believed it would change for the worse! Where was George now when he needed him the most?

Startled at Pete with concerned eyes, Don said, "Whatcha showin' on that iPad of yours, Clay?"

"My God!" Clay said. "My God!" He shut off his iPad and began packing it up. It was only 8:35 a.m.

Sue Beth's fingers were on her lips as she whispered, "We've known Clay since we moved here. Even when we had that bad tornado last year, and that flood two months ago, I've never seen Clay look this terrified…this overwhelmed."

"Yep," Andy agreed.

"What's wrong, Clay?" Don asked.

"Lemme think for a few seconds," Clay said, thrusting his iPad into his jacket.

Her hands clasped and fingers clenching in worry, Sue

J.P. Osterman

Beth whispered, "It's as if the entire city of Amarillo's going to be hit by a comet!"

Andy slid the pitcher of water to the spot where Clay had been typing. "That email must have contained some pretty bad news," he whispered, sipping some ice water and then setting down his glass. He had an expression of doom.

Sliding out of the booth and scooting Sue Beth's chair in front of the decorative partition, Clay called in an order on his Bluetooth, "I need to find a safe haven for these people, now!"

"What happened, Clay?" Don asked again.

Clay was walking away quickly while also glancing back at Pete. Don moved out the booth and began walking toward Clay, but Clay motioned for him to sit back down, fast! "I don't want ya getting hit by a stray bullet," he said sternly.

Pete could read every anguishing line on his fretful face. Feeling sick, he said, "From what I'm seeing, something terrible is coming at all of us, and soon."

Andy huffed and peered out the window. Traffic was picking up, but spectators were still watching the police. He said, "if all those people don't clear a pathway, we might not make it out alive."

Don said, "Clay's working on that. Just let's all hold on tight. Something bad happened, and obviously he doesn't want to tell us about it yet." He was gripping his seat.

Pete remembered his conversation with George. George had told him that a model home would save his life. They weren't anywhere close to one of those? And where was George now when he could use him?! Furthermore, he also had his sister's life to be concerned about. If Sue Beth's professor, Kimberley Turner, was in fact his sister, her life might also be in danger. Touching the arrowhead that Walks-With-Dreams had given him, he closed his eyes and whispered a prayer of protection. "Please, God, help."

"I've been praying too, Pete," Sue Beth said. She had her fingers on the little gold cross around her neck and her arms were slightly shaking. "I've been praying real hard." She touched her charm bracelet with Sandy's skater charm.

Pete's Crossroad

Clay returned and said with serious eyes and terrified pale skin, "Those two agents who were supposed to be coming here to question and protect you…Agents Sidney Armon and Leslie Boseby…they're dead, Pete, murdered, their throats slit and bodies left in the desert in Albuquerque.

"My God!" Pete gasped, almost falling back. Andy and Don reeled in shock.

"The FBI's working on another solution to help you," Clay said, "but for now, they've put me and my team in charge of protecting ya."

Pete was speechless. He had no one but Clay and Clay's two guns to help defend him and defeat a gauntlet of hit men now after him.

J.P. Osterman

Chapter 17 – The Bomb

A bomb suddenly exploded in the parking lot—a furious fireball—the rumbling sound sending shock waves through the restaurant. Pete thought his ear drums might shatter.

"Take cover!" Clay screamed as they dove under a counter and booth—shrapnel and glass piercing the walls.

Pete grabbed Sue Beth's arm and pulled her close. He believed the entire ceiling might collapse, as did happen during a California 7.2 magnitude earthquake.

"Get to the truck!" Don cried, crawling up and standing.

Pinned under a beam, Clay shouted: "My laptop, we need it, take it!" Gasping in pain, he handed it to Don as Andy and Pete heaved off the beam, freeing Clay's leg.

Andy grabbed the shotgun and looked out the window: "I see three guys heading this way!" He was ducking and bobbing to catch a glimpse of them. "They're not cops."

Don lifted Clay off the floor. "Get movin' now!" And they limped to the back exit.

Running with them, Pete could hear the sounds of sirens, screams coming from outside the restaurant, guns firing, and the car horns blaring. The engine was revving a grinding call at the rear exit, beckoning them. Throwing open the back door,

Pete's Crossroad

Pete felt as if he were moving in slow motion. The sun was just beginning to peek over the top of the restaurant; the wind was picking up and whipping. The weather was changing for the worse. "I'll get in the bed of the truck!"

Sue Beth shouted: "I'm with Pete!" She slammed shut the tailgate.

Clay, Andy and Don dashed into the front seat. Don punched the truck into drive and goosed it, flinging up shafts of dust and pebbles from the unpaved alley. Don opened the sliding back window and called, "You all right back there?"

Sue Beth yelled, "Yeah, okay, just drive!"

"Step on the pedal, Dad!" Andy yelled, peeking over his shoulder. "From what I can see through a hole in the restaurant, Stan's parking lot is filled with balls of tar!"

Through the spaces between houses, Pete could see speeding police cars flashing their red and white lights as ambulances bounced over potholes. "No one's following us so far," he called through the truck's sliding glass window. He looked into the sky, through tall branches with their canopies extending into the streets. "But that doesn't mean the enemy won't track us down by way of airplane or helicopter."

"I'm putting in a call to secure the airport!" Clay shouted.

Don called back to Pete and Sue Beth, "You two hide under one of those brown tomato nets, ya hear?"

Sue Beth reached over to a bundle of them and handed a corner to Pete. "Got it, Dad," she yelled.

Don made a sudden sharp turn, and Pete steadied himself on the rear wheel well cover, but still hit his head on the steel frame. "Ahh!" he cried, rubbing out the sting as he reassured Sue Beth, "I'm fine…really." Remembering what George had told him that morning, he said, "Is there a new subdivision around here? One with model homes?"

Andy called back: "We need to get you to jail, Pete. That seems like the only place you're gonna be safe."

Clay pointed down another alley and ordered Don, "Take the next left." After Don turned, Clay added: "Even the jail's not safe for this guy. Dangerous and powerful hit men are

J.P. Osterman

after Mr. Turner…big time!"

"Who?" Don asked.

The wind feeling akin to an approaching thunderstorm, Pete called: "Wherever the nearest model homes are, head there!" He didn't want to leave any trace behind for the enemy to follow. "Who would think we'd seek refuge in one of those places, right?"

After Clay discussed his idea with Don, he quickly agreed, and Andy said, "There's that Star's Edge subdivision that went bankrupt a year ago. It's completely vacant."

Turned another corner, Don added: "Yeah, Clay, most of those model homes haven't been vandalized, and they're pretty far outta town."

"A twenty minute drive at least," Clay said, his voice desperate sounding. "Star's Edge became a development about a year and a half ago. Before that, it was a deserted town called Edge City, before that—" He scratched his head.

"Nothing for about fifty years," Sue Beth said, "but I do know that Edge City was a stopping point for the Pony Express back in the 1860s." She stretched toward the cab window as she continued: "The developer wanted to resuscitate the old ghost town. They were hoping a *real* ghost-town image might attract retirees."

Don shut the window on the cab. "Clay needs to make a few phone calls. I'll keep ya posted as he receives more information from the station."

Lying down, Sue Beth reached into her handbag and pulled out a bottle of water. Holding it on her red cheeks, she opened it, took a giant gulp, and then gasped in relief. "This tastes so good. Here, have some."

After handing it to Pete, Pete said, "I guess that idea of resuscitating the ghost town fizzled out since no one bought into the place."

"A ghost town is a dead town for a reason," she said as the truck drove through a small dust twister and skidded a bit. Coughing, she said, "You see a lot of these dust devils here, Pete, especially out of the city where the wind can really pick up hard and wild."

"Uh-huh," he agreed, covering his face. "Orange-yellow everywhere," he coughed and gagged a bit.

Pointing at the blurry sun almost high in the sky, she added: "The word 'Amarillo' means yellow…and the place seems like it's in the middle of the Sahara…but at dusk and dawn…it's beautiful, Pete."

Now lying close to her, Pete saw his eyes reflecting in her eyes. When he thought of the possibility that those oriental men might have killed her, he felt angry. "Well, when this is all over, I hope to see one of those beautiful scenes you've been talking about." He rolled on his back and stuck his jacket under his head. When the truck bounced through another bulge in the road, he collided with Sue Beth. When he saw Sue Beth's pained expression, he shouted at Don, "*Ahh*, take it easy up there!" He shoved a brown gunnysack under her back.

"I'm all right," she shouted to her Dad, "just keep flooring it!" She grabbed the edge of the truck, lifting herself up to get a look at their surroundings. "So far, I don't see anyone behind us." She plopped back down and sighed. "I was supposed to be meeting a classmate for a study group."

"I'm really sorry for all this," Pete said, feeling dismal. If he had any inkling of ever becoming more than an acquaintance to her, he believed he had dashed that hope.

Before he could muster up the nerve to tell her that, she said: "Pete, your life's in danger. You're more important than some study group! Don'tcha know that?"

Glancing up, he could see a black helicopter. "Get down!" He covered her with more camouflage. Then he spotted the star on the side. "It's law enforcement, Don!" he called into the cab window.

"Clay's working to identify the craft," Don returned.

Pete wondered why the police were flying above them: Maybe battling the people who were after him, or maybe they had succeeded in stopping the hit men. Looking at Sue Beth, he felt he had imposed too much on her, and now her day at school was ruin—a day she needed to make up for missed work. "Sue Beth, your classes *are* important, and your studies, and your grades—"

"Pete!" She had tears in her eyes. "I don't think you've ever really had a family…and you believe that if someone takes time for you, or is inconvenienced because of you, that you don't deserve their attention." She wiped her eyes. "You've done so much for our family, Pete. I'm so thankful and grateful to have you in my life."

Hugging her, he said, "Anyone would have—"

"No, *you* did," she said, "you've been so kind to us."

"Ah, come on, Sue Beth—"

"No!" she insisted, the lines in her brow pinching. "You're a kind man, Pete." She sniffled. "You need to know that, because *we do*." She said the last word with emphatic importance. Then she turned away.

The rattling of the shocks and the pinging and clatter of stones hitting the wheel wells made Pete's insides toss in confusion. Before when a woman tried to analyze him, he disappeared like smoke. But now? Sue Beth was right. People were really seeing him and getting to know him under the worst circumstances and conditions, and they were still helping him. No, he had never had that…not even from his own father. He lay back down on the steely truck bed and covered his forehead, every now and then peeking at her. They were under thick camouflage, and it was getting warmer in spite of the bursts of cold air and roars of thunder in the distance. After having spent only been a couple of days with Sue Beth, how could he have such strong and uncontrollable feelings for her? It didn't seem possible! Love? Nawww!

Suddenly, the truck jolted to a stop as the *ding ding* sounds of a railroad-crossing alarm sounded. A train rushed by— *clickity-clack clickity-clack*; the sound waves from its loud horn piercing his chest. Dust flew into the air, and Sue Beth turned and kissed him on his lips. "This is all going to be okay, Pete," she said tenderly. "I know it will."

He hugged her—a melting feeling flowing through him. "Yeah," he returned her kiss. "I'm going to make sure of that,

Pete's Crossroad

Sue Beth." He could repeat her name forever! As he kissed her again and the train noises receded, he could hear a muffled conversation coming from Don, Clay, and Andy:

Clay said: "Take this next road north to the Star's Edge subdivision, Don. We've got about another ten minute drive until we get there." Cars passed by, but they were minivans and country-sturdy trucks.

"What's Star's Edge like now?" Andy asked.

Clay replied, "The developer completely abandoned ten acres. There are paved streets, but the street lights don't work, and there about ten homes, and a block's worth of homes half-built."

"That part probably looks like a zone of pick-up sticks by now," Andy laughed.

"How many model homes are there?" Don asked.

Andy replied: "I remember that a friend of mine worked construction there. I believe they built three model homes before they abandoned the project."

"Are they furnished?" Don asked, turning the truck again.

"I think two of them are," Andy replied, "so we might have a bit of comfort when we get there. It all depends on what the developer left behind."

His keys jingling, Clay said: "I have a master lockbox key. We can decide which place is best to hole up in when we get there. We'll need to make sure we pull the truck into a garage that doesn't have windows, if possible."

Don asked, "Clay, have you figured out yet who the hell's after Pete?"

Pete heard that. He let go of Sue Beth, sat up straight and opened the sliding glass window. "Yeah, I'd like to know that too!"

After a long pause and a gloomy sigh, Clay said loudly, "The Snakeheads have orders to hunt you down and kill you, Mr. Turner." His words sounded as dangerous as the threat. "I didn't want to tell you that back there...I didn't want ya panicking, but, I'm telling ya now."

"What the heck's a Snakehead?" Andy asked.

J.P. Osterman

"Oh my gosh!" Sue Beth cried with knowing eyes filled with terror. She had her fingers tight around the straps of her handbag. "You think you'll be safe in a model home, Pete?" she asked, "because 'hunt you down and kill you' sounds like you won't be safe anywhere!"

"Not even a church," Don said, gunning the engine and passing a van.

Imagining she might call him crazy but also having faith that she might believe him, Pete whispered so that no one else but Sue Beth could hear him: "Your grandfather told me that a model home would save my life...that's why." As he watched her mouth drop open in disbelief, he slapped dirt off his shirt, picked a few sparkling shards of glass off Sue Beth's collar and added: "Considering what just happened to us back there...I believe that's where we'll all be safe." Watching her flat expression, he waited for her response.

Clay interrupted. "The Snakeheads are Chinese gangs that that smuggle people out of the orient to other countries."

"You mean those human traffickers Pete talked about?" Andy added.

Clay took out his iPad, wiped off the cover, inspected it for damage, and then turned it on. "That's about right, basically. The Snakeheads make deals with illegal crime syndicates who exploit immigrants in terrible and unspeakable ways." He flashed them INTERPOL's home page on his iPad screen. "Those dead guys at Stan's were members of a Chinese Triad Snakehead gang. Their tattoos are giving us their life stories as well as their rank and position in their gang."

"Horrible!" Sue Beth said, covering her stomach. "How demoralizing...and happening in America! Sick."

"It's all about making money, Sue Beth," Andy said, shaking his head in disgust. "That's why those criminals in L.A. don't want Pete to testify against them. Their illegal sweatshops get closed up and they lose billions—"

"And their lives will be in danger in prison because of the shame of their failures, even though what they've done is completely criminal," Clay said, peering again at his watch.

Pete's Crossroad

"About five more minutes to Star's Edge, and then I'll show you just what the FBI emailed me." His body rocked as Don's truck veered around an obstacle in the road. "It's pretty bad."

Don kept glancing out of the rearview mirror, his eyes fixing on several spots in the terrain in an effort to spot anything suspicious looking. "So is this Snakehead gang like the Mexican coyote?" he asked.

"That's right," Clay replied, his head tilting as the truck made a jagged maneuver. "The FBI believes that the Snakeheads are responsible for most of Los Angeles' human trafficking. They've put out a contract on ya, Pete, as well as on a few other witnesses." He wiped the dirt-speckled area under his eyes and gave a quick jerk of his elbow as he groaned slightly in pain. "I'll explain it all when we can get holed up in one of those model homes."

Don called, "So maybe Pete's right…that a model home in the boondocks will be the safest place for us to hide out."

"At least for now," Clay replied.

Andy had his cowboy hat cockeyed on his head and his shotgun pointed and ready to fire. Every now-and-then, he peeked over his shoulder, obviously trying to spot anyone who might be tailing them. His eyes filling with fear, he suddenly looked at everyone in the truck. "I just thought of something!"

"What?" his dad asked.

"Does everyone have your cell phones off? These people hunting us might be able to trace our signals!" he replied.

Clay shut down his iPad. "Good point, Andy. Everything off, everybody…iPhones, iPods, even this GPS."

As Pete shut off his phone, he heard the ring tone on Sue Beth's phone. Quickly, she pushed the *Ignore* key and thrust her phone into her purse. She called out to Pete: "It's just a friend…trying to get a hold of me."

Pete said, "Of course! They're probably worried sick about you after hearing what happened at Stan's." He held her hand and felt the smooth soft surface of her skin. "When we get to the model home, ask Clay if it's safe to call them and let your friends in your study group know you're all right."

J.P. Osterman

Leaning her head on his shoulder, she said, "Yeah, I'll do that." Then she peered at him with added interest. "And maybe Clay will have some information on Kimberley Turner."

"Oh yeah, my sister," Pete gasped. He didn't really want to face her, but he also couldn't wait to see her. "Kimberley…it's been a long time since I've seen her."

The tires speeding down the stretch of near-empty highway to Star's Edge licked the hot pavement like melting wax. The wind streaming over the truck's cab made low and high-pitched whistling sounds.

Don called to the back of the truck, "Any sign of anyone following us, Pete?"

Sue Beth called, "A helicopter now and then."

As the truck turned onto another two-lane highway that disappear into a mirage in the distance, Pete peeked out the back. Never having ridden in the back of a truck, he believed that if he lifted himself any higher, he might fly out the back and end up as road kill. Still, again, he peered above the trick's frame but could only see a sparsely populated section of Amarillo—parched front lawns, brown splintered fences, and the visitor's sign: Welcome To Amarillo! "We're out of town, now. No one's behind us," he said, craning his neck to speak through the sliding window. "Over there's a cemetery…with a few hearses, and people walking to funerals."

Sue Beth fell back into the bed of the truck. "That's where we're burying Grandpa, on Thursday morning."

Pete exhaled in dismay, ran his fingers through his hair, and shielded his eyes from a loud crack of lightning. Soon a wild thunderstorm would be upon them as well as hit men if they couldn't outwit and outrun them. "You feel so sad about his death, even though you never met him."

"Of course," she said, "I wanted to meet him. My grandma talked about him often when she was alive." She sat up a little and took another sip of water as Clay shouted that they were almost at Star's Edge. "My grandma told me stories about him…about them." Her throat reddened, her lips quivered, and more tears filled her eyes. "Even though he

Pete's Crossroad

wasn't there, my grandfather was always in the house with her, and with us."

This time Andy called back, "You two see anyone inside the cemetery who might be following us?"

"No one is exiting or entering the cemetery, Andy," Sue Beth shouted, drying her eyes.

Pete remembered the packages George had showed him, and he told her, "Hey, don't forget...your grandfather left you that gift you haven't opened yet." He believed he was giving her some important information about her grandfather—a little piece of George to get to know.

"Yeah, I can't wait to open it!" she said. Scooting closer to him, she had a restless expression on her face as she asked, "Did you *really* hear my grandfather's voice and *really* see him since he's been dead? As a ghost?!" She lifted herself so that her lips were next to his.

"Yes...I *really* did." he replied, kissing her, then smelling her herbal-scented hair. "I really did...honest!"

Chapter 18 – Star's Edge at Edge City

After turning a quick left, Don called, "Okay, I'm pretty sure we're not being followed."

"You can sit up in the back then," Clay shouted to Pete and Sue Beth.

Pushing away the camouflaged netting, Pete and Sue Beth sat up next to the window cab, wadded up all the brown burlap and netting, and packed it against the tailgate.

From the middle seat, Andy peeked around, pointed north, and said: "We're about to drive through the ghost town the builder left half-developed." He ran his fingers through his ash-blond hair. "About a mile up, we turn right, then we're at the model homes."

The stretch of highway suddenly transformed into a narrow paved road with a large billboard that appeared as a line drawn in sand, cutting off humanity from civilization: Star's Edge: A Piece of the Past Still in Your Pocket!

Pete said to Sue Beth: "I can't imagine anyone ever living out here. It'd be like traveling back in time to the Wild West."

Sue Beth laughed and bumped against him in a joking gesture. "Are ya afraid Indians might jump out with bows and arrows and start shooting at us?"

Pete's Crossroad

He thought of Chuck and Walks-With-Dreams. "You know, everything those old movies portrayed about Native American Indians is completely wrong." As they transitioned into the antique town, he added, "This place looks like it came right out of a movie set."

As Don drove through town, he passed a two-story saloon with batwing doors boarded up and windows shuttered. Below its frayed neon sign trembled a long line of plastic tumbleweeds in front of a brown plastic water trough. On both sides of the main street were various types of multi-hued stained shops and stores: Dan's Dry Goods, a small post office, several half-constructed clothing and souvenir shops, and a small improvement center.

"I don't see one sign of modern civilization, except for that streetlight across the street in front of the renovated hotel…but even *that* looks like a telegraph pole," Pete said.

As they slowly made a detour through a small section of town, he noticed that the developers had used wooden planks for sidewalks and painted signs for parking spaces. They had also planned for a pharmacy and a convenience store. Pete had an idea when he spotted a flickering neon sign on the store. "Clay, that place has a permanent electrical supply! It must be infused with Smart technology! How about if we open the store and reposition the light. If hit men come after us, this could be a temporary diversion." Don said he also knew how to rig a warning alert on his iPhone. He had such an alarm system at Gibby's to warn him of an intruder. The model homes were now only a few minutes' drive away from them, and they could at least quickly prepare for a fight should any hit men trigger the alarm.

After getting permission to proceed from Clay, Don said, "Lemme pull over and do just that." It took two minutes to readjust the light, open the shop, and connect Don's iPhone app to the Smart system in the shop.

As they finished rigging the warning system, Pete spotted a vulture feasting on road kill as a tumbleweed rolled out from behind a red water drum and knocked Don's truck. The wind began blowing hard, and above the heat-wavering air, thick purple-and-black clouds were gathering. Encroaching rain was approaching from the earlier thunder rolls and lightning claps. "We better hurry up and head to the model homes," Clay said. "I see a big downpour coming! We need cover."

After driving past banners advertising models homes, Don turned down a main-paved road that branched out into several fishbone-like streets. "Look at all these streetlights, and electrical poles—"

"But not one house," Sue Beth interrupted, staring with sad eyes at the lifeless landscape, wind-tossed tumbleweeds, and dust rising along the arid land and barren streets.

Hearing the sounds of dry brush and whistling winds scraping over the streets, Pete suddenly spotted red-white-and-blue flags. "Over there! The model homes!"

After driving down three streets and over a small hill, Don pulled into the middle home and put the truck into idle in the driveway. He said, sighing, "Here at last…and no one behind us."

"Yet," Clay corrected, telling Don to wait. "I want your truck in the garage, Don. Lemme see which side is the best to park it in." He got out, opened the lockbox on the front door, and entered the two-story model home. After the garage door lurched open, he pushed aside some dry wall, and waved for Don to maneuver inside. There were a few garden tools setting alongside an unfinished wall covered with spider webs. The builder must have planned to put in a lush landscape to fill in the now bumpy patch of dark sand. The house had a front sideway leading to the front door, but only partially completed with two-by-fours right up the arched entryway. Clay stopped everyone from walking on anything other than the driveway, warning: "You could leave footprints. You'd be surprised how trackers can detect a human presence." He even threw some dirt on the driveway before closing the door!

Once inside, Andy doffed his cowboy hat, wiped away sweat off his brow, and plopped down in a kitchen chair next to Don. The house smelled of a tinge of mold and stale cinnamon air freshener. "We should check around for a phone and a working land line. We have to contact the marshal, or FBI, right Clay?" Andy asked as Clay connected his cell phone and iPad tablet into a socket for charging.

"Amazingly, the electricity is on!" Clay said. He couldn't understand why, but he said, "I'm not looking a gift horse in the mouth"

"I'm going to work on directing law enforcement to us as soon as I get my laptop up and running," Clay said, "but I have to use an encrypted line." He made a *tsk* sound. "It's gonna take some work…and possibly some fancy hacking."

Sue Beth had already run up and down the hardwood steps; and when she returned, she exclaimed, "This place is completely furnished with beds and everything!" Darting into the bathroom, she turned on the faucet and water gushed out in spurts. "This hasn't been used in a while though I can tell. The water coming out is a little moldy smelling, like it's been standing in pipes for quite a while. But I'm sure we can drink the water after we flush out the system. I'll check the kitchen!"

Pete turned on a light switch in the dining room and took out his laptop. So many options came to his mind, but the best one was to call Chuck in Albuquerque. Chuck might know what to do. "Can I make a call on my cell phone now?" he asked Clay.

Clay shot him a cautious glare. "Not yet," he said, powering up his iPad. "These gangs that are after ya know how to locate you through cell phone towers. The second you dial, they've gotcha. I'll try to direct the calls to ping off several cell towers…that should confuse 'em."

Pete scrolled down to Chuck's cell phone after checking the time: 9:46 a.m. But Albuquerque is on mountain time—an hour behind Amarillo's central time. After asking Sue Beth if the model home had phone service, he said, "I'm calling a guy I met in Albuquerque named Chuck."

Drinking a glass of water, Don pushed up his rimless glasses that had slid down his nose and asked, "Who's Chuck?"

"A Native American Indian I met," Pete began as he

dialed the number. "Chuck's pretty high up in his tribe…an elder. He's a great guy and gave me some good advice while I was laid over in Albuquerque. I'm hoping he might have some good suggestions about this mess I'm in."

Andy turned around and gave him a perturbed glare. "This is *your* mess, Pete."

"Yes, I know…and I'm trying to fix it!" Pete snapped.

"Stop, both of you," Don ordered, his voice then turning calm. "We're all in this now, and we're *all* gonna work to get out of it and find a way to stop the hit on Pete."

"The hit out on all of you now," Clay said somberly.

Andy sighed, "Sure, Dad," and then pounded his empty water glass down on the table. "Hey, Clay, these are foreign gang members you're talking about right?"

"Yeah?" Clay replied, glancing at him askance.

"They're after Pete, right?" Andy asked, pointing at Pete. "Not us…so we shouldn't even be involved in all o' this. I disagree with my Dad that's this is all our problem!"

"Andy!" Sue Beth said as Don groaned through the argument.

Hmm, Sheriff Clay moaned. He stood up straight and nodded toward the picture window in the living room with its tinted reflective coating. The blinds were open, obviously enabling sales agents to see buyers while not permitting them to see inside. "From that earlier email I received from the FBI, those two Snakeheads were just scouts, Andy," Clay said.

"You mean testing us?" Pete asked, his chest pounding. "I wonder just how deep this gang has been able to delve into my personal business. God…help me! Maybe I'll never be able to ditch the hit!" He began pacing around the great room, trying to find a work area for his laptop.

Clay said, "If they were doing more than testing, Pete, you'd be dead by now." He began opening up home pages and secured sites on his iPad. "That's what I want to find out…whether or not we've been able to ditch the gang, or whether they're on their way here to no-man's land." He peeked up from the small screen as if spotting them. "I'm intend to get precise information from airport security, rental car agencies, gas station cameras, and anything else I can think of. If I have to, I'll hack my way into everything and take the heat for it later!"

Sue Beth walked up to Pete and grabbed his shirt. "We're going to help you, Pete. And Clay's gonna keep you alive," she said, putting her hand on his shoulder.

Through the slight fog in his brain, Pete suddenly calmed. "All right," he sighed.

"Clay," Don began, "my neighbor said his German shepherd was really barkin' last night." He had found blank paper and was preparing to jot down notes. "So these gangs must also know about my family too...not just about Pete. Maybe I should call my banks? My employees? Shouldn't I warn everyone I know?"

Tapping open the picture folder on his iPad, Clay said, "I don't think the gang knows about everyone you've come in contact with, Don, or the FBI would have included them on a list they sent me." He showed Don an email he had received. "And back at Stan's Drive-In, those two guys didn't have time to blast *all* your information over the internet to their bosses. Suddenly, Clay's eyes widened, and he bolted from the table.

"What the heck's wrong?" Don cried as Sue Beth dashed over to him.

"They're coming!" Clay said, running to the blinds, looking in between them. After Andy said he couldn't see anyone outside from the living room and Don said the back yard appeared deserted, Clay quickly rolled shut the blinds in the dining room, scrambled back to the table, and clicked on four pictures. "I hacked into this file. Thank goodness at least we know they're on the way!"

"Ya sure they're coming *here*?" Pete asked, "To *this* place?"

"Yep," Clay said, still hunt-and-pecking for data.

"How did they find us?" Andy asked, his broad shoulders rolling as he looked out a side window. He stopped, stun-faced at his Dad. "It has to be *your* truck that led them to us, Dad!" He raced to the kitchen door leading to the garage and opened it.

Following, Sue Beth asked, "Is there some kind of tracking device on it?"

Still seated in front of his iPad and opening private security footage, Clay said, "See these men?" He double-tapped the photos, enlarging them. Don and Pete leaned in to get a good look. "There's a pyramid tattoo on this one. He's a top boss. And this guy's got a Phoenix tattoo on the back of his bald head."

Peering into the garage, Pete said, "I remember reading about the Phoenix. Like the city in the desert, the Phoenix is the bird that rises out of hot ashes, representing death, to become reborn." Hitting the doorframe, he added: "That Snakehead gangster is implying that he won't die...that he's untouchable." Pete felt all his breath exhale out of his lungs. "I'm so sorry...terribly sorry for getting everyone involved in all of this!"

"Those men are going to be working to their deaths to kill us all!" Andy said.

"Pete, just go check the truck with Sue Beth, okay?" Don asked, leaning into Clay's iPad screen to get a better view of the gangster's location.

As street footage opened up, Clay scanned for comparisons. The gangster hit men were driving two Cadillac SUVs that appeared bulletproof. The iPad app retrieved their license numbers and their progress since leaving Amarillo. On a side map on his iPhone, Clay began tracing their current position. "That's the Quick Mart. This one's the B of A. This one's Tyler's Pharmacy, and this picture is the Shell station on the outskirts of Amarillo. We passed all of these...one-by-one on the way here. Each one's a little closer to us right now. They're taking the same route we took here." Peering at each other, Clay and Don had a look of terror in their eyes.

"Snakeheads *are* comin'." Clay said. He was like a revving engine. "We gotta power up, now." He wiggled in his seat and patted his holster. "Get out all the guns." He stood up like an old western marshal preparing to fight bank robbers.

Pete's Crossroad

"Load 'em, lock 'em, and prepare to fire!" He perked up in the direction of Don's truck. "Oh! I remember! I stashed the two guns I took off the dead guys behind the seat in your truck!"

"Take it easy, Clay," Don said, breathing deeply, waving for him to settle down. He added, "According to this date/time stamp, they're an hour and forty-five minutes away from us."

"We've got twenty minutes," Don repeated, slowly.

Sue Beth finally found the switch to turn on the garage light, and Pete felt the humidity settle on his sweaty shirt. They began rushing around the truck, inspecting under the frame, checking under the hood, and rummaging under all the burlap in the back.

Sue Beth said, "I see nothing, no tracking device."

Brandishing a flashlight, Clay appeared and began searching the wheel wells, finally stopping at a thick line of steel. He exclaimed, "Here!" He extracted a little black box with a sensor chip on top. "A GPS tracker." He lifted it up into the light. "One of those Snakeheads found your truck, Don, and planted this on it."

Don said, "So hit men *are* on their way here!" He breathed as if inhaling his last bit of oxygen. "And no cops...no FBI."

"Me," Clay said.

Glanced into the rafters, Don leaned against his truck. "Cripe!"

After crushing the chip under his boot, Clay called everyone back into the dining room. "I've put in secured calls to every agency I can think of. Now, we have to wait for—"

"But me, Sue Beth and my Dad are okay, right, Clay?" Andy asked. "These hit men are just after Pete. I mean, if they do find us before people who can help us, maybe we can try and reason with 'em."

"Huh? Are you nuts, Andy?" Clay asked. "After everything I've shown ya, you believe we can reason with 'em?" Andy slouched and walked away, downtrodden.

"Chuck!" Pete suddenly exclaimed. "He's our answer, I

just know it. I'm calling him on the landline!"

"There's a phone on the kitchen wall," Sue Beth said.

"There's no way those goons can tap into a telephone line so quickly." Running to the kitchen, Pete could still overhear their conversation as he peeked through the sliding door, watching them. He found Chuck's card in his wallet and dialed his number.

Sue Beth sounded spitfire angry with her brother. "What are you saying we do, Andy? Leave Pete?" She thrust her fingers in the air as if swatting a fly. "Just abandon him in the desert? Let him fend for himself?"

Andy bent down to her face. "It's *his* fight!" He pointed at the kitchen. "You wanna get killed? How about Dad? And—"

"Stop it!" Don cried, and both of them sat down in their dining room seats. "Let's wait and see what Clay says. Let's wait for his advice."

Andy's head was tossing back and forth in abject disgust. "I wanna get the hell outta here, Dad, and fast. This isn't our fight."

"Well I don't wanna leave!" Sue Beth said, standing up. She began searching through nearby cabinets. "I'm going to see if there's any food around here. I already plugged in the refrigerator, and it works."

Don said, "We sure could use some ice, so fill up some trays and stick 'em in the freezer."

Clay peeked up from typing and said, "Ice is a good thing to have around, in case Andy there gets a bloody nose."

Don laughed at the joke, but Andy kicked a table leg. "Hah!" he scoffed.

Pete waited through another ring as Sue Beth walked into the kitchen and began filling ice trays. Pete knew she was eavesdropping. "Never mind me," she began, "just pretend I'm not here."

"Okay," Pete whispered.

Finally, Chuck answered, "Hello?"

Pete leaned on the counter after he Chuck returned his

greeting. "Hey, it's me, Pete Turner."

Sounding surprised, Chuck said, "Hey, Pete, what's up?"

Pete hated asking anyone to go out of their way for him, especially this far out of their way! Still, he had to protect Sue Beth; he'd do anything for her, even if it meant treading on very uncomfortable territory. "I need some advice...maybe some help, Chuck."

"Oh yeah?" After a pause of shock, Chuck asked: "What's going on? You all right, Pete?"

Pete could hear what sounded like jukebox music in the background and men laughing. He surmised Chuck might be in a bar. "Remember when I was fired?"

"Yeah, Pete."

Pete rubbed his throat. "Remember I told you and your grandfather that I had some information that could put powerful people in jail?"

"Yeah...what's wrong?! You sound like someone's about ready to murder ya," he said in a concerned tone of voice.

Pete reeled a little and replied: "That's about what's going on here in Amarillo, Chuck. I have information that could stop human trafficking on the West Coast for good. I just found out I could really make a difference and help people. I could help save lives, Chuck."

"What!"

Pete could hardly catch his breath as he continued: "I've got a big problem right now. One bad *bad* gang is after me... Snakeheads the sheriff calls 'em. They're part of the Chinese Triad or the Chinese Mafia. These people who are after me— who want to kill me—"

"Hit men," Chuck said.

"Yeah! They're involved in human trafficking, and they're real hunters, Chuck," Pete began. "I'm as good as shaking hands with the saints at St. Peter's Gate if these gangsters nab me, Chuck." He wiped sweat off his forehead and breathed. Sue Beth was right next to his ear now, listening in on the conversation. Pete turned the phone so she could hear.

"Words fail me, Pete!" Chuck gasped. "I know a little bit

about these types of gangs." He inhaled and exhaled hard. "My God...You're gonna need an army to stop 'em. They're tyrants! You're looking at Kung Fu, Muay Thai, Combat Jujitsu!" The noise stopped on his end. "I'm leaving the building right now, Pete. Where are ya? Huh? Where?"

Pete believed that if wormhole transportation were possible, Chuck would be with him right now. "I'm holed up in a model home, in a defunct development north of Amarillo." Walking over to the kitchen window, he noticed a six-foot high brick wall. It was about twenty-five feet away from the back door and had no exit gate. He believed he was safe, at least for that moment. "I don't know what to do, Chuck. The sheriff has his iPad connected to all sorts of websites and resources. We're trying to get a good indication of how many hit men there are and where they're at...how many exactly are hunting me down."

Giving out a sarcastic laugh, Chuck said, "You're looking at a whole barrage of 'em, Pete. When one stops, their boss, or bosses, just send out more. It's like an ant trail!"

Pete could hear Chuck's car keys jiggling. He knew Chuck was now in a hurry.

"You're dealing with instant death, Pete," Chuck said, his car door slamming in the background. "When that gang puts a hit on ya, ya have just hours to live."

"Hours," Pete panted. Terror shot through his chest like an arrow, and he put his hand over his heart. "The sheriff's here—"

"Sheriff, marshal, FBI...nothing stops these guys, Pete," Chuck groaned. "Snakeheads are here in this country illegally, but they blend in as if they're third generation Americans."

"You mean like those deep-cover Russian spies the FBI arrested...the ones who were living as regular citizens while infiltrating policy making circles?" Pete asked.

"Yeah, but the Snakeheads carry out assassinations from their Triad bosses back in China," Chuck added. "You must have really pissed off some multibillionaire mobster!"

Pete coughed as if someone had poked him in his Adam's

apple, "Assassinations, hits…what am I gonna do, Chuck?"

"I'm coming, Pete," Chuck said firmly. "Just send me your coordinates…I got contacts, Pete…*big* contacts and fast planes!"

Whew, Pete sighed, telling Sue Beth to get Clay's secured iPhone. "I don't want to put your life in jeopardy, Chuck, but I had to call you. You seem so level headed and calm under hot situations—"

"Like the one you're in now?" Chuck said, laughing.

Pete couldn't find humor in his dire situation. "Well, yeah! So what do I do?"

"Give me your address," Chuck said.

Peeking around the doorframe into the dining room, Pete asked Clay: "Hey, what's the address here?"

Clay ran over to him with frightened eyes. "Who ya tellin'? Who is that?"

Chuck said, "Can ya put me on speaker mode, Pete?"

Pete pressed it, and Chuck's voice came in loud and clear. "Hello?"

The sheriff whisked the phone away from Pete and said: "This is Sheriff Clay Carter. Who is this?"

After Chuck gave him all of his pertinent information, Chuck said, "Sheriff Carter, I suggest you get the local National Rifle Association to back you up, especially if you can't trust the FBI."

"The NRA?" Clay asked. He was biting his lip again as if he had chewing tobacco tucked between his gum and teeth.

Chuck said: "They're your grassroots barricade, Sheriff. That's who *I'm* bringing along with me to nail these sons-a-guns who are after Pete."

Immediately, Clay typed in a secure message to the Amarillo chapter of the NRA.

Pete felt suddenly uplifted. "You're coming then right now?"

"After I hang up! I'm calling five buddies of mine who arrest illegal poachers on the reservation," Chuck began. "They have flying power and rifle power."

J.P. Osterman

Clay shook his head, "I don't know about this."

Pete met him eye-to-eye. "I trust him, Sheriff. I met this man...saw his home and everything he stands for." There was a great pause as Pete could hear Chuck talking over his CB radio. "I know Chuck can help us. I trust him."

"Pete wouldn't have called this man if he wasn't safe, Clay," Sue Beth added.

"How fast can ya get here, Chuck?" Clay asked, and then he told him to call the Amarillo Police for him since the hit men had obviously blocked his call for help—and had diverted his police officers—after he left Stan's.

After Chuck agreed, he said: "It's about 272 miles from here to Amarillo, and I'll be flying straight there in a..." He was arranging the final detail. "Looks like it'll be a Cessna 210 Centurion."

"The single engine plane...I know it...I'll be lookin' for ya," Clay said. He walked over to the window and Pete pointed to an area where a small plane could land.

"We've got a spot for it to land," Pete said.

"A lot of spots!" Sue Beth added. "The whole darn development could be turned into an airport."

Pete asked, "How long will it take you to get here, Chuck?" Glancing north out the window as Clay gave Chuck their exact latitude and longitude, Pete noticed dark clouds at high altitude, and he couldn't see the horizon.

Chuck said, "I'd say an hour and a half. But maybe sooner 'cause we'll be flying with the wind."

Clay said, "I'm checking on our precise latitude and longitude for you, Chuck. You should have our location."

"Waiting for it," he said.

"I hope the storm won't cut you off from us, Chuck," Andy said, gazing at a weather website. "This forecast I'm looking at now predicts a big thunderstorm dropping its load of rain on us in the next half hour."

Pete remembered seeing thick clouds as they entered Edge City's ghost town. "I'm surprised we haven't been rained on yet."

Pete's Crossroad

Sue Beth set a box of variety potato chips on the table. "That's just great," she said, opening up the box and throwing everyone a small bag. "We might have to fight off gangsters through thunder, lightning, and rain!"

"I just received your coordinates," Chuck began, "and I'm on my way to our airport where I'll meet my four buddies."

Believing a cavalry to be on the way, Pete sighed when he heard Chuck's truck accelerate, the tires whipping up rocks. "Good, thanks, Chuck."

"Keep this line open, Sheriff. I'll be calling you every now and then to give you updates." Now, it sounded as if Chuck was speeding down a long highway.

Clay had his iPad opened up to the email message he had received from the FBI at Stan's Drive-In. He began shaking his head. "We're in for one helluva long dark dangerous night here, Chuck...so I hope you'll make it here fast, 'cause we need ya," Clay said. "I got it your number, Chuck, but I gotta hang up now so no one can infiltrate this call."

"Bye, Sheriff."

Then Clay hung up.

Leaning over Clay's shoulder, Sue Beth said, "From the look on your face, Clay, it seems like no one from the station can make it hear on time to help us, and we're gonna be fighting this gang all by ourselves."

"That's not totally true, Sue Beth," Clay said.

Andy began scooping up wrappers as if angry about a little mess. "Sheriff...Sue Beth, me, and my dad are outta here...*now*."

Pete reached out and touched Sue Beth's arm. "He's right. You need to go...*all* of you."

"Not me!" Clay said, pointing to his badge.

"Everyone except you, Sheriff," Pete said. "This is *my* fight. I never intended to get anyone else involved."

"Good," Andy heaved, "I'm glad you agree."

Don stood tall and glanced at his watch. "Just hold on a minute, Son." Patting Andy on the back in a show of comfort, he then walked over to Clay and peeked over his shoulder.

"Aren't more FBI agents coming, Clay?"

"They should be comin', but where are they?" Clay turned full circle. "Maybe the hit men are blocking their phones and devices...or leading the agents on a false trail!" He opened up another email attachment. "Look here." Pete's picture popped up with Chinese characters under it.

"That looks like a wanted poster," Sue Beth said. She had her fingers over her lips, her bangs a little thick from sweat.

Clay nodded seriously as he dabbed perspiration off his neck. "That's Chinese. You can read the translation here."

Peeking around him, Andy read the words: "Two million dollars, dead-or-alive."

Wow, Don exclaimed, "powerful people want you dead, Pete."

"There's more!" Clay said, opening another attachment. A picture appeared of two dead people in a parking lot at the Albuquerque airport.

Recognizing the faces and the location, Pete felt instantly sick. "That's Tina Bowlett...and Fred Aspon!" He touched Fred's bloody image.

"Who are they?" Sue Beth asked.

Pete quickly explained. "Fred Aspon is the guy I told you about who caused me to lose my job by making himself look good and me incompetent." He sighed, covering his face. "Dead! And Tina Bowlett was the closest person to a friend I ever had!" Remembering what she had given him, he tapped his pocket. "She was such a positive person, and encouraging, like you Sue Beth." He turned, trying to cough back tears. "She gave me a cross." It jingled when he tapped it. "She told me about how Easter represents new beginnings. I'm partly here because of Tina."

"I'm sorry, Pete. I'm—"

"My God...I know I wanted revenge, but I never wanted anything like this to happen to Fred!" He thought he might have to run to the bathroom and vomit. Clay quickly turned the laptop screen away, and the food Pete felt rising in his esophagus sank back to his stomach. "I was supposed to go to

Pete's Crossroad

Vegas with Fred after the convention in Albuquerque, but your grandfather's death happened, and bringing his things here to you in Amarillo—" Pete couldn't speak any further.

"Oh my gosh!" Sue Beth cried, patting Pete's shoulder. Slowly she slid a bottle of water in front of him.

Pete felt terror rolling through his muscles, immobilizing him. "Terrence Frapley fired me. He was my boss at Fossil." Drinking some water while staring out the window into the desert breeze tossing tumbleweeds across the dry soil, he said, "I wonder if *he* had something to do with all of this…with this gang coming after me…hunting me."

Don patted Pete on the back of the neck. "Did you ever think that maybe if that Frapley guy hadn't fired you, you might be lying dead in parking lot with those people, Pete?"

Pete nodded in agreement, as Clay ordered, "Spell the name of your former employer."

Thinking hard through a brain fog, Pete spelled Terrence's name and asked, "Do you believe Terrence Frapley has something to do with all of this, Sheriff?"

Clay's shoulders rose in confusion as he brought up another picture on the laptop. It was one of the pictures Pete sent to the D.A., but much clearer and sharper. "Is that Terrence Frapley in the background, behind these three women at their sewing machines?"

Pete squinted as Clay enlarged the picture. The FBI had obviously sent him a much clearer resolution than what he had obtained while on the job. "Yeah…that's him…with two other guys I don't recognize."

Andy folded his arms. "Well, there's your answer, Pete." He began pacing the area on the opposite side of the dining room table. "That Frapley guy, and those oriental guys, are the ones who want you dead."

"My God," Pete huffed. "I remember Chuck pulling me aside after Frapley fired me"

"Yeah?" Sue Beth said.

Pete began recalling all the details. "If not for Chuck buying me a drink, and taking me out to meet his grandfather,

J.P. Osterman

I might have been gunned down in the convention parking lot!" He heaved breaths of disbelief along with a long sigh of gratitude for being alive. When Clay turned his screen and enlarged Tina Bowlett's bloodied body, tears welled in Pete's eyes. He felt Clay accusing her! "She was a nice lady, and kind. In *no way* was Tina involved in trafficking people!"

Turning the screen back around, Clay said, "I just want to confirm that you recognize her, that's all, Pete."

Andy said: "Those...those brutal animals! They slit her throat!" He ran to the bathroom and puked.

Sue Beth wrapped her arm around Pete's shoulder and said: "I'm sure your friend wasn't involved in this, Pete. She was probably collateral damage...someone those gangsters killed to make sure she wouldn't talk...along with the man you knew, Fred. I'm sure the FBI will investigate—"

"Are investigating!" Clay interrupted.

"Yeah," Sue Beth said, "so I'm sure they'll find her innocent, Pete. You wait and see."

Brushing his fingers through his salt-and-pepper hair and pushing his rimless glasses up the bridge of his nose, Don said, "This Snakehead gang is killing witnesses like insecticide dropping mosquitos." His head shaking, he had a hopeless and helpless look on his face as he slid a high-back chair from the living room into the dining room and plopped down. "The FBI or the cops better get here, *and fast*."

Andy walked over to the living room window and peeked through the blinds that snapped back into place. "I don't see anyone coming to help us yet," he said angrily. "Gosh...I'm so ticked off!" Finally, he appeared angry enough to remain and fight the hit men.

Sue Beth shook in fear when Andy opened the front door to better appraisal their situation. It had turned dark outside, with purple cloud cover.

"Shut that door!" Clay ordered, and he slammed it.

Pete believed they were on the verge of becoming human targets. "Who's going to be bringing us reinforcements, Sheriff? Have you received any emails yet?"

Pete's Crossroad

"The U.S. Marshalls," Clay said. "I created an encrypted code and am emailing them our coordinates. If your friend Chuck did the same as I asked him, we should receive word soon from someone who's on the way to help us."

Pete sighed and sat down on the sofa. "That's a relief.

Andy took a swig of water, wiped off his lips, and said: "Clay, you said help should be on the way. Can't my Dad, Sue Beth and me go?"

Clay laughed sarcastically, whipped his gun out of his holster, and set it on the table. "Until I have agents escorting you out of here, you're not safe to even step outdoors. You wanna end up as wild-wolf fodder in the desert?"

Through angry eyes, Sue Beth said, "We have to help Pete, Andy." Her small thin frame seemed to clench with fight. "We just have to!" She walked up to Andy and glared at him. She was obviously bound and determined to make her last stand in the middle of the dining room. "We can't leave Pete here alone with Clay." She began crying.

"He's right though, Sue Beth," Pete said, grabbing her hand. "I couldn't live with myself knowing that something terrible happened to you because of me. I wish you'd *all* go…everyone *except* for the sheriff that is. He has guns, and we have a fighting chance."

"I'm working on getting us all outta here," Clay said, "so just hold on to your breeches."

Pete made her sit down next to him. The wind increased in intensity. A few bottlebrush branches were scraping against the gutters as tumbleweed pummeled the windowpane and brick façade.

Just then, an alarm tripped on Clay's iPhone. "It's the shop with the neon light!" he said. "The hit men are there." He began gathering items to barricade themselves inside.

"They're about twenty minutes away," Don began, helping him, "and we'll buy time because we crushed the tracking device and they need to find the model homes."

Andy pointed at the garage. "I saw some wallboard in there…and I hope some nails and a hammer too so we can nail this place down!"

After minutes of setting up boards and furniture barricades, Don said in an ominous tone, as another roll of thunder roared above them: "The storm is here."

Andy's cowboy boots thudded across the laminate floor as he walked back into the dining room. He appeared worn out as he gestured at Pete and the guns. "Sue Beth, why should *we* put our lives on the line for *him*? I'm pissed off that a crime syndicate is buying and selling young women and children, but we're in no way equipped to fight off hit men...with only four weapons?"

Sue Beth gave Pete an inquisitive glance, then a coaxing expression, prodding him to open up pictures on his laptop.

Pete realized she was remembering what he had told her while they were in hiding in the back of Don's truck—that he had actually seen and talked with her grandfather, George.

Pete gestured no, but she stood up and said: "We need to help Pete because our grandfather told Pete to help us. He also told Pete to send those photos to the Los Angeles District Attorney. Pete can make a real difference in the world by doing that. He's helping people, and we need to help him. Grandpa Gibson's orders."

Whipping off his glasses, Don said, "What?"

"Okay, okay!" Pete said as if George were right in the room with them, except he hadn't seen him since morning. He opened up George's picture on the laptop. "You can talk now, George. Everyone's in the room."

Nothing, only the wind.

"George, come on, say something, anything!" he pleaded.

The picture Hideki had taken of George holding a cup of coffee at the rest stop popped up.

"God," Pete began, rubbed his forehead, "God, I feel like a complete fool!" He sipped water and then jiggled his laptop a little, hoping ghost George might jostle loose. "I'm telling you the truth! How else would I know that this model home would be a perfect hiding spot, huh? Coincidence?" He watched Don's head turning in disbelief as Don wiped his

Pete's Crossroad

glasses with a Kleenex and then slipped them back on.

Clay's mouth dropped open in skepticism as Andy huffed out a laugh and said: "Come on now, Pete. You need a mental ward." He waved at him as if proclaiming him insane.

Sue Beth said, "I believe Pete." She walked up beside him, took him by the arm, and gave a sharp nod of her head.

Ahhh, Don sighed, "this is pretty far-fetched, Sue Beth. Pete, I've known ya for two days now, and you appear to be sane, but I don't—"

"I took that Native American religion and philosophy class, Dad." She began pacing the floor. "You'd be surprised at some of the things people have seen and heard…and many of them invisible. Nature is a very mysterious medium, y'all…and science has been talking about the existence of many dimensions, not just the four we have around us."

They grew silent. An airplane was flying low. "Maybe that's Chuck!"

"Not this fast!" Clay said, checking his watch and un-holstering his gun. "He and his NRA guys are still twenty minutes away from here."

"FBI? Or marshals maybe?" Sue Beth asked.

Peering through the blinds, Clay answered, "Could be, but I don't know 'cause it's dark." He checked to make sure his gun was loaded and then re-holstering it, barely taking his hand from its secured position.

Cocking his shotgun, Andy said, "Well, Pete, I've been thinking about what you said." He put the two guns Clay had brought with him on the table and made sure they were loaded.

"What?" Pete asked.

"Maybe me and my family mighta been dead by now if we hadn't come to this place with ya…I don't know." Andy took a swig of his water. "If my grandfather trusted ya, and told ya to turn in those criminals, then I guess we can back ya up. Besides—" He cocked a gun—the stroking sounds resonating his anger: "I'm pissed off that those jerks have exploited innocent people…time for payback!"

"Maybe it's my dad's way of making a difference in our

lives," Don said, rifling through a telephone book. He had done that several times, obviously a new habit to calm his nerves. "It's not a coincidence that this place will save our lives, like Pete said." Dropping the book, he began looking at the picture of his father on Pete's laptop, and tears welled in his eyes. "My dad—my own father—must have led us here."

Pete sat down next to him. "I never did think much about God, until a bunch of coincidences began occurring in my life," he laughed, "and a ghost! Now, I *definitely* believe in God!"

Sitting at the dining room table with the palms of his hands under his chin, Don stared into the image of his father as if recalling childhood events. "Pete, I believed you heard a supernatural message. I believe you heard my dad."

Touching her father's shoulder, Sue Beth said, "I know you wish things could have been different between you and granddad."

"That's right," he said, peeking up at her. He wiped his eyes with the backs of his hands. "I regret that we never had the chance to make up face-to-face…but I really hated him for being on the road so much…and for not being there when my mom got sick."

"I know Dad," Sue Beth said in a comforting tone of voice as she sat down next to him.

Aaa, Clay exhaled. "It sounds to me like George is trying to make up for all the *I shoulda couldas*."

Shaking his head in disappointment while peering at the picture, Andy bent over Don's shoulder, tapped the image, and said, "Grudges are living hell." He heaved a breath of sadness. "Grudges kill opportunities, but opportunities are what give people life."

"Yep," Sue Beth agreed, "and forgiveness as well."

Leaning over his chair, Clay added: "At the end of a person's life, a fool looks back with only regrets while a wise person says: I made the best choices under the circumstances." Then he turned back, assessing his guns and ammo.

Sue Beth pulled her chair next to Pete. "You think you'll

Pete's Crossroad

ever look for your own family again one day?"

"*Hmmm*," Pete replied. Seeing Don and Andy together and talking about George, he realized how much valuable time they all had wasted to grudges. Now, all they have are pictures, he thought, when they could have had so many happy memories, and George could have died among them.

A sound of thunder and a crack of lightning startled them. They glanced at the ceiling. Rain was beginning to fall.

Sue Beth said, "At least you made up with Fletch, Dad."

Bumping his dad jokingly, Andy said, "It's never too late!"

"And remember...the gifts are still back at your house, Don," Pete said, walked up to him.

Clay still seemed a little spooked by the whole idea. Peering around the kitchen door, he said, "A real live ghost." He popped a potato chip into his mouth.

Pete said, "I wouldn't have believed I saw George myself, Sheriff." He tapped his forehead—an expression of knocking in some sense. "Except that two other people saw George besides me, and Chuck is one of them. He'll be here soon; and after this is all over, he can tell you himself!"

"Okay, all right," Clay said in a placating tone of voice.

Sue Beth's eyes lit up in excitement. "That's it then," she said. "My family believes that you *really* saw my grandfather, Pete."

The sound of a car interrupted them.

"Someone's coming!" Clay said, un-holstering his gun.

Sue Beth crouched down, Andy darted toward the boarded up picture window with his shotgun under his arm, and Don swiped his gun off the table and sat low under the windowsill. Most of the opaque windows were nailed shut, but Clay purposely positioned the boards so as to steady their weapons, aim and fire. Clay snuck behind a wall and motioned for everyone to get down. "Those aren't cops driving up and down the block," he whispered loudly.

Don said: "Pete, call Chuck. Ask him when he's gonna get here 'cause we need him now!" As Pete left for the kitchen phone, Don pointed at the interior of the house. "Get to the bath tub, Sue Beth, and stay there!" She ran upstairs.

The black SUV suddenly stopped, the windows opening.

"Down everyone!" Clay shouted. "They'll most likely fire their best and strongest right at the beginning…so let up waste their ammo!"

The men in the SUV began firing their semi-automatics at all three model homes. The windows cracked and popped. The wallboards covering their windows were absorbing the hits, but not for long, as long lines of polka dot bullet patterns began sieving the outside air. The outside façade was taking D-Day bullet strikes, making pinging sounds on the bricks. Cotton from the sofas and chairs began billowing in the air. The side of the wall by the door exploded with holes. The firing suddenly stopped.

"They're reloading their semi-automatics," Clay said, peeking up over a gnawed-up chair. "Fire, now!" They began firing their guns—the powerful snaps and cracks of their bullet firepower pierced the SUV, pummeling it with lines and holes of mass destruction. "Hit 'em again!" Clay cried, discharging his gun as acrid smoke filled the room.

Andy had his shotgun perched on the windowsill and aimed steadily at the black sedan's window. He fired again, the kickback raising the shotgun barrel. The SUV's window exploded. "I can hear people…but I can't tell if we wounded or killed any of 'em!"

Glass began shattering in the kitchen. Clay said, "I don't know…but they've got us cornered!" Before running to the kitchen, he called: "I'm gonna go defend the back. They're charging us from there too!"

Hearing the sound of an airplane, Pete dialed Chuck's number on the landline. "I know it's him…it's gotta be Chuck, please God" Chuck finally answered his cell phone. "Thank God!"

The plane was flying low like a crop plane spraying pesticides. Chuck said, "We're here, and we got your back, Pete!"

"Do you see the black car, Chuck? That's them! There's

Pete's Crossroad

another black SUV down the street, coming straight for us!"

"We've got a total of two in our sights!" he began. "One in front of the place you're holed up in, and another racing toward ya. That one must be their back up." Chuck was above them now, and circling low as his buddies opened up fire on the SUV in front of the house. "Drop down now!" he called.

Pete called out to Don and Andy, "Chuck's about to fire and says to take cover!"

Just as they fell to the floor, powerful bullets from Chuck's team struck the hood of the SUV parked out in front, blowing the hood off the car. Metal flew like shrapnel from a bomb.

Clay looked through a small hole in the wall. "Five men are exiting the back door!" He shot two.

Andy fired on another two, hitting them, and they dropped dead on the ground. The last man began shooting from behind a green electric box across the street. "I can't see him…too dark!"

Suddenly, the approaching SUV exploded in a plume of yellow flames and black smoke. The green electrical box exploded in the heat, killing the hit man hiding behind it. Chuck had flown low and unleashed a special incendiary bomb, the detonation reverberating like a sonic *boom*, rumbling the ground, shaking the house. Lamps and vases fell as shelves collided. Engine parts splattered on the roof as if a nail gun unleashed all its projectiles. The SUV's door whirred through the air like a Frisbee as a spinning piece of window shield licked the bottlebrush tree, snapping it in two. Chrome bumpers skipped across the dirt like a rock on water. Across the street, a hubcap sliced through a strongbox filled with streetlight bulbs, emitting hissing gases. Part of a hubcap pierced the garage door like an arrow in a bullseye. The last thing to land was the spinning steering wheel, in the center of the dirt lawn.

The noise subsiding, Pete spotted a rear-view mirror that lay rocking, beading with rain water in front of the windowsill.

J.P. Osterman

Pete had the phone on speaker mode, and Chuck called out: "That was a special grenade! I think we got 'em all!"

"Great Chuck!" Pete called. "All five hit men that were firing on us from the front are dead! And everyone had to have died in that other SUV you targeted. Great work, Chuck, whewee!"

"I see more people coming at ya though," Chuck began, somberly, "but according to what I'm hearing over my radio...and my guys who are talking to them, most are cops."

"Oh no," Pete moaned, knowing that Chuck couldn't help him from the air any longer.

"One of my guys says it's a real chase scene...with the cops speeding as fast as they can to chase down some more bad guys," Chuck said. "I'm landing, but I can't get to ya for another five minutes or so, so I hope ya got enough ammo—"

"We do!" Clay said, re-loading his gun, "but not much."

"So this isn't over," Pete gasped; and Andy, Don, and Clay began salvaging whatever objects around them they could find to shield them against another pending invasion.

Pete's Crossroad

Chapter 19 – Snakehead Gangsters

As Chuck landed his plane in a distant field, another gauntlet of cars sped into the abandoned housing tract. Police sirens were shrieking, the cars racing toward them, and ambulance lights were flashing red and white in the distance. But the ambulances weren't moving toward the model homes; obviously, the drivers were maintaining a safe zone from which to operate. Pieces of the ceiling fell down around them as Sue Beth ran downstairs.

Don called to her, "Get back!" He reloaded his gun. "More hit men are coming!"

"Chuck couldn't take out the enemy by way of air 'cause the cops are chasing 'em!" Pete said.

After hearing the sounds of squealing car brakes and door opening and closing, several people darted out of a tall line of brushes from across the street and began firing their semiautomatic weapons. Clay had two guns in hand and began shooting out of several gaping holes in the kitchen walls and windows—the pops and cracks of his guns smoking up the air. Coughing now and then, he ducked and then bobbed up, firing like an expert gunslinger. "Got two of 'em!" he yelled. "Now I'm gonna try shooting those snipers behind the street poles!"

He aimed at the barricaded assassins. "Take this ya Snakehead slingers!" He began bombarding them with a stream of bullets – *pop, snap, snap.* "You can't mess with us in Texas!" he screamed through the crossfire.

From down the street, Chuck and a line of helmeted men began charging down the street. The enemy's firepower suddenly ceased in the realization of an pending battle. The police had cloaked themselves behind metal shields like medieval warriors. They began firing at the hit men.

Over the phone with Chuck, Pete screamed out a safe approach: "The side of the home has the best offense. Divide into groups. Be careful not to expose your rear flank so the enemy can attack you from the back. That's been their strategy thus far."

A police helicopter with a bright-white circle of light suddenly darted out of a dark cloud and began maintaining a static position high above the house. Lightning clashed. The rain was falling heavily. Pete said, "I think we've got Nature on our side." Without more help, they were outnumbered, even with Chuck and his NRA warriors.

After Chuck and a few of his NRA friends scaled a sidewall and vaulted into the model home, Pete grabbed a gun from Chuck and said: "I've never fired a weapon before now, but boy have I learned fast!" They only had bullet holes in the walls and a light from above to help them shoot their targets. Andy, Don, and Clay were now at the front of the house, aiming and shooting at the Snakehead assassins firing on them. Pete could hear grunts, groans, and screams of those outside who had taken direct hits. They were dropping right and left in the street and driveway. The helicopter was landing, somewhere. Pete couldn't hear its whining blades or droning engine anywhere.

After ordering an assault on the model homes next door to them, Chuck cocked a powerful gun, thrust it into Pete's hand, and said: "Just aim and pull the trigger, Pete. That's it. It's semiautomatic and will do all the work." Chuck had the power of his ancestors in his strong arms. With black crayon

Pete's Crossroad

under his eyes and on his brow, he had obviously spent the time between Amarillo and Albuquerque in deep spiritual prayer. He looked austere and mighty in his every move and command. "This is turning into a suicide run, for us *and* for them," Chuck said through angry eyes, "but no one makes slaves out of human beings and gets away with it…never in America again!" He continued to fire.

"*Ahhh!*" Don cried, falling, as Pete continued firing alongside Clay at the back of the house. A bullet grazed Don's shoulder, and Andy stopped firing to hold the wound.

Running at him to help, Chuck launched an arrow this time, striking one of the attackers between the eyes. The man fell to the driveway, writhing. Five more gang members toppled down in the street. Chuck's team had taken them down. Loading another arrow into his crossbow and aiming, Chuck inhaled and said: "These attackers keep charging us like soldiers assaulting Normandy. That's their strategy. We're killing a lot of 'em, but they believe that by striking at us en masse, they'll eventually get one sniper to penetrate this place and take out Pete."

Andy called, "I guess it just takes one to do that…but over my dead body!"

Chuck stuck another clip in Pete's hand. "Let's take these bastard hit men down!"

An oriental group of warriors charged toward the three model homes. With his steel bow cocked, Chuck began firing arrows with precision into the enemy's line of assault. With each arrow strike and gun discharge, an attacker fell, but two made it on to the porch until Don and Andy shot them at point blank range—one in the belly, one in the chest—just as they were about to break into the house.

Suddenly, a second-story window broke. Glass shattered, followed by a the sounds of footsteps.

"Someone's inside!" Andy whispered loudly.

Putting his finger over his lips as if motioning for Pete to stay put, Chuck sidled up the stairs, his body encased in shadow. Pete realized he was setting himself up as a decoy.

J.P. Osterman

Suddenly, a masked man with a black bandana over his face pounced over the stairs into the living room. Drawing out a long sharp blade, he aimed the shiny steel, directing it in an expert fashion towards Pete's face. Staring into the man's slanted eyes, Pete felt cold death ticking, until Chuck jump-kicked the air and launched himself around a support beam. He struck the Snakehead gangster in the chest, thrusting his bowie knife into his heart. The man fell with a thud down the stairs as Clay shot another intruder who had managed to sneak into the house and had targeted Don.

With a shell-shocked expression on his face, Don said, "I don't know how much more we can take!"

The sounds of screeching rubber filled the rainy air. The red and white lights and cycling sirens sounded like an army of police officers. Andy shouted. "The cops! Finally!"

After a sudden spray of gunfire that quickly ended, a row of men clad in black began surrendering.

Breathing deep gulps of air, Sue Beth peeked out of the bathroom. She had a gun dangling in her shaking hand. Obviously, she had shot someone and was in a state of shock. "Can I come out?" Her hair was frazzled, her eyes terrified.

Don ran to her and embraced her. "Yeah, sweetie." He kissed her forehead. She was like a doll in her father's arm. "It's all over now."

A chunk of drywall fell, and a pillow of dust rose into the air just as drops of rain began seeping through the ceiling.

Glancing around while leaning on half-a-counter separating the dining room and living room, Pete said, "This fight's over…but I have a hunch, not for long."

"Why do you say that, Pete?" Sue Beth asked.

He gestured at the street now illuminating with giant battery power lights. "Looking at those gangsters that the cops are hauling in, they keep looking this way…like they're searching to see whether I'm alive or dead."

Clay holstered his gun after making sure the safety was on. "They haven't given up hope in killin' ya, Pete. But I'm sure someone will figure out a solution."

Pete's Crossroad

Chapter 20 – Agent Valarie Tilston

After FBI agents and Amarillo law enforcement officers began rounding up the Snakehead gangsters, a tall brusque female agent walked into the half-bombed out model home. Pete felt almost afraid of her as of the hit men! He wondered what she had in store for him.

"Hi, Mr. Turner, I'm Agent Valarie Tilston," she said, lifting her iPad out of her briefcase. It was decorated with beads and glitter, so opposite of how she was projecting herself to the world.

Pete said, "Hi." His tongue felt numb, his teeth chattering, his arms and legs cold.

Agent Tilston twisted open the shredded blinds, removed her bulletproof vest and sat down at the dining room table. "Take a seat, Mr. Turner, we have a lot of ground to cover and not a whole lotta time to solve your problem." The microphone over her ear hissed off as she tapped it, and her iPad played a lively activation jingle. "I'm gonna call Witness Protection."

"Witness Protection!" he countered. "But I don't wanna go anywhere else right now." When she didn't respond, he checked the time: 2:17 p.m. on a Friday afternoon, but it felt like 10 p.m. "Have you found out who's coming after me?" He began picking at his fingernails, felt self-conscious, and then clenched his fists to stop panicking.

"No one we captured is talking yet," Agent Tilston replied, "but because the entire human trafficking ring extends internationally, we've got the CIA flying in from Washington and L.A. We'll get some answers...you can bet your bottom dollar on that!" She had a torturous glint in her eye as she glanced outside at the pouring rain, the red-and-white flaring lights, and the large groups of federal agents and local police officers collecting information and evidence. People had erected three large tents, and had a bomb squad and CSI vans positioned in strategic locations.

Inside, the downpour sounded like bullets on the windows and roof, the noises reminding Pete of the gunfire, making him twitch now and then. All around them, water was kerplunking into buckets. Don and Andy were setting them up and emptying them, also working around the agents who were collecting evidence. In the kitchen, Clay was giving his statement while sitting alongside Chuck and several other agents as Sue Beth continued sweeping up glass.

Pete watched Agent Tilston direct more FBI agents to collect shell casings and check for fingerprints. Dressed in a black pant suit, she looked near middle age and athletic. With straight lips, she told Pete: "Mr. Turner, we have a plan that we're putting in motion to get you free of this gang for good."

Feeling relieved that he might not have to spend the rest of his life attachment-at-the-hip to the FBI, he asked, "What plan is that?"

"You'll see," she said, waving for people to enter the house. "Wheel it in!" She put in another call on her microphone, and two ambulance drivers stormed through the doorway with a gurney. "You have ten minutes to make Pete Turner look dead."

"What?!" Pete shouted, putting his hands on his throat.

She folded her arms, sat back in her chair, and a flat expression appeared on her face. "Just what I said, Pete...I *can*

Pete's Crossroad

call ya, Pete, right?" After he nodded yes, she said. "We need to make you appear dead...*appear* is the operative word, Pete, so don't worry, and don't fight us on this. Just give us some time and you'll see our plan."

"Fine, okay, I'll play along," he said.

Carrying small make-up cases and suitcases, several men and women entered after the paramedics. She turned to Pete and added, "This is a professional make-up crew we use. They're so good, sometimes Hollywood requests 'em," she laughed.

He didn't think the joke was funny. "How long's it gonna take to make me look dead?" he whispered, peeking out the window. Agent Tilston pulled him down.

Overhearing from the kitchen, Sue Beth took a well-needed break. "Pete, that's a great idea!"

"That's right, Miss Gibson," Agent Tilston said, "because if we can make the gang believe that Pete is dead and buried, they'll leave him alone."

"Buried now?" Pete gasped, thinking that there might be two funerals on Thursday: his *and* George's!

"That's right...buried," Agent Tilston emphasized. A tall poised woman sat down in front of Pete and whipped a plastic drape over him, obviously preparing to cut his hair. Agent Tilston added: "We have to show proof of death first. It's the only way these powerful Snakehead gangsters are going to leave Pete alone." The woman began combing his hair back, her expression analytical as if trying to decide which look and style to give him.

After setting down another empty bucket to catch the rain dripping off the ceiling, Don asked, "Agent Tilston, are *we* all right? Me, Andy and Sue Beth? I also have a son...Fletch Gibson." He told her that Fletch should be showing up any day from his service in the Army.

Agent Tilston turned her iPad tablet around. Showing them the FBI file displaying Pete's evidence, she said, "From the intelligence I've received, your family is okay, Mr. Gibson. The Snakehead gang never discovered that you were assisting

J.P. Osterman

Mr. Turner. You were here with him, but they never linked any of your family members to Pete."

"Thank God!" Don said, wiping his face.

Suddenly, Pete remembered other members of *his* family. "My sister!"

Sue Beth said: "Oh that's right! Did you investigate Dr. Kimberley Turner?"

She and Pete told Agent Tilston that Sheriff Clay Carter had entered in all the information on Dr. Kimberley Turner. The FBI was supposed to be checking to see if Sue Beth's professor was indeed Pete's sister, Kimberley. Meanwhile, the make-up artists had applied a ghostly-gray paste mix to Pete's face, and then instructed him to lie down on the gurney. A TV crew and a female reporter were ready to begin reporting live once Agent Tilston gave them the word.

Pete was twisting and turning his fingers but trying to hide his anxiety as he inhaled deeply, waiting for Agent Tilston to give him the news on his sister. Agent Tilston kept tapping his hands and legs, ordering him several times to remain still as a make-up artist glued a fake hole onto Pete's skull. Pete told Sue Beth, "I don't know what to do...what to say to Kimberley."

Kneeling alongside him, Sue Beth brushed her bangs away from her eyes and said: "You just talk to her, Pete. She's your sister." She shrugged and gave him a little confused twist of her lips. "Just talk to her like I talk to my Dad and brother, that's all ya gotta do...be yourself...you're a nice person!"

Pete sighed and smiled.

"No smiling...you're dying, remember?! You're gonna crack your make-up, and we'll have to apply it all over again." Agent Tilston reprimanded him, gently.

Pete whispered through closed lips: "You act like it's so easy, but I haven't seen my sister in...gosh...about eight years?" An ambulance driver rushed into the house, whipped out a tube of red liquid, and began squirting Pete's hair and shirt with the blood. Trying to avoid the spill, Pete asked him, "Is that blood *real?*"

Pete's Crossroad

"You bet, Sir," the driver replied. Like an artist, he began brushing the blood all over him.

"Just don't look," Agent Tilston said, "and you won't vomit."

"Great...now ya tell me that," Pete said as a male FBI agent excitedly popped his head into the house.

He called to Agent Tilston: "Valarie! Two more minutes and we can get this show on the road." His voice turned to a near whisper through the clamoring rain shower playing drum rolls on the gutters. "The cops have spotted a few Snakehead hit men hiding in the tall brush across the street. They're wearing night vision glasses. We're not going to apprehend them until we're certain we can tap into their internet connections and phone lines. We wanna also try to trick them into reporting Mr. Turner's death to their boss. If we can do that...we nap all of them!"

Agent Tilston's eyes widened and her lips open in amazement. "Great! The trail *could* lead us to all sorts of locations in the orient, and some Eastern countries, if we're lucky." She patted Pete on the leg. "Mr. Turner...I think you found a wedge into an entire global human trafficking operation! Wow! You're a hero!"

"But nobody can know that," Pete said firmly.

"Of course...but too bad 'cause you will have saved an army of people all around the world," she returned.

Pete thought of the pictures he sent the district attorney. "To think I mighta been able to stop a lot of suffering a long time ago—if only—"

"You stopped it now, Pete," Agent Tilston said softly. "*Now* is what matters."

As two more FBI artists tore Pete's clothes and plastered his arms and legs with soot and black chalk, Sue Beth said, "How was the relationship between you and your sister before you left home, Pete?"

Pete had to talk over two artists changing his shoes, ripping his pants, and brushing him with more blood. They were just about through with their endeavors of portraying him dead. After Pete asked Agent Tilston again if she had been able to ascertain the whereabouts of his sister, Pete said to Sue Beth: "Kimberley's a little more than three years older than me. She was going to college when I left home at eighteen."

Agent Tilston interrupted them. "We're about ready for this production to begin," she said, "so let's roll 'em!" She whispered to Pete: "All you have to do, Pete, is stay still, try not to breathe, and do not move...at all." She retreated into the shadows as more agents scattered blood around the scene.

Dressed in paramedic wear, FBI agents lifted Pete to the center of the room among wild bullet holes in the wall as Agent Tilston waved camera operators into the dining room. She then told everyone to hide and remain calm. "Shhh!" she ordered Pete, who told Sue Beth before she disappeared around the corner: "I think Kimberley was upset at me for leaving...even though I had no other choice but to go."

Acting as if she were a movie director, Agent Tilston said to Pete, "I wouldn't normally tell a person something like this now, but perhaps tell you might make you relax and play along with this part."

"What?" he asked, feeling as if his face was turning purple under the make-up.

"Sue Beth's professor at West Texas A&M *is* your sister, Kimberley Turner," she whispered, patting his arm.

"Really!" Pete said, remembering that George and Walks-With-Dreams had told him that being in Amarillo would change his life. He had no idea the change would mean reuniting with his sister. Now he began to wonder about his mother and father.

Patting him again in a gesture of trying to ease all his concerns, she added, "Agent Glantag rode to her home this morning. We're in close communication with Dr. Turner. Thank goodness she kept her maiden name! And we're in the process of locating the rest of your family as well."

He couldn't wait to tell Sue Beth. She was nowhere in sight, neither were Don and Andy. He tried sitting up to see them; Agent Tilston shoved him back down. Now he felt

Pete's Crossroad

panicked. "When will I be able to see the Gibsons again?"

"Later this afternoon...or tonight...after we've secured you a new identity," Agent Tilston replied, waving in a television news crew.

Pete tried to picture Kimberley's face, but he didn't have pictures, and the thought of meeting up with her, his mom, and his dad made him do what Agent Tilston ordered him to do: "Just play dead...like you did when you were playing cops and robbers, or frozen statues, as a kid. Let your arm hang halfway out of the stretcher. Don't move. Don't breathe! And when I tap your foot, hold your breath. Medics will then rush you into the ambulance. Remember, Pete, you're dead...and this is your life we're also trying to save. After I tap your foot twice, you can at then breathe, but remain completely still! The attendants will drive you to the morgue where I'll meet you, and give you the next plan of action. I have an gauntlet of agents guarding you, Mr. Turner. You'll be okay now, I'm sure, but you have to do exactly as I say, understand?"

Nodding slightly, Pete replied, "Got it."

A bright flood light illuminated as a reporter clasped on a microphone, positioned herself in the doorway and brushed back her hair. "Ready when you are," she said.

Agent Tilston pointed her finger at the reporter and whispered, "Action!"

The Hispanic reporter began broadcasting in a solemn voice: "The car chases in Amarillo have ended here, at Edge City, at the abandoned housing tract that developers once dreamed would become a burgeoning retirement community of Star's Edge."

Pete felt a tap on his foot, and he exhaled deeply as the camera focused on his perceived lifeless torso. Red splotches of blood were oozing through his torn sleeves. The make-up artist had placed a fake sack there to show a gaping wound. After the reporter cautioned people watching from the comforts of their homes, she continued: "Members of the Chinese Snakehead gang clashed with FBI agents in this model home between the hours of 10:00 a.m. and 1:45 p.m., which as you can see is now completely decimated by gun fire." The camera focused on holes and bullets lodged in the ceiling, shattered glass, blood stains, a table broken in two, and splintered support beams. "One man lost his life in this battle, Mr. Pete Turner." When she gestured at the body, the camera panned over Pete's lifeless remains—briefly focusing on his face—and agents dressed as coroners wheeled Pete quickly out the door. "But according to Amarillo City Sheriff, Clay Carter, Pete Turner is a hero. He risked his life to expose foreign and domestic corruption by providing evidence to the FBI."

The reporter held up a picture of Pete smiling as if he were alive and well. "But this hero is very dead instead." Suddenly the camera lens shifted to Pete's spilled blood on the floor. "Mr. Turner's evidence will lead to the prosecution of a giant human trafficking ring in Los Angeles that operated several sweatshops in the garment district. The CIA has traced the corruption all the way to Far Eastern countries, extending into the realm of internet theft in Russia." An FBI set director crept up stealthily and slyly positioned a board displaying three pictures. The reporter continued: "We have breaking news: FBI agents have just arrested Terrence Frapley, a Los Angeles corporate icon in America's fashion industry, and two Snakehead gang members who go by the aliases Jianjun and Feng. For more on this story, watch our nightly news broadcast at ten. This is Meagan Dallwinger reporting. Good afternoon."

Agent Tilston motioned to the crew to cut their lights and cameras. The reporter and camera operators dashed out the door as Agent Tilston yelled, "That's a great take!" From inside the ambulance, Pete watched the broadcast from on the FBI's secure videoconferencing screen. "Mr. Turner," Agent Tilston began, "you're almost free of the Snakehead gangsters. Just a little bit longer and we'll unite you with your sister, Kimberley, and the Gibsons. See you later, Pete."

As the ambulance sped down the highway, Pete sat up but then plopped back down on the gurney. He felt relief, but also

Pete's Crossroad

agitation that he had hoped would be gone the second all the trouble abated. Seeing the Skype connection still active but almost about to de-activate, he asked Agent Tilston, "Is everyone all right there?" He was trying to see around her. "Sue Beth? Sue Beth?!" All he could see were forensic investigators collecting evidence.

Suddenly, Sue Beth ran out from the hallway and said: "Here, Pete! We'll all come and see you later...okay?"

"I can't wait!" he said.

She looked energetic, although a bit sweaty and smudgy. "Just hold tight, Pete. It looks like all these terrible things'll soon be over."

"And you can go on and live your life as if none of this had happened, Pete," Agent Tilston added. "You can go anywhere...do anything...except you'll have a new name."

Pete felt speechless. *Do I really wanna go somewhere else?* Agent Tilston's comments kept repeating in his mind like a bad irritation that he had to address: "What do you mean by *a new name*? Yoy mean, like a new identity?" The ambulance hit a bump, and the FBI's giant laptop tilted sideways until Pete caught it.

Agent Tilston laughed. She had white teeth even though they were a bit crooked as if she had once worn braces but her overbite was returning. "Don't worry, Mr. Turner. The people close to you will always know your identity, but the Amarillo coroner is currently filling out Pete Turner's death certificate. You are now officially dead, pronounced dead today on April, 15, 2011 at 1:55 p.m. You'll see the certificate in a few hours," she exclaimed.

Pete gasped in dread, "Huh!"

Her white face enlarged as she stepped closer to her screen. "Peter Michael Turner has no valid social security number, no valid driver's license, and no valid ID card," Agent Tilston said emphatically.

"Okay, enough," Pete said.

Sue Beth's face appeared next to Agent Tilston. "It's the only way you'll be safe, Pete." She turned to Agent Tilston and asked, "What's Pete's new name?"

"Don't know yet," Agent Tilston began, "they're putting together his new identity right now, and should have a new name and new numbers ready for him when he arrives at the morgue."

"You're not going to stick me inside on one of those slats at the morgue, are you?!" he groaned, his body jostling as the ambulance bounced over another bump. The sirens were still shrieking as the driver turned around to tell him they were almost at the county hospital. He told Pete that they had to play out his death all the way...even to the cold slat and even close the door. Shaking, Pete protested.

The driver ordered him to lie down. "Anyone could be at the morgue to take a second look at your dead body, Sir. We need you still, and playing very dead until we tell you otherwise."

Pete began rubbing his forehead. "God...I feel like this is all one bad joke...one huge mistake...one terrible bad dream!"

"Nope," Agent Tilston said.

"God, wake me up when it's over," Pete said, half-praying. He felt so sore all over that his teeth hurt. "I never thought I'd ever see the florescent lights and metal slabs of a morgue, *ever*," he laughed sarcastically. "And as far as a new name and a new identity? Ha! I thought only babies get names in hospitals. Not me!"

Agent Tilston and Sue Beth laughed.

"I'm leaving now, Mr. Turner," Agent Tilston said. "I'll meet with you at the morgue in about forty-five minutes."

She left, but Sue Beth remained on Skype. "Hang in there, Pete," she said, smiling with the innocence of a calm spring day. "They're driving us all back to Amarillo later, after they make sure the coast is clear of gangsters.

Pete felt her encouraging spirit penetrating to the heart of him. "I will," he said, lying down on the gurney.

An agent moved to the back of the ambulance, every so often surveying the exterior to make sure they weren't being followed. The agent told Pete: "Sometimes gangs are ordered

Pete's Crossroad

to bring back physical evidence after a kill, like a finger or toe."

At that comment, Pete tucked down close to the rail. He called to her, "I can't wait to see you, Sue Beth!" He then thought about George. If George were sitting alongside him, he might mistake him for dead and whisk him off to the spirit world right along with him. "And when all this is over," he told her, "I'll ask your dad if he still wants me to work that temporary job in his shop...at least until after we bury your grandfather."

"Oh, yeah, I'll ask him about that as well. I'm sure the offer is still open...whoever you turn out to be," Sue Beth said, her head lowering, expressing disappointment. Then she perked up. "Okay...we'll all see ya later, Pete."

Chapter 21 - Aleksandar Trochenkov

Late Saturday afternoon, at 4:45 p.m. in the coroner's refrigeration section of the morgue, next to the autopsy and forensics lab, Agent Valarie Tilston met Pete. She had on civilian wear instead of a black suit and bulletproof vest. Picking up objects, inspecting them, and scanning the room with a device capable of gleaning eavesdropping signals, she was attentive to every noise, her senses keen on spotting trouble. She kept touching her holstered gun, obviously prepared to fire. Her brown hair curling at her shoulders, she had a flowery purse strapped around her shoulders that matched her salmon-pink lipstick, short Hawaiian print dress, and blooms on top of her flip-flops. When he first met her, she half terrified him with her Special Forces personality. Now, she appeared feminine and muscular athletic.

"You look like you're going on a vacation, Agent Tilston," Pete said, huffing out a laugh. "Either that, or you're retiring to Florida."

"Funny, Mr. Turner," she said, sarcastically, "but there is a method to my madness."

"You mean a method to this show we've been staging since I left the model home," Pete said, donning a bowling shirt, a style he'd never be caught dead wearing in the past.

"Correct," she said, pacing in front of him. "I want to make your transition into a new identity as easy as possible. And I'm dressed this way as also part of the show. Having agents walking in and outta here might make hit men or gangsters suspect you're not dead. We don't want that."

Having had a shower to remove all the blood, make-up, glued-on gore-sores, and fake bullet holes, Pete brushed his fingers through his hair and said: "When will it be safe for me to walk outside? Do you have my new identity yet?"

Lifting up a brown satchel and setting it on the metal table next to him, she tapped it. "Right here!" She unzipped a pouch, several IDs scattered, and she fanned them out like a card dealer. "May I be the first person to greet you into this beautiful world, Mr. Aleksandar Fadei Trochenkov." The name *Aleksandar Fadei Trochenkov* appeared magnified in every type of font on all the IDs. She swept up his new driver license containing his picture and showed it to him, but the pictures had him wearing a mustache. "Ya gotta grow one of these as soon as possible," she said, pointing at the facial hair.

"Huh?" he blinked in disbelief. "What? Ya gotta be *kidding* me!" He took two steps back. "A Russian?" He careened into a steel door. "You're giving me a Russian identity? That's bull—"

"No it isn't, Mr. Trochenkov," Agent Tilston said. "If you let me explain the logic behind this choice in ID, I think you'll agree that your new name will provide you with the utmost protection from the Snakeheads who could possibly recognize you if you go by an American name, pronounce you undead, and put another bounty on your head."

"But I can't even pronounce the name…Troch— Chekov…who?!" He wanted to tell her to shove her new identity "where the sun don't shine," but instead he said: "Let me guess, Val, ar, ie," he returned curtly as she folded her arms like a teacher waiting for her pupil to finish his sissy fit. "If a Snakehead gangster hears a name like Trochenk…whatever, that gang member will think Russian then leave me alone? Is

J.P. Osterman

that your strategy?!"

"That's correct, Aleksandar," she said, emphasizing the name. She picked up his wallet that he tried wrestling out of her hand, picked out his old IDs, and with a scissor, began cutting up everything with the name Pete Turner.

"Oh no...not that one too!" he cried.

Slice, snip, cut...

"Oh no...*that's* my gym membership card—*darn* you!"

She turned around so he couldn't see her, cutting up the last one. "Sorry, but I have to."

"What about all my college credits?" he asked, panicking. "I spent years—"

She set all the chopped cards on the table and pointed at a black carry-on next to the door. "We're in the process of transferring all your academic records and diplomas, Pete. I'm leaving you with that black carry-on. It contains a few articles clothing, a pair of shoes, and some toiletries to get you by for the next few days until you can do some shopping."

"My size is—"

"Our agents sized ya up with the things they found in your carry-on at the Gibson's."

"All my things...gone!?"

"Yep, everything...we have to expunge *everything* that lives and breathes Pete Turner, but we *did* gather some replacements for ya." She then handed him a new birth certificate.

Again he read the Russian spelling of his name: Aleksandar Fadei Trochenkov.

"Say it," she ordered. "Say it like you mean it and know it...like you were born with it, 'cause that's how it's gonna haveta be, or we'll be forced to make you *really* disappear. This is the middle ground, Pete...I mean, Aleksandar." She tapped the ID firmly.

He thought of Sue Beth. He didn't want to disappear. Tasting the sour-stale aftermath of last hour's sandwich, he said: "Aleksandar Fadei Trochenkov."

"Again."

"Aleksandar Fadei Trochenkov!"

Pete's Crossroad

"Good, Aleksandar."

The new name repeated in his mind like a blossoming headache. Slapping the birth certificate on his thigh, he said, "How am I ever going to get used to...this hell-of-a name?!" He wanted to pull his hair out, until he had an idea. "I know! I'll introduce myself as Alex," he shrugged, "after all, it's the American version of that Russian name, so at least I can ask people to call me Alex, right? Or, how 'bout Al?"

Agent Tilston appeared deep in thought as her eyes rolled upward. "I guess so. Alex or Al is okay as a nickname, but you'll have to memorize the correct spelling of your Russian name, and you'll have to make sure you tell people that first! You have to know that name and *all* its corresponding ID numbers by heart, perfectly."

Pete exhaled in dread. "How am I ever gonna get used to this?" As he watched her sweep his old IDs into her brown satchel for disposal, he felt as if were watching someone pouring handfuls of dirt over a dead body. "How am I ever gonna get used to Aleksandar Fadee...no, Alexandar Fadi...Fado, Fadum—crap!" He hit the wall, and the florescent light wavered a bit.

Agent Tilston walked over to him and grabbed him gently by the shoulder. "Time, Alex," she said, emphasizing *Alex*. He realized she was trying her best to help him. Then she walked to the door. "Over time, you'll adapt."

Pete felt as if she were abandoning him. She couldn't do that now! "What about references for jobs? Employment history? My money in the bank?" The mounting panic was bringing him to the brink of hyperventilating. Everything was being stripped away, not a new beginning at all, as the FBI had promised.

Agent Tilston dashed over to him and looked him in the eye. "Everything's in the carry-on, Alex...all the documents you need, including bank statements, credit cards, debit cards, and savings account." She opened the carry-on and showed him a few. She also slid all his new ID's gently into the far reaches of the packed suitcase, except for his driver license.

"You name it, it's here," she said, pulling out a bank packet in the pouch. There are even codes for when you use the ATM set right inside each card's encasement." She showed him the card and a small paper with a pass code written on it.

"I have money then?" He felt a little bit of relief.

"We gave you the equivalent of what you left behind in all your accounts—but not what Terrence Frapley left you, 'cause that's evidence," she whispered.

"I didn't want that anyway!" he said.

"But we replaced those funds, and Witness Protection gives you a *great* monthly stipend until you can procure a new job." He felt even more at ease. "Your worker's name and phone number are in a packet on top of that desk in the bedroom at the Gibson's house."

"Okay…"

"Tonight, when you have the time," she continued, "just look through everything. I think you'll be pleased…even happy since you no longer have to be looking over your shoulder for hit men who want to kill you."

"Yeah, right," he breathed, his composure returning. That money will help, and give him time, and freedom."

"If you have any questions," she said, sliding her business card out of her dress pocket, "call me…anytime, you hear?"

Pete felt as if the light was enlarging and shrinking. "So there's no other options other than Aleksandar Trochenkov, huh?" he asked softly, standing up and staring at his new picture and new name on his driver license.

"Nope," she sighed, "all other options might mean death!"

"I see…"

"Life could be worse, Alex," she said, "or, as I mentioned, another alternative would be disappearing all together."

"Witness protection," he said, trying to imagine all the consequences.

"Yep," she began, stepping back and staring him down. "You'd have to leave Amarillo completely, not even say goodbye to the Gibsons." She turned and began slowly

Pete's Crossroad

walking toward the door.

Pete looked askance at her. "That means I couldn't stick around and bury George, or work at Don's home and garden center, and not even see my sister, or—"

"Or your parents in the future, Alex," she interrupted, handing him a cold Starbuck's mocha latte that someone had quickly handed to her. She and the agents seemed to know every detail about him. "It's your choice." After glancing at her watch, she began sipping her Frappuccino. "But please hurry up and decide, 'cause I'm starving and I have an appointment...actually, a date," she winked.

"Hmm," Pete said. Staring at the carry-on stuffed full of new things, he thought of Sue Beth. "Gosh." He crossed his legs, folded his arms, and tapped his shoe on the base of the metal table. "Hmm." Memories of her grew into an unstoppable river. Sue Beth's soft skin, brown eyes and short bangs made her look a little like Audrey Hepburn. He remembered her soothing voice, thoughtful disposition, the way she played her fiddle, her giggle, and the she slight tilted of her head whenever she was trying to be encouraging and positive. She was heaven sent! Finally, he remembered that sad look of disappointment on her face when he told Andy he would be leave after George's funeral. "George's funeral!" He sat up straight. "I have to attend that! I don't want a ghost lingering around me forever!"

"Ghost?" she laughed. "Some people *like* starting over. Some people *want* to be rid of all the ghosts in their pasts. They like leaving brothers, sisters, mothers and fathers."

Shaking his head because she was misunderstanding him, he said, "I don't mean those kinds of ghosts, I—"

"From what I've read about you, you've always been the type who always leaves." She pulled a brown file folder out of her purse. "Fourteen roommates in the past four years. Two wrecked cars. Sixteen addresses—"

"Stop it, Valarie," Pete shouted, rubbing his aching forehead. When he saw her paused at the door as if implying that he'd never be able to reverse his decision, he said, "Okay,

I'll be Alex. I don't want to leave. I don't know what's in store for me here…but I'll stay." He felt himself stepping on a new pathway through that crossroad that Walks-With-Dreams had described to him…but he could still step back.

Turning around and extending the carry-on to him, she said, "I knew you'd take the new name and not Witness Protection." She put the carry-on's handle in his hand and patted it. "Good luck with your new life, Mr. Trochenkov. And call me if you need me."

Pete felt a weight lifting off his chest, so unexpected, like inhaling fresh air. "I'm sure I'll have questions, Valarie, and I'll call you if my assigned rep doesn't work out." Just give me a few days to check out all this information." He clicked the handle to the carry-on in place and called to her, "Thanks!"

"You're welcome," she replied, "and now I'm off to Maui!" She did a tiny hula wiggle. Before she closed the door, she said, "Wait here. I'll send someone in to escort you outside. You also have a surprise waiting for you at Don Gibson's place, Alex. Enjoy!"

"What?" he called. Valarie Tilston was gone.

Two minutes later, an agent he recognized from the model home put a fake mustache on his face and combed his hair in a different style. He then sprayed him so he appeared to have a few gray hairs. Now, he looked more like Sam Elliott, the narrator of the Dodge Ram commercials! The agent motioned for Pete to walk straight out the door. "Just a precaution," he said, "I don't see anyone who could be tracking you, and we scoped the area, but we need to make sure you're safe."

Another agent dressed as a maintenance worker handed Pete an envelope. "Your new car's over there with everything inside the glove box," she said. "We'll be tailing you for a few days, Mr. Trochenkov, to make sure you're safe and that everything's going well for you." Quickly, she pushed down the brim of her hat and walked away.

Pete opened the door to his new car and checked the glove box. Someone had taken special care to make sure his

Pete's Crossroad

new name was on his registration and insurance card. Everything was in place. Still, he couldn't believe he was Alex. He didn't look like an Alex, or feel like Alex, and he wondered how long it would take to form some type of an affinity to the name and blank-slate of Alex Trochenkov.

J.P. Osterman

Chapter 22 – Filling the Blank Slate

It was past dusk. Only a few cars and trucks dotted the parking lot as evening song of birds piped their calls through the air. As he was about to drive away, Sheriff Clay Carter walked up to the window and tapped on the glass. "Hey, Pe— I mean, Alex!" He tapped the side of his head, an acknowledgement that he'd made a bad slip of the tongue. "Sorry!"

Rolling down the window, Pete glanced around him to make sure no one else was approaching them. "Hey, how's it going, Clay?" He realized it might take a while before he'd feel safe and secure.

When Clay whipped of his sheriff's hat, his toupee almost rolled off. Smiling and crossing his arms on the window frame, he said, "Pete, you know the MacDonald's across the street from Stan's Drive-In?"

"Yeah," Pete replied.

"Can you go there now? We had to debrief some o' the people in that accident," he said, winking. "People are waitin' to meetcha there, right now."

Pete did want to tell Chuck thanks and to exchange new information with him, so he said, "I'll be there in about ten minutes."

Tipping his hat a little, Clay whispered, "Actually, I'm here to escort you there." He peered over his shoulders, obviously assessing the parking lot.

Nodding, Pete said: "I know, I get it...you're just taking precautions."

"So follow me then," Clay said.

Trailing close behind him and then approaching McDonalds, Pete noticed that some snippets of crime-scene tape were stuck and wavering in a few tree branches in front of Stan's. Memories of what had happened to him earlier flooded his thoughts, and he felt instant panic. Putting his car into park, he bumped his head on the steering wheel and breathed into it. *Where am I gonna go? What am I gonna do for a job? Should I head off into the sunset...sunrise? Stay here...in Amarillo?*

Sue Beth's face popped into his mind. He realized that every time he debated whether to leave Amarillo, he became inundated with thoughts of her and feelings for her. Shutting off the engine and getting out of his car, he glanced at his reflection in the window. He ran his fingers through his artificial salt-and-pepper hair. He looked ten years older with the fake mustache; and another day's worth of hair growth on his face made him look entirely different from when he had arrived in Amarillo. He believed he might snap! He didn't recognize himself...except for his white teeth. He sighed in relief...at least they were the same, and his lips and smile. They were like grounding wires to his old familiar identity. Even his styles of clothes was completely different! He used to wear starched shirts and dress pants. Now he had on blue jeans and a cowboy shirt. Turning from side-to-side, he said to his reflection, "God I've changed in just two days...two days! I look like Sam Elliott...almost an old man!"

Everything was different, except for the Rolex. Quickly, he pushed down his sleeves, concealing it. The Rolex was his—his manager symbol—in case he might decide to strike it big in some grand city like New York. They forgot to take that away from him, and he wasn't going to call Agent Tilston and offer it up to her. Shivering, because the night had created a blanket of white on the tile roofs and black pavement, he grabbed his denim jacket and walked towards McDonalds.

Out of the back seat of Clay's unmarked car stepped a woman who was glancing around the parking lot with a frenzied expression on her face.

Noticing her, but barely recognizing her, Pete ran to her, "Kimberley?"

"Oh my!" She had her arms outstretched as she ran to hug him. "Alexandar!" Reaching him, she embraced him, whispering into his ear: "I know about your new identity. It's okay. The FBI counseled me."

Feeling suddenly safe, he pushed her away so he could get a better look at her face. "Kimberley! It's really you!"

She hugged him as if holding on for dear life. "It's been so long! I've missed you! I tried to locate you, but couldn't."

"About eight years," he said.

"Too long," she said, pulling away from him and then inspecting him from head to toe. Wiping her eyes, she continued to cry. "I can't believe we both know Sue Beth!"

Pete wiped tears out of his eyes. "Oh my God," he began, "you haven't changed a bit." He inhaled deep gulps of air. "Seeing you is the best thing that's happened to me in a long time, Kimberley!"

"You can say that again!" she said. "Let's get inside so I can get a better look at my little brother."

Walking toward the yellow light illuminating her face, he noticed Kimberley hadn't changed much, except for having an different hairdo and a few age lines around her eyes. "You look great. Do you still run a lot?"

"Marathons," she replied, "that's how I first came to Amarillo."

"What made you stay though?" he asked, holding the door open for her while glancing around; but he couldn't see Chuck or Sue Beth.

He was about ready to turn around and ask Clay were everybody was sitting until Clay said: "You go order.

Pete's Crossroad

Everyone's in the kid's area. We closed it off so we could all meet in a place we knew would be safe."

Glancing over his shoulder, Pete saw opaque windows with a large jungle gym. "Okay," he said, pointing out crawl tunnels, "but I passed the four-foot height limit years ago."

Clay and Kimberley laughed.

"I can't fit into those tubes," Pete chuckled as he slapped his bicep. "See ya in a second."

Scanning the area, Clay quickly disappeared behind the partition leading into the children's play area.

The line to order was long, but he dashed toward Kimberley who was walking there and waving for him to join her. She had her short brown hair pulled back behind her ears in plastic headband, and she had the elegant and sophisticated posture of a model. He said again, hugging her: "This is all so unbelievable. I met this man—a shaman in Albuquerque.

"Really, wow!" she said.

"He told me that being in Amarillo would change my life." He shook his head in disbelief and then looked her over from head to toe. "Boy has my life sure changed!" George had told him that as well, but he didn't want to tell Kimberley he was seeing a ghost, even though he was convinced beyond any doubt that George was real...and God...and the afterlife!

Kimberley giggled as if someone was tickling her. "I am *so* happy to see you, Alex! Gosh...my little brother...right here now, and standing in front of me." Then she whispered into his ear as she eyed the room suspiciously: "I have to get used to that name, Alexandar. Everyone has to call you that or else—well, you know." But then she shrugged as if avoiding all the terrible possibilities of what could happen to him should his new identity be compromised.

"You were never the pessimist, Kimberly," Pete said, keeping his arm around her shoulder while peering down into her eyes. She was about a foot shorter than him, and he told her: "I expected that ten years would make you grow up, or me grow down." She laughed. "But you still look the same as you did eight years ago, Kimberly." Suddenly, he felt a thick fog of avoidance move through his mind. He remembered why he'd left home. He looked up at the menu for relief.

"Aren't you going to ask me?" Kimberley said, pulling her large black Chanel purse in front of her.

Pete exhaled. "*Ahhh*...Mom and Dad." He swallowed hard, his throat dry and stinging.

"Just a minute," she said, battling a sudden cough, until the cashier asked to take their order. "I'm paying, Alex," she said, pushing him away, her lips vibrating, her face blotch-red as if she might cry. "My little brother...all grown up. I missed so many years." She cried.

The French-fry air cooled when the air conditioner whirred on as Pete wiped his eyes and began filling a white paper cup with Ketchup, telling her, "It's my treat next time, Kimberley." When she began to protest, he stopped moving and added: "You always took care of everything when we were growing up. You took care of me and even Mom sometimes. But now that I'm not planning to leave anytime soon, and I don't know how long I'm going to stay in Amarillo exactly...but next time we get together, it's my turn to take care of *you* a little bit." He watched her as they waited for the cashier to bring them their order. Eight years had gone by; and now, she was a college professor, and maybe married. Could he be an uncle? Uncle Pete? No, *Uncle Alex.* He kept forgetting his new identity. He hoped he wouldn't slip up and reveal his old self one day. "My gosh!" he exclaimed.

"What's wrong, Alex?" she asked, repeating the name as if trying to hammer in the new identity.

He put down his food. "Nothing, I'm just wondering if you're married? Do you have children? Where do you live?" He couldn't blurt out the questions fast enough let alone wait for the answers.

She laughed. "I'm married." She picked up her tray and they headed toward soda fountain. "His name is Stewart. We've been married five years." She filled her cup with ice as she added: "He's a chemistry professor, but we don't have any children."

Pete's Crossroad

"You mean, not yet," Pete said. "I know when we were kids you used to say you wanted five."

She laughed. "No, just one now."

He hugged her affectionately. "Then I'll be Uncle Alex." He sighed when he said that name. "Alex. I'm never gonna get used to this," he whispered. "What am I gonna do?"

She laughed as the stream of Coke filled her cup. "You'll get used to all this, Alex. It'll take some time, but before you know it—one day at a time—all the pieces will fit together. Your life will turn out." When she set her full cup on the tray, she pulled Pete a little closer to her, out of the earshot of others. "That's what life is, change." She grabbed his shirt and braced him against her. "But I have bad news."

"What?" He stepped back.

"Dad's dead, Alex," she said, flatly.

"Oh." He remembered his father, gripped the counter, and shut his eyes. "What a violent man. He always used to hit us, and Mom. I don't know what to say. I wanna say…he deserved it." He felt a knot in his stomach, eating away at him.

She laid her head gently against his arm. "He's buried in Colorado."

"Did he ever sober up?" he asked.

Through watery eyes, she replied, "Nope." She picked up a napkin and swept it up her cheeks so as to miss her mascara.

Leaning on a steel bar separating two booths, he asked: "Where's Mom?" He glanced around, hoping to spot her.

Kimberley perked up and smiled. She had straight white teeth and smooth skin. In the glow of her tears, she looked twenty again, her age when he last saw her. "Mom's living in Dalhart, Texas, about seventy miles from here. She's a court reporter for Dallam County."

Pete felt stunned. "Wow, she was a waitress when we were growing up. Now she's a court reporter?" He sipped his Coke. "That's great!" He felt a surge of curiosity and a longing to see her. Years ago, he couldn't wait to leave home. Now he was beginning to feel a tug of attachment pulling him towards his mother.

J.P. Osterman

Steadying her tray on the edge of a table, Kimberley said, "Mom went back to school after Dad died six years ago."

"Six years...*hmm*," Pete said, shaking his head. Next to the Coke machine, he broke down crying.

"What's wrong?" she asked, patting his back.

Turning around, he fell into her arms. "I thought hearing that Dad was dead would make me feel better. Like I'd be finally free of him." He sobbed. When he saw a few people pointing at him, he quick pulled away from her and breathed deeply. "I don't feel any better though. I never knew him. He never knew me!"

Softly, she said, "Dad never really lived at all, Pete. He was, as the expression goes, a dead man walking through life."

As they sat down in an empty booth, he felt another burn sting at his eyes. "What a drunk!"

"I know, Alex," Kimberley said, obviously trying to comfort him. "He died an alcoholic death. I was there when his liver failed." She shook her head as she spoke. "It was a terrible, painful way to go."

Pete felt his jaw clench and he tightened his hands into a ball. "He deserved it," he said, hitting the table.

Kimberley tapped him again and said: "He was sick Pete, that's all...real sick."

Suddenly, a deep revelation occurred to him. As George had been haunting him to make amends with his son and grandchildren, maybe, through Kimberley, his father was making amends to him. "Maybe, through you, Kimberley, because you're here with me now...our dad is trying to tell me he's sorry for all the bad things he did to us."

"That could be," she said, "if so, it's working. I'm happier now than I've been in a while, especially since seeing you again. A family entered the restaurant to place their order. The father was laughing with his children, the mother playfully shuffling them away from the quarantined play area. Gesturing at the contented family, Kimberley said: "I know we never had what *they* seem to have, but we have each other, Alex. Now is what counts. And if you want, I'll call Mom. I'll tell her we can drive there and see her, if you're willing..."

"Oh, tomorrow is Easter," Pete said, wanting to see her immediately but remembering he had made plans for the week with Don and his family.

Kimberley ate a French fry. "Is next weekend all right then?"

Pete sighed. Whenever someone brought up the topic of staying in Amarillo, he felt so confused and unsettled. He wanted to create roots in one place, but staying also meant not moving! "Okay, I guess. I guess I'll stay that long."

"What's wrong?" Kimberley asked.

"I don't know whether I want to stay here in Amarillo or leave," he debated. When he glanced past her, he could see an outline in the cordoned off play section: Sue Beth!

After taking another sip of her drink, Kimberley said: "You don't have to decide that now, do you? I mean, you've had a ton of bad things happen to you in the past few days."

He gasped and whispered, "So the sheriff told you everything?"

Her eyes were blue and wide, her gaze wandering everywhere. "Yes, *and* the FBI." She pulled out a business card. "Agent Tilston said for you to call her. The Department of Defense is hiring civilians to help relocate people. With your degree, Agent Tilston said you'd be an asset. I think you'll get extra protection by staying close to the FBI."

His mind racing, he said: "A government job? Wow! That certainly would be steady, *and* secure!"

Kimberley winked. "It would mean a permanent job, Alex." She emphasized those words. "A lot of people now-a-days would be more than happy to have a position like Agent Tilston's offering you."

"*Hmm*," he said, glancing beyond her to the outline of Sue Beth's figure behind the partition.

Turning around, Kimberley nodded toward the play area: "I've met them. They're nice." Then she gave a sly glance to Pete. "And she likes you...a lot. Sue Beth."

"Think so?" he asked, trying to get a better look at Sue

J.P. Osterman

Beth. He felt like running to her.

"I sure do," Kimberley replied, "and I think you like her too…a lot," she said, emphatically. "It just sounds like you don't want to admit that."

"Me?" he chided. One more time, his big sister had succeeded in revealing one of his secrets. She was being truthful, and he liked hearing it. He had needed some of that necessary medicine.

Rubbed her finger on the table, she said: "Do some serious thinking, Alex. Talk to Agent Tilston. Maybe there's a place for you here, in Amarillo."

"Here, in Amarillo," he repeated.

"You do have *me* now, you know," she said, stealing another French fry and eating it. "And Mom."

"Have you told her about me?" He held his breath, waiting to see if he could read a response in her blue eyes.

"Yep." She sat back, smiled, and folded her arms.

"What did she say?" He wished they could have a computer mind connection so he could have an instant answer.

Kimberley glanced around again, obviously suspicious of their being overheard. Leaning over the table, she whispered: "The FBI talked to her about two hours ago. She knows everything, including all the information about Alexandar." She said his new name slowly as if it was a new word in the dictionary. "But what I'm trying to tell you, Alex, is that you have family now if you chose to have us in your life." She had a look of sadness and loss on her face.

Grabbing her fingers, he clenched them. "I'm so sorry for running. So many wasted years—"

"It's okay, Alex," she began, "everything will get better with time. Just put one foot in front of the other, and in no time, you'll have answers. Things will fall into place."

Suddenly, the words that Walks-With-Dreams had told him popped into his mind. The shaman's face rounded clear and crisp. "Kimberley! A guy told me those exact same words a few days ago."

"Who?" Kimberley asked.

Pete's Crossroad

After telling her about George's sudden death on the Greyhound bus, George appearing everywhere and bugging him, and his futile attempts at exorcising George's spirit, Pete replied, "Walks-With-Dreams said that the best way to tell if you're going in the right direction in your life is to see how things fall into place...people, places and things aligning just right," he said, gesturing in a straight line.

Standing up, Kimberley motioned for him to walk toward the cordoned off play area. "That makes sense. You said that man is a shaman?"

Pete nodded an emphatic yes. "With wisdom that I've never heard of before."

Stopping at the door, she said, "Well, things sure *are* falling into place for you, Alex." She lifted her eyebrow and gestured coaxingly at Sue Beth's outline behind the opaque window. "I guess you'll have to consider Amarillo as a big turning point in your life...a positive thing that's happened to you in spite of the hardships you've experienced since leaving home."

"*Hmm*," he sighed, thinking of the wasted time he'd spent forcing himself to pursue the wrong career and the wrong people in his life. Now, he had Kimberley with him, and his mom was an hour's drive away. Maybe, he'd soon have a new exciting career! Walking into the high play area that reeked a bit like stale socks, he glanced at a set of monkey bars and two blue and red tunnels that looked like pieces in a park.

Kimberley laughed. "Maybe someday, you'll have a child who'll be playing in these exact same tunnels while your friends and family will be sitting around watching and visiting."

"Wow!" Pete gasped, blinking in the realization that his life was definitely changing. "Not yet, Kimberley, please, you're scaring me half-to-death here!"

She tapped him jokingly on the arm as he waved to Sue Beth who began walking toward him. At another table, he saw Chuck waving hello. Chuck's NRA team spotted him and yelled, "Hurrah!" Don, Andy and Clay began toasting to their health with Cokes and root beers. Everyone were his friends.

His friends! "Maybe staying here isn't such a bad idea, Kimberley," he whispered, just out of ear reach of Sue Beth. "I wonder how Don, Andy, and Sue Beth will feel if I bring up the idea."

Shrugging, Kimberley said, "There's only one way to find out...ask them."

Making the area into one giant table, Don pulled over a table while Andy slid over four chairs. "Here, Kimberley, take a seat," Don said.

Sue Beth took Pete by the arm, quieted the crowd, and said, "I'd like to introduce y'all to Aleksandar Fadei Trochenkov!"

They raised their Coke cups into the air and toasted him.

Feeling embarrassment, Pete said, "Call me Alex, okay? Pleeease?!" They all began eating and chatting, like one large happy family.

Leaning over to Pete, Kimberley said, "Alex, that girl, *my* student, Sue Beth, is the best thing that could ever happen to you. I know her. She's real nice."

For a moment, he believed he saw the glow of an angel's halo around her. "Maybe...I have to think about that some more. I have to decide whether I want to stay here...see if I can get a job."

"Well, I can see one thing. She can hardly take her eyes off you," Kimberley said.

Pete suddenly thought of his mother. "Oh, I want to give you all the information about where I'm staying and my new numbers." As Kimberley rifled through her purse for writing implements, he searched his pockets. His thumb hit metal. After pulling out the piece, he looked at it and said, "This is the cross that Tina Bowlett gave me a few days ago!"

"The girl who was murdered, right?" Kimberley asked, softly.

Through stinging eyes, he said, "She gave this to me, obviously right before she died." The small cross glistened in the light. "She said the hands represented a crossroad for me. She said...she hoped I'd find happiness and a new direction for my life after Frapley fired me."

Kimberley said, "That's beautiful, Alex. The FBI told me all about Tina. She was a victim in that whole human trafficking scheme. Terrible!"

Clenching the cross, he breathed through his tears as he remembered Tina Bowlett. "She told me that Easter is a time of new beginnings." He put down his hamburger. Even the French fries looked unappetizing. "She's gone. Nothing new for her."

"But there is for you, Alex," Kimberley said, "and Heaven is for her."

His sister's tender taps on his hand brought back feels of security, and he sighed as he touched her smooth forehead. "Here," he began, "I want you to have this cross." He put the silver symbol into her hand and folded her fingers around it.

"Me? I—I can't—"

"You have to," he demanded. He pushed her hand away. "This is probably the most special thing I have, and I want you to tell the story of it to your own kids someday. All right? Please?" Peering up, he noticed that Chuck and his friends were about ready to leave. He stood to say goodbye, as he watched Kimberley pull the cross close to her heart. "I'll be right back, Kimberley," he said, scooting out of the booth. "I wanna give Chuck all my information and set up a time when I can see him and his grandfather in the future."

Kimberley unclasped her chain necklace and slipped on the cross. "I'm going to keep this cross forever, Pete…and cherish it…thanks!" She put on the necklace and sat down with Sue Beth who slid into the booth next to her.

Stretching out his hand for Pete to shake, Chuck said, "I can't wait to tell my grandfather about this *great* reunion. *And* the shootout. *And*—" he whispered, "your Russian name."

They laughed. After saying farewell to Chuck and his friends, Pete and the others continued to eat, talk, and celebrate until the restaurant closed at midnight.

J.P. Osterman

Chapter 23 – George Returns

"Wake up, Pete! Wake up!" Someone was shouting right into his face, jostling him out of a deep sleep.

Pete checked the time: 7:15 a.m. "Huh? What the heck?" He squinted into the early light, smacking his lips to get out the stale taste of night breath. When he could finally see clearly, he recognized George. "George! Finally!" He sat up straight. "Where the heck have ya been? I called for you yesterday. All hell broke loose! A couple o' agents thought I was nuts or drank peyote-spiked juice!" He scooted back into Fletch's headboard, hitting the edge. "Ouch!"

"Pete, get up. It's Easter morning…come on!" George said, bending down close, nose-to-nose with Pete. He was still yellow transparent with his blue-green eyes, his face showing the excitement of a child on Christmas morning. One moment George was next to him; the next second, at the door!

Pete realized that his body was only an aura that he could pass right through if he would just stand up and walk to the bathroom. Pete did noticed one thing different with George this time: he was less visible and bright than the last time he'd seen him. "You're fading," Pete said, sitting on the edge of the bed. He turned his laptop around on the desk so he could get

Pete's Crossroad

a good glimpse of the picture Hideki had taken of him and George. "I always like to compare what I see on this screen to you so I can judge how close you're getting to leaving and letting *me* rest in peace." He yawned and ran his fingers through his hair. "Gosh I need a haircut!"

Laughing, George waved, gesturing that they were wasting time with petty talk. "It's Easter! And my son has my big suitcase open. He's about to give everyone my presents!" He was dressed in blue jean overalls and a bright white t-shirt. Pete remembered when he had first seen George. He always looked sad and dejected. He walked around as if in a state of permanent sag, and the lines and frowns on his face shown all the tatters and rips of mistakes and regrets. But now, George was almost dancing a jig!

Chuckling and amazed at his complete transformation from sullen and sunken to perky and child-like, Pete said: "Heaven sure must be good for you, George. It almost makes me not feel so afraid of death." That made him think: "I guess that's why God doesn't allow spirits to show themselves all the time, 'cause people wouldn't be afraid of dying and wouldn't care about living!" What a gift George had received from God, and he felt grateful for being a recipient—most likely, a most unusual case!

Suddenly, George turned solemn. "No need to be afraid of death, Pete." Then he began pacing over the carpet in front of Fletch's bed. "I mean, Alex. Death is just a transition…but ya wanna make the best of your life."

Pete walked into the restroom and splashed water on his face. "So you know about my new identity?"

George laughed from his round belly and his echo caught in the curtains, making them flicker a little. "Of course I know about Aleksandar Trochenkov. I was here yesterday, in your computer, when the FBI cleared this place for spyware and installed that emergency speaker phone next to the doorframe." He pointed to the white box as he sat down on Fletch's bed. Never once did George leave an indentation. "It seems you're all set for a new life." He rubbed his hands, a gesture telling Pete that his old dirty life was now nice and cleaned up.

"Uh-huh," Pete huffed, "but I still have no idea how I'm ever gonna get used to the name." Again he splashed water on his face as he glanced into the mirror. Now he had thick black stubble, and his hair had grown over the tops of his ears. "Whoa! Yuck!"

"A great disguise for ya!" George added, laughing.

Then Pete peered around the door at his cowboy clothes and scuffed boots at the side of the bed. "I have no idea how to shine those things." He picked up his shirt. "And I'm not used to these kinds of clothes." He exhaled in exasperation. "This isn't my style. It's not me!"

George waved him off. "Ah, Pete, you're bein' silly. Ya still look like a race car driver." He disappeared and then reappeared right next to Pete.

"*Nah*, I look like Sam Elliott! And with this temporary hair style and gray highlight those agents gave me, I look like I'm thirty-five instead of twenty-six!" Pete said, careening.

In a display of deep thought, George peered upward, his forefinger tapping on his lower lip. "I remember seein' him on TV." He had an expression of pride on his face as if pleased that he still had a good memory. "Still, Pete, ya put too much importance on how ya look. Ya look fine...ya look twenty-eight." He winked at him and then whispered, "I know Sue Beth likes ya just fine—*ha ha ha*!" He leaned into Pete's reflection in the dresser mirror and then shot him a sly smile.

Feeling a bit embarrassed, Pete said waved him off this time. "I don't know how I'm gonna do all this." As drops of water trickled down his forehead, he rubbed them off his nose. "I have a new identity. All my stuff is gone...some had sentimental value because they belonged to my dad, who I found out is dead." Helplessness wafted through him.

"Sorry to hear that, Pete." George was now hovering next to him.

"I *hope* they're still in storage." Pete took out Agent Tilston's card. "Tomorrow, I'll call and ask her, but for now, I

Pete's Crossroad

have a jalopy for a rental car, and still no job." He felt pressure increasing in the blood pumping through his neck.

George put his transparent hand on his shoulder. "Well, Pete, some of those things ya said aren't really true."

"Yeah, like what?" he asked, sighing. "Everything feels so darn hard...so insurmountable." He felt tired even though the day had only just begun.

Spinning around like a top, his yellow ghost aura creating streaks of light, George said: "That's life, Pete...I mean, Alex. It's moment-to-moment stuff ya gotta deal with." He still had his hand on Pete's shoulder, but Pete felt nothing. "You'll survive...just like everyone else who calls Earth home." He rubbed his big belly and glanced at it as if he had heard a growl. "Life...your circumstances...could be worse." He gestured from his lips to his hips. "Ya could be dead!"

"No thanks!" Pete exclaimed.

George moved closer. "Everything's fallen into place for ya so far."

"Uh-huh," Pete said.

"And ya have friends now," George said, tapping him again. "They'll help ya. And just call that FBI agent. What's her name?"

"Agent Tilston," Pete replied, sighing, realizing he was creating more distress—making his own misery. Then he remembered some good things that had evolved out of the seemingly bad events. "I *did* see my sister Kimberley again."

"That's great! See? A good thing," George said.

Pete dried his face and spread toothpaste on his brush. "I never thought I'd ever see her again...or my mom. I'm probably going to see her next weekend."

"Great! See?" George said, bobbing in the air. "I told ya your life would change in Amarillo." He snapped his fingers and began dancing in place. He seemed to be preparing for a much larger party.

"So when will you leave, George?" Pete parted the curtains and opened the blinds as he brushed his lower molars. Through the minty foam, he asked, "Don't you think it's time for you to leave?" He saw George's pale outline reflecting off a blind as he walked back into the bathroom. "You really have to give this place up, George." Motioning around the room, he suddenly stopped, put his hands on the sink, and said, "Just like *I* have to give up my old life of Pete Turner." He rinsed his mouth out and wiped his lips. "I know it's not easy to let go…to start over somewhere else." He pointed to an early childhood picture of his family that Kimberley had given him last night. "Since leaving home, I've spent years stuffing down old hurts, ruminating over bad memories, and holding grudges," he huffed. "I wasted *years* moving around, not talking to my sister and my mom, and using and abusing all sorts of things to escape from facing my feelings, and them."

His arms and legs suddenly numbed. His throat stung; his shoulders pinched, and he rolled them, trying to stop the panic and sadness from inching up into his spine, immobilizing him. "I told myself I was never going to see them again." He shut his eyes and clenched his fists, movements to fend off a deep well of tears. "All these years, all I did was hurt myself when I believed I was punishing them." He felt the gloom of shame and remorse wrenching in his stomach like an infectious computer virus—prodding him to isolate—driving voices enticing him to pack up his things and leave. Imagining the disease as a bad worm on his cheek, he wiped his face again and flicked the hand towel into the sink. He spit into the toilet bowl, and slop gurgled down as gray dregs from his toothpaste. "Not anymore! The past is dead. I've learned from it. Now, I move on, George. You should too."

Still sitting on the edge of Fletch's bed but not leaving any impressions, George said, "Maybe that's why all this happened for you, Alex." He put his hands palm-side down and began moving his fingers as if trying to smooth down the fabric. "My meetin' ya on that bus and bringing ya here helped change your life." George now had intense eyes, large and blue green.

The more Pete looked into them, the more he became lost in a trance. He began to see a vision of what would have happened to him if he had continued to live on his old

Pete's Crossroad

destructive path through life without ever meeting George. "*Ahh!*" he cried, grabbing his chest, his back hitting the wall. The vision was impossible to stop:

It was late night, in a Las Vegas alley, with lights flaring in the distance. He had gone to Vegas instead of Amarillo. The Snakehead gangster with the Phoenix tattoo had him pinned down in a grimy alley. With his gun cocked and aiming at Pete's face, the tattooed man was about to shoot him between the eyes.

Snap! "Pete!" George shouted, snapped his fingers again in Pete's face.

"Okay…okay," Pete said, gasping, wiping some sweat off his temples. "Whoa, what a completely different reality," he inhaled. "Is that what would have happened to me if I hadn't met you on that bus?" He exhaled. "Wow."

"Whatever ya saw, Alex," George said, his yellow ghostly body pacing, "that's what woulda happened."

"Death." Standing, Pete dashed into the bathroom and splashed more water on his face. But when he peered into his reflection in the mirror this time, he sighed in relief. "I guess I should be happy to be alive." Returning to the bedroom, he asked, "So, what about you, George?" He stood in the doorway, leaning on the frame. "If I have to get used to being here…living in this new skin of mine…what about you?"

With a sad round face and his bald head shining as if it were reflecting sunlight, George stepped back toward the door leading into the breezeway. "The presents first," he said. His voice sounded low and throaty as if it were running on a slower frequency. "Prrreessennnttsss," he said.

Grimacing, Pete said: "Your voice sounds like it's a long string being pulled to the breaking point. What's wrong?"

George began flickering in and out of existence.

Pete thought of him as a hologram signal that the Divine Maker was slowly recalibrating in order to take George to Heaven. Pete said, "Do you still think that Don and your grandchildren don't forgive you?" He walked over and stood over George's slightly sunken face that kept hissing and wavering in and out of reality. "They do forgive you, George." He sat down in front of him and put on his cowboy boots. "They told me they forgive you...several times, and your son, Don, really regrets not making up with you." He pointed at Don's part of the house. "Don's going to have to live for the rest of his life with rejecting you after you tried so many times to apologize to him...*and* for keeping you away from your grandchildren."

George was nodding as if understanding.

"But Don's made up with Fletch," Pete continued. "He should be here, and home from Afghanistan any day now." He had to infuse George's spirit with hope. "So, a lot of good things have come out of my meeting you on that Greyhound, George." He felt the sting of incoming emotions burning in his throat, his eyes welling with tears of gratitude. Swallowing hard, he added, "I think it's time for you to move on, George...to Heaven. I think staying here is only suffering for you." He walked over to the window, opened the blind, and let sunshine blast into the room. "Your family forgives you. Pain and punishment time is over." He unclasped the window stops, heaved up the window, and let crisp air whoosh into the room. "Smell that," he breathed. "It's a brand new day! A whole new twenty-four hours filled with moments of opportunities." He imbibed oxygen into the bottom of his lungs. "And I'm taking in all of them!" For a second, he believed he saw Heaven in the God rays beaming out of a few gilded clouds on the horizon.

Beneath a blue blanket of sky, a white frost had settled on the ground, and a few songbirds were perched on bushes outside the long breezeway leading into Don's house. On the terrain, there was a gentle rolling of umber and deep burnt-orange mounds speckled with cacti. Texas oak trees seemed to stretch on forever as did the thick tall weeds, vibrating in sheets in the wind.

Seeing that the giant Texas oak tree on the side of Don's house was dotted with snow, Pete spotted green buds on some of the branches. "Look, George," he pointed, excitedly, "Sue

Pete's Crossroad

Beth said *that tree* out there would come back to life when Fletch comes home." He wiped his eyes. "It's like overnight that tree began turning green! Amazing, huh, George?"

George didn't answer.

When he turned around to see him, he heard buzzing on the new loud speaker. Throwing on his shirt and pressing the speaker button, he asked, "Yes?"

Click. "Alex, am I bothering ya?" It was Don. "Can ya hear me all right?"

"Loud and clear, Don," Checking his watch, Pete noticed the time: 8:33 a.m.

"We're goin' to church this mornin'. We're wonderin', well, if ya wanna come along with us," Don stammered, obviously trying not to be pushy.

Knowing he hadn't been to church in years but also thinking he might meet some people, Pete said: "Sure, just let me finish dressing. I'll be out in a few minutes." The speaker clicked off.

Sitting on the edge of Fletch's bed—the spot where George had once sat—he finished dressing and fastened the clasp on his Rolex. He recalled some of worries he had mentioned to George…worries about his car and a job. And he'd never see Tina Bowlett again. Gangsters killed her! And his sentimental possessions? Stuck in storage in Santa Monica.

He laughed as he began polishing his boots with the damp towel on which he had dried his face. "At least I have my life! Thank God! Like George said…things could be a helluva lot worse." He noticed he was discoloring the leather. "Gosh darn!" He tossed the cloth and began blowing on the boots, hoping to get rid of the tie-dyed streaks. "*Everything* about this new life is like sitting on one of those cacti outside!" He pulled his smudgy boots on anyway. "Gosh, I hope I don't look like an idiot!"

As he entered Don's kitchen from the breezeway, the doorbell rang. Don called: "Hey, Alex, take a seat at the dining room table. I'm having breakfast delivered."

"Okay," Pete called pouring himself a cup of coffee from

a huge silver carafe setting on a sideboard.

Suddenly, he heard Don gasp as a car door opened and closed. "It's Fletch!" he called.

Pete ran out the door and stopped when he reached the last step. It was Don's moment. He wanted to make sure Don basked in the reunion for as long as possible.

Beyond Don's wooden sculpture of an angel and his manicured frost-speckled lawn, Fletch stepped over the curb and ran into his father's arms. Pete could hear the pats of their hands on their backs as they greeted each other. Don was crying and seemed as if he might never let go. Fletch was dressed in camouflage wear. Obviously, he hadn't had time to change from arriving home from war. Sue Beth's little Honda rolled up behind the Taxi, and Andy's pickup truck pulled into the driveway. Hearing a sudden creaking of the porch swing on its chain, he glanced at it, and there sat George.

"It's over," George said, wiping his eyes. He glanced over his shoulder at the sun.

Pete knew that if he'd look at the sun that way, he'd go blind. "They all look happy, George," he said. "I wish I had that myself." He took a step down the stairs, but stopped and grabbed the handrail. "My dad's dead now, so I'll never will." He swallowed down a lump that felt like sadness in his throat.

The swing creaked on its chain as George said: "Nothing ever dies, Alex. We all just go on to a different place." He gestured at the sun.

Pete covered his eyes. Slowly, the light was exchanging its brightness with George. "So I guess I might see you again."

George laughed as he stood up, walked through Pete, passed through the porch rail, and stepped on the grass leading up to the budding Texas oak tree. "Yep, one day, we might see each other again." When he took another step toward the tree, his clothes changed from overalls to an immaculately pressed shiny black suit.

When he saw that change, Pete said, "You look like a cartoon character now." He looked past him to the Gibsons who were still hugging and talking to Fletch at the curb. He

Pete's Crossroad

didn't want them to see him talking to air, so he walked over to the other side of the porch where he could watch George take small steps toward the sprouting Texas oak tree, beyond it, the sun. What Don once proclaimed "dead" was now speckled with green burgeoning leaves. The Yellow Cab pulled away after the driver left Fletch's suitcases in the driveway. "I thought you were going to leave after they opened your presents, George."

Shaking his head as he continued to meld with the sunlight, George said, "I've seen all that I need to see." He touched his heart. "I know they're all fine now." He pointed at Pete. "And you'll be here with 'em."

"Me? What?" Pete asked, feeling confused.

"Bye, Alex." George turned around and began walking towards the sun as rays of light wound around his body. "What a wonderful world!" He had his arms raised in a celebratory gesture. "I was so blessed to have been here. The odds are few-and-far-between ya know…but I had life."

Pete wiped away tears as a burst of sadness rushed through him. "Bye, George, I'll never forget ya!" He stepped up to the swing and plopped down in the seat, the hinges creaking. "I never thought of life that way," he said, gazing into the blue sky. A blue jay sailed down onto the wet grass and began pecking at a purple flower.

"Have a great life…Alex!" George said, waving. He was smaller now, the sun soaking him up. "You're a good guy, Alex. Tell my family I love 'em!" George Gibson disappeared in a flash of sunlight, gone for good.

"Well, now I'm alone without a guide, and a new life. I wonder what's gonna happen for me next?" he whispered, staring at the sun's effects shimmering off flowers, grass, leaves, and birds.

Chapter 24 – Fletch Gibson, War Hero

"Alex!" Sue Beth called to him from the curbside.

Still squinting and feeling captivated by the sunshine that had snatched up George to the afterlife, he whispered, "Is that Heaven?"

"Come here, Alex!" Sue Beth called again. From his place on the porch, he could see a sparkle of light reflecting off her charm bracelet. Maybe George was etching a little piece of himself—his peaceful spirit—into his granddaughter's bracelet!

Rubbing his eyes, he had to stop thinking about the deep cosmic puzzles surrounding life and death. The Gibsons might want to call an ambulance if they saw him stalled on the porch and gaping into the sunlight! Turning away, he felt changed. He had stepped beyond that crossroad Walks-With-Dreams had talked about and onto a new path as George had transitioned to new life. Now, it was his turn to walk away from Pete Turner and become Aleksandar Trochenkov—Alex. *After this point*, he thought, *when I walk down those steps toward the Gibsons, everything will be different. I will be, Alex.*

Alex walked down the steps and down the long walkway until he came to a smiling Don. Dressed in his Sunday best, Don said, "Alex, this is my son, Fletch."

Pete's Crossroad

"Pleased to meet ya, Alex," Fletch said, standing eye-to-eye with Pete, shaking hand firmly. Fletch was muscular-thin and shorter than Don. He had a light scar running down the side of his neck, a military crew cut and a deep tan with light-circles around his eyes from wearing sunglasses during the scorching Middle Eastern days.

Alex said, "You look a bit like your grandfather, George."

Fletch laughed and glanced at Don. "That's funny, 'cause everyone in this house says I look like my grandma, Sue Lynn." He closed his eyes and inhaled as if it were his first breath. "God…it's great to be home. And I can't wait to fix one of grandma's dishes from her old recipes!"

Andy slapped on his cowboy hat and said, "You won't believe how Amarillo's changed since you've been gone, Fletch." He began rattling off lists of shops that had closed and opened throughout the city as he lifted up a suitcase and began rolling it up the stone-paved walkway.

As they reached the steps leading to the porch, Fletch stopped and peered around at the ranch and house. The day was warming up, the sun inching higher, songbirds perching on a sprouting grape arbor in the middle of the front lawn, and melting snow releasing fragrances through the spring air. "This place hasn't changed one bit since I left, Dad," he said, wiped away tears. Again he hugged Don. He was like a child grabbing hold of his father after hitting a home run. "I'm so glad to be home for good!"

"I'm glad you're here too, son," Don said, patting Fletch's back. "That war's been going on for so long, but now, it's over for you. You're home."

Pulling a suitcase behind her, Sue Beth added, "For good!" Standing by the carved wooden statue of the angel, Sue Beth suddenly had a startled expression on her delicate round face. She stopped, pointing at the Texas oak tree. "Look!" Surrounded at the base by patches of melting frost, the tree was no longer black and skeletal. "It has green buds all over it…wow!" She hugged Fletch and grabbed her father's arm. "I *knew* that tree would come back to life." She breathed into her brother's arm as if wanting to remember his touch forever. "I just knew it...when you came home, Fletch. We're all together now. A family again!"

Fletch's cheeks reddened in obvious embarrassment. "*Ahhh*, I just wanna get inside and spend time with y'all...catch up on the years I've been gone, and what I've missed."

"Wow, you sure have changed son," Don said, stunned and inspecting him from head-to-toe. He touched Fletch's tanned red cheek. "Before ya went off to the Army, ya wouldn't have even wanted to stay and say hello. But now, you want to spend time with us." He tapped his eyes on his cuffs. "Wow...I got my son back!"

Fletch had a shame-faced expression as he replied: "Dad, I've just grown up, that's all. It's amazing what going off to another country will do to a person. Now, being back here, I wanna kiss the ground!"

Remembering yesterday when he met his sister for the first time in over eight years, Alex said, "I sure can relate. When I saw Kimberley, I felt so dumb for wasting so many years not talking to her. I definitely grew up myself and changed." He and Fletch again shook hands and laughed.

After stepping inside, Don glanced at the time. He had a rugged outdoor appearance even though he was wearing his black Easter suit, starched white shirt, and bright blue tie. "Well, I think we can make the 11:30 service, can't we?" he asked.

Peeking at his watch, Andy said, "It's 9:30, Dad."

"That's fine," Sue Beth said, opening the door for Stan's delivery driver and paying him as Andy took food to the set table.

Sitting down at the table and rubbing his hands as if preparing to feast on the best meal ever, Fletch said, "I wish I had a watch." He patted his left wrist. "A bullet took out mine."

Removing the wrap off the serving dishes, Don said, "Better to lose the watch than to have lost your hand!"

Alex stood observing them all from the archway between

Pete's Crossroad

the dining room and living room. He suddenly remembered George's pocket watch. "Hey, Don," he began as he walked over to George's carry-on. "There's a black plastic bag in here that contains your dad's watch he was wearing when—"

They had all paused statue-like.

"When he died," Alex coughed. As Andy felt through the small carry-on, he suddenly spotted the bag, untied it, and pulled out the watch still attached to its gold chain. "Does it still work?"

Andy opened up the face as he walked over to Don who was seated next to Fletch. "Yep...wow, this is real nice."

"And old!" Fletch said.

"Yeah, I think your grandfather said he bought it during World War II," Alex said.

Don took the watch gently out of Andy's hand and set it softly into Fletch's hand. "Since the enemy busted yours, you can have this one, son. It's yours. I'll go through the rest of Grandpa's stuff in that black bag later."

As the chain tangled through Fletch's fingers, his hand began to tremble, and Fletch said, "Thanks, I'll keep this forever!" He leaned on his father's arm in a tender gesture as Andy patted his back.

Alex felt a bit like an intruder. Glancing at the breezeway leading to Fletch's room, he said, "Well, I'll go read my email while you all spend some good quality family time together." He motioned to George's luggage that Don had opened at some point earlier. "Just call me before you—"

"No way!" Sue Beth said, dashing up from her chair and grabbed him by the shirt.

"Alex, you come here, sit right down, and eat with us," Don said, sitting at the head of the table and then gesturing for Alex to take his old seat alongside Fletch. He began passing around the main dish of scrambled eggs with fried rice. "You're, well, part of the family now." If Don said it, it was a done deal.

A sudden sting hit his eyes, his throat tingled, and he swallowed down dry air. He felt uncomfortably vulnerable, until he remembered what Sue Beth had told him after he first arrived: that he had never really been part of a family while growing up. Glancing around at all of them, he remembered times when he had said something wrong—something that ruined everything and made him an instant outcaste so he could go and hide like an ostrich in his room or move away to another place. Possible responses flooded his thought: *"No way are you my family,"* or, *"My dad's dead,"* or *"I have a mom and sister who are my family, but thanks for the offer."*

He probably would have said one of those things before, but seeing all their faces—Sue Beth, Don, Andy, and now, Fletch—he felt an emotion that brought tears to his eyes, right smack in front of everyone. "Thanks," he said, sitting down.

Andy waved at Alex with an expression of exasperation. "Fletch...I didn't like this guy at first."

Chuckling, Fletch said, "Oh really?" He glanced from Alex to Andy.

"But I got to liking Alex here," Andy continued, "because I really believed our grandfather sent him." Pointing at Alex, he added, "You tell him, Alex. Tell all of us, one more time."

Fletch listened as Alex told him about his bus ride with George, and that he had procured evidence that had saved lives.

Without saying Alex's old name, Andy said in a protective tone of voice, as he perused the room for eavesdropping equipment, "I'm proud of Alex." He sat back, folded his arms, and had a friendly expression on his face. As Don motioned for him to cut the talk about gangsters, Andy whispered, "We have to all remember to call him Alex."

Pete intervened with his knife cutting the air like a conductor. "Aleksandr Fadei Trochenkov," he exclaimed, then laughed.

They all laughed, until Sue Beth choked down her chuckle with a sobering expression on her face. "Hey, if not for Alex, I don't know if we'd all be sitting here together and talking like this right now." She talked about the shootout at Star's Edge, and Chuck and his band of NRA warriors.

Pete's Crossroad

With his head low and repentant, Andy nodded while Don added more details, and Fletch said intermittently, "Huh," and "Wow!"

Playing with the dregs of his scrambled eggs, Alex said, "I believe Divine intervention was at work here." He set down his fork. "Things you see on TV, or in movies, about ghosts and spirits, really happened to me." He picked up his half-full glass. "And because of your grandpa, George, everything has turned out better for everyone." He lifted his glass toward Don. "Here's to George." He then tipped his glass toward Fletch and Sue Beth, proposing a toast. "To George—your Grandad—he really brought me here. And since I've been here, I've been talking to him in spirit," he said, and he didn't care if they believed he was crazy.

Don put his hand on top of Fletch's arm.

Alex said, "Look how well y'all are gettin' along."

"Y'all?" Sue Beth said with a show of surprise in her brown eyes. "That's Southern," she added as they laughed. "So Alex *is* already acclimating. He's a Texan!" Again they laughed as Sue Beth turned serious and said: "I think Divine Intervention's everywhere. People just have to look for it." She raised her glass. "To our grandpa, George…finally resting in peace with our grandma, Sue Lynn." She sipped and then sat down. When Alex saw her peer at her grandparent's picture on top of Don's side board, he saw a peaceful look in her eyes that he hadn't seen before. As he felt differently now, she appeared so different too.

Obviously responding to a call for another toast, Don stood and said: "To everyone here. To my son, Fletch, home with us safe and sound." Their crystal glasses pinged. "And to Alex…a new member of our family…at least for as long as he wants to be. Thanks for bringing all of my father's things here to Amarillo."

"You're welcome," Alex said, drinking. "I guess I'll start by asking if I can still have that temporary job you offered me at Gibby's?"

Chuckling, Don said, "Of course!" He set down his glass

and reached across the table for more food. "I assume you want to start tomorrow."

"Yep," Alex said.

Brushing back her bangs, Sue Beth asked, "What about the job Agent Tilston might have for you?" Kimberley must have told her.

Pete nodded enthusiastically as he imagined himself back to wearing business suits and ties. "I'll call her tomorrow and set that up. But I'm sure that position won't start for a couple of weeks." He rubbed his fingers together, gesturing that he needed money. "I need cash…although I guess I'm not as worried about the money situation as before. I get a stipend until I can secure work."

With a concerned expression on his face, Andy put down his fork and asked, "How much cash ya need?" He tapped his wallet on the table.

"Oh, no thanks though," Alex replied. "The only things I'm worried about really are the things in storage. I'll call Valarie, and hope she can get them to me." Fletch began showing everyone his Bronze Star. "Right now, I don't have to relocate somewhere." He glanced at Sue Beth and smiled. "So now, I have extra cash. I can get an apartment, if I decide to stay."

Sue Beth said, "That's a good thing that came out of all the terrible things that happened."

Alex huffed and said, "I guess you could say that. Unfortunately, a lot of people died, or have suffered terribly because of all that human trafficking and sweatshop activity." Gently setting down his spoon after stirring his coffee, he felt guilt wave through him. "I should have reported what I saw a long time ago, when I first noticed that things weren't what they seemed to be at that place."

Sue Beth said, "But you took pictures. And you said you just couldn't believe anyone could treat people that way, so you really just didn't see what was happening, right? I mean, people see things every day, but the realization of what those things represent doesn't always register."

Pete's Crossroad

"Yeah!" Alex said, looking askance at her.

She had her fingers on the back of his hand in a show of support as she added, "So all those pictures you took helped break up *two* big crime rings."

Fletch straightened up and exclaimed, "You're a hero!"

Pete wiggled bashfully, "I don't—"

"*And*," Sue Beth interrupted, "because of *your* pictures, Valarie Tilston said police apprehended *five* white-collar criminals who INTERPOL had listed on their Red List."

After Don handed back the Bronze Star award to Fletch who then set it in a cushioned box, Fletch said, "Alex, I don't know you that well…"

Andy reached around Sue Beth and gave Alex a slight hit on the back. Laughing, he said: "We don't know him that well either, but we like the dude."

Dabbing his lips with a napkin, Fletch said, "I've been in war…experienced live shootouts daily, Alex." He emphasized the name, strengthening Pete's new identity. "There were times I wondered why I was fighting." He clasped his fingers and pushed his plate away. "But I knew I was doing good. Maybe the good I was doing wasn't good enough—" He turned red in the face—a memory or onslaught of feeling. "I dunno," he said, peering down at his half-empty plate and glancing up under his thin brow. "Sometimes, while fighting the enemy, and one o' my buddies died, I thought, what if I woulda moved my buddy over just an inch or two so that he coulda dodged the bullet?" Fletch's head vibrated. He was reliving a bad experience. "I blame me all the time, but really, who's the one who did all the killing? It was them…*they're* at fault for starting it all…on September eleven."

Standing up, Don dashed over to him as Sue Beth hugged him, comforting him. "It's all right, Fletch," Don said. "You're home now. You're with your family."

"And we love you," Sue Beth said firmly.

Nodding and breathing deeply, Fletch said: "I'm okay. I'm fine."

Everyone sat down and continued to listen to him.

J.P. Osterman

"What I'm trying to tell you, Alex," he continued, panting, "is that I've never met anyone who doesn't have regrets or feel guilty...or wish they woulda taken path B over path A...or vice versa." He gestured with his hands, making two paths out of a fork in a road. "You weren't at fault. The people who committed those evil acts were at fault."

Sue Beth said, "So, I guess the moral of the story is—"

She glanced coyly to the ceiling and her thin lips lifted as if she were in deep thought.

Don broke the silence and said bluntly, "What happened happened." He had an uplifting voice that sounded hopeful and encouraging. "Both of you...Fletch and Pete. Now, *bury* the past, *and live*." He bent down toward his plate and said, "Oops, Alex, I mean." He had a commanding presence as a wise patriarch of the Gibson family. "You took pictures that are now saving lives. The FBI has information now that'll stop human trafficking. Like Fletch said...you're a hero. I think *you* deserve an award."

Sue Beth said: "Me too, Alex, and from what Agent Tilston said at dinner last night, because of you, they also have more leads that'll lead to bringing down a major sweatshop operating in the outskirts of New York City!"

With large eyes, Fletch said, "Maybe I oughta give Alex my Bronze Star!"

They laughed.

"'Cause it sounds as if you were a hero in one helluva war here in the States!" he added.

Slapping the table and straightening up tall, Don pushed his rimless glasses up the bridge of his nose and said, "Now...are we all done with all this regret stuff?"

Fletch lifted his glass, maneuvering for another toast. "Well, I have all of you to talk things over with," he began, "so I have to say...the past is gone and dead." He took a sip of his water, the glass sweating drops down his shaking fingers. "We only have this moment."

Sue Beth drank and said: "Given all this information, Alex, you helped a lot of people. Their futures are going to look bright because of you."

Glancing at the time, Andy said, "Hey Dad, we have an hour before church starts." He gestured at the living room. "Are those presents I see on the coffee table?"

Don said, "I guess we'd better go and open them up." He coughed, choking back tears.

"Grandpa's presents to us!" Sue Beth exclaimed. She was standing up with her arms on the back of her chair, her eyes wild with beauty, strength and innocence.

Walking over to George's gifts, Fletch picked one up and turned it over, squinting at the writing. "This one has a tag with my name on it." He turned the small box in his fingers. "Grandpa wrapped this gift in horsey wrapping paper...huh!" He laughed as if George was with him, tickling him.

Sue Beth walked over to him, rifled through three more packages, picked one up and held the long box into the light streaming in from the window. "Grandpa wrote my name on this one," she sighed. "Gosh, his writing looks cockeyed and crooked. He must have been shaking when he wrote my name." She plopped down on the sofa, and Don hugged her. "It's okay, Dad," she said, "I don't blame you anymore."

"I'm sorry," Don began, "sorry for keeping him from y'all."

"You were angry, Dad," Fletch said.

"You believed you were protecting us, Dad," Andy added. "I see that now, so don't be so hard on yourself." He patted him on the shoulder. "Like ya just told us...the past is the past. You did the best you could."

"You did what you thought was right," Sue Beth said.

Fletch walked up and joined the small circle. "Just like me, Dad. Remember when I was sneaking outta the house and disobeying?"

Nodding in disapproval, and with a look of terror on his face, Don said: "You bet I remember! I thought several times you were lying dead somewhere!"

"Right," Fletch said. Then he hit himself on the side of his head. "Stupid of me! I'm sorry for that now, but back then, I believed *you* were wrong and *I* was right."

"Ya sure did ya little scoundrel!" Don said jokingly.

Fletch knelt down in front of him. "It's amazing how smart you've become since I left home," he said, chuckling." Through his father's surprised scowl, he waved and said, "But seriously, Dad, I was wrong. I did wrong things."

Sue Beth said, "At least now though, you recognize what you did and you're taking responsibility. Some people *never* do. They go through life blaming everyone else, and never look at themselves."

Alex sat down in a tall armchair. "You grew up, Fletch. That's what you did."

"We all change, and the stages of our lives reflect our perspectives," Sue Beth said, glancing at her grandfather's wrapped gift. She picked it up and lightly shook it. "Mine has these beautiful roses all over it. I'm gonna keep this paper to line the bottom of my dresser drawer." Then she set it gently on the sofa. "Oh, I forgot!"

"What?" Don asked, peering around the room as if he were searching for something lost.

Sue Beth went to her briefcase and pulled out a picture. "I had this enlarged yesterday morning," she began. "A friend of mine used a software program to cut and paste pictures of Grandma Sue Lynn and Grandpa George." She held them up.

Pointing at George's face, Alex said: "This is one Hideki took. You cropped his figure out of the rest-stop photo and combined it with your grandmother's picture. Nice job!"

"My mom's background is the farm in Indiana...before my dad took off for a job in Los Angeles," Don said. "Gosh, I think I remember taking that of her back in 1985!"

Andy added, "Before grandma got sick, but after we all moved to Albuquerque."

Sue Beth had tears in her eyes. "I posed them together and facing each other. They seem so happy."

Andy swallowed hard and his mustache twitched uncomfortably. "Maybe they *are* that way now...in Heaven."

Don huffed out a grand sigh and then said: "It's Easter, a

time for new beginnings, for all of us…and for my parents." He picked up the photo and placed it against his chest as if wishing he could touch them—hug them—one more time. "But they'll always live on in these pictures, and in us."

Taking the photo and setting it on the coffee table behind George's gifts, Sue Beth sat down on the couch and picked up her gift. "This box is long." Unwrapping the present, she opened the faded white box and exclaimed, "A Barbie doll!"

Alex said: "Oh yeah! I remember George telling me he bought you a doll."

She slugged him jokingly. "And you kept that from me?"

"Sure," he said, "I didn't want to spoil the surprise."

As he flipped over and inspected his gift, Don asked, "So you know what's in *all* our boxes, Alex?"

"No," he replied, "I was so occupied at the time with trying to pay attention to George's physical symptoms, that I wasn't really paying attention to which box contained what."

Andy said softly and slowly, "That's when he was dying, huh?"

Alex nodded. "Yeah. That's when he also told me that these gifts were so important to him. He believed the presents would make a difference in your relationship with him."

"That we'd forgive him!" Sue Beth exclaimed, holding her Barbie close to her heart. The doll was donned in a white wedding dress with a veil streaming down to its tiny white shoes. "This is beautiful," she said, crying. "I love it! I'll always treasure it!" She looked toward the ceiling. "Thank you, Grandpa. I love you…and Grandma."

They were silent as Fletch opened his gift. Peeling back the brown and frayed box, he had look of shock on his face. "My gosh! A pocket watch!" He lifted it up and spun it in the air. "This one looks brand new." He laughed as he pulled the other one out of his camouflage pocket. "Now I have two of 'em." It was on a long gold chain and Fletch touched the front face with a gentle brush of his fingertips. "I guess I could use this one too."

Holding up a baseball card, Andy said through the sounds

of crinkling wrapping paper, "A 1963 Topps Pete Rose rookie card! I don't believe it!" He leaned back into the couch cushion. "And it looks brand new, in mint condition. This is probably worth hundreds—"

"No, try thousands of dollars!" Don interrupted, leaning over to get a good look at the rare collectible.

Andy pulled the card into his shirtsleeve. "I'm not selling," he exclaimed. "It's going to the bank." He glanced at it again. "I know—I'll save it and give it to my own kid someday."

"A tradition you'll start then," Sue Beth said as she set down her Barbie in front of a lamp on a side table.

Don lifted off the box top to his gift. Everyone sat breathless as he peeled back thin crinkling white paper. "It's a Lenox bird!" he said.

"Huh?" Andy exhaled, craning his neck to see.

Don nodded toward a porcelain bird collection on shelves against the wall. "A beautiful cardinal!"

Andy said, "Grandma used to love cardinals."

Don said: "She was a prolific birdwatcher. She could hear a birdcall and match the sound to the correct species." He walked over to the collection and moved over a set of porcelain birds with their wings spread as if in flight. "I remember her telling me right before she died, that she was waiting for my dad to bring her the last bird from the specialty shop in California." He set it gently among the multi-tiered collection. "*This* is *that* bird, the last one I needed." His shoulders heaved as his voice changed through his tears. "Now…the collection's complete." Stepping back, he glanced at the collection as if it were a priceless and irreplaceable menagerie. He cupped his hands over his face and cried.

That reminded Alex of the moments just prior to George's heart attack. Motioning to all the opened gifts and neatly folded wrapping paper, he said, "Now, you can all start over." He pulled out George's tractor magazine that had the date, June 7, 1962, and set it on their coffee table. "This has finally found home."

Pete's Crossroad

As Don perused the magazine, Sue Beth said, "We won't let grudges keep us apart anymore." Her eyebrows lifted in caution, and she tapped her father's arm. "What lesson's we've learned. Dad, you and Grandpa sure made some *big* mistakes, but none of us have to do the same to our children someday."

Andy stood up and glanced at his watch. "Mistakes *I* don't ever wanna make," he said firmly, his expression reflecting fear of consequences.

"Whew," Fletch added as he walked to the door and swooped up his duffle bag. "Me neither." He glanced at the pocket watch he had just finished setting and said, "Hey, it's about time to leave, isn't it? Church!"

Don wiped his eyes, slid on his glasses, and said: "Oh yeah! We gotta get outta here." He scooped up his wrapping paper, folded it neatly so that the corners all matched, and set the paper speckled with little train engines gently on the dining room table. "Fletch…so many people are gonna be so happy to see ya, son."

"A lot of people from high school attend our church," Sue Beth said, lifting her sweater off the coat stand. "They'll probably wanna throw you a huge welcome back picnic party next weekend."

Don stopped in front of the door, turned around and cleared his throat. Emotions had choked him up, but he appeared determined to express them. "I wanna say one last thing before we all leave this house."

Everyone stopped to listen.

As Don put his thumbs through his belt loops, Alex remembered George pulling at his suspenders in almost the same manner.

"We learned some hard lessons, as Sue Beth said," Don began, nodding at the picture of his parents. "Any hurt feelings…any slights, or bruises, or angry behaviors…we talk about 'em." He glanced at each of his children as if he were correcting a bad habit. "Everyone hear?"

After a moment of silence, Andy said, as he slipped on his cowboy hat, "Sure thing, Dad. I think we pretty much all get that now."

Fletch nodded emphatically and through teary eyes said: "No more disobeying from me, Dad." He waved as if he fanning off a bad stink. "I learned one big lesson."

"What's that, son?" Don asked.

Fletch reached into his suitcase and whipped out a shirt and pair of pants. "You've lived a helluva lot longer than I have, Dad. You're wise. I shoulda listened to your advice a long time ago." He huffed out a sigh of exasperation. "I'll listen from now on!"

Don laughed and picked up his coat. "Come on, y'all. Let's get on over to church. I wanna be early so I can talk to the reverend about my Dad's funeral this coming Friday.

Pete's Crossroad

Chapter 25 – Gibby's

Gibby's Home and Garden store was a block north on 6th Street and five blocks east of Stan's Drive-In. It was now under renovation from the Snakehead gangster shootout. Nestled among tall crape myrtle and crooked Texas oaks, Gibby's looked like a Hansel and Gretel German cottage. Behind the store, Don had an outdoor section with a high wrought-iron entryway.

Walking on the job early Monday morning, Alex meandered through several pathways edged with red-and-blue gnomes, wand-weaving elves, pottery, and angelic decorations. He stopped and scratched his forehead when he saw three gigantic boxes containing pieces to a cascading waterfall. Don had asked him to assemble the display and then fill it.

Never having constructed a fountain, Alex spent that entire Monday, and the following two days, cutting black tarp, gathering pebbles, and snapping together plastic parts. Every night, he returned to Don's place tired and exhausted, but a bit closer to accepting his new name and identity. Customers had been calling him Alexandar, Alex, or Al! At first, he had trouble responding, but as each day passed, he grew accustomed to his name. Several times, while sitting behind a huge berry bush so that no one could see him, he tossed hoses, aluminum slats, and rods into the air. "*Rrrr*," he grumbled. "I should just quit!" It was Wednesday, and he only had the tarp and round bowl assembled.

Suddenly, he spotted Don, waving at him and giving him the A-Okay signal.

Smiling, and feeling embarrassed, he waved back and returned to erecting the pick-up-stick waterfall.

After calling Agent Tilston twice, wondering when he could begin his new job at the FBI, she finally returned his call. He would start his job as an Employment Specialist on Monday. But that good news didn't relieve his frustration with trying to piece together the water fountain and make a good impression on Don, so he dialed Sue Beth. "Ah, I know we're going out tonight," he began, glancing at his watch. It was 3:30 p.m. "I'm just wondering, are you busy right now?" Taking a giant gulp of water, he swallowed hard and wiped sweat of his forehead. He could hear the sounds of kitchen trays being stacked and utensils clattering. She had to be eating a late lunch in the college cafeteria.

Sue Beth replied: "No, I'm free. Are you at Gibby's?"

Holding a connecting rod to a water pump and trying to force them to fit, he replied, "Yep, I'm here for another two hours." Yards away, he noticed Don talking to a customer. After their exchange, Don might check in on him! He told her, "I really need your help here, Sue Beth." He quickly dodged behind a tall hedge. "I have no idea…well…how to assemble this fountain your dad told me to put together." He hit his arm on a clay pot. "Ouch!" He began rubbing it. "I wanted to prove that I can do this, but—I'm trying—"

"Are you all right?" she asked.

Huffing, he kicked a pipe with his foot and said, "I'm a salesman. I never learned how to put things together." He tossed a grease-covered nut onto the tarp that he believed was supposed to function as some sort of protective guard to keep water from seeping out of the finished fountain. "I don't know how the heck to seal all these fabrics…I think that's what they're called. And all these rods, and steel pipes, and rubber fittings are supposed to go somewhere…darn!" he cried. "I'm like lost in a jungle!" He panted as each piece seemed to magnify three times. "There's no beginning," he said, picking up a hinge, "nor ending," he added as he looked down at a little plastic door.

"Alex! Are you all right?" Sue Beth asked again.

"*Wheew*…yeah," he replied, "but I won't be for long when your dad fires me." He felt like a failure again, and hated it. "I thought this looked easy…that I could do this *simple* job! So simple!" He clenched his fists.

"Did you set out all the parts first?" she asked.

He didn't hear her light advice. "I just know he's gonna fire me!" he repeated, taking another drink of water. Looking at the fountain pieces spread out on the ground, they appeared as Lego blocks mixed with Tiddlywinks and clear plastic hoses. "I've been working two days on this one fountain…*one* fountain, Sue Beth," he exhaled.

"Uh-huh, Alex," she said, consolingly, "my dad's *not* going to fire you."

"Yeah, right! You sound pretty sure of that, Sue Beth."

"I am," she said, softly and slowly. "My dad *isn't* going to fire you. You know better than to believe that. You just don't like asking for help, that's all. If you can't put the fountain together, it's no big deal. Just tell him."

"Gosh," he moaned through her long pause. "Okay, maybe you're right." Feeling defeated but encouraged, he peeked around the large bush he was using to cover up his entire botched project. He whispered: "Even so, can you please get over here and help me? Will you…please? When you're done with school." He peered around another corner. When he met Don's eyes, Don waved at him, and again gave him the A-Okay signal. Realizing he could fool Don for only so long, and that Don had already been more than patient, Alex said, "If you can call Andy and see if he can come over here with you, maybe together, you two can help me get this fountain together…teach me a thing or two about assembling things."

J.P. Osterman

She was obviously eating as she spoke through chewing food, "What model is it?"

"Model?" he replied, glancing around for the box he'd thrown away yesterday. "I don't know. I'll have to go out back to the alley where I threw the box away and check."

He could hear her car keys jingling as she got into her car. "I'm leaving school right now. You go and look around for the model number on another box, and when I get there, hopefully with Andy, we'll search the internet for the design, or call the manufacturer if you can't find a box."

"Uh-huh, good ideas," he said. "I have the design, but not the instructions."

"A piece of cake then!" she exclaimed. "I'll call Andy and tell him to meet us there when he can. I'll be there in about twenty minutes."

Feeling relief, he said, "Thanks, Sue Beth, I owe ya one."

"Lunch tomorrow then," she said, laughing. "Oh, and you owe me nothing, Alex. Nothing."

After taking a drink out of a stream of cold water from drinking fountain, he asked, "Ya wanna have dinner with me tonight? I know it's only been a week, but, ya know, if we keep this up—" He coughed. "People might say that we're, well…a couple."

She cleared her throat. "A couple? *Hmm*…I can see that." She sounded surprised, but happy in her little pause. "Yeah!"

"Yeah what?" he asked as he swept up a rag and wiped off sweat and dust off his face and neck.

"I can see us as a couple," she said quickly.

"That's it then," he said dabbing his hands dry on his shirt with the cell phone tucked under his chin.

Above him, a large thick net was reflecting the strong sunlight and keeping plants alive while outside, the Amarillo air was heating up. The sun was beginning to bake the tops of trees and bushes, but the cacti blossoms were acclimated— their small ink prints of yellow, red, and orange appearing like indelible impressions in an expressionist's oil painting.

In spite of the adjacent lot that looked as if it might crack

Pete's Crossroad

in the heat, Alex felt like dancing. "Couple we are then!" he exclaimed.

She gave out a coy laugh. "See you in ten minutes, Alex." Then she hung up.

Don popped his head around the corner at him. "Hi!"

"Hey Don!" Alex said, reeling. He dusted off his blue jeans and fit his cap on his head.

Don walked in front of the large green hedge, covered his mouth—disguising a good chuckle—and said, "Well Alex..." He sighed, his eyebrows lifting in confusion. "Building things may not be your forte."

Shuffling his feet, he said: "I'm getting help, Don. Sue Beth's coming." He cleared his throat in embarrassment. "She's bringing Andy."

Don slapped him jokingly on the back. "Look, Alex, I know you've been having a little trouble with this fountain assembly." He waved at the jumbled mess as cool air from the ceiling fans curled around them. "I just didn't want to interfere...make you feel bad."

Alex stood tall and pushed back his shoulders. "Well—" He rubbed his chin—the tubing, rods, and washers sprawled out on the floor looked unsolvable. "I'll get it together. Sometime, before supper, I hope."

Don laughed. Taking him gently by the shoulder, he led him to the checkout area. Customers were standing in queue in front of the long steel counter, and shopping carts were rickety-rackety rolling in front of him. The aisles were bustling with patrons asking for help concerning their springtime lawn-and-garden issues. Landscape designers and contractors were conversing about property layouts and fixer-upper projects.

Alex didn't know what Don was expecting of him. "Mr. Gibson—"

"Don," he corrected him.

"Don," Alex said sternly, "if you know I wouldn't do well putting that thing together, why didn't you put me inside, working with customers in the first place?" He felt a little ticked off, as if, on purpose, Don had put him through all types of misery for the last three days.

"Alex," Don began, pushing his rimless glasses up the bridge of his nose. His full salt-and-pepper beard was well-manicured, like all his hedges and evergreen sculptures in his home and garden shop. "I think every father likes to, well, sort of test the man his daughter's datin'." He had a little smirk on his face as he folded his arms, like one of those gnomes he had setting at the entryway.

"Uh-huh," Alex said, shifting in place, peering into his testing but friendly blue-gray eyes lined with crow's feet.

Standing between two rows of hibiscus bushes, Don glanced around the interior of his store. "See all this?" A light mist from a misting tube began spraying cool water on the tops of their heads, dispersing miniature rainbows in the hot air. "Someday, my children will own this place," he said.

Alex nodded, but didn't see what that had to do with him. "Yes, Don."

"I know you're dating Sue Beth," Don finally said, pointblank. He was obviously waiting for an answer.

Alex swallowed hard, his Adam's apple thickening. Before meeting Don, or Sue Beth, or George, he would have denied the truth, excused himself, packed up and left town. He hated complicated things…commitments! But, he decided to stay. *I can face this…I can handle this*. Muscling up and folding his arms, mirroring Don's stance, he said, "Sir, yes, I'm dating Sue Beth…exclusively." He stretched, his back hurting him from having been in a crouched position for so long. When he saw that Don was about to interrupt him, he put up his hand and said: "I *am* dating Sue Beth and I'm *not* leaving." He had to speak faster. "But before you stop me, Sir, I mean, Don…no, Mr. Gibson—" He closed his eyes, not wanting to see any disapproving facial expressions. "I have the best of intentions. I really like your daughter." He could feel the blush in his cheeks, and he glanced up into the mister for cooling relief.

"Yes?" Don said, coaxingly.

He breathed hard as past event flashed through his mind

Pete's Crossroad

like prices on a cash register. He recalled the moments he clicked the button on his camera and took all those incriminating photos at Fashion Diva. He recalled Terrence Frapley saying, "You're fired." He remembered being drunk at a bar in Santa Monica and his last girlfriend dumping him, coldly. He remembered slipping out through the window of his parent's home when he turned eighteen. He had always been on the run. Not now. Not anymore.

"I know it's only been a week, but I think I'm falling in love with Sue Beth," he said.

Don's jaw dropped as he starred at him.

Alex stepped back a little. He didn't know whether Don was going to hug him or slug him. "Sir, I don't know about next week...or ten months from now."

"Uh-huh," Don finally said, with a skeptical look in his eyes.

Alex realized that Don wasn't the type of man to run on sudden impulse or temper, so he added, "And maybe, six months from now, Sue Beth might not like me."

"Uh-huh," Don said, "go on, Aleksandar."

He hadn't heard Don say his full name, ever. Still, he felt as if he were half-way to convincing him of his good intentions. "All I can tell you, Mr. Gibson, is that when I imagine my future—" He paused and began peering around the garden shop as the misting system swooshed on again, dispersing rainbows. He saw colorful roses vibrating on their bushes, and laughing customers who were happily conversing about planting their very first gardens. He imagined himself, momentarily, one day, standing among them.

"Uh-huh, but I'm a bit confused with what you're trying to say," Don said, his tone of voice rising. "Go on."

"When I picture my future, I see myself with Sue Beth," he finally said. "*When*—there!"

Don laughed as he nodded toward the far end of the store. "And there she is!" he gestured at her.

Alex panicked. "But Don...don't tell—"

"I'm not gonna tell 'er," he said, hitting Alex jokingly on

J.P. Osterman

the side of the arm. "I've been in love myself, Alex." He sighed, and then a look of deep sadness swept over his face.

Alex believed he had just said something wrong. "I'm sorry, Don." Having never discussed Don's past or asked Sue Beth about her mother, he jostled a few pipes and tubes on the ground, hoping the noise might close the uncomfortable topic. Sue Beth had spotted them, and began walking towards them; and he didn't want her sad by talking about past pains he believed should be buried, as would George's body, tomorrow.

Don picked a yellow leaf off a hibiscus bush. "Sue Beth's mother left when Sue Beth was two." He glanced at her as he quickly relayed the facts.

"I'm sorry," Alex said.

Don turned red in the face, obviously shrugging off the hurt. "Those types of things happen," he said, "but I've dealt with it." Peering at the sky, he seemed to enjoy the mist lightly spraying his face. "I survived, and made this place my life. Someday, I hope to give it to my children." He stood tall and proud of the years of obvious self-pruning he had endured to accomplish his dreams. Again, he patting Alex on the back. "And if you end up with Sue Beth, well, someday...this place'll be partly yours."

"I hope so, Don, I really do, 'cause I like her a lot," Alex said, breathing deeply. He didn't want to make promises; but then again, a life with Sue Beth certainly sounded ideal. "I could definitely see us together permanently...in the future." He felt perked up and energized. "And I have that job with the FBI starting Monday."

"Great!" Don said through an expression of relief. "That job will probably be best for you," he laughed, kicking a plastic tube for the fountain display.

Laughing as well, Alex said: Agent Tilston offered the job to me—ah..." Seeing Sue Beth pass through the wooden archway leading into the outdoor area, his breath left him—she was that beautiful, dressed in a light-blue flowered dress; and he called out to her, waving her toward them. If Don hadn't been there, he would have run to her, swept her off her feet and kissed her. "I'm getting an apartment tomorrow, after your dad's funeral. I'm going to ask Sue Beth to help me look for one." Don smiled. "And my things should be arriving any day now from Los Angeles. Agent Tilston procured them in secret for me, so I have a few of my dad's things."

"Great!" Don said.

With her fiddle case around her shoulder, Sue Beth bounced as she craned to kiss her father on the cheek. "How y'all doing?"

She appeared bubbling over with energy as Alex replied, "Fine." Then he hugged her. "What are you going with your fiddle?"

Don asked, "Are your classes over the day?"

"Yep," she replied, wide eyed. "I'm gonna play here at the store while Andy and my dad help you assemble that fountain."

"Oh, wow, entertainment!" Alex exclaimed. "Your playing will draw people into the store for sure."

Sue Beth tilted up her fiddle case and added: "Oh, and Fletch says he'll meet you for dinner, Dad. He'll call you later to set up a time."

"Where's he now?" Alex asked.

Pushing her purse strap up her shoulder, Sue Beth said: "At Texas A&M. Fletch gets VA benefits now, so he's visiting with a counselor to see which classes he wants to take."

Don reached over and lightly pinched her on the cheek as if she were his little girl. She would always remain that way to him. "You seem to have everything in order, Sue Beth." He pointed to a dying plant and a fried fern that he had obviously been trying to resuscitate. "Your music should help bring those poor little creatures back to life." He laughed as he walked over, picked up a hose, and began watering them.

"Well, ya ready, Alex?" she asked, her lips curled into a smile over her white teeth and her little shoulders straining under the weight of her fiddle and purse.

Taking her fiddle case to help her, he replied, "I don't know how I'm ever going to put that fountain together."

J.P. Osterman

"Oh yeah?" she said, glancing at him askance, her brown eyes appearing to entice him into joining a seductive dance.

He couldn't take his eyes off her. "I want to listen to you play," he said. There was a little stage alongside the arched entrance area that someone had erected just for her sole performance. They walked over to it, and he helped her set up speakers. Stepping on the stage as she donned a microphone, he added, "I could listen to your music for the rest of the night." He waved off the fountain and all its pieces scattered on the ground in the distance.

Her head turning in a little twist of disapproval, she said, "Now, I know you wouldn't just leave a job uncompleted, Alex." She took the fiddle out of her case and set it gently on the stage. "So here comes some help for you." Andy walked into the store, and she gestured for him to join them.

"I know…I'll finish it." As Sue Beth tuned her fiddle, he felt disappointed. He'd rather listen and watch her perform.

With his cowboy hat tilted low and his sleeves rolled up as if he had been working all day on Don's ranch, Andy walked up to him, dropped his hat to his side, and dusted off his light jacket. "Hey, Alex." He quickly greeted a few customers and drank cold water from the drinking fountain. "Ahhh!" he said, basking in its coolness. After pouring trickles on his neck and arms, he straightened up and said, "Where's this project you need help with?" He looked as if he were trying to regain his balance and energy.

"Thanks, Andy, I know you've worked all day, so I appreciate your helping me."

Don walked past Sue Beth, patted Andy on the shoulder, handed him a bottle of cold water, and said, "Andy, go easy on Alex here when ya help him assemble that fountain." He gestured at the fountain in the distance, parts scattered crisscross. "He's a salesman. I gave him a job a little harder than what he could do. My fault."

Alex laughed. "You can say *that* again, Don!"

Sue Beth began playing the *Sally Ann* rendition she had played at the roundup, and customers began applauding and

Pete's Crossroad

tapping their feet to the beat of the music.

Glancing at all the happy and excited faces, Alex saw people placing calls on their cell phones while some other people began activating their video apps. News would get around shortly about Sue Beth's performance, and Gibby's would be bustling with customers and sales. Their voices were homey, friendly, and inviting: "Come on down to Gibby's. She's playin' right now!"

Watching Sue Beth move gracefully to the rhythm of the music as she imbibed each note, he said into a bougainvillea bush that was brimming with salmon-colored flowers, "I think I'm going to ask her to marry me...someday soon." He smelled the mist-filled air. Every color of each flower looked so sharp, clearing his mind, and he felt really alive. The scent of gardenia wafting from bushes at the front of the stage imprinted Sue Beth into his mind. "I never want to leave her!" he whispered. "Maybe tomorrow I'll ask her to marry me," he said, touching another flower. He spotted a singing sparrow engaged in a dance with a mate up in the rafters. Walking behind Andy toward the fountain, he whispered: "Yeah, tomorrow. I know it's soon, but what the heck, I love her. I'm gonna ask *that* girl, standing *right* there, Sue Beth Gibson, to marry me."

He never felt happier about tomorrow!

###

J.P. Osterman

Pete's Crossroad

ABOUT THE AUTHOR

J.P. Osterman was born December 21, in East Chicago, Indiana. She graduated from the University of San Diego with a BA in English (emphasis Writing) and obtained a teaching credential, and an MA in Education from Azusa Pacific University. She taught high school English and writing for 8 years in Southern California. She won the prestigious Rupert Hughes Award at the seminal Maui Writer's Conference and First Place in the Southern California Writer's conference for her one-act play, *The Man Next to Me*. She also won a very important award as Outstanding Teacher for her student's literary prizes in writing, 4 years in a row, at the Los Angeles County writing competition. She spent a year and a half in the Licensed Professional Counseling program at Texas State University. She considers herself a research scientist, and likes studying statistics, testing, and research results. She writes because writing is her passion and identity.

For more information about these stories please visit Amazon.com or my website: http://www.jposterman.com

Other Books by J.P. Osterman:

First Communication (Book I, the Nelta series) and *Battlefield Matrix* (Books II in the Nelta Series), *Cosmic Rift*, *Dimension Mind*, *The Screaming Stone*, and *Corporate Revenge*.

Books in the Works: *Nanobot Invasion,* Book III in the Nelta series. Strange occurrences happen onboard spaceship *Sagan* on the voyage to Nelta! Books IV and V are in editing mode.

J.P. Osterman